PERCEPTION
OF DEATH

Louise Anderson

PERCEPTION OF DEATH

arrow books

Published by Arrow in 2005

1 3 5 7 9 10 8 6 4 2

Copyright © Louise Anderson 2004

First published in the United Kingdom in 2004 by Hutchinson.

Arrow
The Random House Group Limited
20 Vauxhall Bridge Road, London SW1V 2SA

Random House Australia (Pty) Limited
20 Alfred Street, Milsons Point, Sydney
New South Wales 2061, Australia

Random House New Zealand Limited
18 Poland Road, Glenfield
Auckland 10, New Zealand

Random House (Pty) Limited
Endulini, 5a Jubilee Road
Parktown 2193, South Africa

The Random House Group Limited Reg. No. 954009

www.randomhouse.co.uk

A CIP catalogue record for this book is available from the
British Library

Papers used by Random House are natural,
recyclable products made from wood grown in sustainable forests.
The manufacturing processes conform to the environmental
regulations of the country of origin

ISBN 0 09 947126 4

Typeset by Palimpsest Book Production Limited,
Polmont, Stirlingshire
Printed and bound in Great Britain by
Cox & Wyman Ltd, Reading, Berkshire

Acknowledgements

I have many, many people to thank for their help and understanding in, what probably seemed to them, my endless endeavour to write *Perception of Death*.

My sincerest thanks to all at the Darley Anderson Literary Agency, particularly my darling agent, Darley Anderson and Lucie Whitehouse.

I owe a huge debt of gratitude to all at Random House, most especially to my brilliant editor, Paul Sidey who has shown remarkable patience and encouragement. Also Tiffany Stansfield, copy-editor Jacqueline Krendel and proof-reader Neville Gomes.

To John Connolly for his inspirational and enviable talent.

To my wonderful friends Caroline Sutherland and Nick Wilkes, Catriona and David Harris, Ceinwen and Mark Lombardi, Eileen and Robert Skinner, Sheila and Douglas Kinnaird, Lynn and Paul Newman, Fiona and Russ Crawford, Krysia and Terry Brennan, Jennifer and Mark Watson. Girlie hugs and kisses also to June McGeachy, Kate Lough, Dorothy Ritchie, Ann Girvan, Liz McRobb, Beth Thornton, Irene Martin and David Henderson.

To all at Martin, Aitken & Co., Accountants. Especially Jim McInroy, Jim Copeland and Adrienne Airlie – unbelievably you make accounting fun!

Thanks also to my aunts and uncles and cousins, too numerous to mention, but rest assured you'll all be getting a copy for Christmas!

To my wonderful parents David (Papa) and Elizabeth (Nanny) and fabulous, cherished siblings Marty and Simi.

And finally, all my love and thanks to my husband (the saint) and our two special boys.

To anyone I have missed, I apologise. You know who you are.

Prologue

It's not what actually happens that matters but how we perceive it. We all witness the same thing but see it differently. We see it from our own perspective. While we suffer possibly the worst day of our entire lives, we do grasp that throughout the world others are also enduring catastrophe.

We recognise it in terms of a baby starving in Africa every minute, a school kid shooting his classmates, an earthquake in Eurasia, but we tend not to linger on the broader picture. We give our pound to the *Big Issue* seller and we applaud charities for their efforts. The world is too big a place to consider the mountain of human misery. It's only when it pulls up a deckchair and stretches languidly in our own backyard that we truly focus.

I do care about the world, believe me, but I care more for those that I love than for those I have never met.

Our lives are linear. While I am in the shower, you are brushing your teeth. While my neighbour is spreading butter on his toast, I am putting on my suit. While the paperboy rushes to school, the lollipop man drinks tea from a Thermos. Our lives are linear and metaphorically parallel. Thousands of thin lines packed so closely together that you cannot see the gaps.

While Alex fucked Mrs McCaffer, I poured a cup of fresh-brewed coffee and Lucy Grant breathed her last. A finely choreographed ballet, each event seem-

1

ingly separate yet glancing off one another with every new step and change of tempo.

. . . laceration of anterior neck which perforated the trachea, oesophagus and larynx . . . severing of the frenulum lingae and tongue removed . . . abrasions, bruises and contusions of the mons and labia . . . evidence of sexual assault . . . rape kit used . . .

I looked forward to Fridays and the end of another week. I had since I was a child. Time to kick back. I made a pact with myself to work hard during the week and relax at weekends, but it didn't work. The more diligent I was, the more rubbish landed in my lap. Being efficient and conscientious simply left me open to others' negligence. I wanted to be a slacker, but in my desperation to prove myself worthy and equal to any man, I inadvertently gave myself a legacy. I was the be-all and end-all in the firm my grandfather had created. I also cosseted my family so effectively that they could no longer cope without me. Or so I thought.

I was perfectly aware that many people did not like me because of my abrupt and confrontational manner. If I were a man I would be described as forthright and incisive. I was also attuned to the fact that I was born not only with a silver spoon in my mouth but a whole canteen of cutlery, in solid silver with matching teapot and sugar tongs.

The morning of Lucy Grant's rape and murder changed things for me, but not because I suddenly realised life was short and 'this was not a rehearsal'. I didn't rush out and decide to find myself as all those other thirty-five-year-old career women were doing. I didn't purchase cast-off sperm and take up knitting matinée jackets. I didn't have a radical haircut and join the VSO. I didn't do anything reactionary. I took it all in my stride.

The Friday morning, in early October, of Lucy Grant's death knocked my particular linear course into another and another and another. And as our corresponding lines bumped and ricocheted, we were forced to look at ourselves. Nobody liked what they saw.

There are some things in life better not known – some things that should be left where they rest.

ONE

It was a glorious morning and I enjoyed the brisk ten-minute walk to the office. The crisp sunshine and icing-sugar frost made me feel I could be anywhere. It was one of my secret pleasures, pretending I was walking the streets of Boston or New York. A feeling helped along by the newly arrived Starbucks coffee shops.

I only brought my car to the office if it was partic-ularly foul outside. I had a designated parking space but driving through the city centre was torture. In their wisdom, the city fathers had littered the streets with bus lanes and cycle paths. That might have worked in a European metropolis with a functioning public transport system and slightly more clement weather, but in Glasgow it made the same amount of traffic move even more slowly.

During the previous weeks I had arrived at work later and later. My boyfriend was the cause of my tardi-ness, which made me furious and pathetic in equal measures. I had been forced to hang back until he looked like he was actually going to set off for work before I could leave.

He had the education, background and good looks required, but severely lacked professional motivation. Bluntly, I had discovered him to be a lazy bastard.

During the initial months when I naively believed he had potential, I had arranged for him to work for one of my many contacts as a recruitment consultant. He wasn't actually trained as a recruitment consultant but,

5

as far as I could tell, there didn't seem much training necessary. You interviewed prospective employees for prospective employers. How hard could that be?

Alex had seemed to settle down but recent reports of four-hour lunches, days off and general piss-taking had been filtering through to me. I was tired of him. The sheen had rubbed off to reveal a very dull interior. And I suspected the feeling was mutual.

I had worked in my grandfather's law firm since graduating but still felt a small surge of pride as I swept up the stone steps, past the gracious Georgian pillars and into the marble reception of The Paterson Building. It was built in 1875 for my great, great grandfather, one of the original Glasgow tobacco lords, and now housed Paterson, Paterson & Co., Solicitors.

William, the concierge, opened the door and greeted me. I returned the greeting as he called the lift. He had worked for us for forty years and knew better than to involve me in small talk. I was busy in those precious moments ticking off mental lists and formulating strategy. It was not an awkward silence – well, certainly not for me, it was reassuring in its ritualised repetition.

My office, which had been my father's before me, was on the top floor beside the boardroom. The lift opened directly on to an open-plan area for the assistants and secretaries. It was already buzzing.

I acknowledged my staff and went straight to my office. Friday was a strange day. The start of a new business day but the end of a business week. The two didn't sit well together; the feeling of wrapping up for the weekend but still the promise of a rewarding day. I knew I was alone in believing that just as much work could be achieved on a Friday as any other day.

I had rather a busy handbag and realised it was due

for a clear-out when I couldn't find my hairbrush. I liked to be immaculate and was forced to empty the contents into my out-tray. Naturally, the hairbrush was at the bottom, under my Psion, my wallet, make-up bag, keys for my apartment, keys for my parents' home, keys for my car, keys for the office, and my mobile phone.

After I smartened up I went to the office kitchen to get a cup of coffee. I didn't believe in omens or any of that nonsense, but the window in the kitchen sprung open suddenly and gave me a fright. I splashed boiling coffee on my hand and scalded myself.

As I ran cold water over the burn, my expression set for the day. A grim no-nonsense face that my colleagues had learned to cross at their peril.

I sat back at my desk with my coffee and was shifting through the dross from my handbag when Michael McCabe knocked on my open door.

'Morning, Erin.' He entered my territory and tried to look friendly.

'Morning, Michael.' I did the same but with conspicuously less effort.

'Did you get a chance to finalise the details of the Murphy versus Broadwood settlement last night?'

'It's all in my briefcase.'

'And we're going to go for five hundred thousand?'

I shifted in my seat. Since when was Michael so interested in my cases?

'I believe so.'

'Good, good. They're due at ten.'

'I know.' Of course, I knew. I had arranged the meeting. Michael hovered for a moment more, so I arched an eyebrow.

'Is there something I can help you with?'

'No. No. Good luck.' Michael said with jovial insincerity and left.

Luck had nothing to do with it. I was a good lawyer. Damn good. I did my homework. Michael was acting strangely, but then again around me he was always odd. We tended to keep out of each other's way – as much as two senior partners could who were once lovers. What had once been mutual admiration and romantic interest had curdled to distrust and dislike. He was an ass but he was also a fine lawyer, and, although it would have suited me, I didn't want him to move on. But I did wonder about his sudden interest in the Broadwood settlement, which had been ongoing for three years.

Five hundred thousand pounds didn't seem enough for the loss of a husband and father, but it was the industry standard for a fatal accident of this type. Mr Murphy had died because of alleged negligence on Broadwood Ltd's part.

Purely to reassure myself that I hadn't missed something fundamental, I opened my briefcase and shuffled through the files. Hammersmith versus Duguid & Masters Ltd. Morris versus Donald. McGowan versus Francinelli & Sons. No Murphy versus Broadwood Ltd.

I searched again, slammed my case shut and glanced at my watch. Eight fifty-five. I could get back to my apartment, pick up the file and return within half an hour.

In my haste I knocked my coffee over my desk and keyboard. I breathed deeply, snatched up my keys and raincoat and headed back to the lift.

'Karen, I've got to go out,' I sighed at my PA on my way past, 'and I've spilt coffee on my desk and keyboard. Can you get somebody to clean it up?'

8

'Certainly, Miss Paterson. When should I expect you back?' Karen called after me.

'Half an hour.'

I realised I was brusque but I didn't have time to exchange pleasantries that morning.

The streets were busy with office workers, shop assistants and hairdressers scurrying to work. I was slowed down by the flow of human traffic and had to jostle past them all the way, mumbling 'excuse me'.

As I reached the far end of my street, I looked up towards my apartment building. The sunlight ricocheted off the windows and toasted the blond sandstone. The whole building radiated warmth and beauty. It was a reclaimed Victorian warehouse overlooking the re-claimed river that ran through the heart of the reclaimed city.

They had done a wonderful job, particularly on the penthouse lofts, one of which was mine. It was an exclusive building with only twelve apartments and fully occupied by other professionals. We steered clear of each other's lives but were civil enough to lend the building a feeling of superficial community.

I reached into my raincoat pocket and pulled out my parents' house keys. It was turning into a perfect day.

I buzzed the caretaker, Mrs McCaffer, but got no answer. Dispiritedly, I buzzed all the other flats until I reached the two penthouses but, as I had expected, everybody was out.

I took a deep breath and buzzed penthouse number 2. Half of me wanted no answer and the other half was desperate to get in.

'Yes?'

'Hi. It's Erin Paterson. I've forgotten my keys and Mrs McCaffer is out. Could you buzz me in, please?'

There was an odd pause. It was typical of Paul Gabriel, my immediate neighbour, who saw himself as something of a comedian.

'OK, but the lift isn't working,' he said eventually.

'Thanks,' I muttered, but I checked the lift anyway. Telling me it was out of order was the type of puerile joke Paul might play.

I stared at the stairs. I hated exercise, at any time and in any way. Exercise was rubbish. I would do anything rather than exercise. I had no desire to be down at the gym sweating my pants off, pretending to enjoy it when all I wanted was a glass of wine. To keep my perfect, size-eight figure I used a revolutionary dieting plan. I ate less.

I began the ascent to the fifth floor but needed oxygen by the third. Little beads of perspiration gathered on my hairline. I shrugged off my raincoat, left it on the third-floor landing and made a determined effort to spring up the last two flights. I had discovered that I recovered more swiftly from a quick burst. I had never mentioned the fact for fear that the fitness bores who surrounded me would tell me in tedious detail that it was something to do with cardiovascular recovery times.

I took a deep breath and hammered up the stairs two at a time. It was a big mistake. As I rounded the corner to the fourth, I caught the heel of my left Gucci and tore it clean off. By the time I reached my floor I was singing expletives under my breath. To add to my annoyance, Paul Gabriel was waiting for me.

I couldn't understand why he bothered because I certainly didn't have anything to say to him.

He was leaning against his doorframe in what he probably thought was a casual, debonair manner.

Admittedly, he was very attractive. Early forties with a peppering of grey hair, tall – well over six foot – and fit. In every sense of the word.

'Everything OK?'

'Yes. Thank you,' I panted.

He watched as I hobbled past him, as elegantly as I could when missing a two-inch heel. I retrieved my spare set of keys from the large potted fern creation that sat in the corridor between our lofts. I felt obliged to say something, although it was obvious what had happened.

'I forgot my keys.'

He nodded smugly.

Privileged New Yorkers had the right idea: the only downside to this building was that you didn't get to veto prospective neighbours. How a disreputable hack like him could afford an apartment here was beyond me.

'Thanks for buzzing me in,' I said, and unlocked my front door.

'Would you like to come in for a cup of coffee?' he asked suddenly.

'Much as I would like to pass the time of day with you, some of us work for a living. Thank you, but no.'

'You're not still angry about that piece in the papers, are you?'

I shrugged. 'Not at all. Freedom of the press and all that.'

He had written an article about dubious compensation lawyers who promised 'no win, no fee', but required you to take out exorbitant insurances. And he had the audacity to cite me personally as a specialist compensation lawyer. He hadn't said I was unscrupulous, but the very mention of my name in his diatribe was enough. I worked for one of the most prestigious and prominent law firms in Scotland. That was certainly *not* how we worked. We took a percentage.

He grinned. 'That's not what you said at the time! You called me a vicious, ill-informed, two-bit hack!'

I batted my eyelashes facetiously. 'I'm sorry. I really am behind schedule.'

'Come on,' he urged, 'come in and have a coffee. Let's bury the hatchet.'

Bury it in your head, I thought, but said quite firmly, 'I'm sorry. No. I'm late for a meeting. I have to go.'

'One little cup of coffee?'

'What part of "no" don't you understand?'

'Is that hostility I'm sensing?'

'I'm very glad you're sensing something. No. I. Do Not. Want. A. Coffee.'

I marched into my apartment and attempted to slam the door shut. It didn't catch and bounced back open, but mercifully he didn't follow me in.

I went over to my computer station while simultaneously kicking off my wrecked shoes, but didn't spot the Murphy versus Broadwood file.

Irritably, I glanced around my living room. The air smelled stale and almost sweaty.

A wall of French doors ran along the entire south side of my apartment and opened on to a large decked terrace. When I was tired, frustrated or bad-tempered, which was most of the time, fresh air usually helped. I opened a door and stepped outside in my stockinged feet.

From the edge of my terrace I looked across the city, taking deep slow breaths and trying to absorb warmth from the weak sunshine. I glanced at my watch and cursed. It was nine twenty.

12

Going back inside I searched angrily for the Broadwood file, which I located finally under a magazine on the coffee table. I was sure I hadn't left it there. I carefully put the file on my computer station and hurried to my bedroom for a fresh pair of shoes. The sight that greeted me was astounding.

A naked woman astride Alex jumped off him with a shriek. It was Mrs McCaffer. I stood in the doorway blinking in astonishment as they both squirmed about the bed grabbing sheets to cover their modesty.

'Get out,' I managed to say.

'Erin, it's not what you think . . .'

What? I snorted in disbelief. Mrs McCaffer had accidentally tripped and impaled herself on him?

'Get out. Both of you,' I hissed and reeled into my dressing room.

I supported myself against a shelf until I could concentrate. My heart was thundering in my chest. I was completely stunned.

Find a fresh pair of shoes. Alex and Mrs McCaffer? Who would have thought it? Find fresh shoes. Find another pair of shoes. This was a trick I had taught myself for moments of crisis. I would focus on a mundane task, consciously detaching myself from what was around me.

Dr Eunice McKay, my psychoanalyst, would have turned in her wing-backed chesterfield if she had known about my diversionary tactic. 'You must face your emotions,' she warned. But treating them with complete detachment was the safe option because it put me back in control.

My shoes were carefully organised in styles and colours. It was far too easy to locate another pair of black heels.

13

'Erin, we need to talk about this. It's not my fault.' Alex's voice reached me.

I sat down on the dressing-room chair and put on my shoes. My pulse raced and sweat collected on my lip. I closed my eyes for the briefest moment and focused on poor Mrs Murphy and her two little boys. Focused on how they had been denied their father for three years. They needed me at my best. That's what they paid me for. I had to get a grip of myself. Mrs Murphy needed me.

It had been over between Alex and me for months. I didn't really want to sort this out. How could I? My pride was at stake. He had slept with another woman. It was the excuse I had needed.

I marched out of the dressing room.

'Erin, we need to talk. We need to talk about what this is really about.'

'There is nothing to talk about!' I snapped. 'Get out. We're finished. Leave *my* apartment. I want all your things gone by tonight.'

'You can't just throw me out! I have a right to be here.'

He threw back the sheet and grabbed his boxer shorts.

Mrs McCaffer looked smug and that really got to me. A low-life like her daring to look smug at me? Me? Scotland's tenth most eligible woman according to last year's *Sunday Herald*.

I sauntered towards the door with more poise than I felt.

'From where I'm standing, you've blown your rights. Get out or I'll throw you out.'

'You can't make me!' Alex bellowed.

I wasn't used to men shouting at me. And I was well versed in being thoroughly nasty to Alex because I held all the cards. It was my apartment, my car, my money. I wasn't accustomed to him shouting back. Normally, he attempted apologetic conciliation. But that morning he came after me.

'You can't push me around! You can't make me do anything.'

I didn't respond. I simply picked up my keys.

'Erin, you're not leaving. You'd better stay here and sort this out . . .'

He gritted his teeth and barred my exit. I could see he was furious but I wasn't sure whether it was the thought of losing me or the fear of being chucked out.

'This is my apartment. I don't want you here. I want you to leave.'

Annoyingly, my voice was high pitched. Emotional confrontation had that effect on me. I could win a legal argument hands down, but when it came to personal conflict, I was way out my depth. I backed away from him nervously.

'You stupid, conceited, frigid little cow! You can't get rid of me! I've got things on you. You're an arrogant, spoilt, fucking misfit. "Don't touch me, I don't like it!"'

He matched me step for step as I backed towards the terrace. I felt cornered and very scared.

'Alex, it's over. Please leave. I can make you leave if I have to. You don't really want that, do you? A big scene?'

He laughed in my face.

'You'll make me? Will *Daddy* sort it out? Will *Daddy* make me? Only if the old bastard lives long enough!'

His spit landed in my eye.

'Is *Daddy* going to sort out *bad* Alex? Will *Daddy* fix it?' he sneered.

'Shut up Alex! Shut up! Don't you dare mention him.'

Triumphantly he smiled down at me. 'You think your father gives a damn about you? He couldn't care less about you. What's left of his fucking brain only cares about fucking ducks! He's history! Is that what's wrong, Erin? Daddy doesn't love you the way he used to?'

Before I knew what I was doing I had picked up the heavy bronze cast of *Seated Female Figure* and smacked him across the head with it.

He fell to his knees, clutching the side of his face.

'Jeezus Christ . . . Jeezus . . . Jeezus . . . God . . .' he moaned.

I wanted to smash his skull in. I wanted to bring the statuette down on his soft fair hair. I wanted him to feel the pain my father did. I pushed him on to his back and bent over him.

'You ever mention my father again and I'll kill you. You ever come back here, I'll kill you. I'll bloody well kill you. Do you understand?'

I gave him a hard kick in the ribs and he moaned again. I could see drops of blood ooze between his fingers.

'You had better be gone by tonight.'

I tossed the bronze statuette at him and glimpsed Mrs McCaffer, now decent in some tacky leopard-print dress, gawking from my bedroom.

I ignored her and calmly picked up my file, but found Paul Gabriel blocking my exit. His face was ashen. He stared down at Alex, curled up on the floor.

'I think you'd better call an ambulance,' he said.

'You were trying to cover for them!'

I pushed past him but he caught my arm.

'Erin. I think you should call an ambulance. He's hurt!'

I yanked my arm away.

'Fuck you! Fuck the lot of you!'

On the third-floor landing I picked up my grey silk raincoat and glanced at my watch, but a noise escaped from my throat. Tears filled my eyes. Now I would have to run to be back in time for the Broadwood settlement.

Tears and running. Two of my least favourite things.

TWO

The managing director of Broadwood Ltd, Mat Cohen of Cohen Freidmann, Solicitors, my assistant Douglas Thomson, and Michael McCabe were already seated round the boardroom table when I swept in uttering apologies. We got down to business immediately.

They droned on about the settlement, itemising the details for the hundredth time. I could see that they were getting mildly agitated by my apparent disinterest.

The sun streamed in, making it hot and uncomfortable on their side of the table. I could have put the blinds down but I wanted them to sweat. I wanted them to sweat as much as Bernadette Murphy had during the last three years.

Poor Mrs Murphy. Terrified of lawyers, terrified of the future without her Danny, terrified of what would become of her and the two small children. This settlement had been on the table for two years, and only now, with a court date finalised, were they willing to actually sign. It disgusted me.

I was also irked that Michael had continued to sit in on the meeting. He had only needed to cover for me while I rushed back to the office. This was my stage; I didn't need prompting from the wings.

'Gentlemen, I think we've heard enough.' I smiled benignly around the table. Mat Cohen and Mr Broadwood visibly relaxed.

I smiled again.

'I simply cannot recommend this settlement to my client.'

There was a stunned silence. Mat Cohen gasped.

'I thought we had an agreement.'

I sighed heavily and shut my file. 'We did. Two years ago.'

'Are you now saying you want to go to court?' Mat glanced at his client. I noticed with satisfaction the patches of sweat on Mr Broadwood's shirt.

'Mat, all I am saying is that two years is a long time.'

Mat glared at me and then at Michael. The hairs stood up on the back of my neck. Something was afoot.

'I would like to consult my client in private,' Mat said grimly.

I nodded and indicated for Douglas to leave with me. Michael followed us out.

'What the hell do you think you are doing?' Michael hissed as soon as the door closed behind him.

'I'm playing hard ball.'

'For God's sake! We've got to settle. If this goes to court and she's awarded less than the five hundred thousand on offer, she'll have to pay their costs. And ours. She'll end up with two hundred thousand if she's lucky!'

I noticed the heavy frown lines at the corners of Michael's mouth as he spoke. Strange how you see someone every day, but you stop observing them age.

'I am well aware of the law, Michael, but they could have settled two years ago. The interest alone is worth forty grand. They wait until three days before we go to court to finally sign an agreement. Come on?' I tried to sound nonchalant, but Michael's tone had put my back up and Douglas's ears were flapping; it would be round the office by tea break.

19

'You've made a bad call,' Michael muttered.

Douglas coughed to indicate the door to the boardroom had opened. We silently filed in and took our seats. Mr Broadwood was flushed.

Mat Cohen cleared his throat. 'We are willing to offer your client a further twenty thousand in good faith.'

I nodded and let his words hang in the air.

'Thank you, Mat. That is kind of you and I appreciate the good faith with which it is offered.'

I watched them relax again. I lived for this – the drama, the bluff, the sabre-rattling.

'However, I would say a further seventy-five thousand would be more appropriate.'

Mat Cohen nearly jumped out of his chair.

'What? You are way out the ballpark! Our original offer plus twenty is more than generous.'

'And I do appreciate that, but gentlemen, we are two years further on. Two more years in which Mrs Murphy and her two small children have been denied the love, comfort and financial support of a dedicated husband and father. I would reconsider your position, especially in light of the fact that at this moment in time we are not pursuing an admittance of negligence.'

Those final three words were my caveat and they both knew we had a case.

If they were found negligent, then Health and Safety would be all over them like a rash, but more importantly, the insurance company would be disinclined to pay the damages. Broadwood would be liable, probably forced into bankruptcy to make the pay-out, and neither Cohen, Mrs Murphy nor I would see a bean.

It was a risk, but one I felt was worth taking. People didn't hire me to say yes to the first offer.

Silence. Douglas shifted in his chair and Michael glared out of the window. I saw a muscle twitching in his cheek, but I couldn't figure out why he was so irritated.

I stood up.

'If that's all, I suggest we end this meeting.'

I made my way to the door; Douglas faltered slightly before he rose to his feet, glancing from me to Michael and back again. I made a mental note to reprimand him. He was my assistant, not Michael's. What I said, went.

Mat Cohen thumped his fist heavily on the table.

'You play a hard game, Erin. Five hundred and fifty thousand. Not a penny more.'

I allowed myself a smile. 'Done. Thank you. I have all the papers ready to be signed. It was a pleasure doing business with you.'

'The pleasure was all ours,' Mat Cohen muttered.

Mr Broadwood looked thunderous, but I knew the money wasn't coming out of his pocket. Employers' Liability would pay the compensation. The insurance company instructed Cohen and he would have been given a top line. I knew the business.

Michael had been pressing me for several months to change sides and act for the insurance companies. There was a part of me that wanted to throw my hat in with the big guns of litigation, but there was also a part of me that enjoyed the mild celebrity that came with being the lawyer to whom the maimed and bereaved could turn. I liked being the champion of the plaintiff. More truthfully, though, I didn't want to dance to somebody else's tune. With the big, fat, insurance conglomerates I would just be part of the chorus line. On my own I always got to play the lead.

I was anxious to get to my office and call Mrs Murphy with the good news. Once we had taken our twenty per cent, she would be left with four hundred and forty thousand, clear. It felt good to know it would mean a new life for her.

Karen had a peculiar expression on her face as I approached her desk.

'Please get Mrs Murphy on the phone for me,' I said, as I waltzed past.

'Miss Paterson, Miss . . . there're two men to see you . . . I've put them in . . .'

I held up my hand to silence her. 'They'll have to wait. Have they an appointment?'

She shook her head.

'This isn't a drop-in clinic. Send them away and get Mrs Murphy for me.' My moment of glory was being chipped away.

'But, they're . . .' Karen glanced anxiously at my office door.

'You put them in *my* office? I don't believe it! You must never put anyone in my private office without an appointment.'

Karen's face reddened.

'And get Mrs Murphy on the phone.'

I marched into my office. The two men who were sitting opposite my desk stood up and turned as I entered.

'Gentlemen, you must excuse me. There has been a small misunderstanding. You have to make an appointment to see me.'

I smiled frostily while holding the door open.

The elder man reached into his inside pocket and pulled out a credit-card holder. 'Miss Erin Paterson?'

I nodded. Why couldn't they take a polite hint?

'I am Detective Inspector Stevenson from Stewart Street Police Office and this is Detective Sergeant Marshall.'

DI Stevenson held out his ID card. I stared at it in momentary confusion.

'We would like a few words, Miss Paterson, about an incident earlier this morning.'

This I had not foreseen.

I closed my door and went to my desk.

'Please, take a seat. Would you like some coffee?'

'No. Thank you.'

'You don't mind if I do?' Before they could answer, I buzzed Karen on the intercom and asked her to bring me a coffee.

'Miss Paterson, this morning your, em, partner, Mr Alexander Faraday, reported you for assault,' DI Stevenson stated plainly.

'Yes?'

The police officers glanced at each other.

'You're admitting it?'

'No, not at all.'

'Mr Faraday is in the Western Infirmary, suffering from a suspected fractured skull and a large wound to his left temple. It required eight stitches.'

'Oh,' I whispered lamely.

'Mr Faraday claims that you assaulted him in an unprovoked attack and that you also threatened to kill him.'

'Right, right . . .' I nodded several times.

Karen appeared with my coffee. She glanced at the two policemen. The staff would have a field day with this, I thought miserably.

'Miss Paterson, did you threaten Mr Faraday?' DI Stevenson shifted the weight of his huge frame from one buttock to another.

How did policemen get so fat? I sipped my coffee and felt it scalding my mouth.

'Miss Paterson? Are you all right?' DS Marshall asked.

'Yes. Sorry. What was the question?' It was taking me some time to regain my composure.

'Did you threaten Mr Faraday?'

'Yes, I did, but it was purely rhetoric. I may have said "I'll kill you", much as an angry parent says that to an errant child. It was not meant literally.' I winced at my own bad choice of words.

'Was this before or after you bludgeoned him with the bronze statue?' DS Marshall enquired.

'After, I believe. However, I only hit him in self-defence.'

'Self-defence?'

'Yes.'

'After you caught him with another woman?'

'Yes and no. I didn't hit him until he chased me into the living room and cornered me. Then I hit him.'

'You were in a state of fear?'

'Great fear. Terror, in fact.'

'Mrs McCaffer, a witness to the event, said that you hit Mr Faraday in a frenzy of jealousy and threatened to kill him.'

'Mrs McCaffer? Oh, yes. That would be the care-taker who was taking care of Mr Faraday,' I said lightly.

DI Stevenson took up the baton. 'Miss Paterson, I don't think you grasp the seriousness of the situation. I'll have to ask you to come down to the station.'

My phone buzzed and blinked. It was Karen. I ignored it for a moment.

'Am I being arrested?'

'Yes,' DI Stevenson replied grimly.

I nodded and picked up the receiver.

'Mrs Murphy on line two,' Karen whispered.

Instinctively I whispered back, 'Put her through.'

'Hello, Mrs Murphy? Yes. It went very well. Very well. Exactly what we had hoped for . . . Yes . . . Thank you . . . No, thank you . . . Please don't cry, Mrs Murphy . . . I would love to speak to little Danny and Eamon, but maybe another time . . . Yes, yes . . . I'll come over on Sunday. Yes . . . At five o'clock . . . I'd love to . . . Yes. I'm sorry, I'm very busy right now . . . Yes . . . Thank you . . . Goodbye Mrs Murphy . . . bye.'

DI Stevenson read me my rights and I said that I understood. I picked up my handbag, got my raincoat and left my office in a stupor.

My floor had ground to a halt. The assistants and secretaries tried to look busy but they were all watching me. I walked ahead of the two arresting officers and maintained a dignified calm. Karen was waiting at the lift, looking wide-eyed and pale. I smiled reassuringly.

'Forget about earlier, Karen. I didn't realise it was Strathclyde's finest. Could you put a call in to Marcus Mayes? I may need his help. He'll be in court right now, but alert him to my situation.'

Karen gave a sob, which surprised me. She seemed genuinely upset by my misfortune. I had always been rather cool towards her and had imagined she thought I was a patronising cow.

I didn't speak to the officers in the car journey to Stewart Street Police Office for several reasons. I wanted to find out exactly what they had on me. I wanted to make them uneasy with my polite self-assurance. And I was scared. I didn't fancy being locked up in a stinky police cell one bit. I was scared of handcuffs and ill-treatment. I was scared of real criminals and what they might do to me.

Lawyers specialise. I specialised in compensation claims for victims of accidents, medical negligence, and also class actions for multiple claimants. Some lawyers specialised in corporate law, some in tax, some in criminal work. We knew very little about one another's field of expertise. And as police stations were not places I frequented, I wasn't entirely sure of the procedure. I knew as much about police matters as anyone who has ever watched *The Bill*. Would they fingerprint me? Would they take away my belt? Would they make me wait for hours in a cold, grey cell smelling of faeces and boiled cabbage?

DI Stevenson and DS Marshall, however, were the epitome of politeness. They ushered me into an interview room after the desk sergeant took my details. It was surprisingly civilised.

We went over the events of the morning again. It was vaguely depressing telling complete strangers about coming home to find my boyfriend shagging the domestic help.

'And you didn't return to your apartment because you suspected something?' DS Marshall asked again.

'No. I came home because I had forgotten an important file for a compensation case that was due to settle today.'

'You went straight up to the flat?'

'Yes. I had to use the stairs because the lift was out of order.'

'But you claimed that you buzzed Mrs McCaffer's flat. Were you checking to see if she was there?'

'*Yeesss*, because I had forgotten my keys – and she

has keys because she cleans for me.' My tone bordered on condescending.

'You were forgetting lots of things this morning. Your files, your keys . . .' DI Stevenson let the sentence hang. I ignored it.

'Mrs McCaffer did a bit of cleaning for you?'

'Yes. Cash in hand. Twice a week. She also cleans for several of the other residents. You could say she's a bit of a scrubber.'

DS Marshall's lips twitched and I sensed a potential ally.

'In her statement she says that you went into the living room, picked up the statue and attacked Mr Faraday.'

'She's lying. They have concocted the story together. I went into the living room to get my keys and the legal file. I wanted to leave. Mr Faraday followed me and threatened me. It was then, and only then, that I picked up the statue. I was under severe provocation.'

'Mrs McCaffer and Mr Faraday's statements tell a different story. They say that you launched an un-provoked attack on him, which has put him in hospi-tal. You also threatened to kill him.' DI Stevenson leaned forward, pressing his beer belly against the desk and stared me out. He had a face like a bag full of spanners and was obviously enjoying this. 'You are in a lot of trouble.'

I stared back at him but said nothing.

There was a knock and a constable popped his head round the door. He mumbled something to DI Stevenson who, with a grunt, heaved himself out of his chair. He terminated the interview and switched off the tape, but gave me a smirk as he left.

DS Marshall smiled awkwardly at me. I smiled back. He was quite attractive in an institutionalised way. He was about my age, clean-cut and smartly dressed. When the silence became too much we spoke in unison.

'Would you like a cup of tea or coffee?' he asked.

'Have you any idea how long this will take?' I asked. We smiled again.

'I would love a cup of coffee. Thank you.'

He got up. 'Milk and sugar?'

'No, just milk, please. Quite a lot of milk, thanks.'

'Baby coffee?'

That took me by surprise. Baby coffee was an unusual expression, not used by the masses. Maybe DS Marshall had hidden depths?

'Detective?' I called. He turned back and waited for me to speak.

'I know this looks very bad and I know I shouldn't have hit him, but truly it was in self-defence. I was scared. He's much bigger than I am, and he had lost his temper because I told him it was over. He really was behaving in a threatening manner.' I looked down at my hands sorrowfully.

'I suppose I should have hit him with my hand, but then he could still have attacked me. Self-preservation took over. I needed to give myself time to get away from him . . .' I let my voice trail away.

DS Marshall sat down opposite me and said softly, 'You needed time to escape from the danger?'

I knew he would understand. 'Yes.'

'And you used that extra time to kick him and threaten him?'

I narrowed my eyes slightly. So DS Marshall wasn't just a pretty face? Obviously, recruitment standards in Strathclyde Police were rising.

I shrugged. '*Touché.*'

He winked. 'You'll get community service.'

DI Stevenson returned to the interview room a moment later. He looked like someone had died and for an awful moment my mind went into overdrive. It would be bloody typical of Waster Alex to quit early. I could just see myself in *Prisoner Cell Block H*, surrounded by dodgy haircuts.

'Another witness to this morning's incident has come forward,' DI Stevenson said.

I blinked at him. I didn't know what he expected me to say. It was a ménage à trois and number three was hiding in the yucca plant?

'A Mr Paul Gabriel, your neighbour.'

My heart sank.

'He said he heard everything.'

'He's a journalist! You can't believe a word he says! This is just more copy.' I folded my arms huffily across my chest. I could see the headline: TOP LAWYER IN LOVE-RAGE ASSAULT.

DI Stevenson perked up visibly.

'So you say he's lying?'

I thought for a moment. Why would old Beefy look perky?

'No, because I have no idea what he has said. I have to presume that in this instance he has told the truth and confirmed it was self-defence.'

If I had stuck a pin in DI Stevenson, he couldn't have deflated faster.

They released me, pending further enquiries, half an hour later.

DS Marshall offered me a lift back to my office but I said no, that I would prefer to walk and relish my freedom. He told me to steer clear of the art gallery, as there was an exhibition of Rodin sculptures.

I walked back towards my office and switched on my mobile phone, which had been off since the previous evening. There were eight new messages. Three were from clients, one from Marcus Mayes, one from my mother (whoever had told her was in for it) and one from Karen saying she had cancelled all my appointments until after lunch. Alex had left one saying that he wouldn't press charges, which explained why they had suddenly let me go. All these messages were standard and unremarkable. Except the third.

It sounded very like a man masturbating. For a moment, I envisioned Alex and Mrs McCaffer getting a weird kick from sending it to me. There were grunts and moans and finally a throaty climax. I didn't want to hear it, but I couldn't turn it off. I wasn't good with intimacy, whether talking about it, doing it, seeing it or thinking it. Intimacy had no place in my life. Hearing a man's orgasm was way out of my league. It made me wince. I was about to delete all my messages when my mobile rang.

'Erin? Erin?'

My mother had the quaint idea that mobile phones didn't work very well and you had to shout. I supposed one could blame it on people yelling, 'I'm on the mobile,' on trains and buses, but as my mother had never set foot on public transport, she was unlikely to be aware of that. I held the phone away from my ear.

'It's your mother. Are you all right?'

'Yes, I'm fine. It was all a simple misunderstanding, nothing for you or Dad to worry about.'

'What on earth were you doing? Getting yourself into such a mess!'

'It was a simple misunderstanding.'

'But think of the firm! Think of the bad press. We'll take out an injunction to stop them!'

Only my mother could make any situation worse.

'Mother, please! Please don't do anything. You don't know the whole story. Mother, promise not to do anything.'

There was silence.

'Mother? Promise me!'

She tutted angrily. 'You'll regret this.'

I was regretting it already.

I switched off my phone for the sake of some peace. I knew I needed to go back to the office, but I was worn out and jittery.

That was the huge downside to my crisis-control technique; it left me with a load of issues that were never dealt with.

I knew I should only use it to get through post-mortem reports and harrowing testimony, but it was so successful in that department that I increasingly relied on it to guide me through the quagmire of my personal life.

I wanted to find a quiet, dark corner in a bar to sip a glass of ice-cold wine, but there was little chance of that on a Friday lunchtime. I racked my brains for somewhere I wouldn't meet anyone I knew. Glasgow was filled with style bars and restaurants. It was a running joke that a new one opened every week. But I didn't want style. I wanted comfort and anonymity.

I sifted through the morning's events while wandering the streets, turning each new corner in the hope of spotting just the right place.

I had hit Alex and wanted to kill him. That unfamiliar fury truly scared me. I had a difficult and fiery

31

personality, but had never resorted to physical violence. The presumed safety of my office exerted a magnetic pull. I found myself in front of The Paterson Building. William opened the door for me and looked like he was about to say something comforting but then thought better of it.

I stepped into the lift, rallied my strength and expected most of the office to be out to lunch, but I was greeted by a cacophony of phones ringing, calls beeping on hold and faxes spewing paper.

Karen was standing by her desk, unopened sandwiches in hand, answering one call after another. My heart leapt. I had been out of touch for three hours tops, and something major had happened. I shrugged my shoulders quizzically at Karen, but she instantly combusted to a beetroot colour.

'Miss Paterson is unavailable. Goodbye.' Karen hung up the phone. Immediately it rang again.

'Good afternoon. Miss Paterson's office,' she sang.

'No. I'm sorry. Miss Paterson is unavailable. Goodbye.' Karen put down the phone again. It rang at once.

I glanced at Douglas and the two other secretaries who were missing their lunch break. They, too, were fielding calls.

'Ignore it.' I indicated the phone. 'Come into my office and tell me what the hell is going on.'

Karen sat down, still clutching her home-made sandwiches.

'It's the press. They know about ... about ... this morning.'

'I see.'

And I did see. I saw Paul Bloody Gabriel standing in my doorway, watching the whole drama unfold.

'Has it been going on long?'

'Since about twelve thirty. We heard you were released, a reporter phoned, and then we were deluged. The main switchboard is simply transferring all calls for you to here,' she explained.

'Send a note of my clients' names to the switchboard and tell them to hold all calls for me apart from anyone on that list. We'll never be able to work with this going on. And eat your lunch.'

Karen nodded gratefully and closed the door quietly behind her, cutting out some of the noise. I slipped off my shoes, rubbed my tired feet on the thick carpet, and put my head down on my desk.

The only reason Paul Gabriel had offered the police a statement was so he could run this story. If I had been charged, his statement would be *sub judice*.

For an insane moment I had actually thought he might be all right.

THREE

By 5 p.m. my staff and I were exhausted. Not only did we have every hack within a two-hundred-mile radius calling us, but also well-meaning business associates. In one sense that was a good thing.

When my professional acquaintances picked up tomorrow's papers, none of this would come as a complete surprise. But it was very bad in every other sense. I didn't fancy my name and my love life being splashed all over the tabloids.

I gazed out of my office door and saw Douglas and Karen yawn in unison. I flirted with the idea of taking them for a well-earned drink, but it wasn't my style and they had lives outside the firm.

Wearily I began to pack up for the weekend – not at all the weekend I had planned – and switched off the computer.

I knew I couldn't go to my apartment, the very place I longed to be, in case Alex had already been released from hospital and was waiting for me. I racked my brains for some other safe haven, but my mind kept throwing back the same suggestion. Go home. Not as easy an option as it sounded. It was a bit like handing oneself over to the Spanish Inquisition.

'Let's call it a day,' I said to Karen as I came out of my office. 'There's no point in trying to field them any longer. If somebody does call about a pending case, they'll call back on Monday.'

Karen breathed a sigh of relief. She looked worn out.

I cleared my throat and said loudly, 'I want to thank you all for your outstanding help today. Hopefully by Monday, everything will be back to normal.'

The assistants and secretaries stopped to listen.

'You have all been brilliant and I can assure you it is much appreciated. I am also sure that I don't have to remind you that your contracts of employment contain a confidentiality clause, and if the press do contact you, a simple "no comment" will keep you right. Thank you once again. Good night.'

I nodded towards Douglas and Karen and went to the lift.

I felt bad about mentioning the gagging clause, but I was fairly certain I couldn't rely on loyalty alone to keep my staff silent. Loyalty requires respect, of which I had plenty, but it also requires a quiet dose of affection, on which I could not rely. It didn't bother me that many of them saw me as arrogant and demanding, but on a professional level I needed to trust them, and if clauses and threats were the way to do it, so be it.

Karen scuttled up to me as the lift arrived.

'Miss Paterson, a man called several times. He was very insistent that I tell you he called . . .'

Alex. Alex begging for forgiveness. Alex begging for another chance. The prospect of going through the severing process again was depressing, but I accepted the notion of his apparent heartbreak. Not that I would change my mind. Mrs McCaffer was merely the catalyst I had been waiting for. I nodded for Karen to continue.

'A Mr Paul Gabriel. He said it was absolutely crucial that you speak to him.'

I gave a shriek of disbelief. Karen jumped.

Tentatively, she held out a sheet of memo pad. 'He left his phone numbers and several messages.'

I took it without looking at it, crumpled it up and put it in my raincoat pocket. I would bin it in the lobby.

'Thank you, Karen. You really have been a wonderful help today.'

I held out my hand and shook hers.

Coyly, she smiled back at me. 'I hope I'm not speaking out of turn, Miss Paterson, but I think you've been remarkable. Not many people could hold themselves together the way you have.'

If she only knew the half of it.

Instead of going straight down to reception, I stopped at the second floor. I wanted to speak to another lawyer in the firm, Elizabeth Miller. She had risen up the ranks quickly and had been made a junior partner last year. She was a corporate lawyer and very good. I liked her candour and wicked sense of humour. I also knew she would tell me what was really being said about the whole debacle.

A partners' meeting had been held earlier in the afternoon and everyone had made sympathetic noises about my predicament, but I knew that, if it had been one of the other partners involved in such a sordid mess, I might have been less than understanding.

Liz looked up from her computer as I knocked on her open door.

'Hold on.' She indicated for me to remain in the doorway as she leapt to her feet. Then she gathered up a vase, a Lladro figurine and photograph frame. With a flourish, she carefully placed these on the shelf behind her desk.

I strolled in and shut the door behind me. 'Very droll.'

'How are you coping?'

'As well as can be expected. Do you mind if I cut to the chase? What's the word?'

'Not very good. They're worried about how it will reflect on the whole firm. Then there's the Law Society to consider. McCabe was making the most noise. He's not your biggest fan, is he?'

'Was there any discussion about what they'll do?'

'Matthew Stuart is advocating a wait-and-see policy. He seems to be the voice of reason. He said that all press is good press. He is very much of the opinion that you are a star player.' Liz leaned forward conspiratorially. 'You have my complete and utter support. If you had asked, I would have decked him for you.'

I smiled. Good old Matthew. As the chief executive his views were of great importance.

'Thanks, Liz. You fancy going for a quick drink?'

She grimaced. 'I would love to, but we're going to Allan's aunt's seventieth birthday party tonight. I'm helping with the food.'

'Party animal! Have a good time. Would you keep your ear to the ground for me?'

'Of course. One other thing – but I'm not sure what it means. My assistant saw Michael McCabe and Mat Cohen in a very animated conversation earlier. I didn't think anything of it, but I thought Cohen was one of your lot?'

By that, Liz meant a compensation specialist. Michael was a tax lawyer. Cohen and he were not natural associates.

'I don't know,' I said vaguely, but all this crap with Alex was forcing me to take my eye off the ball. Yet another reason to resent him.

The lift was crammed with my colleagues. The hush that fell over the small space was unnerving. I was acutely aware of seven pairs of eyes boring into the back of my head. Normally I was treated with obvious respect; I hated this feeling of smirking, nudging familiarity. I prayed that it would be short-lived. I stepped out of the lift first, head held high, and made straight for the front door only to be deflected by William.

'Miss Paterson, if you please. I have organised for a car to collect you in the basement car park.'

I nodded, mildly perplexed, and allowed myself to be directed towards the stairs. William opened the door for me and then insisted on going ahead of me, 'in case of any nastiness'. It seemed an odd turn of phrase.

I wasn't expecting any nastiness apart from a couple of reporters, perhaps. I doubted that members of the public would be incensed enough by my sorry tale to hurl rotten eggs. However, I appreciated William's concern and followed him to the blacked-out Mercedes. I instructed the driver to take me to my apartment because I wanted to pick up my own car.

It was only when we drove out into Bath Street that I realised what William was concerned about. Three press photographers ran forward and began snapping ineffectually at the blackened windows. I turned my face away and felt a sharp pain in my chest.

It was worse, much worse, than I had expected. This could damage my family's good name. It all went hand in hand with damaging the firm. I could imagine my mother's reaction.

I collected my car without any trouble and headed for my parents' town house in a South Side suburb. They had wanted me to remain in a large Victorian flat that was within walking distance of their home, but I had seen too many American sitcoms and was determined to have my 'Manhattan' loft. I found my loft and Manhattanised it as much as I could, but there was no getting away from the fact that I lived in Glasgow.

Pollokshields was known as the garden suburb and was the original model for Hampstead's own garden suburb. It was the largest, intact, Victorian district in Europe. With its wide tree-lined avenues, large gardens, grand houses and surrounding parks, it was an oasis of greenery in the city.

The low October sun glinted off my Jeep as I drove past glorious, sandstone villas alongside Maxwell Park, but the wintry sunlight didn't comfort me. I was dog-tired and bewildered by the fuss that had blown up around me. It must have been a very quiet news day.

My parents' house was in a cul-de-sac that over-looked the duck pond. I noticed several cars parked outside and was maddened by the idea of our family home being staked out by reporters.

I drove my car straight up the driveway, but it was remarkably quiet. Only after I put my key in the front door did it dawn. This was far more sinister than the press – it was my mother's bridge club.

I beat a hasty retreat and let myself in through the back door. I wanted to go quietly upstairs and lie down before any of my family berated me. The dogs, Smith and Jones, had other ideas and bounded from their baskets beside the Aga to apprehend the intruder.

Apprehending intruders was their life. It involved ferocious barking, followed by knocking to the ground and licking to death. They were two, fat, old, black Labradors and about as vicious as a pair of angry tortoises. I tried to shush them but they were ecstatic to see me. I then tried to bribe them with a Bonio.

I crept from the rear of the house into the wood-panelled hall and attempted to sneak past the door that led from the dining room to the ballroom.

'Erin? Erin? Is that you? Come and say hello, dear,' my mother called.

I cursed under my breath. Facing the Law Society would be preferable.

There were twelve of them, three tables of four, the matriarchs of the good and the great. It was an intimidating sight. They all smiled at me, saying hello, but I could see the gleam of anticipated gossip in their eyes.

I dutifully went round each table until finally I reached my mother. I kissed her proffered cheek.

'How are you, dear? Was it awful?' she asked, without actually taking her eyes from her hand of cards.

'Terrible. They strip-searched me, then used a cattle prod.'

'Oh, my God! Well, that's it, then! We'll sue!' Mother looked up at me, her mouth wide open.

I smiled and her eyes narrowed. 'You made that up.'

'Mum, it was fine. A little misunderstanding. OK? Nothing to worry about. Is Dad up?' I wanted to kill the conversation stone dead.

'Yes, dear. He's in his study.'

I went back round the tables, saying polite things to several of the ladies, then made my excuses.

'He was never good enough for her,' I overheard my mother say as I left.

'Yes, Georgina, but time isn't exactly on her side now, is it?' clucked another. Their inevitable discussion of my biological ticking was odious. I closed the door and went upstairs.

My father's study was at the front of the house, nestled between two large bay-windowed bedroom suites. The stairway to the billiard room, which was on the floor above, cut a chunk out of the room, giving it a pleasingly odd shape.

I loved his room with its papery smell, its mahogany panelling, plush sofa and serious desk. My father sat in the semi-light close to the arched double window, staring out over the pond and the park beyond. In his good hand he clutched a pair of binoculars. He might have been asleep.

I entered quietly and whispered, 'Dad?'

He beckoned me with a flick of his binoculars.

I stood behind him, resting my hands on his wheel-chair. 'What is it?'

'Look. In the top of the berberis.'

He pointed a trembling finger at the front garden. I peered out the window, desperate to please him.

'Oh, wow! It's a gold crest!'

'I think I might get a pair this year.' When my father spoke, the words only came out one side of his mouth.

The enunciation was not clear but I understood every single word he uttered. The second stroke, the big one, had left him paralysed down his left side, with severe tremors. I refused to believe my family when they claimed it had also robbed him of his faculties. He was lucid to me. I thought they used it as an excuse not to spend as much time as they should with him, as an excuse to ignore him. Admittedly, sometimes he was ponderous, but what he said made sense. It wasn't his mind that was impaired but the frail body that housed it.

'Got a lot more ducks now. And a pair of swans come and go,' he mumbled.

'So all that work they did on the pond helped?'

Land Services had planted the edges of the pond

41

with bulrushes, water irises, marsh marigolds, variegated reeds and water lilies. They had created a small nesting island to protect the ducks from the large urban fox population. I watched as a dozen mallards swooped low across the pond, circled and finally landed.

'Got more seagulls, too.'

'Are they a problem?' I leaned over his shoulder slightly so I could let my cheek lightly touch his hair.

'In the mornings. With the bread. Smith and Jones soon put paid to them.'

I could envisage the two black monsters hurtling into the park and chasing the gulls. They worked as a team. Smith would go out wide, with Jones cutting a swathe through the middle. Next to intruder-apprehending, chasing gulls, squirrels and magpies was their speciality.

'Dad, something happened today. I, I . . .' I didn't know how to tell my father that I had assaulted a man.

'I've spoken to Mother. The press won't come here.' He held the binoculars up to his eyes. 'I'm sure that's a grebe.'

The conversation was over. In the fading light I gazed at the crowd of ducks bobbing on the pond. They all looked the same to me.

'Can I get you anything?'

'No. I'm fine.'

We sank into companionable silence. He never asked me about the firm these days. In the weeks after his stroke he had still wanted to know, but now it was as if that part of his life, our lives, was over. A distant memory. I sometimes tried to talk to him about cases and problems, but he would change the subject. I wondered if it was painful for him to talk about his loss.

'Is Max home?' he asked suddenly.

'I don't know. Do you want me to check?'

'Yes. I want to show him the grebe.'

I left his room and went in search of my four-year-old nephew, namesake of my father.

I went back down to the mid-landing where Max and Brontë, who was my younger sister, had their bedrooms. There were no lights on in either room but I could hear Max's little voice jabbering away. I opened his door silently and watched him playing.

He had lots of tiny Lego men on top of his pine toy boxes. They were involved in some sort of complicated battle. He had medieval knights fighting cowboys and Indians, who in turn were in cahoots with ancient Egyptians, who were fighting a rearguard action against Vikings and astronauts, but the real heroes were tiny figures from *Star Wars*. He sang little nonsense songs under his breath and then changed to dialogue, each character receiving its own comic voice.

It was a wonderfully vicarious pleasure observing his unselfconscious play. I didn't spend enough time with him, my only nephew, but neither did the rest of the family. His upbringing was shared between anyone who was available. He was well loved and secure, but the demarcation between Mummy, Granny, Papa, Auntie and the hired help was slightly blurred. It worried me, not for now, but for his future. He was far too willing to dole out his affection to anyone who showed the slightest interest.

'Max,' I cooed.

For a moment he gazed at me with his innocent, blue eyes, before his face split into a grin and he bounced to his feet.

'Ern! Ern!'

I gathered him up and swung him round, burying my face in his warm neck, and stroked his fine blond hair. His father must have been blond, not that we had ever seen him. The rest of us were all blessed with dark hair and deep brown eyes.

'Darth Maul's trying to kill Lookout Skywalker, but Handsome Solo's going to sneak up behind him and kill him with his life-saver! The astronauts are helping!'

He struggled free of me and dived back over to his game. 'Look, this knight's got a machine gun. Take that, you animal! Ratatatata . . . ratatatata . . .'

'Have you had your tea yet?'

'Nah. Mum's out.'

'Papa wants you to go up and see him. He's got a surprise.' I picked up one of the Lego men and examined it. They were amazing, so intricate. Lego had come a long way since my day.

'Is it a duck?' he asked.

'If I tell you, it won't be a surprise. Tell you what, I'll give you a piggy-back.'

That swung it.

I crouched down and let him scramble up my back, pulling my hair. We messed about on the stairs in fits of giggles before I deposited him at my father's door.

'Bet it's a duck,' Max whispered as he went in.

I wanted to go in with him to share the moment, but was worried that if I shared it that would take something away from my father. Moments were finite in my view, just like emotions. They didn't come from an endless resource. Instead, I went downstairs to the kitchen.

Martha, our housekeeper, was packing up for the day.

'Martha, what's for Max's tea?' I asked, as I opened the fridge and peered in.

'Your sister went to Safeway's, but that was ages ago. I wonder what's keeping her?'

Martha pointedly looked at her watch. She didn't need to say anything further. It was par for the course. Brontë would pop out on an errand and return hours, sometimes days, later. I didn't understand why my parents put up with it. Having a child on her own at age twenty-four hadn't affected her social life whatsoever. She was even more selfish and irresponsible, if that was possible.

I opened the freezer and took out Dinosaurs and chips. I spread them on a baking tray and popped them in the oven. The dogs' tails thumped expectantly on the tile floor. Martha stuck her head back round the door.

'That's me away. I don't want to disturb your mother.'

'Have the dogs been fed?'

Martha shook her head. 'Dog food was on the list.'

I had tea with Max, stealing his chips and laughing at his awful knock-knock jokes. We went upstairs so I could change out of my suit and put Max into his pyjamas. We curled up together on the sofa to watch *The Simpsons*. Listening to his laughter was therapeutic; it lulled away my spin cycle of worries. We were in a cocoon. I even felt distanced from the bashing-Alex fiasco.

Brontë finally swanned in at seven thirty.

I blinked at her in shock. I could tell she had been drinking. She rushed over to Max, who was almost asleep on my lap.

'Mummy's baby! Mummy's baby!' she shrieked and covered him in gin-soaked kisses.

'Mummy! Mummy!'

He leapt up and hugged her, his eyes gleaming. I wanted him to be surly and petulant. I wanted him to punish her for her disregard and self-indulgence.

'What have you done to your hair?' he asked.

'I've gone blonde. Just like you! I wanted to look just like you, angel boy.' She turned to me, not noticing my disgust or choosing to ignore it. 'Because he's so blond, people often don't think I'm his mother!'

'I wonder why?'

'Oh, don't be so grouchy! D'you like it? I think it suits me.'

She fluffed up her new platinum locks.

Max reached up and touched her hair. 'I think you look beautiful, Mummy.'

'It will be hell to keep,' I observed.

She tutted and slumped down beside me.

'You're such an old killjoy. You'd think you were thirty-five going on fifty.'

I shifted away from the smell of cigarettes, peroxide and gin.

'Thank you. Where's the car?'

'Oh, God! I forgot! I left it at Safeway's. I met some friends and we decided to go for a drink and catch up on old times, you know, so I left it there.'

'With the shopping?' I could feel irritation tickle in my throat.

'I did the shopping,' she said indignantly.

'Big of you!' I snapped, as I stood up and left the room.

The sound of Max giggling and Brontë telling him that Auntie Erin was an old pooh-bum followed me.

I went back down to the kitchen where my mother was heating something unidentifiable for Dad's dinner.

'Brontë left the shopping at Safeway,' I sighed.

'I know, dear. The dogs are starving. But I can't collect it. I've had a couple with the girls.' She stirred the pot absent-mindedly while she read the paper.

'Do you want me to go? I could take the dogs.'

'Would you, dear?'

Supposedly, opposites attract, a fact borne out by my parents. My father was solid and rational; he seldom lost his temper and retained a remarkable equilibrium. My mother, however, oscillated wildly between hysterical overreaction and complete disinterest. She was sometimes so laid-back that she was almost horizontal. I put it down to her artistic temperament. Obviously, my fifteen minutes of her attention were up.

Nobody had asked me what it was all about. Nobody had enquired after my state of mind. It was my own fault, I supposed. Having discouraged them from invading my privacy, I had inadvertently given them the completely wrong impression. They had mistaken my need for independence as a declaration of self-sufficiency. I lingered for a couple of minutes in case she was suddenly gripped by a wish to comfort me, but she continued to stir and read.

'If you've got time later, can we go over the quarterly reports for the firm?' I asked.

She blew air out her cheeks and didn't even glance at me.

'Do we have to? Can't you just sign them off on your own?'

'Yes,' I said tightly. 'But I thought you might like to go over them, so you know where you stand with regards to projected profits this year.'

'I'm sure they're fine.'

47

She began to root around the kitchen for a tray. Cue to leave, I thought irritably.

I collected my sister's car keys and the dogs and walked to Safeway's. It made a change from my usual Friday-night routine of a long hot bath, a glass of expensive wine and dinner in a lovely restaurant.

Brontë had gone out again by the time I returned. I didn't need to ask where. It was Friday night, therefore she would be at The Granary with the other post-twenty-five lonely hearts. Max was tucked up in bed with a variety of cuddly toys. His devotion to Elmer the Elephant and Tracker the Beanie Baby was particularly heart-warming because they were from me.

I unpacked the shopping while stepping over the circling dogs. I hadn't lived at home for a decade but I still knew where everything went.

I poured myself a small glass of Penfold's and began the onerous task of telephoning people I was due to see over the weekend. I couldn't face anyone; so I cancelled lunch with Cecilia on Saturday and visiting the annual Royal Glasgow Institute art exhibition with Catriona later in the afternoon. They were both very understanding. Ironically, I had purchased the statuette of *Seated Female Figure* at the RGI the previous year.

My mother was in the drawing room playing Chopin's *Fantasie Impromptu* on her concert grand, and my father was in bed. I loved the sound of her playing as it drifted through the house. She was a talented pianist when she met my father, their romance budding by the light of a candelabrum. I pictured them seated side by side at her Steinway. When he had his second stroke, I had tape-recorded her playing his favourite pieces but he said it wasn't the same.

I went upstairs, switched on the TV and settled down

to watch *Friends*, like so many other unattached women on a Friday night. It made me ache for my loft.

Frantic barking alerted me long before the doorbell rang. I swore the dogs could hear a mouse sneeze at the bottom of the garden. I had visions of the paparazzi blinding my poor mother with their flashbulbs, so I leapt off the sofa and spilled white wine down my grey cashmere turtleneck and trousers. As recompense, I decided to set the dogs on the cheeky bastards.

My mother was hovering at the drawing-room door as I came down.

'Are you expecting company?' she asked.

'No. It's probably Jehovah's Witnesses.'

With mother watching, I had to put my dog-attack plan on hold. I opened the door, pushing my leg into the gap so that Smith and Jones couldn't barge out.

'Yes?' I said haughtily.

'Miss Erin Paterson?' A middle-aged man looked past me, seemingly unconcerned by the two barking monsters.

'What do you want?'

He held up his ID. 'I'm Detective Superintendent Kelman, from Lothian and Borders Police.'

I closed the door slightly because Smith was jumping up at me. 'And?'

'I would like to ask you a few questions about an incident this morning.'

I sighed pointedly and silently wondered what it had to do with Lothian and Borders.

'I've been through all that at Stewart Street. The charges were dropped.'

The officer looked bemused. 'You spoke to Strathclyde Police about Lucy Grant?'

'No. About Alexander Faraday.'

DSI Kelman leaned forward. 'This is another matter, miss. It is very important that I talk to you. I have a car waiting and use of Govan Police Office, if that's more convenient.'

'Lucy Grant?' I asked. The name vaguely rang a bell.

'Yes. May I come in?'

'I'll put the dogs away first.'

I closed the door and forced the dogs back into the kitchen. I recited the name over and over in my head hoping to ignite some spark of recollection. *Lucy Grant? Lucy Grant? Lucy Grant?*

I went back into the dark hall, pausing to turn on a side light that cast long, dull shadows.

I hesitated at the front door, my hand on the Yale. *Lucy Grant?* I repeated as I opened the door to the police officer.

A blast of cold air followed him in. It made the hairs on my arms stand up.

FOUR

I showed him into the dining room and smiled apologetically.

'I'm afraid I don't recall Lucy Grant.'

DSI Kelman seemed surprised. 'You don't know her?'

'I don't think so. May I ask what this is about?'

'Lucy Grant went to the same school as you,' he replied.

'Did she? I'm sure she wasn't in my year . . .' As I spoke it suddenly came back to me. 'She was called Lucy Granville-Grant at school. She was in my sister's year.'

It was a strange thing, but I could probably name most of the girls that had attended the exclusive Edinburgh boarding school.

'Brontë, isn't it?' he asked.

'Yes, but my sister isn't at home right now.' I couldn't see what Lucy Granville-Grant had to do with me.

'Lucy Grant was raped and murdered this morning,' Kelman said plainly.

I gasped.

'Good Lord! What on earth happened?'

'I'm afraid I'm not at liberty to discuss that, Miss Paterson. However, we recovered Miss Grant's mobile phone from the scene and the last calls appear to have been made to your home phone and mobile phone. What were the calls about?'

I blinked at him and shook my head. I might have

51

been a bit out of it earlier in the day, but I certainly didn't remember taking a call from Lucy Grant. I hadn't taken any calls from lunchtime onwards.

'I don't know,' I said genuinely. 'I don't remember taking a call from her today, but my mobile phone was switched off for most of it. She may have left a message that I haven't yet picked up.'

DSI Kelman looked at his notebook. 'There was a call at 9.32 a.m., and another at 10.37 a.m. which lasted for forty-six seconds, Miss Paterson. Something must have been said.'

I shook my head again. 'No. I am positive I didn't speak to her. My answering service was on all morning, but I checked the messages and there were . . .'

I stopped mid-sentence. Kelman narrowed his eyes ever so slightly.

'What exactly was the message?'

'I didn't get a message from her but there was one that was . . . disturbing. I had rather a stressful morning. It may still be on my messaging service.'

'May I hear it?' he asked.

'Certainly.' I stood up and went towards the door. 'My mobile is in my handbag in the kitchen.'

'I'll come with you, if you don't mind.'

He followed me. What did he imagine I was going to do?

I got the mobile from my handbag and began to dial my voicemail.

'May I have it?' he asked and held out his open hand.

I gave him a look. 'There are private messages on here. I'll get you to the right one.'

'Miss, this is a murder inquiry. May I have the phone?'

This time it wasn't a request. I shot him a glare as I handed him the mobile.

Chopin flooded the house as we returned to the dining room. *Prelude in B minor* was my favourite piece. It added a strange, unearthly quality to the surreal circumstances.

I was aching to put him in his place. This was a gross invasion of my privacy. The quiet insinuation that I was hiding something provoked my less amiable streak.

'How do I get the messages?' Kelman asked.

I snatched the phone irritably and keyed in the number again.

'This is quite out of order. My clients may have left confidential information.'

'I'm not interested in your clients.'

He sat perfectly still as he listened to my messages. I tried to recall exactly what each one said. It was painful to have him intrude into my personal life. I knew there was one from my mother shrieking about the debacle with Alex. And one from Alex pleading for forgiveness. I cringed inwardly.

Suddenly DSI Kelman went rigid, his face tightened and his colour drained. Was there a message from Lucy that I had missed?

He listened to the rest of the voicemails and then said, 'How do I repeat them?'

'You press seven.'

He began to listen to them all again, but his eyes rested on me. Irrationally, I felt guilty. What had he found?

'Listen to this.'

He held the phone up to me. I had to bend down to hear it.

'That was a crank call, the disturbing one I mentioned. I didn't get a chance to delete it. Surely that wasn't from Lucy Granville-Grant?'

'It was received at 10.37 this morning. Exactly when Lucy Grant phoned you.'

'Lucy sent me a crank phone call?' I said dubiously. Kelman stood up and began pacing the room. Something I was inclined to do myself.

'Miss Paterson, Lucy Grant was murdered this morning. At the approximate time of her death, a phone call was made to you. Would you care to explain that?'

'I can't explain it. I really didn't know the poor girl. There may be some tenuous connection through my sister but I really have had no contact with ... with Lucy Grant.' Her name stuck in my throat like a dry bone. I could vaguely recall her now. She was into horses and outdoor pursuits.

'Why would your number be programmed into her mobile phone?' he asked insidiously.

'I honestly don't know.'

'And the call at 9.32 a.m.? Why is there no record of the message? Did you delete it?'

'No,' I explained patronisingly. 'When the phone is switched off and a caller hangs up without leaving a message, the phone doesn't register it. If the phone is switched on, it registers a missed call.'

'Why did she call your home at 8.45 this morning?'

'I don't know! I never spoke to her. I haven't been home to pick up my messages. And as far as the crank call goes, I had no way of knowing that came from Lucy's phone. She didn't exactly leave her name.'

Kelman gave me a sour look, which irked me. I was sorry that Lucy had been murdered, but it had damn all to do with me.

'I will have to take your phone, Miss Paterson. Could you write down your access code?' He pushed a notepad across the dining-room table in my direction.

'OK, but I'll need it back by Monday.'

'Could the call be some sort of message to you?'

'Message to me? Are you suggesting that I might be in danger?'

He ignored my question. 'Are you aware of any shared acquaintances?'

'I really don't know. I presume that we must have known some of the same people, given our . . .' I hesitated for a second, 'our social connections. My sister might know who Lucy's friends are. She might know who we have in common.'

'When will she be home?' Kelman glanced at his watch.

'Good question. She may or may not reappear tonight. She's a bit, em, unpredictable.' That was putting it politely. She was out being a good-time girl. It all depended on whether she pulled or not.

'Are you OK? You look a bit pale,' he said.

'I feel sick,' I replied honestly.

The piano had stopped, which should have alerted me. Mother knocked, stuck her head round the door and smiled for a brief instant. Then her eyes narrowed.

'Mother, this is Detective Superintendent Kelman,' I explained, but she didn't bother to acknowledge him. I had never understood my mother's bizarre hostility to policemen.

Her voice was distinctly cold. 'I thought we had that all sorted out?'

'It's about something else,' I said. 'Mother, do you remember Lucy Granville-Grant? She was in Brontë's year.'

'Of the Granville-Grants?' She shifted uncomfortably. I knew she wouldn't want to discuss them in front of a mere policeman. I hoped she would at least be civil.

'Yes.'

'I don't really know. There were so many girls at your school. It's hard to recall each one.' I knew she was being deliberately obtuse. It was one of her favourite methods for avoiding unsavoury discussions.

'Well, did Lucy speak to Brontë lately?' Impatience strained my voice.

'She may have. I don't know. Your sister has lots of friends calling and such.' Mother gave me a hard look. 'You will have to ask her.'

'Where can we find your daughter?' Kelman said curtly.

'Erin knows where Brontë will be. Is Lucy in some sort of trouble?'

My mother's eyes had visibly darkened. Did she sense something was wrong? I cleared my throat. 'Lucy's dead. She died this morning.'

A tiny noise escaped from her. 'How?' she whispered. 'How did she . . . ? Did she . . . ?' She couldn't bring herself to say it.

She wanted to ask if Lucy had committed suicide. She had never recovered from Leland taking his own life. To her it was worse than an illness or an accident, which one could blame on God or fate. Suicide deposited all the guilt on those left behind.

'She was murdered,' I said softly.

'How awful . . . how truly awful . . . her poor parents . . .' Her voice trailed away. She cast a fleeting glance at DSI Kelman as she left the dining room. I heard the drawing-room door shut ominously and knew she would be hitting the gin.

'My elder brother committed suicide. My mother has never recovered.' I felt obliged to explain, but he immediately started on me again.

'You said you haven't been home to pick up your messages?'

'That's right. After I left the office I collected my car, but I didn't go up to my apartment.' I didn't add 'because I was afraid of meeting Alex'.

'But you were in your apartment this morning.' He pointedly checked his notebook then glared at me. 'Between 9.05 and 9.45.'

'I was there but I didn't pick up my answerphone messages. I was getting a file.' My tone bordered on insolent. He had obviously done his research. 'You can ask Mr Faraday or Mr Gabriel, my neighbour. They were both there.'

'Mr Faraday? The man you assaulted?' Kelman couldn't keep the dig out of his voice.

'No. The man I hit in self-defence.'

'You've got quite a temper on you. Family trait?'

I was taken aback by his presumption.

'My personality and family traits have nothing to do with you or your enquiries.'

Kelman leant back in the chair and weighed me up. I was familiar with this. Men frequently had to adjust their outlook on my account. They were struck by my natural beauty, but I could be as forceful or obstinate as any man. They seldom found trembling femininity.

'We'll need to check your answering machine back at your flat.'

'Fine.' I folded my arms across my chest. 'Alternatively, we could call my answering machine and use remote access. If there's anything on it of interest, you are welcome to it.'

'Right, then,' he snapped.

I got the cordless phone from the hall and dialled my machine. We then went through a repeat procedure

57

of earlier. Kelman listened to all my messages and then let me listen. All the messages were fairly innocuous, even the one from Lucy Grant. She simply said she would try me on my mobile. That was it. Nothing sinister or unusual. I could tell that DSI Kelman was disappointed.

He then had me call T-Mobile and authorise the police to access my phone and retain all my messages. Here I was, for the second time in one day, helping the police with their enquiries. But my mind kept repeating: *Lucy Grant was murdered, Lucy Grant was murdered.* I found it hard to concentrate on anything else.

There were so many questions I wanted to ask the dour policeman, but I doubted that he would tell me anything. Oddly, I felt I had a right to know because she had called me, but I knew it was a trivial link.

I was troubled by the silent inference that I knew more than I had disclosed and that Lucy Grant had some significant connection to me. Kelman asked me to help him locate Brontë, but apart from my directions, we drove in silence to The Granary.

He followed me through the crowds of Friday-night revellers who packed the popular bar. I knew from experience that Brontë would be in the larger main bar. I was self-conscious because people were staring at me and possibly not for the right reasons. Not for my height and appearance, not for my expensive casual clothes, not for my long, glossy hair. My stomach tightened as I silently wondered if I had made the local TV news. As the Glasgow saying went, it would be the talk of the steamie.

I saw Brontë at the far end of the bar where she was flirting with a group of three men, patently enjoying the renewed attention triggered by her ridiculous hair.

She was obviously well gone because she tottered a bit and sloshed her drink when she laughed.

I recognised two of her companions. They were a couple of low lifes I had seen before. They always seemed far too willing to buy Brontë another round.

'Brontë!' I called from behind her. She turned slightly and rolled her eyes.

She swung back to her admirers and said something that they found very amusing. I didn't want to imagine what it was. I put my hand lightly on her elbow and turned her towards me.

'Brontë. I need to talk to—'

'Go away! You're just an old spoilsport!' she sang loudly for the assembled company. She pointed at DSI Kelman. 'Who's that? Your minder!'

'No. He's a police detective. We need to talk to you.'

'Policeman! What have you done now? Have you been arrested again?' she shrieked.

There was a ripple of laughter from those nearby, but I wanted to slap her sneering gin-flushed face. Thankfully, DSI Kelman stepped forward.

'Miss Paterson, I would like to ask you a few questions. If you could come with me, please.'

'No! What about? I had nothing to do with her decking Alex. I wasn't even there this morning. And if he says anything different, then he's lying!'

'For God's sake, Brontë! This isn't about Alex.' I snapped. The mirth that had surrounded us disappeared and people began to step away.

Brontë glared at me. 'What is it, then?'

'We can't talk here. Come home,' I urged.

Kelman was shaking his head in disbelief.

'No! I'll bet he's not really a policeman. I'll bet you just hired him to make me come home.'

Kelman pulled out his warrant card and held it close to her face.

'Now, miss,' he said impatiently, 'why don't you put down your drink and come with us.'

Brontë scowled at him, downed her drink in one and slammed the glass on the bar.

We left by the side door, Brontë staggering slightly as she walked. I was mortally embarrassed.

She chattered all the way back to the house. It was like sitting beside a Furby on speed. Not once did she ask what it was about. Not once did she seem remotely concerned. I couldn't comprehend her or her way of life, limping from one unsuitable man to the next. She hadn't worked since university and even then she had dropped out in the third year. I couldn't understand her complete lack of direction. To drift aimlessly terrified me.

I wasn't allowed in the dining room while Kelman quizzed her and I wondered if that was significant. I had automatically presumed that by 'a message to me', he meant a threat, a warning. I made myself a coffee and decided that I was being paranoid.

DSI Kelman came into the kitchen.

'Could you make your sister a strong coffee?'

'Would you like one?'

'Yes, please. Black.'

I put two mugs on a tray. 'How's it going?'

He rolled his eyes.

'See what I have to put up with?'

'She says she hasn't seen Lucy for ages. And she keeps going on about traffic wardens . . .' he grimaced.

I handed him the tray of coffee. 'Maybe Lucy wanted some legal advice?'

He shrugged, took the tray and went out the door.

I sat down at the kitchen table and laid my head on my arms. Lucy and I were merely passing acquaintances, so she hadn't wanted to catch up on old times. Why hadn't she come through the office? Because she must have wanted to talk to me personally, therefore it could only be in relation to a legal matter. But that didn't make sense because Lucy must have known lots of lawyers.

I sat back upright.

Perhaps she needed specialist advice? Perhaps she was going to sue somebody for compensation? Did she have a great case and was killed for it?

I hurried through the house to the dining room and knocked on the door before entering. Brontë was sprawled over two chairs. Her gracelessness appalled me.

'I've just thought of something,' I said.

Kelman nodded and indicated for me to sit. 'I think we're about finished, Miss Paterson.'

Brontë yawned and nodded at the same time.

We waited awkwardly for my sister to get the message and leave. It was too much to hope for. Kelman cleared his throat. Brontë examined her nails. Kelman tapped his notebook. Eventually, I couldn't bear it.

'Brontë, I think you can go now.'

She looked from one of us to the other. 'Why?'

'Because we're finished,' Kelman said through gritted teeth.

She sat up slightly, spoiling for a fight. 'But Erin's still here.'

'*Jeezus, Brontë!* Go away!' I barked.

She leapt to her feet and spat, 'I hate you!'

I gazed at her pityingly; she probably did hate me.

There was an uncomfortable silence as we listened to her swearing and then slamming the front door.

'Sorry about that,' I apologised.

'She's not easy, is she?' Kelman stretched slightly in his seat. It must have been a long day for him. Almost as long as mine.

'What was it you thought of?'

'I'm a solicitor,' I began. 'I specialise in compensation claims for serious injury and death, medical negligence, that sort of thing. I also do class actions. Lucy Grant would have had access to lots of lawyers, so she must have been after my expertise.'

He nodded.

'Maybe she was going to sue somebody and they killed her to shut her up?'

Kelman eyed me curiously. 'Why rape her, then?'

'So it didn't look suspicious? To make it look like a sex crime. Aren't they usually random?'

'Your sister mentioned some gossip about an ex-boyfriend. Did you know about that?'

I shook my head. 'Maybe she wanted an interim interdict to stop him from bothering her, but she wouldn't come to me for that.'

Wearily, Kelman folded his arms across his chest.

Lucy was twenty-eight, the same age as Brontë. It was horrible to think about her death, her frightful, violent death. I forced the thought from my mind.

'I'm sorry I can't be of more use.'

Kelman got up to leave.

'Thank you for your help, Miss Paterson. And thank you for your candour.'

I assured him that I would get in touch if I thought of anything. He promised to send me a transcript of my messages.

I closed the front door and leant my back against the cold glass. I glanced at the grandfather clock and saw it was only 11.45. It felt much later. I put the chain on the door and then took it back off.

It was pointless double-locking it because I wasn't sure if Brontë would come home, especially after her histrionics. The thought made me shudder.

If Lucy Grant wasn't safe, then nor were we.

FIVE

The house I had grown up in now seemed vulnerable and exposed.

I went round the ground floor checking windows and doors. As I had suspected, the door to the basement wasn't locked and neither was the door that led from the basement to the back garden. My parents relied too heavily on the dogs as an early warning system, although I was glad of their reassuring presence as I crept through the damp basement.

It was the full size of the house and had six rooms, which had never been fully utilised. Two rooms still retained the original fireplaces from the days when it had been the domestic servants' quarters. Now it was filled with discarded belongings: prams, sports equipment, school trunks, the boiler, an ancient, rusty oil tank, and the collective debris of four grown-up children.

The dogs sniffed in dark corners with half-hearted interest. This confirmed that there was nothing more frightening than a lifetime of memories and spiders. I recalled scary games of hide-and-seek played with Brontë and various neighbours, the real fear being the spiders and mice. Finlay, my youngest brother, was still a baby then.

I locked the garden door, called the dogs and ran up the stairs. The single bulb that lit the cavernous space blew just as I reached the top. I locked the door and decided to wait until morning to replace it. I suffered from a fear of the dark and was in too foul a mood to search around the house for a torch and light bulbs.

My mother had irritated me with her disinterest in the quarterly accounts. She was forever telling me how poor they were, what with their losses as Lloyd's Names. It was hard to justify my father's continued share of the firm's profits when he was no longer able to consult. None of the partners had dared to say this, but I knew how business worked. If you couldn't pull your weight, then you were out. I tried to redress the balance by doing more than my fair share in bringing in fees.

Senex bis puer – the old man becomes the child. I felt a compulsion to look after my parents and wondered if all children eventually exchanged places with theirs to become the responsible adult.

In truth, though, it was my family's ungratefulness that irked me. I was indirectly financing the entire household, but was treated with a mixture of disregard and suspicious hostility. Brontë, Finlay and I earned a small income from the trust funds our grandparents had set up but, as far as I could see, my siblings used this as pocket money without making any contribution to the general household.

Before I went to my room I checked on Max. His soft breathing reassured me. My own bedroom hadn't altered since I was a teenager. Lying down in my four-poster bed, I tried not to dwell on my day but distorted images kept flashing behind my eyelids.

I could see Alex and Mrs McCaffer on the bed, but his adultery was an insignificant detail. The real issue was my violence. It had scared me so completely that even thinking about it was too frightening.

I turned over and buried my face in my pillow. I still

had to consider the fallout from my momentary insanity. The deluge of reporters indicated a fair degree of coverage, but there was a good chance it would blow over.

My fifteen minutes of ignominious fame.

I could only hope that the Law Society would avert their horrified eyes.

I let my mind drift. Brontë would be smarting for days after tonight's episode. Maybe, if Brontë got a place of her own, she would become more accountable and stop taking advantage of everyone for childcare. I could even offer to help her look for a suitable property.

And her drinking worried me. We had argued about it before. I couldn't remember the last time I had seen her one hundred per cent sober. And that wasn't all. I suspected she was dabbling in drugs, and could only hope they were 'soft', if there was such a thing.

I didn't like the people she associated with and not for the first time suspected her of pilfering. Little things would disappear: a solid silver Mappin & Webb bonbon dish, an antique tortoiseshell shaving set. Not only from here. I rarely lost my belongings, but had still managed to 'mislay' a Chanel clutch bag and a digital camera.

My parents had not taken the matter in hand. They seemed content to treat her like a wayward child, merely shaking their heads and throwing up their hands as if there were no other course of action. She had sponged off them her entire life and showed no signs of changing her ways.

I knew it was cynical, but I had always been sceptical of her motivation in naming Max after our father. It had the whiff of manipulation about it, forcing my parents to accept more readily an illegitimate grandson. His very name handed responsibility for him to his grandparents. And what about his biological father? Who and where was he?

I realised that over the next few days my mother would be in a foul mood. The spectre of her firstborn's death had returned and she would dwell on it relentlessly. I didn't think about Leland, my elder brother, very often, although only a year separated us. He was the last person anyone expected to commit suicide.

He was doing exceptionally well at Edinburgh University, lining up for first-class honours in law. He sailed through life, relationships and friends, where I struggled. Then, quite suddenly, he was dead.

Dead, like Lucy Grant. Her name crept insidiously into my mind. Why had she called me? I felt unwittingly involved in her death, as if I could have prevented it. If I hadn't thumped Alex, would I have taken her call? But the call could have been about anything. What did I have to do with her? What weird connection had been made?

My hands and feet felt unnaturally cold. I knew I had to shake this or I would never fall asleep. I closed my eyes and thought about my forthcoming cases, but they led me back to Alex and then to Lucy Grant. After an hour of turning and fretting, I switched on my bedside lamp and picked up *The Shipping News* by Annie Proulx. Not the cosiest of bedtime reading.

I woke with a start. Max was standing silently by the side of my bed, watching me sleep.

'What is it, honey?' I asked.

'I'm hungry.'

I glanced at my watch. It claimed it was eight thirty. I was expecting it to be the wee small hours. I felt I had hardly slept. I yawned noisily as I sat up.

'Is everybody else asleep?'

'Granny and Papa are having a lie-in and Mummy's gone somewhere.'

Max fixed his great pale eyes on me. There was something worrying him. I reached over and pulled him up on to the bed beside me.

'What's wrong, pumpkin?' I whispered.

'I'm lonely.'

'But you've got me!' I gave him a bright smile but my heart broke for him.

'Are you lonely, too?'

I didn't reply. I threw him back on to the pillows and tickled him until he begged for mercy.

We got dressed and went downstairs. The dogs were waiting at the back door, desperate to get out. Max spooned down some dreadful chocolate cereal and I made coffee. It was quite pleasant, his gentle, chattering company. My mother made an appearance half an hour later.

'How's my best boy this morning?' She gave Max a kiss.

'Ern's lonely,' Max replied.

My mother gave me an odd look. 'Are you?'

'No,' I sighed. 'It's a game Max and I were playing.'

'A game?' Max asked.

'Yes. It's called "eat up or I'll tickle you again".'

Max giggled.

'You're silly! Silly billy! Silly billy!' he crowed, then jumped from his seat and ran out of the kitchen. I sat down at the table with another cup of coffee.

'I think you're supposed to chase him,' my mother explained helpfully.

'Where's Brontë? Isn't that her job?'

'She didn't come home last night. Her bed wasn't slept in.'

I wondered how often she had to check Brontë's bed for signs of occupation. Mother busied herself getting a tray ready for my father.

'Mother, you really need to do something about her.'

'And what do you suggest?' There was an edge to her voice.

'Give her some rules. Parameters that she must adhere to.'

'She's not a child,' my mother snapped.

'My point exactly.'

'You're too hard on her. You're too judgemental. Not everyone can be as self-sufficient as you.'

'Nobody is hard on her! That's the problem. She gets away with murder!'

'Isn't that more your forte? Or are you just sticking to assault?' she replied blithely, as she carried my father's tray out of the kitchen.

Cheeky cow. I remained in the kitchen contemplating my protest.

It was never like this when my father was in charge. If we weren't spending the weekend at the cottage, then we were all up by 8 a.m. on a Saturday and had an organised day of tennis, horse-riding or sailing ahead. The family home was not the sanctuary I had envisaged. It came jam-packed with its own problems. I wanted to go back to my apartment, but first I needed to check if Alex had left. I had intended asking Brontë to phone – but clearly that was now out of the question.

Martha was standing in the doorway of the kitchen, clutching a pile of newspapers to her chest. I nodded a greeting but she just blinked at me and blushed. I stared back at her. She blinked again.

Martha had seemed perfectly sane when she began

working here, but evidently long-term, close contact with my family had a contagious effect.

'Martha? What on earth is wrong?'

My eyes had strayed to the *Sun*'s screaming headline: TOP LAWYER IN LOVE RAGE . . . EXCLUSIVE! Exclusive?

'Let me see that!'

Martha jumped a foot in the air and scattered the newspapers all over the kitchen floor. We both dived on them and began to gather them up. Martha tried to snatch away the most offensive colour exclusive.

'Give it to me!' I demanded.

She blanched and handed me the pages. I crouched on the floor and my own face stared back at me.

I skimmed through the type. Words like 'jealous', 'frenzy', 'unstable' and 'cold' jumped out at me. I was stunned.

There was a photograph of Alex and me at some charity ball, looking remarkably happy. I knew the photo. It was from my own photograph album.

I flicked to the next page where there was a picture of Alex, with a bandage round his head, holding the bronze statuette, and another of my loft living room.

He had let them into my apartment to take photos! He had sold me out.

I flung the paper aside and grabbed another. The *Daily Record* had a short article about the incident and the blacked-out Mercedes leaving the office. So the *Sun* really did have an exclusive.

The conniving, spineless, two-timing bastard! How could he?

I snatched randomly at the newspapers, looking for mentions in the quality ones. The *Scotsman* had a small article and an old photo of me on page five, but the *Herald* had a large article and had used the photograph from their '100 Most Eligible'. I closed my eyes. Tenth most eligible and first most idiotic . . .

I flung the paper away and picked up the *Sun* again. Next to the TOP LAWYER IN LOVE RAGE was a smaller headline: 'Heiress Murdered'. Lucy Grant and I were juxtaposed together.

In my mind's eye, I could just see Judas Alex cutting the deal. I wondered how much he got for selling me out. I hoped it was a lot. I hoped I was worth several thousand. It would add insult to injury if it were only a couple of grand. I toyed with telephoning our libel department, but I was pretty sure that the *Sun* would have worded its piece with extreme care. It would be punctuated with 'allegedly'.

I got up slowly, leaving the newspapers scattered about the floor. I was appalled.

'Are you OK?' Martha asked gently.

'I'm fine. Could you tidy these up? I don't want Mother to see . . .' I stopped abruptly. 'Why did you bring them?'

Martha shuffled the papers into some sort of order.

'I thought you'd rather see them here than anywhere else.'

I nodded, not entirely convinced. 'Bin them.'

'There're things in them that you ought to see.'

'Martha, I was there. I know what happened.'

'There's some other stuff,' she said.

'Oh, like I'm difficult? I'm cold?'

'There's that and some other *stuff*.' It was the way she said it. She offered me the papers. 'You had better read them.'

I rolled my eyes at her and took the bundle. I didn't

think I had too many skeletons in the cupboard – well, not any that Alex knew about.

My mother swept into the kitchen a moment later.

'Good, you're here, Martha. Can we get everything ready to go to the cottage?'

'You're going to the cottage?' I repeated.

'Yes. Your father wants to go.'

She gave me a look that told me she was still huffy about earlier. She didn't seem to notice the bundle of untidy newspapers I was carrying.

'With Max and the dogs?' I asked hopefully. Maybe I wouldn't have to retreat to the safety of my apartment after all.

'No. Max has nursery. We're going for the whole week, before it gets too cold.'

'Who's going to look after Max?'

'Who do you think? *Brontë*!' She snapped at me again. Twice in one morning. This was getting out of hand.

'OK. I'll see you when you get back, then.' My own tone left nothing to the imagination.

'Are you leaving?'

I smiled falsely. 'Yes. I'll just say goodbye to Dad and Max and then I'll get out of your hair.'

I had her. She wasn't expecting that.

She pursed her lips. 'Could you stay here until Brontë comes in?'

Our eyes met.

'How long will that be?'

The phone rang before she could respond. All three of us looked at it. Martha picked up the receiver and then held it out to me.

'Have you seen the papers?' Michael McCabe hissed with ill-concealed alarm.

'Yes.'

'What are you going to do?'

'Nothing until I've read them fully,' I said patiently. How about, *Are you OK, Erin*? How about, *Is there anything we can do*? But no, all I got was alarm and something that felt suspiciously like glee.

'Is it true?'

'I don't know. I've only scanned them. Tell you what, I'll call you if I'm going to resign.'

That was a joke. Michael was taking this far too seriously. It was a bit of juicy gossip. It didn't reflect on my effectiveness as a lawyer, certainly not in my eyes. I might get a dressing-down or a fine from the Law Society, but I couldn't imagine them striking me off. Me? Erin Paterson, daughter of Sir Maxwell Paterson, MBE. I thought not.

'I would prefer if you handed your resignation formally to Matthew Stuart,' Michael said solemnly.

I nearly choked. He was serious!

'I have no intention of resigning. I was joking. This will blow over in a couple of days.'

'Think of the firm. Think of your family. Erin, for once in your life put them first and do the right thing!'

'Piss off!' I said, and hung up the phone.

Martha and my mother stared at me. Mother spoke first.

'Who was that?'

'Just the residents' committee at my apartment building,' I said airily.

'And they want you to resign because you hit Alex?' Martha shook her head in disbelief, but it was my mother I was studying.

She was frowning. Normally, she would have laughed at the sheer absurdity of the residents' committee.

Something about my mother had changed over the last few months. I had ignored it at first, thinking I was imagining it, but now I was sure. It was the same feeling I had had during the Broadwood settlement. The feeling that all was not what it seemed, that there was a hidden agenda.

'I'm sorry, but I can't stay and look after Max. I need to go and sort some things out.'

'Oh, that's fine, dear. You go off and live your life. We'll be just fine without you,' Mother sniped back.

I chose to ignore her. It was their bed, they had made it and they could lie in it. If Brontë mucked up their plans, then I was merely proving my point. And it wasn't the first time. It was up to them to address it.

'Good. Have a nice week.'

I marched out of the kitchen, still clutching my bundle of scrappy newspapers.

Max was in his bedroom playing his Lego-men game. I watched him silently from the doorway. How many hours did he while away by himself in his Lego world? I could easily have taken him with me; I had done so before, nervously waiting for Brontë to call for his return.

I had been left with him for an impromptu week last winter, while she sneaked off skiing and my parents were in Portugal. Nobody knew where she was.

I hadn't minded looking after him but it was quite a feat of logistics, getting him to and from nursery and entertaining him in the office. It was the fact that she had abandoned him in the sure knowledge that one of us would simply step in to take care of him that irritated me.

I didn't disturb him by saying goodbye. It was selfish, really. He would want to come with me, but I felt

I must make a stand. I said a brief goodbye to my father, but he was engrossed in a new bird magazine that had arrived in the post that morning and hardly looked up. I collected my suit, briefcase and handbag, and left without another word to any of them. It was raining, so I shrugged my raincoat over my shoulders and scurried to my car. I scrabbled in my handbag for my mobile until I remembered that I didn't have it.

I drove to Safeway's to use the public phone. Having dialled my home number, I was told by that smarmy woman's voice that my number was unavailable. I closed my eyes tightly and tried to think of some other way of checking whether Alex was still there.

Everyone's phone numbers were programmed into my mobile. I had very few memorised. It was another twist of the knife. I contemplated ringing my mother and asking her to phone my apartment. A humiliation, but I couldn't think of what else to do.

I thrust my hand into my raincoat pocket, felt about for some more loose change and pulled out the forgotten memo sheet from the previous day.

Expecting some gloating, sarcastic message from Paul Gabriel, I unfolded it slowly.

12.30 p.m.: Call Paul Gabriel.

1.15 p.m.: Call Paul Gabriel urgently.

2.00 p.m.: Call Paul Gabriel urgently. Re: Alex in Dutch auction.

2.30 p.m.: Call Paul Gabriel. Re: Story sold.

3.15 p.m.: Call Paul Gabriel. Re: Damage limitation.

3.45 p.m.: Call Paul Gabriel. Very urgent. Re: Get an injunction.

4.15 p.m.:   Please call Paul Gabriel. Very urgent.
Re: Time running out.
4.45 p.m.:   Paul Gabriel called. Wishes you good
luck.

Wishes me good luck? The bastard. I stared at the piece of paper which had his phone numbers listed neatly at the top. Karen was truly a good PA.

I wondered if he was really trying to help me or if there was an ulterior motive. How stupid did he think I was? So the *Daily Record* had been outbid by the *Sun* and he thought he would pretend to be my friend. As if *I* was going to fall for that old chestnut. But perhaps he could have his uses.

I dialled his mobile but it rang out. I hung up and dialled his home number. He answered eventually, grunting hello. His phone manners were repellent.

'Hello, Paul? It's Erin Paterson here. Sorry I couldn't get back to you yesterday. I was snowed under.'

He yawned loudly. 'I can imagine.'

'I was wondering if you could do me a favour?' I spoke airily, as if it was of little importance.

'The mountain comes to Mohammed?' he laughed.

'Yes. Quite.' I took a deep breath and tried not to rise to his bait. 'Could you please tell me if Alex is still in my apartment?'

He made a strange groaning noise. 'OK. I'm still in bed. Give me a minute.'

I listened to muffled sounds and pictured him in a filthy vest, shuffling to the front door. I would lay money on his apartment being a pigsty of dirty plates and old take-out cartons. It took him an age to come back to the phone and I was down to my last twenty-pence piece.

'Em . . . the place is empty.'

'Did you go in?'

'Yup. The door was . . . eh . . . open.'

'Jeezus! Can't you shut it?' I barked.

'Er . . . no,' he replied, as my money ran out.

Er, no? Er, bloody no? What sort of neighbour was he? He couldn't even be arsed to shut my front door. I'd probably be burgled and it would be his fault.

I swung round and was faced by two old ladies and three youths openly gawking at me. Had the newspapers made me notorious so quickly? I stormed past them back to my car.

Screeching into the underground car park, I flung the Jeep into my allotted space.

I was puce with anger. Every nerve in my body sizzled and burned. I jabbed the lift button and waited, praying that it was working today. I heard it stop at the second floor and willed it to hurry up. Why couldn't they use the stairs? They only lived on the second floor. How hard was it to walk? It opened and the couple from 2B sauntered out.

'Oh! Hello,' the guy said, with conspicuous surprise.

I gave them a phoney smile and viciously pressed for my floor.

My front door was not open. It was completely off its hinges and propped up against the outside wall. Cautiously I popped my head inside. The apartment was wrecked.

'Jeezus H. Christ!' I cursed.

Sheets of paper littered the floor, bits of furniture were upended, lamps lay on their side, earth spilled from toppled potted plants. I felt my throat constrict.

I walked slowly to the centre of the room and glanced into my bedroom. It told the same dismal story.

I swallowed the tears away and searched for the phone under all the debris that had been my life. I found it under a chenille cushion beside the terrace door. I picked it up and dialled 999. It took me several seconds to realise that it wasn't working. Typical. The one day of my life that I desperately needed a phone and none was to hand.

I marched into the corridor and thumped on Paul's front door. I was irritated that he hadn't been waiting for me. For all he knew, I might have been very upset.

He took an age to answer. When he finally did, he had a towel round his neck, a pair of jeans on and an open shirt. He smelled of warm water and shower gel. I tried not to notice his six-pack and attractive scattering of chest hair.

'Hi. Come in,' he said casually, buttoning up his shirt.

I stared at him in disbelief.

'I can't believe you didn't hear this!' I flailed my arm behind me.

'I took a sleeping pill.'

'You look like shit,' I added nastily. It struck me that Paul wasn't the sort I imagined needing a sleeping pill.

'I know,' he said, as he walked away from me. I was flummoxed by his indifference.

'Have you called the police?'

'No. I didn't know if you would want me to.' He shrugged.

'I'll need to use your phone, then,' I snapped.

'It's to your left.'

I glanced around his loft. It was not what I had expected.

The colour scheme was dark and luscious. He had overstuffed sofas and two huge mahogany bookcases.

It was the complete opposite of my place, which was straight out of a *House Beautiful* showcase: understated, expensive and minimalist. His loft was warm, luxurious, tasteful and welcoming. His place was nicer than mine.

I rang the police, gave my name and address and reported the burglary, although I hadn't a clue what might have been taken.

'D'you want a coffee?' Paul's disembodied voice called to me.

'No.'

'Are you in the flat?' asked the woman operator.

'No. I'm in the apartment opposite.'

'Do you think the burglar might still be inside?'

'No.'

She told me that a police car was on its way. I put down the phone and stood aimlessly beside Paul's open front door. I could smell the coffee. I sighed and followed the scent.

Paul was leaning over a scrubbed-oak kitchen table engrossed in the newspapers.

'Admiring your handiwork?' I sneered.

He glanced up at me. 'I wasn't on your case.'

I helped myself to the freshly brewed coffee, but could feel him watching me.

'Are you always this aggressive?' he asked suddenly.

I thought for a moment. There was no point in lying.

'Yes.'

The corner of his mouth twitched with a smile. 'Bullied at school, huh?'

'Of course not!'

How could he laugh at me? My life had turned into a grotesque soap opera.

We stood in strained silence. I felt weak with hatred

towards him because I knew he was waiting patiently for events to catch up with me. Nothing gave my detractors more pleasure than watching me squirm and break down. I rubbed my knotted forehead.

'Don't stare.'

He dropped his eyes. 'Sit down. Relax.'

'Relax!' I shrieked. 'Relax? Have you any idea what I've been through in the last twenty-four hours?'

'Shouting at me won't change anything.'

He was right, of course. But I needed to shout at somebody and he was the only person available.

He pulled out a chair from the table. 'Here.'

Reluctantly, I sat down. He remained standing – right beside me. Hadn't he heard of personal space? Pointedly, I moved the chair away and stole a look at the newspapers.

The bundle Martha had bought was still lying in my car. What had she said? 'There's some other stuff'? I pushed the *Herald* aside and stared at the *Sun*'s front page, but my eyes were drawn to the piece about Lucy Grant.

I tried to recall her from school, but it was such a long time ago that her features merged into the composite face of any schoolgirl. I hoped that I had never been too hard on her. I was a prefect and undertook my duties rather rigorously. I thrived on the rigid schedules and routines. They gave me a feeling of security, of immunity.

My eyes wandered the page until a half-seen word attracted them. 'Eligible'. It was in the first paragraph.

'Lucy Granville-Grant was named in last year's *Sunday Herald* as sixth most eligible . . .' I read it twice. I had to admit I had kept a copy of the original paper to fan my own vanity. I hadn't realised that Lucy was mentioned in it too.

'Did you know her?' Paul asked.

'Not really. She went to the same school but she was six years below me.'

'I was at the crime scene yesterday.'

'Oh, God. What happened to her?'

'She was knocked off her horse, drugged, raped and murdered.'

'How did he . . . How was she . . . ?' I didn't want to say the word. In the back of my mind I could hear the grunts and moans.

'It's confidential.' He fixed his clear grey eyes on mine.

'I'm a lawyer.'

'I would need to be a client for that to count.'

His eyes never left mine. The unequivocal way we didn't trust each other was unnerving.

'I'll get my PA to call you. I'll accept a retainer.'

Paul viewed me speculatively for a moment, then pulled a crumpled tenner from his pocket and passed it to me.

'I'll need a receipt,' he said dryly.

This was the most unusual retainer I had ever received. I wasn't a prurient person but I needed to know how Lucy had died. I felt involved with the crime.

Paul handed me a pen and a Post-it pad, which I duly signed, acknowledging receipt of his meagre retainer.

He looked carefully at the yellow Post-it-note and put it in his wallet. Then he did something strange. He crossed himself.

'Are you religious?' Derision dripped from my voice.

He looked me squarely in the eyes. 'No.'

It made my heart flutter with apprehension. He turned away from me and gazed out the window.

'Her throat was cut and her tongue was removed. That can't go any further.'

I gasped audibly and my hands began to shake. I wanted to deny that I had actually heard it, but my mind was racing. I couldn't think of anything but her. Her gaping neck and hollow mouth.

My eyes filled with unwelcome tears, the tears I had been battling against for twenty-four hours. Once they had fought their way to the surface they were unstoppable.

I blinked up at Paul. He crouched beside me and put his hand on my shoulder.

'It's OK. Don't cry. It's OK . . .'

'But she . . . she . . . called . . . she . . . called me!'

He looked confused, tilting his head to one side.

'She . . . she . . . called me! On my phone! Me! I could hear . . . I heard him . . . him . . .'

I couldn't say any more and began to cry in earnest. Great heaving sobs and gurgles. But they weren't solely for Lucy.

Paul tried to pull me into his shoulder but I roughly pushed him away. I rarely cried and now I was a gibbering idiot in front of Paul Gabriel, of all people.

I was mortified. Inhaling great gulps of air I tried to compose myself, but I was overwhelmed by self-pity. My life was a wreck. All I had was my career and, in a blinding moment of madness, I had probably managed to wreck that too.

I had been suffering from stress and depression for years, and clung to the law as to a lifebuoy. I had lost the respect of my peers.

Through blurred eyes I saw two big shapes hovering by the entrance to the kitchen. To my eternal embarrassment, I shrieked.

82

The police constable was startled.

'It's all right, miss! It's all right. What happened?' He turned to Paul accusingly.

Paul stood up and cleared his throat.

'She and Lucy Grant were school friends.'

'Was she in the flat when it was broken into?' the older constable asked him, ignoring yesterday's murder.

'No. She was staying elsewhere. She only discovered it this morning. About half an hour ago.'

'She seems to be in shock,' the young officer observed fatuously.

I was trying to control myself, but every time I swallowed and took a breath the tears welled up again.

'Who else lives there?'

'Her ex-boyfriend left yesterday. Alexander Faraday?' Paul nodded towards the newspapers.

'Has anything been stolen?'

Paul shook his head. 'I don't know. You'll have to ask Miss Paterson.'

Apparently I was now invisible, as I sniffed into the tissue that Paul handed me. I sniffed once more for good measure and stood up.

'I'm fine now,' I said, but my lips quivered and I started to cry again.

'You just sit down, miss. D'you mind if we take a look at the flat?'

I shook my head and watched them leave.

Paul sat down opposite me and studied my face for a brief moment.

'You OK?'

I nodded. My tears had stopped and my breathing had almost slowed to normal.

'You were trying to tell me something before the cops arrived. What was it?'

I gave him a stony look. Typical man, trying to wheedle information out of me when I was vulnerable. I stood up and left his kitchen.

The two policemen were looking around half-heartedly. It was perfectly evident to me and probably to them who the perpetrator was. Both policemen looked surprised by my sudden reappearance and regained composure.

'Has anything been stolen?' the older officer asked again.

I shrugged and wondered if he read the *Sun*.

'I can't be sure until I tidy up. The stereo and TV are still here. That ought to tell you something.'

'So you think you know who did it?' he sighed.

'I have a fair idea. Alexander Faraday.'

I folded my arms across my chest. Fingerprinting would be pointless.

'Your ex-boyfriend?'

I nodded and moved some of the papers on the floor with the toe of my shoe. I wished I had finished him off yesterday when I had the chance.

'There is something missing,' I realised abruptly. 'My bronze statue.'

At that moment, DS Marshall stuck his head round the empty doorframe and knocked on the wall.

'Come in,' I said wryly. 'The door's always open.'

DS Marshall strolled in and quickly understood the scene.

'Your statue's missing? Maybe Mr Faraday took it as a memento?'

'Will I stick it down on the crime sheet, sir?' the young constable interrupted.

'I know where I'd stick it,' I muttered.

'So apart from the infamous bronze statue, nothing else is missing?' DS Marshall asked.

'Not as far as I can tell.'

'This appears to be a mindless act of revenge,' he said more to himself than me. 'We do have phone numbers for a good joiner and locksmith.'

'Do you have a spare phone?' I asked. 'I seem to be without one.'

DS Marshall gave me a knowing look. 'I heard.'

Realising that I wasn't alone with the knowledge was strangely comforting. I didn't count Paul because I was sure he hadn't understood what I so nearly told him. I was relieved that my tears had stopped me from disclosing everything. I had spent my whole life avoiding moments of weakness like that.

'You report it and I'll take it from here, boys,' he told the two constables.

When they had gone, DS Marshall offered to make me a cup of tea. I idly wondered if it was in the training manual. A: Make cup of tea. B: Appear sympathetic. C: Get confession.

I showed him into my stainless-steel and granite kitchen. Oddly cold compared to Paul's and hell to keep clean. When Max stayed here, I was forced to spend evenings buffing the shiny surfaces clean of little finger-marks. In the end, I had barred him from the kitchen.

'D'you want us to pick him up?' Marshall asked.

'Is there any point?'

'You might get your statue back.'

Marshall smiled. He had a nice smile, good straight teeth.

'It could come in useful if I end up with another cheating bastard.'

I put fresh coffee beans from the fridge into the grinder.

'You gave him an almighty thump with it.'

'You should see me when I'm really angry.'

'Whoa. I'm not ready for that yet.'

The 'yet' hung in the air between us and I turned to the coffee-maker to busy myself.

Paul coughed as he came into the kitchen. He looked DS Marshall up and down once and said, 'Erin, I've got to go out.'

I shrugged.

'Make yourself at home.'

He threw a set of keys at me with a gentle underhand. I caught them, mid-air, above my head.

'Reactions of a snake,' he commented.

'Mongoose. They kill snakes.'

Carelessly, I flung the keys down on the worktop, where they skidded to rest at my stainless-steel bread bin.

I knew I had been outrageously discourteous, so I retrieved the keys and put them in my pocket.

'You've got all my numbers if you need me. Feel free to use the phone.'

'Thank you.'

'See you later, then,' Paul said to me, ignoring Marshall.

There was a moment's silence but Marshall couldn't contain himself.

'Who was that?'

'Paul Gabriel.'

'Didn't he write a nasty piece about compensation lawyers?'

'Yes, but he's also my neighbour. And he told the truth about Alex.'

I poured the coffee.

'So you're friends now?'

'Not really.'

'I've spoken to Lothian and Borders.' It was a swift change of subject. 'They told me about the message.'

I sighed. 'I don't know why she called me.'

Marshall scrutinised my face. 'It must have been very disturbing.'

'It was even more disturbing when I heard what he had done.' As soon as the words were out I wanted to bite them back.

'What did you hear?' Marshall's whole body language changed. He sat up straight and leaned forward.

'I found out she'd been murdered. Until then, I thought it was a crank call. Or Alex.'

He relaxed a little. 'Oh.'

'Were you sent here to question me?'

He smiled again. 'No. I came here to make sure you were OK.'

'I'm fine, but I need to find a new cleaner. The present one is fired.'

We engaged in more chit-chat but my mind was wandering.

I wanted him to leave so I could begin the odious process of tidying up. And I was dog-tired of everything, of Lucy Grant, policemen, family, you name it – I was tired of it. My life only ran smoothly if everything was in its rightful place. Now it bore an uncanny resemblance to a snow-dome. Somebody had taken my life, shaken it vigorously and stood back to watch the fallout.

When DS Marshall left, I made a half-hearted start on my bedroom. Alexander had taken his belongings, which was something. I hadn't fancied stuffing them into bin bags and then dumping it all in the street. I wondered if Bitch McCaffer had helped him. I wondered where she was. Eventually, I went up to the top floor.

Mercifully, the two guest bedrooms hadn't been touched. I went into the room that Max used when he stayed over and lay down on the bed, but my bitterness towards Alex made me feel increasingly agitated.

Had he been here last night when DSI Kelman and I had accessed the answering machine? Had he been wrecking my apartment as we played the messages?

I didn't imagine for a moment he was heartbroken by our split and the vandalism to my home was proof of that. He was angry. Nothing more, nothing less. It was the most recurrent emotion I seemed to inspire in men.

And Lucy. Had she made some psychopath so angry that he raped and killed her? I had got away lightly. Broken ornaments and phones were nothing; inanimate objects to be replaced.

It led back to the same question. Why had she called me?

It struck me suddenly.

Lucy had called my home and left an innocuous message, but it wasn't Lucy who called me later. It was the killer. I had probably heard him raping her. What did that mean? Could it have been accidental? Could the re-dial on her mobile have been accidentally activated?

I was hostage to my own paranoia and self-importance. She had probably called me about something inane. Any link to me was tenuous because I was an incidental, a random factor. It could have been any phone number that was 'last dialled'.

It was simply unfortunate that it happened to be mine.

SIX

I woke with a start clutching one of Max's forgotten teddy bears. I tried to summon the strength to deal with my apartment, then glanced at my watch and leapt up. Three thirty? I had wasted so much time.

It was unnaturally dark outside, so I pushed back the voile curtains. The sky hung low, a soft grey shroud. Some days it never truly got light. I hated those days, living in a half-world of continuous dusk.

I peeked out from the security of the upper floor but nothing had changed. The fairy godmother of housework hadn't deigned to visit.

I needed a door and a phone. I went down to the kitchen and got the numbers DS Marshall had left, making a mental note to ask him his first name the next time we met.

I let myself into Paul's apartment and experienced an overwhelming urge to snoop around, but I had no idea when he would return. Being caught with my hand in his closets was way up there on my list of excruciating moments I could do without.

I did help myself to coffee, though, because I hadn't eaten anything for two days. I survived on coffee and the occasional glass of wine. It might have helped me to remain super-slim, but it wasn't exactly beneficial to my health and general well-being. I ate one of Paul's apples but it made my stomach growl.

I poked about in his fridge and found it well stocked. A range of cheeses, salamis, fruit, vegetables, fresh pasta, wine and milk. This man knew how to treat himself. My fridge held the bare essentials. It was better stocked when I was on my own, but I found living with someone difficult. I didn't want to fall into the 'looking after and cooking for' trap and so was over-zealous in the shared-domestic-duties department. If he didn't grocery shop, neither did I.

Listlessly, I dialled the joiner and then the locksmith. Both answering services promised they would be with me within the next twenty-four hours. Very comforting. Only one more day of no telecommunications and a gaping hole to contend with.

I knew I should tackle my apartment but I couldn't muster the energy. What on earth had happened to me? I was the busiest person I knew.

I picked up Paul's *Yellow Pages* and flicked to domestic cleaners. I didn't fancy French Maids or Mrs Moppit, so I flicked on to industrial cleaners. There I found Clean It All, who proffered an 'after break-in' or 'post-fire' service. I dialled the number and was told that they opened again on Monday. Naturally, all sane people were having the weekend off. It did offer an emergency mobile number, which I noted on the top of the page. I decided that this was an emergency if ever I saw one.

The man who answered was rough to say the least, but, on explaining my dire situation (minor celebrity status), I managed to persuade him to come out in an hour or two. I sat for fifteen minutes and then decided I would have my long-delayed bath. I didn't fancy using my own doorless apartment so I brought my towels, change of clothes and washbag through to Paul's.

I thought it would be polite to use the guest en suite, but found all the doors on the upper level were locked and the keys I had didn't fit. Odd, but maybe they hadn't been decorated. Or perhaps Paul used them for bizarre purposes. I hadn't seen many women entering his apartment in the last year, so I figured there wasn't a group of virgins trapped inside.

The master bedroom, like mine, was huge. It had a massive bed and was extremely comfortable. The furnishings were antique and went very well with the open space. I had to hand it to him: he knew how to decorate. I wasn't a creative person so I relied on others to give a room the style I would like.

I had chosen a modern all-white and chrome bathroom, fully tiled and almost clinical. Paul's, however, had a thick-pile carpet, a walk-in power-shower-cum-steam-room, and a raised Jacuzzi bath. And it was entirely mirrored down one wall. The kinky devil.

I locked the door and turned on the taps. Then I checked again that the door was locked. I climbed in and slipped under the warm water. The gentle lapping soothed me. I washed my hair in the bath, something I didn't normally do. I was phobic about leaving even a tiny trace of shampoo, convinced it would give me dandruff. After drying myself vigorously and putting on fresh clothes, I felt safe enough to return to my own apartment. I unlocked the bathroom door and nearly jumped out my skin because Paul was standing right outside.

'Jeezus! Don't do that!' I shrieked.

'I didn't know you were in there! I've just come home.'

I narrowed my eyes. A likely story. He probably had a secret peephole.

'I couldn't get into the other bathroom.' I flicked my head to indicate the one upstairs.

'It's locked. I use it as a dark room.' He gave me a weird grin. 'Did you find my whip and leathers?'

'Thankfully, no. As if I'd be interested in snooping through your things,' I retorted, as I flounced past him into the living room.

There was a strange little man waiting at the front door. Dwarfs and leathers? Paul was one weird bunny.

'Miss Peterson?' The man asked.

'Paterson.'

'Aye, right yous are. I'm fae Clean It Aw.'

'Oh!' That cheered me up. 'I'll show you through.'

'Aye, right yous are.' He eyed the propped-up front door with interest. 'Samwan forget thur keys?'

'Something like that.' I couldn't be bothered explaining it. All I wanted was for him to clean it up.

He wandered in and looked around. 'Domestic, huh?'

I was surprised by his perceptiveness. 'How did you know?'

'Aye, well, nutting's damaged, like. It's only messed up.'

He righted the sofa with an 'umph' of effort.

'D'yous wantae put the small stuff back and I'll dae the rest?'

I didn't actually want to do anything but I could see his point. He didn't know where I liked things put. We began to tidy up in silence. I didn't really need someone to help, but it felt better to have a companion rather than doing it all on my lonesome.

We had it back to some sort of order after a couple of hours. He was an industrious little man, getting stuck in to moving the furniture and cleaning the whole place. It almost looked normal when we finished. I tried to be positive and think how much worse it could have been. People felt invaded after a real break-in, but this was petty vindictiveness. I was grateful it hadn't been a stranger's hands disturbing my belongings.

'Yous are lucky, ya know,' the man commented while I paid him.

'Lucky? Like the three-legged, one-eyed, black cat?'

'Naw. Yous are lucky he didnae shit in yur bed and piss on yur sofa. Been tae those before. Gloss paint doon the loo an—'

I held up my hand to silence him. 'Yes. I'm very lucky.'

It felt strange to show him out of an open doorway.

It was knocking on eight o'clock and I was at a complete loss as to what to do with myself. Alex and I had been due at a dinner party at one of his colleagues', but that was no longer an option. I couldn't relax. I wandered from room to room rearranging things. I felt exposed and vulnerable without a front door. I moped into my kitchen and peered despondently into my fridge. Some past its use-by date hummus stared back at me. I was loath to do it but I needed to go to the supermarket. Worse was the prospect of asking Paul for his assistance again.

I caught a glimpse of myself in the mirror. My hair had gone big and fluffy, exactly how I hated it. I always dried it mercilessly straight and sleek. How could I venture out, saddled with my new-found notoriety, wearing big hair? It didn't bother me that my neighbour would see me, though, because he didn't count.

Paul looked drawn when he answered his door.

'I'm sorry to bother you again but I need to go to the supermarket. Could you keep an eye on my apartment and also listen for the joiner?'

'Empty fridge?'

I smarted slightly. Was my life that transparent?

'No. I have a date,' I replied tartly.

Paul gave a snort. 'It wouldn't be a certain police-man, would it?'

'No, and it's none of your business.'

'So, you're going to the supermarket and then on to a hot date?' Paul grinned.

'You are *so* rude.'

'Do the words pot, kettle and black mean anything to you?'

'What *is* your problem? Why are you always on my case?'

'Hey, hey. Calm down. I'm only teasing. Of course I'll watch your flat.'

He frowned suddenly.

'Erin, I know it's none of my business, but you've had a helluva two days. Why don't you kick back? Come in, I'll make some pasta and we'll watch for the joiner from here.'

I hated it when people were nice. Genuinely nice. I didn't want his sympathy or pity, but he was right. I couldn't be bothered going to the shops. I wanted to curl up somewhere and lick my wounds, but my own flat was now uncomfortable. I hesitated for too long. He flung open the door.

'Come in. I'll try not to annoy you.'

I made a big show of giving in. 'Promise?'

He held up crossed fingers as I bristled past.

'When's the joiner due?'

'Any time between now and next week, apparently.'

In the dull light I could see his computer glowing at the far side of his apartment. 'Were you working?'

'Yeah. Not getting very far.'

He wandered over to the computer and closed the file.

95

'Was it about me?' I asked timidly.

'Not everything revolves around you, you know.'

'You're annoying me,' I warned.

He held up his hands in mock surrender. 'I'm sorry. Let's declare a truce?'

I folded my arms across my chest and didn't reply. I found it very difficult to climb off my high horse.

'I'll take that as a yes.' He shrugged and went into the kitchen.

I deliberately didn't follow him and instead flicked on his wide-screen TV. It came on at BBC News 24, which he must have been watching. It was a dull interview with some southern English industrialist.

'Would you like a glass of wine?' Paul popped his head round the side of the opening that led to his kitchen. I had glass doors put in mine to stop cooking smells from permeating the apartment.

I thought for a moment. It would put our acquaintance on a new footing if I accepted a drink.

But before I could answer, Paul said, 'I promise not to take advantage of you.'

'As if you could,' I muttered.

'Red or white?'

'White, please.'

I flicked his Sky remote up and down, trying to find something mindless. I settled on an old episode of *Spin City*.

He returned with a glass the size of a small goldfish bowl, filled with very cold white wine. I took it gingerly. I didn't drink much because I liked to stay in control.

'Very novel,' I chirped. 'A pint of wine.'

He ignored my dig and sat down right beside me. Personal space was obviously not an issue for him.

He picked up the channel changer and went back to *BBC News 24*. In that instant, we had turned into an old married couple. Any second now he would start flicking through every channel, trying to find some football, only to settle on the one he had begun with. I could feel a prickle of irritation.

'I need to see a report that's coming up,' he offered as explanation.

I sipped my wine, which was surprisingly good and filled me with reassuring warmth.

'The tragic death of Miss Lucy Grant was the focus of intense police activity today,' said the BBC's correspondent in Scotland.

'The scene was cordoned off within minutes of the gruesome discovery on Friday morning. The Granville-Grants, a wealthy but low-profile family, are at the family home. Early indications are that Miss Grant went out riding yesterday morning, leaving from the horse sanctuary she set up outside Whitburn, West Lothian, three years ago, and the alarm was raised when she failed to return at noon yesterday.'

They cut to DSI Kelman. 'At the present time we have highly trained officers at the crime scene and are following several leads.'

The disembodied voice of the correspondent asked, 'Is there any truth in the rumour that she was badly mutilated?'

'I cannot comment on that,' DSI Kelman replied brusquely. 'As I have already stated, we have highly trained officers investigating Miss Grant's murder. I am not at liberty to say more. Thank you.'

They cut back to the correspondent. 'Paul Gabriel, our Scottish crime reporter, was at the scene yesterday. What did you manage to find out, Paul?'

I stared at his impassive profile as he sat beside me on his sofa. Scottish crime reporter? For the BBC? He was a small-time hack! How he had managed to pull this off? Irritatingly, he looked very handsome on screen.

'At the moment the police are saying very little. Miss Grant was very wealthy in her own right and it may have been a botched kidnap attempt. However, other pundits are linking her murder to the unsolved murder of Abigail Dawes earlier this year.'

My mind raced. Abigail Dawes? Abigail Dawes? I knew her name. What had happened to her? My brain was blank.

The correspondent's voice-over cut in. 'Abigail Dawes. At the time there was confusion over whether she was murdered or the victim of a freak accident, wasn't there?'

Back to Paul. 'Yes. She was an Olympic hopeful for the British fencing team. It appeared that she fell on to a rack of rapiers that had had their safety caps removed. It is highly unusual for the foils used in fencing to be without their terminal buttons. The removal was later proved to have been deliberate. The case is now being investigated as a murder.'

'And what would link these two women?' the voice asked.

'Both women were sexually assaulted and appear to have been the victims of a sadistic and vicious killer,' Paul replied.

I sat utterly still beside him, my heart thundering in my chest. He seemed to be totally focused on the television screen. The Scottish correspondent reappeared to replace Paul's image.

'Thank you, Paul. This is David Hartspring reporting

from Whitburn, Scotland. Now back to the newsroom.'

Paul turned off the TV and stared at the dark blank screen.

I swallowed once, but my mouth was dry and tasted foul. I didn't want to move. I didn't want to blink. Irrationally, I thought if I stayed perfectly still I was invisible. I had practised this for years. I would fold in on myself. It was my ultimate sign of fear.

Paul turned to me suddenly. 'I didn't mean to scare you.'

Still I didn't move. It was creeping around my head. It was opening doors in my mind and leaving a filthy trace. I had buried those memories and wasn't about to exhume them. Stillness was the key.

'Erin?' he said with concern. 'Erin?'

He reached behind me and placed his hand gently on the back of my head. Normally I would have punched him, but I couldn't stop listening to the stealthy footsteps as they crept about my subconscious. Whatever I did, I mustn't follow them down the dark corridors.

'Erin? Listen to me. It's all right. It's OK.'

I turned to him. It was too late. The fears had settled. 'He's a serial killer, isn't he? And I'm next.'

'No. No. It's just a wild hunch.'

'A wild hunch?' I repeated lamely.

'It's a better story if we link them.'

'So it's not true?'

'Well, the stories are true, but . . .' He was leaning towards me, finding my eyes with his. I knew he was lying. I straightened up and flicked my head so he would remove his hand.

'Did you know she had called me when you did this interview?'

He sighed. 'Yes. I thought that was what you were

trying to tell me earlier today. I didn't use it, though.'

I slipped to the edge of the sofa, stood up and took a huge gulp of wine. Then I began to pace. I did my best thinking while pacing. Paul watched me as I walked back and forth.

'What was said in the call?'

'First she called my answering machine. It was just a normal message. It was the one to my mobile that was . . . Oh, God . . . I can't tell you. It's too gross.'

I took another gulp of wine.

'Did she speak to you?'

I shook my head. 'No. No. It was on my messaging service. Nobody spoke.'

'What was it?'

'It was noises. Somebody jerking off or something. Shagging. It was horrible.' I took another gulp. I didn't want to say I thought it was the sound of her being raped.

'And you're sure it was from her?'

'No! I don't know anything. The call was made from Lucy Grant's mobile. They found it at the scene. Then they tracked it to my mobile.'

I paced and rubbed my forehead with my free hand. I had drunk half the glass and felt light-headed.

'But you did know Lucy?'

'Not really. She knew my sister. At school.' I stopped dead.

'Christ! My sister!'

I dived across the room, spilling wine over my hand, and frantically dialled my parents' number. It rang and rang.

'Oh, Christ! Oh shit! There's no answer!'

Paul calmly took the phone from my grip. 'We'll go and check on her. OK? We'll go there right now.'

'OK.' I nodded. 'OK.'

The buzzer behind my head hummed loudly and made us both jump. Paul answered it.

'It's the joiner for Paterson. There's no answer at the flat. Could you buzz us in?'

Paul buzzed him in, but I couldn't wait for the joiner. Not now, not with Brontë in possible danger. The telephone beside me rang and I snatched it up without thinking.

'Hello.'

'Hello?' A voice I instantly recognised said back.

'Brontë! Are you OK? Is Max OK?' I gushed.

'Yeah. Why wouldn't we be?'

'How did you get this number?'

'I was in the shower. I heard it ring, so I dialled 1471. What do you want, anyway?' Brontë was surly to say the least.

My tone softened. 'I was just checking to see that you were OK.'

'I'm fine. Is that all?'

'Well, yes, but just make sure you lock up properly,' I faltered. Giving Brontë advice was liable to backfire.

'Christ, Erin. I don't know how I made it to twenty-eight without you,' Brontë drawled before she hung up.

I leaned against the wall and knocked back what was left of my wine. For the first time in my life I didn't want to be fully functioning. I didn't want to be six steps ahead of everyone else. I didn't want to anticipate the next move. I wanted somebody else to take over.

I hardly noticed that Paul had left his apartment and was instructing the joiner on my behalf.

I took my empty wine glass and went to the kitchen for a refill. If a serial killer was coming after me, I wanted to be so drunk that I wouldn't feel the pain.

I emptied the remains of almost half a bottle of wine into my glass and drank it greedily. I felt giddy and slightly nauseous. Paul appeared in the doorway. I saw him clocking my glass.

'The joiner wants to know if this is an insurance job.'

'No. I'll pay by cheque,' I replied.

'You got hold of Brontë, then?'

'Yes. She's such a bitch.' I was shocked as the words came out. I never usually said anything bad about her in public. I thought it constantly but never said it. Blood was thicker than water. I took another glug of wine.

'Aah. Sibling rivalry,' Paul commented.

'Huh! Like I've anything to be jealous of!' I said contemptuously, but Paul had gone.

I cast my eyes around the kitchen haphazardly. I needed something to do, to rid myself of this feeling. I needed to divert my mind from its inevitable course. I opened his fridge and started rummaging for food.

Paul returned about ten minutes later, after I had emptied almost the entire contents of his fridge on to the worktop.

'It's back on,' he said. 'Good as new.'

He surveyed the food mountain I had created.

'You'll need to pay them,' he added.

I tottered through to my own apartment and eventually found my chequebook. With the door safely locked, I went back to Paul's.

He had put most of his food back in the fridge and was busy stir-frying some chopped vegetables. The smell of garlic, onions and sweet red peppers was mouth-watering.

I leaned against the oak-scrubbed table and watched

102

his back as he flung in plum tomatoes and dropped fresh egg pasta into a pan of boiling water. We didn't speak.

I had drained my glass again and helped myself to another bottle out of the fridge. Then I hunted for a corkscrew.

'I thought you didn't drink much?' he said, as he took the cold bottle from me and opened it deftly.

'Who told you that?' I asked indignantly.

'Everybody.'

'Guess they don't know me that well.'

'I'd say they know you pretty well.'

'What do you mean?'

'You hold your drink as well as a sieve. May I suggest you pace yourself a bit?'

'Don't be so patronising.'

He shook his head at me. 'Sit down and eat something. I don't want to be responsible for you having alcohol poisoning.'

I fluttered my eyelashes at him. 'I thought you liked taking care of me?'

He snorted in horror. 'Come back the real Erin! All is forgiven!'

He placed a steaming plate of pasta verde in front of me. It smelled heavenly, sweet and fresh. He had scattered torn basil leaves over the sauce, which reminded me of a family holiday we had once taken in Tuscany.

I was ravenous. I forked the pasta into my mouth with a rare show of gusto. The food was already making me feel better – better and calmer – but the question was out of my mouth before my brain had engaged.

'Tell me about Abigail Dawes.'

Paul leaned back in his chair and studied me. 'Do you really want to know?'

'Yes.'

'Abigail Dawes was thirty-one and very athletic. I don't mean muscular, I mean fit. Attractive, single and from a very good background. That gave her the financial clout to have an ordinary job – she was a mortgage assistant with the Royal Bank. She didn't appear that interested in promotion and she got lots of time off for competitions. She was talented at archery as well.'

He seemed to frown at the memory.

'She was alone in the sports hall they used for practice. They had been working on a forthcoming event and it was her turn to tidy up. The janitor found her later that night when he noticed a light was still on in the equipment room.'

He paused and took a sip of his red wine.

'It appeared that she had tripped and was impaled on the uncapped rapiers. She was already dead when he discovered her. The autopsy found evidence of recent sexual activity, but no signs of force.'

Recent sexual activity didn't mean she had been murdered, I thought callously.

'Maybe she had a boyfriend?'

Paul glared at me, as if he knew what I had been thinking.

'She had a casual boyfriend but he was away on business in America. Also, she was on the pill. The rapist used a condom.'

'Rapist? How come? There was no sign of force. She might have just picked him up and insisted he use a condom. For safety.'

My thoughts were getting ahead of themselves. I had to remember that Paul was a journalist. Murder and rape made better copy. Freak accidents got one head-line and were quickly forgotten.

'She wasn't that sort. When I said recent sexual activity, I meant within a couple of hours of her being found. The practice had finished at ten and she was found at midnight. You think she had a quick shag with the cleaner on the store-room floor?' His tone had changed. He was plainly annoyed.

I shrugged. One shag and a freaky death didn't make a serial killer in my mind. He glowered at me, as if I was responsible for her death.

'OK. I'll tell you. But this comes under our retainer.'

'Fine by me, Inspector Clouseau.'

He paused dramatically before he said, 'Her bow finger was missing.'

I didn't mean to snort and cringed at my inappro-priate reaction. Paul threw me a look of utter contempt. Maybe I was drunker than I realised.

'I'm sorry,' I spluttered, 'it took me by surprise. I certainly didn't mean to be disrespectful of her death. I am truly sorry.'

'I'll need to note that for the morning's paper. I can see the headline now: ERIN PATERSON IN APOLOGY SHOCK.'

I managed a weak smile. 'And you definitely believe it was murder?'

'No doubt. The rapiers went right through. She must have fallen with huge force. Or was thrown. There was other stuff.'

Paul surreptitiously refilled my wine glass as he spoke, but I wasn't sure if I wanted any more. I wanted my lucid self back. That was the problem with drink-ing. For me, the initial euphoria wore off quickly and was replaced by a desperate need to be *compos mentis*.

'In the broadcast you confirmed that the police initially thought it was an accident. How could they, if her finger was missing?' I tried to figure out which was the bow finger. 'Incidentally, don't archers use two fingers to hold the string of a longbow?'

'The police believed her finger had been sliced off when she fell, but they never found it. The janitor could have disturbed the killer before he managed to cut off the second finger. Anyway, the police never really thought it was an accident, that was just how they played it to the press immediately afterwards.'

'So he took her finger? Like some sort of trophy?' It beggared belief.

'That's how it appears. And they haven't found Lucy Grant's tongue, but that is strictly confidential.'

He began to clear up the plates.

'You mentioned the autopsy report. Did you see it?'

'Yes.'

'What did it say?'

He gave me an uneasy glance. 'I never saw all of it, I only got my hands on a couple of bits.'

'So you've got a copy. Can I see it?'

'No.'

'I've read hundreds. There's nothing in it that will shock me.'

'This would.'

'Let me see it. Maybe I could shed new light on it. I see reports from deaths and accidents all the time.'

That wasn't strictly true, but I had come across some bizarre causes of death in my time. Like when an Angora goat fell off the third-floor balcony of a high-rise block in Sighthill, landed on a refuse-collector below and broke his neck. Now that was unusual.

Paul studied me for a moment, a dark look clouding his face. He slammed the dishwasher closed and went into the living room. He reappeared with two sheets of badly photocopied paper and thrust the pages at me.

'Don't say I didn't warn you.'

'You've been reading too much Thomas Harris or Patricia Cornwell,' I scoffed, before I read the brief excerpts from the post-mortem.

. . . massive haemothorax in chest cavity, 1100 cc of bloody pleural effusion present in the right thorax. The inferior branch of the right main pulmonary artery is perforated and the left lung near the hilum shows extensive parenchymal haemorrhage from perforation. The aorta was lacerated causing cardiac tamponade. Perforation of the trachea and liver . . .

It was a repulsive way to die, but almost instantaneous and not unexpected when you considered that she died from being impaled. Blood from her torn aorta had filled the chest cavity and also flooded the pericardial sac. There were penetrating wounds to the windpipe, left lung and liver. None of it seemed untoward. I flicked over to the second page where there was only one sentence.

Ruptured left and right orbits from impalement and penetration. Eyeballs collapsed.

My stomach lurched. A rapier had gone through each eye.

Could that be chance? She must have fallen so perfectly symmetrically for that to happen. I put the pages down on the table purposely, as if holding them could transfer the horror. I couldn't speak for a minute in case the bile in my throat rose.

'Did they go right through?' I whispered. I hoped

he knew which wounds I meant because I couldn't bring myself to say it.

'No. Only the tips were embedded. All the other rapiers produced exit wounds.'

He was matter-of-fact and I understood why. It was the only way to deal with it.

'So that would have happened after she had ... fallen? Her head would have been pushed down on them?'

'Yes. After. When she was dead.'

Thank God, I said inside. Thank God, she wasn't alive. But what sort of deranged animal would do that? Not only kill her but then mutilate her? Force her limp head down on to the foils.

A picture, as if remembered from a sick horror movie, kept flashing into my mind. Her pliant head pulled back by a handful of hair, her body already collapsed and leaking, only held up by the thin swords that split her skin. Blood puddled on the floor, her flaccid legs bent beneath her. His hand carefully positioning her head above two rapiers and pushing it down, down. Down.

I wanted to gag.

Why had this monster killed her and then Lucy? Abigail Dawes and Lucy Grant? All they had in common was youth and good looks. If they had an obvious connection, surely the police would be on to it?

'Did Abigail have any connection to Lucy Grant? I mean, did she contact Lucy before she died?'

'Not as far as I am aware.'

'This is too weird,' I said firmly. 'Why is it not all over the press? Why haven't the public heard about it?'

He came back to the table and sat down.

'The police have requested a news blackout.'

'How did *you* find out if they're trying to keep it hush-hush?' My voice was accidentally disingenuous. It belied my shock.

'I have friends in low places,' he replied mysteriously.

'Oh, come on!' I cajoled. 'Are you the only journalist who knows or is it common knowledge?'

'Journalist, is it? Thought I was a "two-bit hack"?'

I smiled. 'So you have friends in the police.'

He bristled ever so slightly. 'I never disclose a source.'

'You and DS Marshall did a pretty good job of pretending you didn't know each other.'

'Actually, I don't know him. I know of him.'

Paul cupped his wine glass in his hands. He was drinking a rich red and watched the legs it left on the voluminous glass.

'Were you in the police force?'

He glanced at me and gave a slight nod of confirmation.

'Why did you leave?'

He looked tired and sad. Very sad.

'None of your business.'

I felt an urge to comfort him. I had to stop myself from giving him a reassuring pat on the arm. There were only two people in the world that made me affectionately demonstrative – Max and my father. I didn't count the dogs.

'Are you OK?' I asked gently.

He gave me a bitter look.

'I'm about as good as it gets these days. I hate the wasteful loss of innocent lives. I hate the void it leaves for those left behind. You, of all people, should be able to recognise that.'

I knew not to ask him any more.

I went back to my own apartment a little after eleven. I put the chain on and the alarm, and spent a fretful night in Max's bedroom.

I couldn't bring myself to sleep in the bed that Alex and I had used.

SEVEN

Watery sunshine had replaced the flannel greyness of the sky by Sunday morning. It helped my mood. I got up quickly and went down to my own en suite for a shower. I behaved as if this was any other Sunday. I planned to go into the office, which I regularly did at weekends, and catch up on the work neglected on Friday.

With this welcome return to normality, I felt refreshed and authoritative apart from the hangover I was suffering. I thought about phoning a locksmith because Alex still had keys, and put it on my mental list of things to do. I had a second cup of freshly brewed coffee and made a paper list for the supermarket, starting with the word 'food' followed by 'new phone'.

I drove to the office because of my intended shopping expedition and also because I felt safer in the protective custody of my Jeep. There were already several cars in the Paterson car park, which told me that the office was busy.

I imagined that most departments hadn't got their work finished on Friday, with so much salacious gossip doing the rounds. The weekend concierge let me in after I rang. We routinely kept the doors locked outside normal business hours. I did have a set of keys – after all, it was my building – but rarely used them.

I went straight up to the fifth floor, which was quiet. I was glad not to have to exchange pleasantries with anyone, but vaguely annoyed that none of my department was bothering to put in some extra hours. It wasn't as if we didn't have a huge caseload.

I switched on my computer and went to the kitchen to make some coffee. As I waited for the coffee to percolate, I examined my little scald mark, forgotten in the maelstrom of the last two days. It was raised and red. A vague feeling of a half-forgotten dream passed over me but I refused to let it settle anywhere.

I got down to the tasks in hand. We had three cases due to settle next week, the preliminaries of three more, and several conflicting precognitions to dissect and contradict.

The three cases that were due to settle out of court, which most compensation cases usually did, were fairly well tied up. In the bag, as I was known to say. I skimmed over the notes briefly and felt satisfied that all was in order.

Morris versus Donald wasn't in the same league as Murphy versus Broadwood, but he still stood to receive a £150,000 settlement. That was about the smallest amount I dealt with. I let the other lawyers and assistants dirty their hands with the lesser claims from grannies tripping over paving stones and twisting their ankles. Inevitably, Glasgow City Council had the firm on their most wanted list. Doing anything, however petty, to annoy councillors was always worthwhile in my opinion.

I closed the Morris versus Donald file and noted that they were due here at two o'clock tomorrow.

Mr Morris had both his legs broken when Mr Donald had run over him. Unfortunately, Mr Morris and Mr Donald were neighbours and Mr Donald had managed to knock Mr Morris down in Mr Morris's own drive-way. It had taken me two readings of the initial claim to follow it. Mr Morris was a physical-education teacher and couldn't work for eighteen months, and had missed a promoted post to principal teacher. I liked Mr Morris, he bore no grudge. It was covered by Mr Morris's personal insurance, and they, in turn, were suing Mr Donald's motor insurer for the damages. Compensation and insurance were intrinsically about passing the buck.

I began to read through the precognitions for another case. I pitied Douglas who had taken several of the statements. They were punctuated with slang, which Douglas had translated into the Queen's English in brackets. It brought the twitch of a smile to my lips.

In my days as a trainee, it had been the source of much mickey-taking when I was forced to pass the taking of a statement to somebody else, purely on the grounds that I didn't understand a thick accent or the nuances of colloquial terms. 'Gonnie nae dae tha, gonnie nae, gonnie nae,' had been translated by my good self as, 'There was a horse present, which was asked to whinny several times.' It went down in legal folklore. Literally it meant, 'Going to not do that, going to not, going to not.' Who would have known?

I had my head deep in statements and didn't hear the lift doors open and close. I got quite a fright when Liz Miller knocked on my open door.

She came in loaded down with the Sunday papers. 'How's it going?'

'Now *there* is a question,' I said.

She smiled sympathetically. 'Press still on your tail?'

'No. They seem to have drawn enough blood for the time being.' I stretched in my seat. 'Michael asked me to resign yesterday.'

Liz's mouth hung open in shock. 'You're kidding? No way. How could he?'

'Very easily, apparently. He told me to think of the firm and my family.'

'You need a break. When did you last take a holiday?'

I thought for a moment. I had taken a couple of long weekends but that was all. 'Skiing. Last winter. A week in Switzerland.'

'See? You need to get away. You can't always have your nose to the grindstone.'

Rather obviously, I changed the subject. 'How was Auntie's birthday?'

'It was great. We had her up dancing the Slosh. You would have *loved* it.' Liz had a twinkle in her eye. She knew that was my idea of purgatory.

'Sorry I missed it.'

'Are you doing anything tonight?'

'Oh, you know, the usual. Beating up boyfriends, running from the press . . .'

'Would you like to come over for dinner? It'll just be Allan and me.' Liz coloured slightly as she asked. I realised that it was a big step for her.

I gave her a huge grin. 'Yes. I would love to. But can you cook?'

'Not really,' she said frankly. 'Allan does it mostly.'

'Allan cooks! Wow!' I winked. 'Does he have a good-looking, unattached brother?'

Liz gave me a look. 'Yes, he does, but we're very fond of him.'

I threw up my hands in mock indignation.

'Huh, one statue and a girl gets a reputation! What time? I'm seeing a client at five o'clock.'

'See what I mean? You're seeing a client on a Sunday,' Liz tutted.

'Not really. We settled her compensation case on

114

Friday. It was a relief. I'm only going to see that she's OK.'

'Is that sympathy I detect? Have you been taking the nice pills again?'

'Am I really that bad?' I laughed.

Liz shrugged a 'yes' as Douglas appeared in my doorway.

'Douglas! So glad you could make it!' I teased, but his face was tight and worried. I stood up.

'What is it?'

'Have you seen the Sunday papers?' he squeaked.

'No. What's in them now? I'm a satanist? I'm cruel to cute furry animals?' I didn't really think things could get worse.

Douglas swallowed. 'Maybe you should look at them.'

'Douglas, just tell me. I promise not to sack you. Liz is your witness.'

'They're linking you with the murder of Lucy Grant.'

At that moment my world seemed to stop on its axis. I had looked from Douglas to Liz and back before the earth started spinning again.

'What?' I gasped in disbelief. 'That's ridiculous!'

'I know.' Douglas plucked up enough courage to come into my office and close the door. He lowered his voice to a whisper.

'Michael has called a partners' meeting. They're due in at two. They didn't know you'd be here. I presume they thought you would be in hiding.'

'Jeezus Christ!'

Liz opened the *Sunday Times*. 'It's on page three.'

She handed me the broadsheet. I read, 'Top Lawyer Linked to Heiress Murder', but the words swam before my eyes. I handed the paper back to her.

'I can't read it. Read it to me,' I muttered and began to pace.

Liz cleared her throat, 'Erin Paterson, eldest daughter of Sir Maxwell Paterson MBE, and a top compensation lawyer with Paterson, Paterson and—'

I interrupted, 'Cut to the chase.'

Liz took a deep breath, 'Arrested yesterday for allegedly assaulting her . . . blah, blah . . . was linked to the vicious murder of Miss Lucy Grant. Police investigating Miss Grant's murder interviewed Miss Paterson at her family's substantial home, in Glasgow's well-heeled suburb of Pollokshields. Miss Grant was an ex-girlfriend of Mr Alexander Faraday. Miss Paterson . . .'

'What? I didn't know that! I didn't even know they knew each other!' I hissed.

'Erin, sit down. There's more,' Liz said calmly.

'Sources close to the investigation said Miss Grant had allegedly contacted Miss Paterson on the morning of her murder.' She was silent for a moment.

'Then it talks about your father and family and your, em, sister. The rest is standard background information.'

There was a deathly silence in my room. I closed my eyes.

By implication they were branding me a suspect and by linking it with assaulting Alex they portrayed me as a half-crazed bunny-boiler. It was unbelievable. The *Sunday Times*? The story had gone national. I had hoped it would stay provincial.

'This is so unfair,' I said, but I began to focus on the other obvious fact.

Only me, the police, the killer and Paul Gabriel knew about that phone call. Presumably, neither the psychopath nor the police had alerted the press. I was astonished at how easily I had been duped by his kindness.

Liz came round to my chair and placed a tender hand on my shoulder. It made my heart tighten with rage. Douglas was shifting from one foot to another. It was either excruciating embarrassment or fear at being trapped in a room with a potential murderer.

I closed my eyes again and heard voices drifting down the open-plan office. Simultaneously, we held our breath as they passed by my closed office door.

'How did you know about the meeting?' I whispered urgently to Douglas.

'Michael called me. He wants me to take the notes.'

I narrowed my eyes. I knew what Michael was up to, sidelining me and pulling my assistants into the fold.

'OK. OK. Let me think.'

I needed just one minute to get my mind clear.

'This is how we'll play it,' I said decisively. 'Douglas, you go to the meeting and take notes, then tell me exactly what was said.'

Douglas looked disinclined and I knew why. It was completely unethical to disclose the substance of the meeting to anyone, particularly me.

'Douglas,' I said emphatically, 'you may be about to become the assistant of a suspended partner. Where does that leave you?'

'I still don't want to be a mole.'

'You're not a mole, you're only reporting to your superior. Michael asked you to take the notes precisely so that you would be faced with this dilemma. If you don't tell me what is said, then *I* will be furious with you. But if you do, then *he* will be furious. He's using you for his own questionable agenda. There are lots of assistants he could have called. Why pick you? Think about it.'

Douglas shrugged but remained reluctant.

'Come on Douglas! I promise not to use anything you tell me. All I want is to be forewarned.'

Douglas hesitated. He wore that special, dismal expression he put on when he absolutely did not want to do something.

'What if they say they're going to suspend you? What if it's really, really bad?' he whined.

'That's my point. If it is really bad, I would rather hear it from you than from bloody Michael. *Praemonitus praemunitus,* forewarned forearmed. Please, Douglas.'

Douglas sighed and shook his head. 'I've a bad feeling about this.'

Normally I thrived on all types of manoeuvring, but this was different. I used my renowned brinkmanship for those I represented. I wasn't equipped for having my own life entangled in drama.

'Do you truly believe that Michael will try to get you suspended?' Liz asked hesitantly.

'Yes, yes I do. He's been gunning for me for ages,' I sighed. 'He does have a point. This doesn't exactly look good for me or the firm.'

'But if they do it will look like a vote of no confidence.'

'Precisely. They have two options: do nothing, which could do further damage to the firm; or suspend me, which could still do further damage, but mainly to my reputation.'

They exchanged uneasy glances.

'I don't want you two to become embroiled in this. OK? I'm asking you a favour, Douglas, but that's as far as it goes. If my days are numbered, then I don't want to take you down with me. Understand?'

118

They were already involved. I would try my damnedest to limit their further exposure.

'Is the offer of dinner still open?' I smiled brightly at Liz.

'Of course! Does six o'clock suit you?'

'Yes. Great. Anything I can bring?' I was strangely relieved. If a bomb was about to explode, then I wanted some company during the aftershock.

'Just yourself. Why don't you join us, Douglas?'

Douglas looked unsure. It was a mammoth step, having dinner with a junior partner and me. I smiled encouragingly at him.

'OK . . . em . . . if that's OK.'

Liz gave him a playful punch on the arm. 'Six o'clock. Do you know where I live?'

'Yeah . . . I dropped off files to you once.'

Liz poked her head out of my office to check that the coast was clear, and mouthed 'Good luck,' as she left.

It was a strange shift in circumstances, the whispering and sneaking about. I felt an odd twinge of something – regret, or remorse, perhaps. I couldn't stop the tsunami of change but, had I played my cards differently, maybe I could have altered its course. Hindsight was a wonderful thing.

I began to pack away the work I was supposed to do. It would have to wait until Monday because I knew I wouldn't be able to concentrate.

Douglas was hanging around looking faintly lost. I was rather hoping that for once he would summon up enough courage to come right out with whatever was worrying him.

'Yes, Douglas?' I asked eventually.

He continued to look awkward but finally managed

to mumble, 'Michael asked me if I wanted to transfer to another partner.'

That was strictly taboo. One did not poach someone else's assistant without the green light from the partner concerned.

'And?' I said rather frostily.

'I told him that it was inappropriate to approach me unless, of course, you no longer wished me to work with you,' Douglas replied nervously.

My tone softened. 'Would you like to transfer?'

I could honestly say that I didn't want to lose him. He might not have been the brightest star in the galaxy and was somewhat lacking in charisma, but he was conscientious, reliable, hardworking and uncomplaining. What more could one ask?

He blushed. 'No, but if you want me to, then I'll go.'

'Of course not! I want you to stay. I want *you* to be *my* assistant. Tell Michael to piss off.'

Douglas grinned and went to the door.

'Are you staying to do some work?' I asked.

'Yes. I've got some things to catch up on. Could you sign me out a box of floppy disks because stationery's closed?'

'Sure.' I picked up my keys and flung them towards him. 'Just initial it.'

Trying to steal my assistant was a new low, even for Michael. The hostility between us was legendary and, not for the first time, I wondered what I had done to make him hate me so vigorously. We had been together for a brief period, bound by our ruthless pursuit of legal empire-building. We made a good business and legal team, and a crap couple.

I had viewed our relationship as temporary from the

start. To him, it was the combination of hard work and IQ. I wasn't romantic but even I knew that love was an essential ingredient for a long-term relationship. It had ended acrimoniously upon his proposal of marriage. I freely admit that I shouldn't have laughed.

While I waited for Douglas to come back from stationery, I read the *Sunday Times*. The article was very carefully worded. So carefully, in fact, that to slap a writ on them would only encourage more publicity. It was hardly worth pursuing, which was exactly what they had hoped.

The damage was done. Mud sticks, no matter how much you try to scrub it off. There was one paragraph regarding Brontë that I wasn't clear on, though.

It mentioned 'revelations about her lifestyle that had appeared in the tabloid press'. I presumed they were talking about the birth of Max. It was pretty low to drag her into it. I might not approve of her lifestyle but, as far as my troubles were concerned, she was an innocent bystander.

Listlessly, I began to read other articles because I didn't want to focus on the real issue: betrayal, first by Alex and then by Paul. I particularly didn't want to focus on Paul's back-stabbing. I had imagined that we had reached some sort of unspoken understanding. It was clear that I was mistaken. Rationally, it was hard to blame him. In his line of work I was a legitimate target. But rationality had never been my strong point when it came to men, so I vowed revenge.

I left the office under a cloud of self-pity. I went to the supermarket and haphazardly threw things into my trolley. I had no menus planned and would probably end up eating pasta with cauliflower cheese or lasagne with stir-fried vegetables.

I spent ages in front of the wines, carefully choosing two lovely bottles to take to Liz. I was grateful for the invitation. I also got a large bunch of flowers for Mrs Murphy and a mixed bag of treat-sized bars for her two little boys.

Bernadette Murphy lived in the East End, in an area called Dennistoun, which had originally housed the first Glasgow tobacco lords before they became so vastly wealthy that they built huge mansions in the West End and South Side. It had fallen down on its luck over the decades, but was now slowly being renovated by aspiring young professionals.

I parked next to a dilapidated Ford Escort, and hoped my Jeep would still be there when I got back. Mrs Murphy lived in a two-storey terraced house and her small front garden was tidy if sparse.

I didn't know why, but I had butterflies in my stomach. It was unusual for me to visit a client, unless of course they were in hospital or housebound, but Mrs Murphy was a special case. I knocked on the front door and waited. I was sure I could hear several voices inside, so I knocked again. She answered the door in a flour-specked apron, with a tea towel in her hands. The net curtains twitched in the front room.

'Come in! Come away in!' she gushed.

I stepped past her into a narrow front hall. Stairs to the upper floor directly faced me. The carpet was threadbare. I thanked *fortuna* for her settlement.

She immediately ushered me into the front room. I almost turned and ran; at least a dozen people were crammed in there and immediately burst into a chorus of 'For She's a Jolly Good Fellow'. I wanted to die. I mumbled my thanks and handed Mrs Murphy the supermarket flowers.

'I've brought some sweets for Eamon and Danny . . .'

As I looked about the room for the two little boys, one was shoved through the throng of adults carrying a huge bunch of lilies. He stood in front of me, looking as uncomfortable as I felt, and thrust the flowers at me.

I crouched down to his eye height, 'Thank you. Now you are . . . ?'

He eyed me suspiciously then stuck out his tongue.

'Eamon! You little tyke! Say sorry to the nice lady,' an elderly woman, his grandmother I presumed, chastised him.

I straightened up and smiled. 'I have that effect on people, I'm afraid.'

I kept smiling and swore silently. Dear God, it was going to be one of those afternoons.

I was introduced to the rest of the family, a very extended family it appeared. There were even more hiding in the kitchen.

I really wanted a chance to speak to Mrs Murphy privately. I wanted to tell her when to expect the money and how much she would actually receive. The rest of the Murphy clan were determined to have a celebration and had opened some bottles. I declined politely, gratefully took a cup of tea and a home-made scone, and sat down on the sofa.

A man I had already been introduced to came and sat beside me. He shook my hand again.

'Kieran Donagh.'

I smiled cordially and racked my brains. Cousin? Brother-in-law?

'So you're the lawyer?' he said.

'Yes.' I nibbled my scone and hoped he would go away.

'You do lots of cases like this?' He stretched and rummaged in his trouser pocket for a packet of cigarettes.

'Yes.' I sipped my tea and prayed to be rescued.

'And you make lots of money?' He lit a cigarette and watched the smoke he puffed. 'From other people's misfortune?'

'It's not quite as simple as that,' I said, desperately trying to make eye contact with someone else in the room.

'Not as simple? Don't you take a big chunk of the dosh for doing sweet F. all?'

I cringed but said nothing, to his obvious annoyance.

'Not as simple? Now that's a crack!' He laughed and nudged me violently. My tea spilt into my lap.

It was the pretext I needed. I smiled and said, 'Excuse me,' as I stood up.

'Where you going now? Seen an ambulance to chase?'

I ignored him and headed for the kitchen to mop up the tea. Bernadette rolled her eyes apologetically at me as she bore down on Kieran. I heard her hiss something like, 'That's enough of that', but as I glanced back at him, I saw his hand progress over her buttocks. An alarm bell went off in my head.

The delightful Kieran was moving in on Mrs Murphy and her newly found wealth. My private word with her could no longer wait.

I wiped down my trousers with a damp cloth and hovered in the kitchen until she came through.

'Sorry about Kieran. He doesn't mean it.'

'It's OK. No problem. Would it be possible to have a quick word?'

She glanced around her. 'Upstairs?'

124

I followed her through the milling guests and up to a bedroom, which smelled of damp. She sat down on the double bed and waited for me to speak. I wandered over to the window and gazed out at a row of dreary back gardens. It was getting dark.

'You should receive the money in about six weeks,' I said. 'We have the papers ready to sign, so if you pop into the office as soon as you can, we can tie this thing up.'

She was silent for a moment. I knew exactly what she wanted to know and I didn't want to humiliate her by making her ask.

'We settled on five hundred and fifty thousand pounds. You and I agreed on twenty per cent, so you will receive four hundred and forty thousand.'

She gasped.

I sat down next to her. 'Are you OK?'

'Yes,' she mumbled.

'It's a lot of money.'

'Is it a lump sum?' She stared down at her clenched hands. It could never compensate for losing her Danny.

'Yes. With instalments we might have got more, but not enough to make it worth the wait.'

'Right.'

'What we need to do now is decide the best thing to do with the money.'

'You mean, invest it?' She glanced at me.

'Yes and no. The money is for you and the boys, for the loss you suffered. It might be sensible to put some of the money in a trust fund. You could draw on it, as you needed. Also, that would take it out of the equation should you re-marry. It wouldn't be viewed as matrimonial property, particularly if the emphasis was placed on the children.'

125

'But I've got debts from the last three years.'

'That's fine. We could work out what you need right now to clear your debts and what you might need to tide you over, and put the rest safely away. You could choose to receive an annual income, or withdraw it as you needed it but only up to a certain level, or pretty much any way you choose. The important thing is that it's yours and the boys', nobody else's. You do with it as you see fit.'

'Would you help me? I don't know much about these things. Danny always took care of the finances.'

'Of course. We have a whole department for deeds and trusts. The partner's name is Francis Park. He's a good man. I'll arrange for you to meet him immediately after you've been in to see me.'

She lightly touched my arm. 'Thank you, Erin.'

'There's no need to thank me, Bernadette. It's what I do.' I patted her hand and stood up.

'I've got to go now. Thank you for your lovely hospitality. Say goodbye to the boys from me.'

Bernadette nodded but stayed where she was. I closed the door quietly, slipped down the stairs and out the front door before anyone caught me.

I glanced at my watch and saw that I was already half an hour late for Liz's. This mobileless existence was beginning to get tiresome.

Liz lived in the West End. It was a vibrant and eccentric mix of students, media types, young professionals and old money. There were glorious, red sandstone mansions overlooking private residents' gardens, tenements with busy shops below, and new luxury housing. Close to the city centre, the university, the Western Infirmary and the BBC, it was a sought-after area. Parking was a nightmare.

Liz and Allan lived on an attractive tree-lined

crescent, in a first-floor conversion of an imposing villa. I had to park precariously on a corner, mounting the pavement. That was one of the reasons why there were so many 4 x 4s in Glasgow. They allowed you to park halfway up a tree.

I rushed in, apologising profusely. Liz looked flustered and I hoped that I hadn't ruined the meal.

We went into the drawing room, which overlooked a mass of foliage. Douglas and Allan both stood up to greet me.

'I'm sorry I'm late. I couldn't get away from Mrs Murphy and her two hundred close relatives.'

'Douglas, could you arrange a meeting for Mrs Murphy and Francis Park immediately after she comes in to sign? I'm hoping to get her to put some money in trust. She might have picked up a rather unsavoury suitor already.'

Douglas nodded and the room fell silent.

'Have I really ruined dinner?' I laughed feebly.

'No, no,' Allan said and backed out the room. Liz smiled and mumbled something about helping him in the kitchen. I shrugged and sat down.

Douglas cleared his throat and shuffled from foot to foot in front of the fireplace. I eyed him quizzically until suddenly I remembered.

'God, Douglas! I completely forgot about the partners' meeting. How did it go? Judging by your expression, it was as bad as expected.'

'Worse.'

'Sit down. Tell me everything.'

'Michael McCabe called for a vote of no confidence and your suspension. Matthew Stuart called for an in-house inquiry and Sheila Meredith called for calm.'

'Did they vote?'

'Yes. Eight to six against. Three abstentions.'

That was close – too close for comfort.

'Who were for and who abstained?'

Douglas listed the names. Michael McCabe and three of his henchmen were no surprise, but Jack Jackson and George Carr were. Matthew Stuart, Daljit Nair and Hannah Buie had abstained.

'What was the final outcome?' I asked apprehensively.

'You're supposed to have a meeting with Matthew, but then there was something else.' I waited for Douglas to continue, but he looked over his shoulder as if somebody might be listening.

'Michael said they should move the other issue forward. That the matter was now pressing and this was the ideal opportunity. It would take care of all the mess and make sure everyone had a clean slate.'

My skin prickled with goosebumps. 'What other issue?'

'I don't know. He asked me to leave the room.'

Liz called 'dinner' and we shuffled through. The meal was nice, but tinged with unspoken thoughts and fears. Liz searched my face for clues, but that evening I was the consummate lawyer. My face gave very little away.

I got back to my apartment building after ten. I was as quiet as possible opening my door, because I wasn't in the mood for a showdown with Bastard Paul. As I despondently unpacked my shopping, I looked around my designer kitchen and wondered about selling the penthouse. It no longer held a sense of promise and independence. I could see myself as a successful but single career woman with only a cat for company. I hated analysing and recognising my life. I preferred to be busy, so busy, in fact, that I didn't have time to examine my life as it sped by.

I leant my forehead on the stainless-steel door of my American-style fridge-freezer. My beautiful, expensive, stainless-steel appliances were the sum total of my life. I turned off the halogen spotlights that were strung across the ceiling of the kitchen and wandered through to the living room.

I wanted my mother to stroke my hair as I rested my head in her lap, the way she had done when I was small. I wanted her to sing me a lullaby. I wanted to snuggle my face into Max's perfect, chubby neck and smell his baby skin. I wanted somebody to comfort me.

Law was the only area of my life that could totally engross me, no matter what else was going on around me. I flicked through the files of forthcoming cases. Eventually, feeling slightly more balanced, I stretched and yawned. It was bedtime.

As I went to switch on the alarm, I noticed an envelope had been pushed under my door. It hadn't been there when I came home. Hate mail, perhaps? I wavered for a moment before I opened it.

Dear Erin

I know you will not believe me but I did not sell you out. Try to think of anyone else who might have known about the phone call. Contact DSI Kelman and tell him. Be very careful and observant. If you need me, then you know where I am.
Paul

I locked my front door behind me and went over to

his and knocked. He answered quickly and glanced down at the piece of paper in my hand.

'Do you want to come in?'

I nodded.

'Would you like a drink or something to eat?'

'No.'

I sat down on the sofa in the same spot as the previous evening and rallied my courage.

'I'm scared of being alone in my apartment.'

He sat down beside me. His eyes urged me to tell him, but I knew that if I opened the vault, all the darkness would come tumbling out in an effort to reach the light.

I looked away. I didn't want to talk about anything.

'Can I stay here tonight?'

'Sure.'

I slept in Paul's bed and he slept on the sofa. We didn't discuss the strange arrangement, for to verbalise it would make it worse – could make it real.

There was a killer out there and somehow, inadvertently, I might have caught his attention.

EIGHT

Waking up in his bed felt odd. The pillows and duvet smelled faintly of *Persil* and Paul. It was early, six thirty, but I was wide awake. I got up and crept through to the living room, hoping he was still asleep.

Tangled up in a mess of sheets and blankets, his broad back was visible, with one arm dangling over the side of the sofa. He had muscular shoulders and well-defined arms, and I was vaguely embarrassed for noticing. I wondered why he didn't use one of his spare bedrooms.

I let myself out and returned to my own apartment. I headed straight for the shower and got myself as ready as I could for what promised to be a testing day. I penned Paul a brief note, thanking him for his kindness, and pushed it under his door before taking the lift down to the car park. Until I felt safe in my city again, I would take the car.

It was well before eight when I reached The Paterson Building and it suddenly felt good. I might be adrift in all other departments of my life, but I was still a good lawyer.

I was pleased that Douglas and Karen came in early too, and we got down to business as if nothing had happened. Perhaps I was more subdued than normal, but not much. I had the Morris versus Donald settlement to look forward to and it began to feel like a standard Monday.

I immersed myself in my caseload, and stayed in my

office for most of the morning, hoping that purely by my cool presence the rest of the staff would become immune to the speculation that surrounded me. Partners popped in and out but nobody mentioned anything about my situation, and Matthew Stuart hadn't called me in for a dressing-down.

I planned to pop out to the sandwich shop, on the corner of Bath Street, for a bite of lunch before the settlement. Routinely I sent a junior, but the sun was shining and fresh air seemed like a good idea. I knew that I couldn't hole up in my room for ever. Eventually, I had to face the quizzical glances and sidelong looks.

The phone rang just as I picked up my handbag. It was Max's nursery. The principal, Mrs Orman, asked me to come and collect Max because he was 'poorly'. I explained that I was busy, but she told me quite forcefully that they couldn't get a reply from my parents' house.

Bloody Brontë.

It was one o'clock. It would take me twenty minutes to get there, ten minutes to pick him up and twenty to get back in time for Morris versus Donald. That only left ten minutes for contingencies.

'Karen, I've got to collect Max. He's ill. I might need you to watch him. Also, tell Douglas to set up for Morris versus Donald,' I snapped, as I hurried past.

It was the office-cat syndrome. It wasn't Karen I was angry with, but she bore the brunt of my bad mood. She nodded curtly and muttered something under her breath. Normally I would have apologised to her, but I was overwhelmed with annoyance. How was I expected to do my job and act as an emergency nanny as well?

I swore at the slow-moving traffic caused by the idiots using the Kingston Bridge. Why the government couldn't build another bridge was beyond me. The Kingston Bridge was the busiest in Europe. If they could waste all that money on the Millennium Dome, why not build a bridge?

I pulled up outside the nursery and ran up the steep hill, past the junior school and round the back to the little annexe. The other pre-schoolers were running about in the enclosed playground. They sounded happy and for a fleeting moment my heart lifted.

Mrs Orman was waiting at the front door to greet me. She smiled gravely. 'We're just cleaning him up, Miss Paterson.'

'What's wrong with him?'

'He's got a tummy bug, we think. Poor lamb's been sick all morning.'

She could hardly make eye contact with me as she spoke. I put it down to my new-found notoriety.

'I was wondering if I could have a word about, em, Max's home life?'

'I'm not sure that would be appropriate. I'm his aunt, not his mother.'

Mrs Orman shifted uncomfortably.

'Miss Paterson, we are worried about Max,' she said.

'In what respect?' I folded my arms across my chest defensively. I could be as rude as I liked about Brontë, but I wouldn't allow others to be.

'He often comes to nursery without his snack,' her voice faltered. 'And he is sometimes *unclean*.'

I gasped. I physically gasped. My mother would never let him go out dirty. 'What on earth do you mean?'

'It's very difficult. It appears to be when Max's

133

mother is, how shall I put this, *unsupervised* . . .' Mrs Orman flushed as she spoke.

My heart dipped into my abdomen and rushed down to my feet.

'Have you spoken to Max's grandmother?'

'Yes, we've tried to but she seems to have her . . . hands full. I'm afraid we really must take it further if things don't improve.'

She held my eyes. I nodded. I knew what she meant.

'I'll take care of it,' I said quietly, as another teacher brought Max out from the nursery.

He was as pale as milk, with dark shadows under his eyes. My throat tightened. His clothes were dirty and crushed. Crushed like my heart.

I picked him up and he wrapped his legs round my waist and his arms round my neck. He smelled of stale sick. He didn't return my greeting.

'Thank you for looking after him and thank you for bringing this to my attention,' I said to Mrs Orman.

As we went down the hill, Max vomited over my shoulder and down my back. I tried not to gag, but vomit has that effect on me. I put him in my car, took off my jacket and placed it in the boot.

During the one-minute drive to my parents' house I murmured soothing things to him. As we rounded the corner into their driveway, he gurgled and puked into his lap. I didn't know that much about children, but he seemed very sick to me. I tried not to think about my leather upholstery.

I ran up the steps and unlocked the front door, ticking off Brontë in my head for not using the alarm. Then I dashed back out and lifted up Max, his puke smearing on to my shirt and trousers.

I carried him inside and put him in the downstairs

bathroom. Then I stood in the middle of the hall and shouted, 'Brontë! Brontë!', although I knew she wasn't there.

I was going to murder her when I got my hands on her. I rushed back to the bathroom, but thankfully he hadn't been sick again.

'Max? Where's Mummy?' I cooed.

'Don't know. She didn't collect me at lunchtime.'

I was confused. I thought they hadn't been able to contact her, not that she simply hadn't turned up. 'You mean, she usually collects you before I came?'

'Uh-huh. When the bell goes for lunch, I come home.' Max's lips quivered and the tears quickly followed. 'I want Mummy.'

'It's OK, darling, I'm here. I'm here. I'll make it better.' I cradled him in my arms and rocked him back and forth. 'Let's get you all nice and clean. OK?'

I ran a shallow bath and helped him out of his foul clothes. I took off my equally foul shirt and trousers and washed him, gently soaping his hair and body. He was a better colour now, but that could have been from the warm bath water.

Wrapping him in a huge fluffy bath towel, I carried him upstairs. He seemed so limp and weak. I dressed him in clean pyjamas and was about to put him in his bed, when a thought occurred to me.

'Would you like to lie down in Mummy's bed?'

He brightened ever so slightly.

'OK, then. We'll make you all comfy-womfy in Mummy's bed. Will we take Elmer and Tracker and Leopard? They'll miss you otherwise.'

I carried him through to Brontë's room and, after a surreptitious sniff to make sure it was relatively clean, I popped Max in bed, tucking the covers up round his chin.

'Do you still feel sick?' I whispered as I stroked his fine damp hair.

'A wee bit,' he whimpered.

'OK. Don't worry. Do you think you can sleep?'

He nodded and closed his big blue eyes. I lay down beside him and continued to comfort him. We lay like that for ten minutes, until I was sure he had dropped off.

Stealthily, I got up from the bed and crept down the stairs. Where the hell was Brontë? I checked the hall bureau and the kitchen for a note, but there was no indication of her whereabouts. Livid with frustration, I got a washing-up bowl from under the kitchen sink in case Max was sick again.

As I passed the grandfather clock in the hall for a second time, I let out a shriek.

It was 2.10. I was late! I was late, half naked and nursing a sick child! I grabbed the phone and called the office. Karen was equally frantic.

'Where are you?'

'Max is really sick. I can't leave him. Have they arrived?'

Karen groaned. 'Yes. They were five minutes early.'

'Who is in with them?'

'Douglas and *Michael*.' Karen obviously had her ear to the ground as well.

'Michael? Fuck!' I hissed. 'Can you get hold of Douglas? Tell him to adjourn. Tell him to postpone.'

'I'll try,' Karen said, but didn't sound hopeful.

'Call me at this number.' I gave her my parents' home phone number.

I hung up the receiver and caught a glimpse of myself in the hall mirror. The haunted woman who stared back didn't look like me.

136

I took the washing-up bowl upstairs and placed it by the side of Brontë's bed. Max was fast asleep and I ached to join him. Quietly, I opened Brontë's wardrobe, hoping to find something suitable to wear. The best I could see was a pair of chinos and a chamois fitted shirt.

I took the clothes and hosed myself down with a hand shower in the mid-landing bathroom. The door was propped open so I could listen for Max, the phone and the AWOL Brontë. I was relieved to get rid of the acrid stink of vomit. Industrial cleaners would have to take care of my car.

Once I was clean and dressed I didn't know what to do with myself. I paced about the house, waiting. I picked up the phone a couple of times to make sure it was working. I flicked on the TV and flicked it off almost immediately. American chat shows had never been my thing. Really, who in their right mind was desperate to tell the nation that they had slept with their sister's husband's mother?

I rang Martha, hoping she could help, but her phone rang out.

I went back to the kitchen and heated up some lemonade in a saucepan to get rid of the fizz. I remembered my mother telling me that flat lemonade was good for dehydration. I also made some toast, which I sliced into soldiers, hoping Max would keep down dry toast and flat lemonade when he woke up.

But I didn't know what on earth I was going to do about Brontë.

If the nursery had noticed he wasn't being cared for properly, how had my parents missed it? I knew from experience that my mother looked after him even when Brontë was there. Brontë liked a long lie-in and so my mother or Martha, as often as not, took him to nursery.

Brontë was a selfish little pig. How could she be off gallivanting while poor Max was ill? She must have noticed that he wasn't right this morning. And where the hell was she now?

My anger bubbled away with the hot lemonade. Although I was livid with her, I was unsure of what to do. She never listened to me. Any conversations we did have invariably descended into petty point-scoring and dredging up past misdemeanours.

I was so angry I considered calling Social Services myself, but my sense of shame and unease stopped me. What if they decided to take him away? I couldn't live with that. I had enough problems of my own without confronting a truckload of hers. The phone ringing interrupted my mental diatribe. It was Douglas.

'Christ, Douglas! I thought you'd never phone!'

'I just got out of the meeting.'

'Didn't you adjourn it?' I shrieked.

Douglas's voiced dropped to a complicit whisper. 'Michael wouldn't let me . . . it wasn't good.'

'What do you mean? It was all settled! It was only to be signed and formalised' I hissed back.

'Michael wanted another twenty thousand. They wouldn't move and it's going to court. I did what I could but he just ignored me. Mr Morris was muttering about complaining to the Law Society.' His voice creaked with strain.

'About Michael?' That would serve the meddling snake right.

'No. About you! Michael told him you were missing and that your complicated personal life had interfered with your professional judgement.'

138

'I'll kill the bastard! How dare he? How dare he interfere in my case and cast aspersions on me?'

There was silence at the other end.

'Douglas? Are you still there?'

Douglas cleared his throat.

'Yes, Mrs ... Mrs Murphy. I'll tell her you called. Goodbye.'

The line went dead. What the hell was going on? I had a perfect right to talk to my assistant. Why all the secrecy and clandestine phoning? My God, I was out the office for two hours and it all went haywire. Just like Friday.

I re-dialled Karen's direct line. Somebody else answered. I slammed the phone back down and dialled my own direct line. My own voice spoke back to me, telling me I was unavailable and to leave a message. I hung up and sat down on the bottom step of the stairs.

It was three forty-five and still no sign of Brontë. I stood up purposefully and phoned Liz Miller. Finally, luck was on my side.

'Liz? It's Erin. What is going on?' I blurted.

'Thank God you've called! I've been trying to reach you. There's been meetings and stuff going on since lunchtime. Where are you?'

'I'm at my parents'. My nephew is ill.'

'Is he OK?'

'Yes, just a tummy bug. What are the meetings about?'

'I don't know. Nobody is talking. All normal meetings have been cancelled.'

'Have you seen Douglas or Karen?'

'No. Michael huckled them into the boardroom about ten minutes ago. I was up on five, trying to find you.'

'Liz, don't worry. If it's about me, then you'll be fine. OK? Take down this number and call me if you hear anything.'

I guessed what was afoot. They were lobbying the partners and staff. That meant one of two things: Michael was trying to get me suspended or they were dissolving the partnership.

I had to admire Michael's opportunism. He had seen his chance and grabbed the moment. There was nothing like kicking a girl when she was down.

'Ern! Ern!' Max's scratchy voice carried down the stairs.

'Just coming, darling,' I shouted, and went back to the kitchen for his tray.

He was sitting up in bed, looking tousled and pink. I sat beside him and coaxed him to sip the warm lemonade.

'How you feeling, pumpkin?' I felt his head for signs of a temperature.

'Bit better.' He yawned and snuggled down under the covers.

'Do you want to go back to sleep?'

'No. Will you read me a story?' He flicked his pale eyes up to mine as if I would say no. It made me uneasy.

'Of course. Which one do you want?'

He beamed. 'The ones with Winnie-the-Pooh and Tigger too.'

I went through to his bedroom and found all the Winnie-the-Pooh books.

I sat beside him on the bed, putting a pillow behind my back and my arm around him. Max looked at the pictures while I read. I asked him questions that were probably inane, like, 'What colour is Winnie?' or, 'How many footprints in the snow are there?' We counted them together.

'I like books,' he said. 'But sometimes nobody has time to read them.'

It was exactly what I had feared.

'Granny reads but she doesn't do the voices. Not like you.' He twinkled up at me. I kissed the top of his blond head.

'So, I'm a pretty good reader?'

He sat bolt upright. 'Why didn't you like Joy?'

'Who's Joy? I don't know her.' Was she at the nursery?

Max held his head to one side and studied me.

'Mummy says you killed Joy.'

I gave a snort. 'Of course not! I love joy. Mummy was being silly.'

'Good.'

We read two more books and Max finished his flat lemonade. It began to get dark outside.

I should have been at the firm, but in my heart of hearts I sensed it was already a *fait accompli*. Maybe it was better this way. Maybe it was better to conserve my energy for the war and simply concede this battle. My only wish was that someone would exhibit a bit of backbone and confront me, rather than creep around in the shadows.

My abdomen was knotted with anxiety, but I was afraid to acknowledge it. It was nearly half past five. Where the hell was Brontë? I had so many things to worry about, I didn't know where to start.

Max got up and managed to eat two plain digestive biscuits while watching the Cartoon Network. I paced back and forth, waiting for the phone to ring. I wanted to call one of the sympathetic partners, but I was unsure as to whom I could trust. Matthew maybe? I dialled his direct line and got his voicemail but I didn't leave a message.

I was on my way back upstairs when I heard a car stop outside. My parents' house was the second from the end in the cul-de-sac, so I hoped it was Brontë. I ran back down the stairs, flung open the front door and made ready to give her a mouthful, but a man carrying two, large, white, document envelopes came up the driveway.

'Paterson?' he enquired politely.

'Yes.'

'Could you sign here?' He flipped over a page. 'And here?'

'What is it?'

'Don't know. I'm just the courier.'

He shrugged and handed me both packages. One was addressed to my parents and the other to me, but both were from the firm.

I read mine once and abandoned it on the hall bureau.

My hands trembled as I went round the house switching on lamps and closing curtains against the cold October evening. There would be a mild frost tomorrow, I thought idly. My mouth was dry and my heart thundered in my chest.

In one fell swoop I had lost my boyfriend, been branded a bunny-boiler, vilified in the press, been linked to a murder, and had forfeited my firm. My firm. *Mine.*

I didn't know how to react. I had failed at the one thing I was good at. I was resigned to my relationship failures, my sibling failures, my interior-decorating failures, but this? This was entirely new.

I had lost Paterson, Paterson & Co. My grandfather's firm. My father's firm. My firm.

Of course, it was all perfectly legal, dissolving the partnership. In newer firms, there were safeguards within the partnership agreements that made it possible to sack a partner if they were not performing, but we were an old firm. Our agreements were old-fashioned.

The only way of forcing someone out, if the rest of the partners wanted that, was to go to the extreme of dissolving the partnership. Those who wished to could then regroup and form a new one, excluding those who were out of favour.

Naturally, there were costs involved but they were small compared to what it cost to buy out a partner. My poor father. He might have been a partner in name only, but he had still received a share of the profits.

'Christ!'

I sat down on the stairs to get my breath back.

What would my father say? What would my mother say? They would go berserk. What would I tell them? 'Sorry, but while you were out I accidentally lost the family firm?'

Tears pricked the back of my eyes. I couldn't believe it had happened. I thought they might have suspended me, but this was a severe body blow.

'Ern? What's wrong?' Max's little voice asked from the top of the stairs.

I took a deep breath and forced a stupid smile on to my face.

'Nothing, pumpkin. Just bad news about work, that's all. Nothing for you to worry about. Can I get you something else to eat?'

He shuffled down the stairs towards me, dragging the tails of his dressing gown behind him.

'No, thanks. Why doesn't Mummy work?'

I took his hot little hand in mine muttering, 'God only knows,' under my breath.

It was now clear why nobody had called me back. They had mortgages and families to think of. They would throw their tuppence in with the better bet and who could blame them? I knew what I had to do, but I was scared. I opened a bottle of wine and drank two glasses.

Max watched some more cartoons and was soon yawning beside me on the sofa.

'Time for bed, sleepy head.'

'Can I sleep in your bed?' Max asked as I carried him from the den.

'Sure. If you want to.'

At least somebody loved me, I thought miserably. I put him in my bed and tucked him in, leaving the table light on.

'Can I have one more story?' he chirped.

'OK. Just one.'

I didn't mind putting off the inevitable.

We read a story about Kipper the Dog. He was a cute basset-type creature who acted like a child. I kissed Max goodnight and steeled myself for my chore.

I took the phone into the dining room and sat at the table where we'd had so many family meals, special occasions and Christmas dinners. It seemed oddly fitting that I should deliver the bad news, the momentous news, from here.

I took a fortifying sip of wine and dialled my parents' cottage in Crail. The cottage was a family joke. They actually owned a very large house in the popular fishing village. My mother answered.

'Mum. It's me. Erin,' I said lamely.

'Aahh,' she replied.

'Can I speak to Dad?' I would tell him first before she got all hysterical and shrieky.

'He's resting.'

'Well, can you un-rest him. I need to speak to him.'

'Anything you have to say to your father you can say to me!'

She was such an old pain.

'Mother, it's very important. Please let me speak to Dad.'

'No.'

'Pleeaase. Please let me speak to him.'

'No. He can't help you now.'

'Mother! Something has happened. I *need* to speak to Dad. Please.'

'No,' she said, and hung up.

I gazed at the buzzing receiver. Unbelievable. And she had made me forget the other reason I was calling. I pressed redial. My mother answered within one ring.

'Where's Brontë?' I demanded.

'Leave her alone! This has nothing to do with her. You keep her out of this.'

I held the phone away from my ear and lamented the fact that my life was in tatters and that my mother had finally slipped into senile dementia.

'Jeezus Christ, Mum! Where is she? I can't find her!'

'She's at home with Maxwell,' she yelled back at me.

Very calmly I said, 'No. She. Is. Not. I'm here with Max. I've been here all day. She's not here.'

'Where is she, then?'

'I don't know! That's why I'm calling you. I can't stay here for ever.'

'She was there when we left.'

145

'*Obviously*. But she's not here now. Have you any idea where she could be?'

'No. Try that bar.'

'You're not being very helpful. How can I "try that bar" when I'm here with Max?'

'Phone them. The number is in the book in the hall bureau drawer.'

'Mother, don't you think it's odd that she didn't pick up Max from nursery and just expected me to do it?'

'You're his aunt.'

'That's not the point. What if something had happened to me? Where would she be then?'

I didn't know if she was being deliberately obtuse or if she really didn't see the point.

'She probably forgot that we had gone away for the week.' She sounded impatient.

'I see. So it's quite normal for her to disappear into thin air, and nobody is bothered?'

'Of course we're bothered. How dare you insinuate that we don't care!'

'I'm not insinuating anything. She could have been murdered for all we know!'

My heart missed a beat.

'I've got to go. I hear Max,' I lied.

'Goodbye, then!'

She slammed down the phone. Again.

I laid my head on the table for a moment and closed my eyes. I was a nervous wreck. The big black dog of depression was limbering up in the shadows.

I carried antidepressants and tranquillisers in my handbag, although I hadn't taken them for two years. But I was sorely tempted now.

I knew I must be methodical in my search for Brontë, so I went to the hall bureau and took out the book.

The number for The Granary was on the inside flap under Brontë.

There were several places and friends listed, so I rang them all and wondered how many times my mother had done this. I kept expecting to hear Brontë's derisive tones in the background, but had no joy.

I went upstairs and began to search her room, hoping to discover a place or friend that our parents didn't know about, but her room was full of junk. Flyers for nightclubs, matchbooks, magazines and trashy novels. Maybe Brontë was adopted? I wished hopelessly.

I checked on Max before I went back downstairs and dialled the local police office.

'Govan Police,' a man answered.

'I'd like to report a missing person. My sister.'

'Hold on. I'll put you through.'

'Sergeant Chambers speaking.'

'I'd like to report a missing person. My sister,' I repeated.

'What age?' He sounded faintly bored.

'Twenty-eight.'

'How long have they been missing?'

'I only have *one* missing person. My sister. From nine this morning, as far as I know.' I was blatantly crotchety.

'Adults are not considered missing for twenty-four hours,' he replied.

'She has a young son. She didn't collect him from nursery school. She *is* missing.'

I could feel a dark cloud of fear billowing round me. Was I the only one that had any sense of apprehension? Did everybody else float through life without any misgivings?

I heard him sigh. 'What's her name?'

147

'Brontë Paterson.'

'Have you tried all her friends and places she would normally go?'

'Yes.'

'What's the address?'

I told him my parents' address.

'OK. I've got the particulars. If she hasn't turned up by nine tomorrow, phone us.'

'*What?*'

'If she doesn't contact you by nine tomorrow morning, call us.'

'That's all you're going to do?'

'Yes, ma'am. She's not missing until twenty-four hours have passed.'

'Sergeant Chambers, my name is Erin Paterson. My sister is missing. Please let me speak to somebody in authority.'

'I understand your concern, Miss Paterson, but she is not considered missing for twenty-four hours. Speaking to the chief inspector won't change that. Thank you for your call. I'm sure your sister will turn up.'

'If my sister doesn't "turn up", Sergeant Chambers, I'll be sure to mention your outstanding help.' I slammed down the phone just like my mother.

Bloody policemen. They were quick enough off the mark to arrest me for bopping that bastard Alex. I leapt to my feet and got my handbag from the kitchen.

I found DS Marshall's card and rushed back to the dining room. He wasn't at his desk, so I tried his mobile.

'Hello, Erin. What's up?' He sounded pleased to hear from me.

'It's my sister, Brontë, she has disappeared. I mean she's missing. I tried to report it to the local police office but they weren't interested.' A pathetic quiver entered my voice.

He switched to professional mode. 'I see. How long has she been gone?'

'Since nine o'clock this morning, I think. She didn't collect her little boy from nursery. I'm worried.'

And I really was worried. Brontë was unpredictable but this was extraordinary, even by her standards.

'I'm actually about to come off duty. Do you want me to come round?'

'Yes. Yes, please. Couldn't you put out an APB on her or something?'

He gave a hollow laugh. 'This ain't America, ma'am.'

'OK, OK. What can you do?' I tried not to bite his head off and yell, *This is no laughing matter*.

He must have picked up the anxiety in my voice.

'I'll come right over. We'll take it from there. You sit tight and don't worry. We'll find her. OK?'

I wandered around the house and wondered about karma. I had always tried to be a good person, maybe not very agreeable, but good. I didn't sleep around, I didn't take drugs, except prescription, and I was kind to animals and children. More or less. Didn't that count for anything?

I told myself that Brontë would probably roll up, rat-arsed, at some ungodly hour, and I would look like an overreacting fool, but it gave me no comfort. I felt somehow I had caused this, somehow I was to blame.

I wandered into the drawing room and sat down at Mother's concert grand. I had played the piano all through my schooldays but, as my mother told me, I was never up to much.

Leland, my brother, had played beautifully and I had

resented his gift. Leland, who could play the piano but not cope with life. Poor, dead Leland who had wasted so much potential.

I flicked through my mother's music and found the Chopin piece in B minor. I sight-read it twice before I began to play. The first rendition was hopeless, but I played it again quite nicely and it filled me with hope.

I played it again and again, and gradually began to feel mildly better. I was unemployed and unloved. I was free. I had no commitments other than those I chose. I had a chance to redeem myself. It made the hairs on my neck stand up.

I was a pragmatic person. The beauty of a moment was often lost on me for worrying about the next.

I didn't hear the doorbell and I nearly jumped out of my skin when DS Marshall knocked on the window of the drawing room.

'Nero played while Rome burned,' he said as I let him in, and I found myself flushing.

'Would you like a coffee?' I asked politely.

He shrugged off his crombie. Not the usual attire of a police officer, I thought.

'Something stronger, perhaps. It's been a long shift. Whisky?'

I went to the drinks cabinet and poured him a good measure of Laphroaig. I held up the amber liquid. 'Water? Ice?'

'Just as it comes, thanks.'

He ran his fingers over the keys. 'That sounded nice. What was it?'

'Chopin. Do you play?'

'Not really. I'm more into sports, but I can appreciate beauty when I see it.'

I handed him the heavy crystal glass. Maybe I was

mistaken, but I got the distinct impression DS Marshall fancied me.

'So tell me, what can I do to help?' He sat down on the sofa.

I went back to the drinks cabinet and poured myself a stiff mineral water.

I thought he looked remarkably fresh for having just come off a shift. I would have gone as far as to say that he looked newly shaved and showered.

'Brontë can be a bit irresponsible but this is different. And I have a bad feeling.'

'You rely on intuition a lot?'

I thought about it. To be perfectly honest, I didn't have much to do with intuition. I used it in legal bartering and sizing people up, but I didn't decide what colour of underwear to wear with it.

'Sometimes.'

'Have you tried all her usual haunts?'

'Yes.'

'Have you contacted the hospitals?'

'No. I never thought of that.'

Strangely, that was a comforting question. She could have been in a car crash or knocked down. She could be injured.

'Let's try them first.' He motioned towards the door.

I went through to the dining room and opened the *Yellow Pages* at 'Hospitals'. He smiled at me and shook his head, then picked up the phone and dialled a number.

It was a brief conversation. He told someone to try all the Glasgow hospitals for a Brontë Paterson, then added if there was no one of that name to try a Jane Doe. I gave him her age and description, which he passed on. He advised them to call back on his mobile. I admired his command of the situation.

'What now?' I asked.

Marshall shrugged. 'We wait and see.'

'What if the serial killer has got her?' I blurted out.

'What serial killer?'

I knew Paul had said it was confidential, but this was Brontë we were talking about. My sister.

'I know about Abigail Dawes. I know what he did. And now Lucy Grant . . . I'm scared in case . . .' I couldn't say the words.

I stared down at the solid mahogany table and prayed. Please, God, don't let him get Brontë. Please.

'Come and sit down.' Marshall gently took my arm and led me back to the drawing room.

I cast a quick glance at his wedding finger but there was no ring in evidence.

'You worry too much,' he said as he sat down beside me. He pushed the hair away from my shoulder.

I didn't know how to respond, but I knew I looked alarmed. He was nice enough, but I had more pressing things on my mind – like a missing sister.

He sat back in the sofa. 'Sorry. I've embarrassed you.'

'No, no. It's just I'm so worried about Brontë that I can't think about anything else.'

'I'm sorry. It was totally inappropriate.'

'No, please. I'm very wound up, right now. I really appreciate you coming here.'

He took a long slug of his whisky and stared straight ahead.

'What do you know about Abigail?'

'I know that she was murdered and he took her finger.'

'And what do you know about Lucy?'

He continued to stare straight ahead.

'Nothing. I just know she was murdered.'

'So how do you figure a serial killer?'

He was nonchalant, but it seemed too well rehearsed.

'I just thought, well . . . because they were both young and attractive that it might be the same guy . . .'

'And because of that phone call to you, you think Brontë might now be a target? But she's been missing in action before, hasn't she?'

When he put it like that, I realised how paranoid I sounded.

'Yes,' I admitted, although I wondered how he knew. His mobile phone rang before I could ask.

'DS Marshall speaking.'

He listened carefully to the voice at the other end, occasionally muttering, 'Uh-huh' and 'Yes, I see.'

He pressed the mobile back off and turned to me. My guts were churning.

'I've got good news,' he said, but he didn't look happy. 'We've found your sister. She's in the Victoria Infirmary.'

'Oh, God,' I breathed. 'Is she OK? What happened?'

He took a deep breath.

'She was found in a back lane off Pollokshaws Road. It looks like a drug overdose. She had no ID. She's got some injuries, but nothing critical.'

I stood up.

'Do you want to see her?' he asked quietly.

'Yes, of course. But I can't leave Max.'

Delicately, he took hold of my limp hand. 'I could stay here with him.'

'Thank you. But if he wakes up he'll be scared.'

My mind was jumping in a hundred different directions. Brontë, drugs, Max – all jostled for space so that I couldn't think straight.

'She's in safe hands just now. Why don't you leave

it until the morning? She's stable. You wouldn't be doing anything constructive by being there.'

He swung my hand gently in his.

'Erin. Sit down. You can't always be the strong one. Let somebody else take the strain for once. You can't blame yourself for the actions of others.'

I was always reading medical reports with the line, 'he or she went into shock'. Was this it? When you could no longer string coherent thoughts together?

He was wrong, anyway. I rarely blamed myself for the actions of others. I blamed them, fair and square.

'Do you want to talk to me about it? I can help you. I know what it's like. Talk to me. I want to help you.'

'I'm just sad. Sad that I didn't know her problem. What will happen now?'

'Social Services, I expect.'

My mind was racing.

'Can we keep them out of it?'

'Doubt it. There's the welfare of a child involved.'

'What if I became his guardian?'

Marshall finished his drink. 'Your sister would have to be declared unfit.'

'Can I get her sectioned? Under the Mental Health Act?'

He seemed taken aback by my suggestion. 'She might have overdosed accidentally.'

'I know. But Max is the most important thing. I have to protect him.'

'Don't you want to know what happened before you pass judgement?' he asked scornfully.

'She takes drugs. Whether she meant to overdose or not is unimportant. Max must be protected.'

'You would do that to her? Instead of trying to get her into rehab?'

'I'll get her into rehab,' I said. 'But I'll make sure Max is safe first.'

He stared at me, his eyes wary and perplexed. I had seen that look on countless men. They were faced with the true me and they didn't like what they saw.

'You're very hard sometimes,' he said.

'I have to be. Brontë's brought this on herself.'

'Isn't this more like revenge?' he asked slyly.

I didn't see how protecting Max could be considered vengeful. I shot him a sour look.

'Thank you for your help. If you wouldn't mind, I'd like to be alone now.'

He stood up immediately and went towards the door.

'Are you angry because I challenged you?'

'I have more important things to consider right now.'

'I just don't get you,' he said as he left.

'Most people don't,' I replied, and closed the door behind him.

I went through to the dining room to look up Susie Newfield, our family-law partner's home number.

I had dialled the first four digits when realisation dawned. I didn't have a family-law partner because I didn't have a law firm. Shit. I hung up the phone and struggled with what to do next.

Should I phone my mother and upset her further? Or should I try to deal with this quietly by myself? I was more familiar with the quietly by myself option.

With all these new complications in my life, any worries I had of a serial killer faded away. Nevertheless, I checked all the doors, set the alarm and took myself up to bed.

Max stirred slightly as I slipped under the covers beside him. I wished he was mine and the thought startled me.

Was Marshall right? Was I hoping to steal the one thing Brontë had that I didn't?

I could start a new law firm and support my parents. I could find a detox programme for Brontë. I could sell my penthouse and move on. I could rebuild my shattered reputation. I could find another boyfriend, maybe even a husband. I could have my own child. I could do anything I set my mind to. I was intelligent, attractive and hardworking.

I lay very still and stared up at the ceiling.

I didn't even convince myself.

NINE

The stench in my car the next morning was unbearable, so Max and I walked through the park to the nursery and counted squirrels – two; wood pigeons – seven; and magpies – ten.

After settling him in I had a quiet word with Mrs Orman, explaining that Brontë was unwell. I didn't expand further and mercifully she didn't press me.

I drove to the Sterling Car Wash, with the Jeep's windows and sunroof open. The full valet lasted half an hour, but there was still a residual smell of vomit. They asked me if I wanted to keep the newspapers but I told them to chuck them.

Back at my apartment, I packed a suitcase. I had the feeling I would be staying with Max all week. I was sorely tempted to speak to Paul and update him on the latest fiasco that was my life, but I wasn't sure he would be interested.

For a couple of minutes I stood outside his apartment, hoping he might come out so I could bump into him casually.

I decided to leave him another note, this time saying my nephew was ill and I was staying at my parents'. I also left their phone number. I pushed the note under his door.

I knew I needed to gauge the gravity of the dissolution of Paterson, Paterson & Co., but my first responsibility was to Brontë. The damage to the firm and me was already done. Leaving it to fester wouldn't change a damn thing. I suspected that they would have cleared my desk, anyway. Picking up the cardboard boxes of my career could wait.

I wasn't sure where Brontë would be at the Victoria Infirmary, so I headed straight to reception. I was told she was in Ward 2B. I trudged up the decrepit stairs and felt sorry for all those in the place.

I glimpsed Brontë from the swing doors. She looked dreadful. Her newly blonde hair had been hacked haphazardly into short tufts. I wondered if it was a form of self-mutilation. She was on an IV and seemed to be asleep.

I sat down on the hard plastic chair beside her cabinet and kicked myself for not bringing flowers and fruit. I was so insensitive.

I remained there for several minutes, idly glancing around the ward. It had six beds on either side and was nearly full, mainly of elderly women.

'You're wearing my clothes,' Brontë croaked.

I took her hand and smiled at her.

'Max was sick all down my suit. You owe me a dry-clean.'

'Where is he?' Her voice was hoarse and her breath smelled like overripe Stilton.

'At nursery. He's fine. He sends his love.'

She looked alarmed. 'He knows I'm here?'

'No. He knows you weren't well and had to see a doctor.'

Tears sprang into her eyes and rolled down her blotchy cheeks. I stroked her damp forehead and tried to comfort her.

'They said I overdosed on cocaine, but . . . I've never touched coke.'

'It's going to be OK. We'll get you into a programme.'

'But it's not true!'

I was sure I had read somewhere that drug addicts always denied it, but her eyes bore into me.

'You don't know what happened!'

'No, Brontë, I don't know what happened and you don't have to tell me.'

She sat up, her face taut with anxiety.

'You don't understand. I don't know what happened. I don't know where I was ...' She began to sob uncontrollably as I gripped her hand. 'I'm sorry, Erin, I'm so sorry ...' She grabbed at my arms and pulled me to her. 'I'm sorry, I ... didn't mean to ... I'm sorry, Erin ...'

'Brontë! Please calm down. It's OK. It's going to be OK. Really.'

Her sobs caught the attention of the nurse, who scuttled over.

'Excuse me. You'll have to leave,' the nurse snapped.

'I'm her sister. She needs me here.'

'You're upsetting her.'

'No, I'm not. Her situation is upsetting her. I am here to help.'

She drew herself up to her full height. 'You'll have to leave.'

Brontë shrieked. 'Erin, no! Don't go! He might come back. He might come here ...'

I pulled her weeping head against my chest again.

'Who will come back, Brontë? Who?'

She looked up at me and choked on the words. 'I don't know ... I can't remember ... I was going to ... I couldn't stand ... I was in a street ... and here ... I'm sorry ... I'm sorry.'

'I'm getting the doctor!' With pursed lips, the nurse marched off down the ward.

'Good,' I muttered. I wanted a word with him.

I drew the curtains around Brontë's bed and tried to calm her down. She hiccuped and cried, and said she was sorry, over and over. I told her it would be all right but she continued to sob and apologise.

'He said . . . then I was . . . I can't remember! I don't know what happened next . . .'

'Who did?'

'The man. I couldn't stand! He made me . . . I couldn't stand. Help me, Erin! Help me! I can't remember.'

Her shoulders shook with the effort of crying. I shushed her and made her lie back on the pillows. I stroked her ravaged hair and kissed her forehead, as our mother used to do, but inside I felt like stone.

A young man in a white coat appeared at the curtain and smiled apologetically. 'I'm sorry, but visiting hours are over.'

I smiled back and held out my hand for him to shake. He looked mildly disconcerted.

'Erin Paterson, I'm Brontë's sister. I am also a solicitor and here in a professional capacity. I would like to know what injuries Brontë has and what was in the toxicology report.'

He looked at Brontë, who in turn looked at me. Brontë then nodded.

He held open the curtain. 'Would you come with me, Miss Paterson?'

'Promise you'll come back, Erin. Promise!' Brontë said.

I gave her hand a reassuring squeeze.

'I promise.'

I followed the doctor to a tatty room off the ward, where he fetched Brontë's file and checked through charts and reports.

'Alcohol and benzoylecgonine,' he said casually.

I wrinkled my forehead.

'Cocaine.'

'How much alcohol?'

'About thirty-five millilitres. That's about the driving limit.'

I knew myself that wasn't very much, equivalent to a measure at most.

'How much benzoyle . . . cocaine?'

'Enough for an OD.'

'Anything else?'

'Traces of several barbiturates.' He shrugged. I supposed this was all routine to him.

'What happened to her hair?'

The doctor shook his head. 'It was like that when she came in. She had lost quite a lot of blood.'

Alarm bells rang in my head. She hadn't looked injured to me. I had presumed minor cuts and bruises. 'Lost blood? How?'

He shifted uncomfortably. 'She has damage to her right foot.'

'What sort of damage?'

'One of her toes is missing.'

I gaped at him. *One of her toes was missing.*

I thought I was going to faint and rattled out the questions shrilly.

'Have you called the police? How is it missing? Where is it? Which toe? Can you sew it back on? Have you got it?'

He pulled out a chair and told me to sit down.

'Are you OK?' The sickly hospital smell from his white coat made me feel worse.

I shook my head. I knew I was ashen because I had felt all the blood in my body rush to my head and then down to my feet like a water flume.

'Are you going to faint?' He crouched beside me and took my pulse. 'Put your head between your knees,' he said, guiding my head down.

I stayed like that for some time, breathing slowly. Her toe. He took her toe. I wanted to scream.

'Have you called the police?' I whispered from my bent-over position.

'Yes. They're coming back later, when she's more coherent.' He was running a tap.

'How was it . . . How did they . . . How was it . . . ?' I swallowed the bile back down.

'Here. Sip this.' He handed me a glass of tepid water. It tasted of too much chlorine. I sat up.

'The little toe was severed. Very clean cut, right at the joint. Could have been a bolt cutter.'

'Will she be able to walk again?'

'It shouldn't affect her mobility at all. It would have been much worse if she'd lost her big toe. I'm afraid that things like removing fingertips and toes are often used by gangs or drug dealers as a warning. She probably owes some money.'

'It's not that,' I said fearfully. 'It's something else entirely. Were there signs of sexual assault?'

'We don't check for that with ODs.'

'Can you check?' I asked.

He grimaced. 'It's difficult. We could check if recent sexual activity took place but whether or not it was consensual is another matter. There wasn't anything immediately obvious when she came in. No vaginal bleeding or such.'

I nodded slowly. But Brontë had said there was a man. Was I leaping to conclusions by linking this to Lucy Grant and the message? Or was I in denial about how far Brontë would go? She had seemed genuinely scared.

The doctor interrupted my thoughts. 'Do you think she was drugged and raped?'

'I don't know . . . Why can't she remember what happened?'

'A combination of things, the drugs, the shock. She might not be ready to remember,' he said with open sympathy.

'But there are drugs that can do that to you. Like Rohypnol,' I said.

'Yes. And Gamma Hydroxy Butrate. But the fact is she overdosed on coke.'

'Just check her. Please,' I said. I needed to establish if there was a link to Lucy Grant's murder.

'You said you were a lawyer. What d'you specialise in?'

'Compensation,' I said dryly. 'Can I use the phone?'

He pointed to an ancient phone in the corner. It took me four attempts to get an outside line.

'Paul?'

'Uh-huh. How's Max?'

'He's fine. I'm at the Victoria Infirmary with my sister. Something's happened. I need to ask you something.'

'Okay . . . '

'You said that Lucy was drugged. Was Abigail drugged?'

He was silent for a moment.

163

'I don't know, Erin. What's this about?'

I ignored his question. 'What did he use to drug Lucy?'

Again he was silent for a moment while he considered his answer.

'He used Ketamine. It's a horse anaesthetic, but produces incapacity and hallucinations in people. It's kinda like Rohypnol, the date rape drug.'

'So they could be raped without defending themselves? Would they remember what happened if they survived?'

'Erin! Please tell me what this is about. Has something happened to your sister?'

'Yes, but I can't explain now. I'll explain later.'

I hung up the phone and slumped against the cabinets that lined the wall. At least she's alive, I repeated over and over in my head.

Before I returned to the ward, I found the doctor and asked him to test Brontë for ketamine and to check for signs of sexual assault. He raised his eyebrows at me as if to say, *clutching at straws*.

Then I sat with Brontë, holding her hands and telling her to rest.

She desperately wanted to see Max and I promised to bring him in later, but only if she was well enough. I told her firmly that it would not be good for him to see her like this. For the first time in her life she accepted my advice. I think we were both equally stunned.

'Do Mum and Dad know?' she whispered.

I rubbed my forehead and cursed silently. I had forgotten to phone them.

'No. They know I couldn't find you, but they don't know you're here.'

'Are you going to tell them?'

'I'll have to. I don't want you to be afraid, but I think

you've been . . . that you're the victim of a crime.'

Brontë closed her eyes. 'I know.'

'We need to find out exactly what happened and let the police take it from there. The doctor said they'll come back later.'

The tears started again.

'No, I don't want that . . .'

'Darling, hush. I won't let anyone hurt you. I promise. OK?'

I knew what she was afraid of. Sometimes it was better not to know the truth. I looked at my watch.

'I need to collect Max. Is there anyone who could look after him for a while?'

She sighed heavily. The tears had left her exhausted. 'Martha, or Mrs Gordon next door sometimes watches him.'

'I have to go to the office at some point. I might take Max with me and then leave him with Mrs Gordon when I come back. Is that OK?'

'So you're not bringing him?' She looked crestfallen.

'Not this afternoon. Maybe after tea. Can I bring you anything?'

'Something to drink. Orange juice. And something to read. And a washbag and nightshirt.'

Brontë sniffed and sat up.

'They said I didn't have a handbag when I was . . . You might need to cancel my credit cards. There's a list at home.'

'Your handbag's missing?' That could be a lead.

'I don't know. They said I didn't have one . . .'

She frowned.

'But I must have had one because I was going . . . Oh, my God! That's where I met him! I was in Shawlands.'

I sat back down immediately.

'Can you remember what he looked like?'

'Not really . . .' her voice trembled. 'Erin, what will happen to me?'

I took her clammy hand in mine. 'I don't know, Brontë, but I'll be here. I'll be with you.'

I left and pulled the curtains closed behind me, hoping my sister would rest and maybe recall some more pieces of her shattered day. I didn't know if she was aware of her mutilation. I was scared for her. Of how she would feel and cope with the truth.

She would bear the scars for ever. Every time she stood up she would be reminded of what he had done.

A still shot of Brontë's maimed foot flashed before my eyes. I had not seen it, but, as with Abigail's eyeless face and Lucy's bloodied mouth, my mind's eye could picture it clearly.

I didn't know exactly what had happened to Brontë, but her mutilation coupled with the phone call from Lucy's killer was enough to send my imagination careering out of control.

I parked my Jeep in front of the hill leading to the nursery. Max skipped down the hill as soon as he saw me. It was a dramatic change from the limp little parcel I had carried the day before. He climbed into the back and immediately started telling me what he had done at nursery that morning.

'I need to go to my office,' I said.

I drove towards the city centre and wondered if the dissolution of Paterson's had hit the journalistic wire yet.

At least I still had my parking space. William opened the door and greeted me with the utmost courtesy. I shook his hand and thanked him for all his wonderful work in the past. It brought a lump to my throat.

Max held my hands as we went up in the lift, swinging back and forth singing, 'One, two, three four five, once I caught a fish alive.'

My floor was quiet. Fortunate that it was lunchtime, although we did receive some curious glances from those still working.

Max ran ahead gleefully. 'This is your office, Ern! Do you still get money for dead people?'

It was just as I had suspected. My office was filled with cardboard boxes. I surveyed it coolly and wondered if everything would fit in my Jeep. Picking up my extension, I called William to ask if he could get someone to help me carry it all.

I had been hoping to see Karen and Douglas, so I could thank them for their work over the years.

While Max whizzed round in my swivel seat I went to Karen's desk to leave her a note. I opened her top drawer looking for a piece of paper and found nothing. I then searched in several other drawers and her filing cabinet, but they were all empty.

'Aah, Erin. I was hoping you would pop by.' Michael bore down on me from the boardroom. I wondered if he had been notified of my arrival.

I looked at him blankly. I felt nothing. No anger, no desire for vengeance, nothing. It was an extraordinary feeling of calm. Not like me at all. Four days ago, I would have decked him. My reaction surprised him too.

'No hard feelings?' He held out his hand.

I raised an eyebrow and ignored him. It was not what he wanted. He was desperate for a fight. He followed me back into my office.

'It was for the good of the firm.'

I shrugged. 'Whatever.'

'Young Maxwell! How are you, young man?' Michael swooped down on him and lifted him up. Max looked nonplussed.

'Fine.'

'How's your mummy?'

'Fine.'

'And Granny and Grandpa?'

'Fine.'

Michael plonked him back in my seat. There was an awkward pause.

'Well, then. I see you're busy . . .' Michael looked at his watch. 'I've a meeting at two . . .'

I continued to ignore him until he bolted from my room.

Max and I took the few things that we could carry and left my office. I said a silent, painful goodbye as we went to the lift.

William was waiting in reception and took my potted plant from me.

'I've sent up the mail-room boys, Miss Paterson. They'll be back down directly.'

'Have you seen Douglas Thomson or Karen McCall?'

'Not since yesterday.' William gave a smile. 'They both handed in their notice.'

'Are you sure?'

'Yes. Cleared them out first thing. And that Liz Miller on floor two. Nice girl.'

'They all resigned?'

William nodded and opened the door to the car-park stairs.

'Yup. Pity. They didn't want to merge with Cohen Freidmann.'

Merge with Cohen Freidmann? The enormity of what

William had just said was lost on him. The sneaky bastards, merging with Cohen. It must have been on-going for months. Mat and Michael were made for each other. And three of my colleagues were jobless.

Max and I played I-spy while the mail boys loaded up the boot of my car. There were far too many boxes for one load, so I told them I would come back for the rest later.

I pressed the button on the automatic gate and drove away. Paterson, Paterson & Co. was no more.

'I'm hungry,' Max whined.

'What would you like?' I said sweetly.

'Happy Meal. Chicken nuggets.'

'OK. One Happy Meal coming up.' I headed for McDonald's.

When we arrived back at my parents' I was dismayed to see a Volvo waiting outside. I hoped it wasn't the press. As soon as I drew into the driveway, two people got out of the car.

'Miss Erin Paterson?' called the woman. She darted up the driveway towards me.

'Yes. How may I help you?'

She fumbled about in her enormous handbag and eventually extracted a laminated photo ID.

'I'm Jane Hobson from Glasgow Social Work Department and this is my colleague, Colin Craig.'

I wished that Max wasn't clutching a Happy Meal.

'We were wondering if we could have a few words?'

The exact words, I thought, were bloody hell and damn.

Once we were all inside, I sent Max upstairs to watch cartoons and eat his disgusting food. Normally I made him eat in the kitchen, but today was an exception.

I showed the two social workers through to the dining room.

'I was hoping you would come,' I lied.

That seemed to disconcert them. Colin Craig shifted in his seat and opened a loose-leaf file. In amongst handwritten notes and various typed forms, I noticed some newspaper cuttings.

'As you will understand, Miss Paterson,' he began, 'with this newest incident and the revelations about Brontë's lifestyle in the press over the weekend, we felt that . . .'

I cut him off, 'What revelations?'

They exchanged glances.

'The ones in the press,' he offered vaguely.

'I haven't read them.' Why, in God's name, hadn't I read them? Fear of their vicious criticism, I supposed.

'Em, well . . .' he shuffled through the file and pulled out a press cutting. 'This one says that she regularly appeared to be stoned and abandoned her son, Maxwell, to your and your ex-partner's care . . .'

'That's a lie to begin with! Alex never looked after Max. May I see that?'

He handed me the newsprint.

I scanned the article. It was part of the *Sun*'s exclusive. Alex claimed that Brontë was frequently drunk or stoned, left Max to be looked after by his grandparents or by us, and we suspected that she stole from them and me. He claimed I knew that she took drugs, but I didn't do anything about it for fear of dragging the family name through the mud. Ironically, I had already.

Those had been private conversations. Thoughts and fears I had been foolish enough to share. How could he? The bastard.

'We presumed you would have already read these articles,' said Ms Hobson quietly.

I rubbed my hand over my mouth. Oh, Brontë, I thought, what have we done?

'Is there any truth in these allegations?' Mr Craig asked.

'No. It's not as simple as it appears.'

'Who is caring for the boy just now?'

'I am. I am perfectly willing to be made his temporary guardian.'

I had thought this would appeal to them, but they exchanged those glances again.

Jane Hobson hesitated before she replied. 'It's quite delicate, Miss Paterson, because of . . . well, other things that have come to light.'

'What other things?' I prayed to God that they didn't cite my arrest as a reason for taking Max into care.

'Have you spoken to your sister today?' Mr Craig asked.

'Yes. I saw her earlier.'

'What did she say to you?'

'She said she was sorry and that she couldn't remember what had happened. She was in a pretty bad way.'

'Mmm . . .' he nodded.

'What does that mean?' I asked.

'Because of the child's welfare, Strathclyde Police contacted our department and we also saw your sister, but she told us some rather disturbing facts.'

I felt the hairs stand up on the back of my neck.

'Your sister remembered some details of the events yesterday . . . and, well, she remembered being here. In the basement,' he said ominously.

'You mean she was in the basement?' A shiver ran through me. Could Brontë have been here all along? Under this very room?

'Em, well, the thing is she claims that you were there.

171

That you let it happen. That you didn't help her when the man cut off her toe.'

'That's ridiculous! I never saw her yesterday. I couldn't find her. I even reported her missing to Govan Police . . .' My voice trailed away. Why would Brontë say such a thing? Why would she lie?

'Do you have a basement?' Ms Hobson asked.

'Yes. But surely if she'd been here I would have heard something?'

'She was vague about the precise details. She's having flashbacks. One of the side effects of the drugs,' Ms Hobson explained, but my mind was racing.

Why would Brontë lie?

'Are you absolutely sure she wasn't here?' Mr Craig asked.

'Yes. No. I mean, I don't know if Brontë was here.' I shook my head in bewilderment.

'Can we check the basement?' he enquired politely. 'Just in case there's anything nasty for the wee one to stumble across.'

'Yes. Of course. Although Max would never be down there on his own. It's through here.'

The two social workers followed me through the house to the locked basement door. My heart thundered in my ribcage as I turned the key.

Collectively, we peered into the eerie half-light.

'Is there a light?' Ms Hobson asked.

I flicked the switch inside the doorframe. Nothing happened.

'It blew on Friday. Sorry. I forgot.'

Tentatively, we made our way down the stairs, which creaked with age. We traipsed from room to room checking for drug paraphernalia or any evidence of Brontë's claims.

'Doesn't look like anyone has been down here for a while,' Mr Craig commented.

'I was down here on Friday, with the dogs, but only to lock the garden door.'

We found nothing untoward and trudged upstairs. As we filed back into the dining room, the front doorbell rang.

I was surprised to see Paul.

'I'm sorry to intrude. I was worried about you and your sister,' he explained.

'Oh . . . em, I've got somebody here just now, em . . .' I wasn't quite sure what to say. 'Come in.'

He was equally clumsy. 'If this is a bad time, I'll call back later.'

'No, em, not at all. The kitchen's through the hall. Make yourself at home.' I pointed vaguely towards the back of the house.

For once, Paul didn't look entirely comfortable. 'Are you sure?'

'Hopefully I won't be long,' I said, and went back into the dining room.

'Sorry about the interruption,' I apologised and sat down.

'This is really odd,' Ms Hobson said immediately. 'Brontë was adamant that something happened down there. She said your brother was there too. Is he at home?'

'No. Finlay's in Thailand. I don't understand why she would say that . . .'

I had shut out the memories for so long that they no longer existed. I was mortified by my own cowardliness and by my guilt.

'Finlay? That's not the name she used.' Mr Craig flicked through the loose-leaf file. 'Leland. She called your brother Leland.'

A chill sliced through me.

I cleared my throat and tried to control the tremble in my voice. 'That proves she's mistaken about yesterday. Our brother, Leland, died more than a decade ago.'

'Oh, I'm so sorry,' said Ms Hobson, mistaking the tremble for sorrow, but Colin Craig narrowed his eyes.

'I imagine that the police will want a statement from you, if Brontë told them the same things.'

'Yes . . . I imagine so.'

'Would it be possible for us to see Max?' Ms Hobson asked.

'Yes. Yes, of course. I'll go and get him.'

'Actually, it's usually better for a small child if we introduce ourselves while they are relaxed, like playing or something.'

'Oh. Right. He's upstairs.'

I showed her up to the den and introduced her to Max as a friend of Brontë's. I wasn't sure if that was the correct protocol but I didn't want to alarm him.

Max immediately told her that his mummy wasn't well and had gone to stay at the doctor's. Jane Hobson threw me a look that made me curse inwardly.

'Do you know what's wrong with Mummy, Max?' she asked.

'Yes,' he said excitedly.

Ms Hobson's eyes widened.

'She's got a sore tummy. I had one too. And I was sick over Ern. And her car,' he said triumphantly.

'But you're better now, eh? I see you had a Happy Meal,' she smiled.

I rolled my eyes. I knew that they would notice.

'Miss Paterson, could I see you a moment?' Mr Craig called from downstairs.

I recognised their ploy instantly. Divide and conquer.

Mr Craig was waiting for me at the bottom of the stairs.

'Would you mind if I smoked? I'll go outside.'

I was mildly taken aback by his request, but politely offered the use of the drawing room and showed him through. He took in the grand piano, the antique furniture, the sumptuous drapes, the Persian carpet and numerous paintings.

'This is a beautiful house. Have you lived here long?'

'It's been in the family since it was built.'

I searched in a sideboard drawer for the set of Hermes ashtrays I had bought my mother one Christmas. I opened another drawer and found a Wedgwood one instead. I handed it to Mr Craig and went back to the sideboard. I opened every drawer and all the cupboards. The ashtrays were nowhere to be found.

'Have you lost something?' he asked eventually.

'Misplaced,' I said vaguely. If Brontë had nicked them I was going to kill her.

'Did you honestly not know Brontë was taking drugs?' he asked.

I sighed heavily. It was pointless lying.

'I didn't know for sure. I suspected she might be, but . . . well, you have to remember, I don't live here. I don't really see her that often.'

'But you do see Max?'

'Oh, yes. At least a couple of times a week.' I didn't add that Brontë wasn't always here because I didn't want to make things worse.

'But not Brontë? Is she normally out?' He threw me a sideways glance.

Damn.

'And that stuff she was saying about the basement

here? There's no truth to that whatsoever?'

'I really don't think she was here yesterday, if that's what you mean,' I said. I noticed that he hadn't actually lit a cigarette.

'I don't want to put you on the spot, Miss Paterson, but if your sister maintains that's what happened, then it will look pretty bleak in terms of Max remaining here . . .'

I closed my eyes for a moment and tried to form the words.

'Something did happen here. Years ago. With my brother. Leland. He . . . he . . . mistreated us . . . her, here.'

I had finally let the words out and they left a filthy deposit on my tongue, they compounded my guilt.

'Were you present?'

I tried to shut out the noise but I could still hear her begging and crying.

'Yes, but I couldn't help her. He had tied me up. I couldn't get free to help her . . .'

'What did he do?' he asked softly.

I could hear her calling my name and begging me to help. I could see myself struggling against the skipping rope that bound my wrists. I could feel the burns it left. I could taste my failure to protect her. I could smell our fear. Subconsciously, I rubbed my wrists.

'What did he do?' he repeated quietly.

'He put bugs in her clothes. In her pants . . . and hair. And in her ears . . .'

'Did he *touch* her?'

'No . . .' I breathed out my shame.

'No. He pulled out her toenail. It bled and bled, but I couldn't help her. I was tied up . . . I couldn't help her . . . I couldn't.'

176

TEN

Veritas praevalet – truth prevails. Brontë and I never discussed the incident, and I thought we had both buried the memories alongside our brother.

I wanted to fold in on myself, physically and mentally, but dutifully drank the hot sweet tea Mr Craig had made me. He told me he had been in social work for thirty years, but I saw that my painful and stumbled account had appalled even him.

'Are you feeling better now?' he asked, like the kindly uncle.

We didn't have any real aunts or uncles because both my parents were only children. Strange that they should have chosen to produce four. I had the notion that the only child begot another only child.

'Erin?' he said again.

'Yes. I'm fine.'

I hated hot sweet tea. I was convinced it was in some sort of handbook. For shock, administer hot sweet tea. Then extract confession.

'Are you up to answering some questions? It may help to put Brontë's overdose into some sort of context.'

He opened his loose-leaf file and glanced down at his notes. 'You said your brother is dead. Do you mind if I ask what happened?'

'He committed suicide eleven or twelve years ago.'

His jaw hung open. Immediately, I realised the erroneous connection he had made.

'It wasn't the same as . . . well, as Brontë. He took

177

a skiff out and drowned. He left a note. My mother had to identify his body.'

I clearly remembered how devastated she was, wandering aimlessly round the house, not speaking for weeks and weeks. She used to wait at the drawing-room window, her eyes scanning the road, as if expecting him to come home.

'I don't think Brontë was . . . I think her overdose was accidental.' Could Lucy's killer have given Brontë the coke? Could he have forced her to overdose?

'Or a cry for help?' he said.

'Maybe. Her toxicology report showed a cocktail of drugs.'

'Did Brontë ever report the things Leland did to her?'

'I don't know. I don't think so.'

'Didn't your parents intervene?'

'They wouldn't have believed it. They thought the world of him.'

Mr Craig raised his eyebrows and I realised how terrible that sounded.

'It was . . . difficult to . . . it's difficult to explain . . .'

'Has she received any form of counselling?'

'I honestly don't know. Surely you have access to her medical files?'

'Not yet. If Max is referred, then we will look into the background.'

I didn't know much about the formalities of child protection, but I had a sinking feeling I was about to become an expert.

'I'm not really clear on the procedures. What happens next?'

'We make a report which goes to the officer of the

children's panel. If he thinks Max may be in need of compulsory measures of care, he'll arrange a children's hearing.'

'Is that what's going to happen?' I ventured. Why hadn't I looked after her?

'No, Miss Paterson,' he said. 'Max may require a supervision order, but the more information we have, the better placed we are to help.'

I knew where he was going. It was well documented that abused children often metamorphosed into abusive adults.

'Brontë has never, ever, hurt Max. In any way,' I said.

He gave me a sympathetic smile. 'I understand, but under the circumstances your assistance could weigh favourably for Brontë. And Max.'

'What do you need to know?'

'Had Brontë displayed any suicidal traits?'

'What are suicidal traits? Reading Sylvia Plath?'

'Self-destructive behaviour. That sort of thing.'

'She drinks too much and is sometimes a bit reckless.' I shrugged uncomfortably. It felt like stabbing her in the back.

'Could her problems be linked to issues in her childhood?'

'Whose aren't?' It struck me that Brontë hadn't mentioned anything about Leland when I visited.

He took a deep breath. 'Is there any possibility that she was here yesterday?'

'In all honesty, I would have to say no. It hurts me to say this but I think she has confused past and present, maybe as a result of the drugs.'

'Do you think she said those things to deflect attention from her own actions?'

I looked down at my cup of tea. A milky film was forming on top. It did seem a logical explanation.

'Miss Paterson?' he urged.

'Yes.' I said sadly. A lump caught in my throat. In some ways it would have been easier if she was entirely faultless.

'Does Brontë ever see Max's dad?'

'No. As far as I know, they have no contact.'

'Do you know how we could contact him?'

'I don't know who he is. I don't think Max's father even knew Brontë was pregnant. She refused to name him on the birth certificate.'

'Would you mind if I took a look around her room?' he asked.

'For drugs?' I said in alarm.

'Not especially, but we have a duty of care to the youngster.'

Mr Craig followed me from the drawing room up the stairs to the mid-landing.

'This is Brontë's room. Max's is next door.'

We went into her room together. He cast about her things, then opened her wardrobe. I felt uncomfortable watching a stranger poking through her stuff, so I quietly slipped away.

The shock of Brontë's revelations had begun to wear off and was rapidly being replaced with anger. Brontë was a bitch. Resurrecting the past like that. It was irresponsible and shabby. Hadn't I been nice to her at the hospital? And this was how she thanked me.

I popped my head round the door of the den, but it was empty. I wondered where they had gone. I went to Max's room, but that was empty too.

Movement on the landing above caught my eye. I watched in disbelief as Ms Hobson disappeared into

Leland's old bedroom. I hared up the stairs after her.

'What on earth do you think you are doing?'

She came back out and seemed rather taken aback. 'Max wanted to show me around the house. He said it was OK . . .'

I gave her a look. 'Max is four and a half.'

She shifted uncomfortably. 'Is this Finlay's room?'

'No. This is Leland's room.'

I caught a glimpse of Max bouncing on Leland's bed.

'Maxwell Paterson. Come out of there at once!'

He immediately stopped bouncing. The use of his full name was a good indication of the degree of trouble he was in.

'It's very . . . tidy. Does anyone else use it?' Ms Hobson asked.

'Not as far as I am aware,' I replied crisply. Use Leland's room? They had to be joking. And of what relevance was that?

The weak October sunshine filtered through the windows, casting a golden glow. My mother had left it exactly as it was from the very day we were informed of Leland's suicide by two young police officers. She came in here regularly to vacuum and dust the tidy remains of his life. The poor cow.

But the smell of Leland had not lingered. He had used an unusual and distinctive aftershave. I couldn't recall the name.

His bookshelves were neat and his bed made. It was the corresponding bedroom suite to my parents'. It had never bothered me that he'd got the best room. Until now. Leland had abandoned his mother and father, leaving them to suffer uncertainty and guilt for the rest of their lives.

'I don't think this is appropriate,' I said.

Max shuffled past me and I closed the door.

'I'm sorry, Miss Paterson. You're right. That was totally inappropriate. I was simply trying to get to know the child. I didn't mean to distress you,' Ms Hobson said.

I nodded my acknowledgement but didn't enlighten her.

Mr Craig came out of Brontë's room and smiled at me.

'Nothing to worry about in there,' he said simply.

I appreciated his candour.

Max was casting apprehensive glances at me.

'Is there anything else I can help you with?' I asked both social workers.

'Not at the moment. We'll stay in touch. Here's my number.' Mr Craig passed me a business card.

En masse we headed back downstairs.

'Max,' I called.

'Yes . . .'

'Do you want to show Ms Hobson and Mr Craig to the door?' He loved doing that.

He skipped down to me. Very formally, he shook both their hands and thanked them for coming.

Mr Craig laughed. 'What lovely manners.'

'Ern taught me,' Max explained. 'She taught me not to scratch my bottom. Unless I'm in private.'

I was relieved they were gone, but anxious about the repercussions. On the surface they had seemed quite satisfied with the current arrangement, but any long-term implications were less clear.

'Ern. I'm sorry,' Max said, and hugged me round my legs.

'That's OK, pumpkin. Just don't do it again. Granny would be really upset. OK?'

'OK. Can I watch *Dexter's Lavatory* on Cartoon Network?' He was already halfway up the stairs.

'I think so,' I said vaguely. What on earth had happened to *Bagpuss* or *Andy Pandy*?

I went to the kitchen. I may have had hot sweet tea, but coffee was still my poison.

I gasped when I saw Paul.

'God! I'm sorry. I forgot you were here!'

'Everything OK?' Paul asked.

'No,' I sighed and put fresh beans in the grinder. I immersed myself in the awful racket it made, hoping the sound would drown out my thoughts. It did. But only for a moment.

'What's happened to Brontë?' he asked.

'She's overdosed on coke. That was Social Services.'

'Because of Max?'

'Yes.'

I bit my lip. I really wanted to be alone. The ghosts of the past were there, marshalling at the breach, ready to come bounding out.

I became preoccupied with the old-fashioned coffee percolator.

'Erin, I may be able to help.'

Avoiding eye contact I placed coffee mugs on the kitchen table. I simply didn't have the strength for another interrogation, for I was sure that was coming next.

'I need to be alone right now,' I said quietly.

'You need to talk to somebody. You can't handle all this on your own.'

I gave a sour laugh. 'I've handled everything on my own, my entire life.'

'But this is different! Brontë needs specialist help.'

He paused for a moment.

'So do you.'

'Yes, I know! I'll get a lawyer for Brontë. I'll organise detox and counselling. I'll work with Social Services. I do know a little bit about protecting an individual's rights!'

'That's not what I meant,' he said.

'Then what do you mean?'

'I, accidentally, heard some of what was said.'

'You eavesdropping bastard!'

'Calm down! It was an accident . . . I . . .'

'You lying bastard! You couldn't wait to hear . . .'

'Stop it!' he said. 'Stop right there! I admit I listened for longer than I should have, but I hadn't planned or . . .'

'Get out! I don't want to hear another word! It was confidential.'

I was shaking. Bad enough two social workers knew, but a tabloid journalist? Christ. It didn't bear thinking about.

'God, Erin. You are some piece of work. I would never disclose—'

'What did you hear?' I said quickly.

He pulled out a chair and sat down at the table. I wavered for a moment and then did the same.

'Your brother committed suicide and, well, there might have been some, em, issues between Brontë and him.'

'Great euphemism,' I muttered.

'OK. Abuse. Happy?'

'Fuck off.'

'Now that's charming.'

'What do you expect?' I hissed. 'My parents still don't know about Brontë! And it will be me that has to bloody tell them. They'll hit the roof and I'll get the blame. Just like Leland all over again. It will be my fault because I wasn't looking after her!'

Paul blinked at me and I truly wished I had never let him in.

'Is that why Leland committed suicide? Because you weren't looking after him?'

'Of course not! But my mother likes to lay the blame at my feet whenever she gets an opportunity.'

'Why?'

'It's easier than accepting any blame herself.'

'Do you blame her?'

'No!'

'But you blame Brontë for what's happened to her?'

'Are you taking evening classes in psychoanalysis?' I stood up and grabbed the coffee jug. Why on earth was I telling him any of this? What the hell did it have to do with him?

'I'm just trying to help. You're obviously upset.'

'I'm not upset. I'm furious.'

'Furious with whom?'

'If Brontë hadn't bunked off, none of this would have happened. I wouldn't be here looking after *her* son while I lost my job, and when strangers come into this house and rifle through her drawers.'

'Your sister's not to blame, Erin.'

'How come?'

'Earlier, when you called me, you thought it might have been connected to Lucy Grant.'

'Earlier maybe, before I realised she began stirring up all this stuff from the past.'

'Aren't you more upset about what Brontë revealed? About what Leland did to you both?'

'It's all in the past! I don't know why she had to dredge it up. So Leland mistreated us. What will be

185

gained from causing our parents even more heartache?'

'I know somebody you could talk to,' he said quietly.

'Thank you. But I'm fine.' I cursed myself silently. I used to be so prudent, so in command.

'I appreciate your concern,' I said. 'But I really must get on with sorting some things out. You don't mind seeing yourself out, do you?'

Paul frowned but I ignored him.

I left the kitchen and went up to check on Max. He was giggling at his ridiculous cartoon. I hoped he was never robbed of these simple pleasures. For a moment, I stood quietly in the doorway trying to structure my jumbled thoughts.

Cancel credit cards. Collect things for Brontë. Get Brontë a lawyer. Find babysitter for Max. Phone Mother. My shoulders slumped. Dear Lord, I still had that joy to face.

Tiredness and self-pity swept over me. Slowly I realised that I could hear Paul talking.

'. . . very cautious, yes, of course . . . well, it's abuse between siblings . . . No, I understand . . . I'll speak to her, I'm sure she'll see my point of view . . . Yeah . . . thanks, I owe you one.'

My blood ran cold. Another exclusive? New, fantastic revelations about the Paterson dynasty?

I didn't know what to do. Go down on my knees and beg? Get an injunction? Beat him to death with a walking stick? At that moment I didn't think I had despised anyone more in my entire life.

He came around the corner from the back hall that led to the kitchen. I couldn't trust myself to speak and ducked away so he couldn't see me. I wanted to beat him with my bare fists.

He let himself out, slamming the heavy front door behind him.

I hared down the stairs and peeked out of the window. I saw him dialling another number on his mobile. He had duped me three times in the last three days. How could I be so stupid?

I leant my back against the cool of the stained glass and felt overwhelmingly alone. Alone and small. I had no one to turn to and no one to trust.

The phone rang. Fearing it was Paul, I hesitated before answering.

'Erin? I was expecting you to call me. Have you found Brontë?' My mother sounded extremely narked.

'Yes. I've found her.'

'Oh, good. See, you were overreacting.'

'Brontë's in hospital,' I said.

I heard her gasp. 'What? What happened to her? Where is she? Is she all right? Is she injured?'

'Don't know. Victoria Infirmary. No and yes.'

'You're not making sense!'

'Well, I suggest you come home and deal with your daughter yourself. I'm tired of being a surrogate parent,' I said and hung up.

The phone rang again almost immediately and I knew she had pressed redial, ready to give me a mouthful about insolence. But I ignored the ringing because I knew it would make her spit tacks.

I went back upstairs and into Brontë's room. I rifled her desk drawers for a list of her credit cards or bank statements, but my sister didn't seem to have amassed the debris of paper that is the curse of adult life.

'Ern!' Max called from the den. 'The phone's ringing.'

'I know, pumpkin.'

The phone continued to ring, cut off, then ring again. 'Shall I answer it?' Max called.

'No, darling. It's a fault on the line.'

I had realised, rather late in the day, that Brontë probably didn't pay her own bills. I went to my mother's bedroom suite. I had to admire her tenacity even if it did drive me mad. I waited for the next time the phone cut off and took the receiver off the hook. That should fix the old bat.

Rubbing my hands over my face, I tried to summon the strength to search my mother's roll-top writing desk.

There were bills, receipts, personal letters and business correspondence all muddled together. How she ever found things was unfathomable.

As soon as I opened the left-hand drawer, I knew I had stumbled on something cherished. The letters and cards were carefully bundled and tied with black ribbons. Two piles of condolence cards and notes, but I didn't bother to look through them. Underneath the two neat parcels were two large manila envelopes, which I cautiously removed.

I went over to her bed and carefully extracted the contents of the larger envelope. I knew I would need to replace everything in precisely the same order. There were certificates and notes of everything Leland had ever achieved, right down to his Grade One piano certificate. All carefully, lovingly kept. I wondered idly if she had kept anything of mine.

Sifting through some press cuttings, it amazed me how times had changed. There was nothing in the newspapers that speculated about anything inauspicious concerning Leland's death. It was viewed simply as a terrible tragedy.

Someone called Jonathan Moncreiffe, whom I

vaguely recalled, had witnessed Leland taking the skiff out and had also discovered the suicide note. I was disappointed not to find the actual note in the drawer, but perhaps it had been too painful for her to keep. I had never read it and had no idea what my brother had written.

I slipped everything back into the envelope just as I had found it and opened the other one, but it wasn't easy to suppress the creepy sensation I experienced as I poked through her most private things. It felt as though somebody was watching me.

The second envelope contained cards and letters that Leland had sent her. The folds of the letters were deep and the cards well handled. How often did mother take them out and lament her loss?

I put everything back and checked the right-hand drawer, but it only contained elastic bands, paperclips, pens and assorted junk. I would need to try the kitchen drawers next.

As I closed the roll-top, a document envelope bearing the firm's name caught my eye. Gingerly, I pulled it out from under the precarious mail mountain that rested on top of it.

The letter and agreement were dated the 2nd September.

Dear Lady Georgina Paterson

Further to our meeting we would be pleased if you could sign and return the enclosed documents, retaining a copy for your files.

The dissolution of Paterson, Paterson & Co., Solicitors is scheduled for mid to end November 1999, dependent on the optimum time for the merger with Cohen Freidmann, Solicitors.

The new partnership shall bear the name of Cohen Paterson . . . Sir Maxwell Paterson shall be retained as a consultant and his share of profits will remain in line with existing arrangements . . .

I read it again and then again.

My mother had signed on my father's behalf.

This was the icing on the cake. My own family had sold me out, betrayed me. What had I done to deserve such treatment?

Max popped his head round the door.

'Ern, I'm bored.'

He clambered up on to the bed beside me.

'What's that?' He pointed at the documents I held in my rigid hand.

I gazed at him blankly.

'It's either the final nail in my coffin or my official certificate of freedom.'

'Ooh, coffins are scary. Let's say it's the free thing. What do you get? A toy?'

'No. Apparently, I get a new start.'

'Not a toy?' he said with obvious disappointment.

'No, darling. Not a toy.'

ELEVEN

Haphazardly, I bundled up a selection of Max's clothes and toys. I left a note telling my parents I had taken Max to my apartment and that they were to cancel all of Brontë's credit and bank cards. I knew I should have waited to explain Brontë's situation to them in more detail, but I relinquished the burden.

We drove away under a threatening sky. I glanced up over the pond where a cluster of seagulls were circling. Seagulls only came inland in such numbers if there was a storm brewing.

'Are we going to visit Mummy?'

'Yes, but not right now. We'll go home first.'

Max sighed. 'I miss Mummy.'

'I know you do, pumpkin, but she's not well enough to see you.'

'Like me, yesterday?' he asked.

'Yes. Like you yesterday.' How could it have been only yesterday? My life was on fast-forward.

'Is she going to die?'

'Of course not! She'll be up and about in no time. I promise.'

'If she dies, will she go to heaven?'

'She's not going to die. You'll be much, much older, with children of your own, before she goes to heaven.'

The storm broke before we reached my apartment building. Great, fat, autumnal raindrops ricocheted off my windscreen and drenched pedestrians. We pulled into the underground car park as the wind picked up.

Icy gusts pursued us and chased leaves around our feet. I surveyed my car and wondered how on earth I was going to get all the boxes up to my penthouse. There were times when a man did come in handy.

We carried our clothes and Max's toys up in the lift. I was secure in the knowledge that Paul was still out, because his car wasn't there. I hoped the two-faced bastard would somehow get soaked and catch pneumonia.

Max scampered up to his room full of excitement at this little adventure. I was glad of his presence, for my beloved apartment now pulsed with unfocused fears. They floated like dust and clung to everything.

He popped his head over the banister.

'Ern? Am I still banned from the kitchen?'

I looked up from my new answerphone, which displayed eight messages.

'Of course not. You can go anywhere you wish.'

'Can I build a den?'

'OK, but only in your own room.'

'Whoopee!' he cried and dived into my linen cupboard for sheets and duvets.

I pressed play on my phone and listened to my messages. The oldest ones were from Liz, Douglas and Karen, each asking me to call them back. I wasn't sure when I would – guilt gnawed at my conscience. They were jobless for a principle. How was I going to sort that out? A reference from me wouldn't come top of other law firms' wish lists.

There was a message from a double-glazing company and one from the secretary of the Law Society. I would definitely ignore both of them. There was also an odd one from a surveyor, wanting to know when I would view a city-centre office property that was available for lease. I presumed that was a wrong number.

DS Marshall had also left a message enquiring after Brontë and apologising for any 'misunderstanding' the previous evening. He asked me to call him back with an update. I would let him stew, I decided. My intestines twisted when I heard Paul's voice.

'Erin. You've just asked me to leave. I don't know what's happened precisely, but you need to contact DSI Kelman with any information. Trust me. You could be in danger. Call Kelman.'

Trust him? I couldn't believe the audacity of the man. I pressed delete and accidentally erased all the messages.

Cursing Paul under my breath, I went upstairs to where Max was making a duvet mountain.

'Will you be OK while I have a quick shower?'

He didn't respond.

'Don't answer the door, or the buzzer, or the phone. OK?'

'Okey-dokey,' he mumbled and plunged head first under a duvet.

Wearily, I ran a hot shower and stood for five minutes under the relieving pulse of water. I needed to recharge my batteries before I got down to the business of rebuilding my life and reputation. No policeman or journalist was going to besmirch my family name with any more innuendoes. I was resourceful. I was educated. I was intelligent. And I hadn't a clue where to start.

Wrapping myself in a bath sheet, I padded back into my bedroom. I was towel-drying my hair when I heard a voice, a man's voice.

I stormed out of my bedroom and yelled, 'What the hell are you doing here?'

Paul was sitting on the sofa with Max.

'I came to offer you my help,' he said.

'I don't need your bloody help. Get out.'

He stood up. 'You do need my help. I want you to calm down and just hear me out.'

'More lies? Great! I've not had enough of those in the last week!'

I glared at Max and then at Paul. 'How did you get in?'

'You said "bloody". That's a bad word,' Max said.

'I did knock, and then let myself in with the keys that Alex left.' Paul looked contrite. 'I forgot to tell you earlier.'

'When exactly did he leave the keys?'

'Yesterday afternoon. About three o'clock. He left you a letter. I put it on the coffee table.'

I didn't bother opening the letter; it could wait.

Max tugged at my towel, reminding me uncomfortably of my state of undress.

'Where is Alex?' Max looked around my apartment as if Alex might miraculously materialise.

'He went to live somewhere else.'

'Why?'

'He didn't want to be my friend any more.'

I sat on the arm of the sofa and pulled Max to me. He looked up at Paul.

'That's OK. You've got a new friend now.'

'Are you still building a den, Max? Shall we go and look at it while Erin gets dressed?' Paul asked.

'Who were you calling from my parents' house?'

'I called you and left a message, and I called a friend. A friend who might be able to help. I'll explain later.'

'It had better be good.'

'Is there anyone you trust?'

I thought for a moment. 'No. Not any more.'

I dressed quickly and gave my hair a short hot blast with the hairdryer. I was impatient to hear what Paul had to say for himself. He soon returned from inspecting Max's hideaway and joined me in the kitchen where I was making fresh coffee.

'DSI Kelman was working on a case with me when Leland's name came up,' he said plainly.

'That must have been years ago.'

'Fifteen years ago.'

Paul toyed with his coffee cup but I stared at him expectantly. I wanted answers.

'There was a series of murders and your brother's name came up along with several others. Leland was part of a quasi-secret sect . . .'

'A secret sect?' I repeated scornfully, but tiny scraps of recollection were filtering back. 'They were nothing more than public-school boys massaging their own egos, like one of those pathetic Oxbridge groups! They called themselves a stupid name, The Masterminds, or something! They're probably running *Daddy's* merchant bank by now.'

'We have strong reason to believe your brother was involved in ritualistic torture and gang rape. He may be dead but somebody is carrying on his . . .'

'Let me get this straight? You and DSI Kelman think that somebody Leland knew, from all those years ago, has started doing terrible things . . . And why didn't you tell me DSI Kelman used to be your partner? When we talked about Lucy and Abigail? Why didn't you say something?'

'Like what? "Excuse me, Erin, but although we've just got on speaking terms again, your dear departed brother was under suspicion as a serial killer"?'

'Leland might have behaved like a monster with me and Brontë, but what's it got to do with now? He's dead! You can't possibly connect him to Lucy and Abigail.'

'We need you to help us build a profile.'

'What on earth for? He's dead! What part of that don't you understand?'

'Because what we have now bears all the hallmarks of the past! It's almost as though the killer is impersonating your brother. If you could help us bridge the gaps . . .' Paul reached over the cold marble table to touch my hand. I snatched it away. Where did he get off, always pawing me?

'I think you should leave,' I said. 'Right now!'

'Stop fighting me. I'm not the enemy!' he yelled and stood up.

'Don't you dare shout at me!'

'You're so bloody aggressive. I'm only trying to help you.'

'I don't need your help. Yours or anyone else's.'

'You need more help than anyone I've ever met.'

'No, I don't. What I need is for everyone to butt out. This is my family and my problem. Go do your social work somewhere else!'

'You're about the nastiest piece of work I've ever come across.' He sat back down. 'And you're rude.'

I opened my mouth to give him a pithy retort, but he got in before me.

'As well as being a complete pain in the ass.'

His sheer audacity stunned me. Paul had showed remarkable restraint in the face of my extreme belligerence. Few people, particularly men, could handle me.

'Can we go back to the beginning?' he asked wearily.

'What beginning? The beginning when I asked you to leave?'

'For Christ's sake, just tell me about your brother!'

'It's irrelevant. Pointless. He's dead.'

Paul put his head in his hands and spoke to me like I was a small child. 'The more we know about Leland, the closer we can get to the killer.'

'I steered well clear of him. And all his friends.'

I had always been afraid of Leland, very afraid. All my teenage and adult life had been spent trying to blot out the pain and the fear. I had buried the memories and I didn't want to exhume them. Now it seemed that Leland would persist in torturing me from beyond the grave.

Paul narrowed his eyes. 'What about his time at Edinburgh?'

'I don't know much,' I said truthfully.

Once Leland had left for university, I had gone the following year, but to Glasgow. I had fancied going to Edinburgh because I had been at boarding school there, but I didn't want to be in Leland's shadow.

'You can't remember anything?'

'He was involved in the debating society. He lived the high life with the society crowd. He hung around with that group of guys that you mentioned. They fancied themselves as intellectuals and Casanovas.'

'Were you surprised when he committed suicide?'

'I suppose I was. He enjoyed his life, well, that was how it seemed. He travelled extensively and expensively during the vacations. Mum would tell me ridiculous stories about him winning some competition for writing or debates, but I suspected my parents financed the trips.'

'What do you remember about his friends?'

197

'Jonathan Moncreiffe was one of them. He was with Leland the weekend he killed himself and he found the suicide note. I read that in an old newspaper cutting at my parents'.'

'If I showed you photographs, would you recognise any of them?'

'I honestly don't know. And what would be the point?'

Before Paul could say anything else, the phone rang.

'Hello. Is that Erin Paterson?'

'Yes,' I replied impatiently.

'This is DSI Kelman. I was wondering if I could ask you some questions?'

'Would it make any difference if I said no?'

'We would really appreciate it . . .'

'Tell me one thing, Mr Kelman, how well do you know Paul Gabriel?' My eyes never left him.

'Very well. May I come up? I'm right outside . . .' I hung up and pressed the security-door buzzer.

'I'm sorry I didn't tell you before—' Paul began to say, but I cut in.

'Before what? Before I was next? When exactly were you going to tell me?'

He held up his hands in surrender.

'Just let me finish. Kelman's a good man, but I couldn't tell you without his say-so. These are murders we're talking about. Common courtesy had to come second.'

I heard Kelman knock but I ignored it. Paul stood up and ushered Kelman into my kitchen. They both sat down opposite me.

'So my brother was a suspected serial killer?' I asked sarcastically.

'Miss Paterson, what you've got to understand is that

after the initial enquiries, all the leads went cold. We were suspicious about your brother's suicide, but there was nothing to prove he hadn't taken his own life.'

'What? You think he might have been murdered?'

'Yes. We suspected foul play.'

'By whom? One of his friends?'

'Maybe. We thought there might have been a power struggle in their group. Leland was obviously numero uno, but once the others had got a taste for it – well, who can say?'

None of this could be real, I decided. This was Scotland, for God's sake. We had drug deaths and sectarian murders. We didn't have serial killers. That was the preserve of the United States.

'This is quite the most unbelievable, bizarre load of crap I've ever heard,' I said to Kelman.

Kelman looked rather taken aback.

'Where is your evidence? First you tell me that my dead brother was probably a serial killer, and he could have been murdered by one of his followers, who might now be impersonating him. And to top it all off, he's coming after me? Have you any idea how ridiculous the whole thing sounds?'

'Yes,' he said.

'Finally we agree on something.'

'Not exactly. Paul told me about Brontë's overdose and mutilation. It could be connected. Serial killers generally work to the same pattern. They have rituals, if you like. They target the same sorts of people and they do the same sort of damage . . .'

Max suddenly came dashing into the kitchen.

'Ern! Come and see my pirate ship.'

He stopped in his tracks. 'Are you Ern's other friend?' he asked.

Kelman smiled. 'Yes. I'm her other friend.'

Max accepted the information without a flicker and grabbed at my hands, pulling me to my feet.

We went up to his bedroom, where I absent-mindedly admired his pirate ship. I was reeling from what I had just been told. It was too much to take in. Serial killers. Brontë's mutilation. The dredging up of our past.

'I'm glad you've got two friends now. You used to be lonely,' Max said as I left.

I kissed his head and prayed that he never found out about any of this.

Kelman was on the terrace using his mobile phone when I returned to the kitchen.

'I'm sorry I never told you before. I never thought it would come back round like this,' Paul said.

'Did you move here deliberately?'

He didn't reply immediately. I knew he was deciding whether to lie or tell the truth, and that alone was all the confirmation I needed.

'Not for the reason you think,' he said eventually.

I didn't want to pursue the matter. The damage was done. He had moved here to be closer to a potential victim. Charming.

'Are you really a journalist and ex-police detective?'

'Yes.'

'Truthfully, why did you leave?'

But my question was left unanswered. Kelman came back inside, wiping the rain from his face.

'Your sister's feeling much better and is ready to be interviewed. She wants you to be there.'

I scowled. After everything she had said? She had to be kidding. And what if more lurid revelations surfaced from the past?

'I can't,' I said quickly. 'I've got to look after Max.'

Kelman was ready for this excuse. 'We've got a specially trained WPC standing by to keep an eye on him.'

Lamely I conceded defeat and stood up, but my phone rang again.

I let it ring five times, vaguely hoping the caller would get fed up before I answered.

'Erin? It's DS Marshall. I'm phoning to see how your sister is. I left a message earlier.'

Pointedly I turned my back on Kelman and Paul.

'She's a bit better, I believe.'

'And how are you?' His voice was etched with concern. I was surprised to feel myself blushing as I recalled his overt pass.

'I've been better,' I said.

'Has Brontë remembered anything yet?'

'Not really. But we're going to see her in a while.'

'Good. Well, if there is anything – and I do mean anything – I can do to help, please give me a call. Even if it's just to talk. You shouldn't be alone at a time like this.'

'Thank you. I appreciate it. I really do.'

Especially as, for Paul, I was the proverbial tethered goat.

Brontë had been moved to a single room. There was a policewoman sitting with her and I hovered in the doorway while Kelman re-introduced himself to my sister. He reminded her of their previous meeting that fateful Friday night, but she didn't appear to remember him.

She looked worse than she had earlier, if that were possible. There were dark hollows under her eyes and some sort of nervous rash had spread over her face and neck.

When she saw me, she immediately burst into tears and held out her arms.

I let her hug me and bury her face in my chest and shoulder, while I patted her back and gently rocked her to and fro. The weight of her grief was monumental. Any wrong she had committed was insignificant by comparison.

A door opened in my enshadowed heart as I tried to soothe away her tears. Pride could be a useful weapon, but to abandon it was liberating.

'I'm so sorry, Erin,' she whispered.

'So am I, Brontë, so am I. I should have looked after you better.'

I took both of her hands in mine and sat on the edge of the bed facing her.

'We have got to forget everything that has come between us. We must stick together. Whatever happens, we must know that we have each other. And Max. That's all we need.'

'Is Max here? Does he know what's happened?'

'He's downstairs with a WPC. He thinks you have a tummy bug. I really don't think we should tell him anything else.'

'But what about my bruises? My hair, my . . . my . . . toe . . . ?'

'We'll tell him you were knocked down . . . by a . . . trolley at the supermarket. We'll think of something. OK?'

She sniffed and wiped her nose on the front of the awful hospital gown. I felt a complete bitch for not bringing the few things that she had requested.

Paul was listening discreetly just outside the door, as Kelman began.

'I've been over the statements you gave my

colleagues, Miss Paterson. I know it's very hard for you, but would you be able to go over a few things with me?'

Brontë nodded and Kelman sat down in the hard plastic chair.

'You said you were in Shawlands and a man approached you?'

She nodded again.

'Did you recognise him?'

'No. Not really.'

'What did he say to you?'

'I think he said something like, "Hi, Brontë. How are you? I haven't seen you for a while".'

'So he definitely called you by your name?'

Brontë looked down at the bedspread. 'Yes. I thought I knew him but I couldn't remember.'

'You thought you knew him? From where?'

Brontë kept her eyes lowered. 'I go out a lot. I meet lots of people. Sometimes I can't remember them.'

'Because you're under the influence?'

She looked up sharply. 'Sometimes I have a little too much to drink, but not drugs.'

Kelman smiled gently. 'That's OK. Lots of us like a good time, Brontë. None of this is your fault. There's a sick man out there. He's to blame, not you. Can you recall what he looked like?'

'He had . . . very dark hair and really blue eyes and . . . and . . . a moustache. He had a moustache!' Brontë's eyes sprang wide open with this new fragment of memory.

'Height? Build?' Kelman was noting it all down.

'Tall, I think . . . and average . . .'

Brontë began to twist the corner of her sheet round and round into a knot.

203

'What happened next?'

'He talked about some pubs I go to, and I thought I must know him. He made a reference to a . . . a . . . night.'

'A night you and he were together?' Kelman asked pointedly.

Brontë swallowed.

'Can you remember the night in question?'

Brontë looked at me with the most stricken expression, and my heart went out to her.

'No,' she whispered eventually.

'But you could have been out with him before? It is a possibility?' Kelman continued.

'Yes. But I'm sure I haven't! I'm sure I didn't! How could I go out with someone who would do this?' Brontë cried.

'But you did, Miss Paterson. You did.'

'Mr Kelman, I don't think I care for your tone of voice.' I interjected, but he ignored me completely.

'Do you remember where he took you?'

'We went for a coffee in The Granary and then I started to feel funny, so he got me a brandy . . . I felt even more giddy, I couldn't stand up. He helped me outside and gave me a mint . . . and then I can't remember . . .'

'Where did he take you? You told the other officers that you were in the basement of your parents' house. Isn't that correct?'

'No. Yes . . . I told them that, but I was still groggy. I was mixed up. I don't think I was there.'

'You also claimed that your sister Erin and your late brother Leland were there. Why did you say that if it wasn't true?'

Brontë couldn't look at me.

'I . . . I . . . was mixed up. I remembered it from . . . the past.'

'So you lied?'

'I didn't mean to! I was confused . . . I couldn't tell the difference between then and now. I thought it was true, but . . .'

'Miss Paterson, is it possible that everything you have told us is a lie? A little story you've concocted to cover up what really happened?'

'This has gone far enough!' I shouted.

Kelman pursed his lips and thought for a moment.

'Let me tell you what I think. OK? I think you scored some drugs. Then you scored some more, but it all went horribly wrong. The dealer wanted to be paid. He wanted cash. But you didn't have any cash, and when you refused – or offered him some trinket you'd pilfered – he cut off your toe. There. Isn't that more like it?'

Brontë put her hands over her ears. I wanted to believe my sister, but had to admit that DSI Kelman's version of events had the awful ring of reality.

Kelman stood up abruptly. 'Your sister has been through a terrible ordeal, for which I have the deepest sympathy.'

'I don't think your style of questioning is helping.'

'A quiet word outside?'

I glanced at Brontë, but her eyes had sunk in on themselves.

'I'll be back in a minute.'

I gave her hand a reassuring squeeze and followed Kelman out, closing the door behind us.

'What the hell was that all about?'

'Erin, I don't think it was the same man,' he said calmly.

'Why? He bloody well called me! It doesn't take

a huge leap of the imagination to link that to my sister.'

'One, he didn't kill her. Two, there's no sign of sexual assault and he could actually be an ex-boyfriend or a drug dealer. Three, he has used ketamine before but never Class A drugs, and four, she's not his type.'

'What do you mean, "she's not his type"?'

Kelman shifted from one foot to the other. 'He goes for *good girls*. She comes from the right background, but she's a bit of a . . . a bit of a—'

'A SLUT?' I spat. 'It doesn't count because she's not a twinset and pearls virgin? Can't you see? He's taunting us! And if she's not his type, why did he call me?'

Kelman and Paul glanced at each other.

'Because you are,' Kelman said.

I was stunned. I had never viewed myself as a twinset and pearls virgin.

'But why did he hurt Brontë? We don't exactly look identical. He called her by *her name*. He knew who she was.'

'Maybe this wasn't the killer. Maybe he is her regular dealer. Maybe he knew her name because he had fucked her before.'

I wanted to punch him in the jaw.

'She got what she deserved. Is that what you're saying? Brilliant piece of deduction!'

I stormed past them both and back into Brontë's room, slamming the door shut before they could reply.

'What was all the shouting about?' Brontë asked.

I took three, deep, cleansing breaths before I could speak.

'Men are stupid, Brontë. Believe me, men are stupid.'

I sat down in seething silence. Brontë leaned her

head back on the pillows and stared up at the ceiling. At least she hadn't been sexually assaulted, I told myself several times.

'Was any of what he said true?' I asked at length.

She glared at me. 'How can you ask that? How can you?'

'I'm sorry. I just had to be sure.'

She tutted angrily and closed her eyes.

We sat for a while without speaking.

'Do you ever wonder if Leland told people what he did to us?' Brontë's eyes flickered open.

'I . . . I don't know. Why?'

'I just . . . wondered.'

I nodded, but she looked away again.

So none of it was my imagination; none of our blighted childhood was embroidered by my own delusions. Brontë and I had dealt with it in the opposite manner. I had become aggressively self-sufficient, emotionally and physically barren, and she had become dependent and needy.

There was a gentle knock at the door and the WPC popped her head in.

'Em, if you don't need me any more . . .' she whispered awkwardly.

I could see that Max was behind her.

She opened the door and ushered him in, saying goodbye. Max stared at his mother as the door closed quietly behind him. His face paled and his eyes brimmed with tears.

'Mummy,' he whimpered and flung himself on her.

Brontë gathered him up in her arms and held him tightly. A lump formed in my throat.

'What happened?' he sobbed. Brontë mutely appealed to me.

'Mummy was hit by a car. You must look left and right, and then left again. Remember?'

'But you said it was a tummy bug!' he wailed.

'It was darling, but then I got hit by a car,' Brontë explained.

Max sat up tearfully. 'I was sick too.'

'Were you? Did it have diced carrots in it?' A single tear trickled down Brontë's cheek.

Max was impressed. '*Yesss*. How did you know?'

'Mummys know these things.' Brontë laughed emotionally, but Max had turned accusing eyes on me.

'Ern said a bad word *and* she lied.'

'Turncoat,' I muttered.

Brontë smiled. 'Did she now? Well, we'll just have to punish her, won't we?'

'Yes!' Max clapped his hands. 'Let's tickle her.'

I made a great show of giggling and writhing around on the hard plastic chair. Over his bobbing head Brontë's eyes met mine.

The fragile threads that bound us had braided into ropes.

Hospitals are awful places. They suck the very life out of you. With a four-year-old child and so many things to be discussed that couldn't be uttered, it was excruciating. After an hour all three of us were yawning and flopping about.

I wanted to go home, but felt that would be tantamount to abandoning my sister. A quiet knock at the door made us all start.

'A gentleman brought these for you.' A smiling nurse held out a bunch of Star-gazer lilies and two Asda bags.

I took the bags and peered inside. There was a nightdress, toothbrush, toothpaste, deodorant and shower gel in one. The other contained apples, grapes, magazines, chocolate, orange squash, colouring pencils, a colouring book and two small boxes of Lego.

'Did he give you his name?' I asked, before she closed the door.

The nurse winked. 'No, but he was quite good-looking. I'll get you a vase.'

I raised my eyebrows at Brontë and carefully placed the bags on her lap. She looked through them quickly.

'Look, Max, Lego! And crayons and a colouring book.' Max scampered to her bedside.

'Who do you think brought these?' Brontë held up a rather unflattering nightie.

'Mmm. Maybe DS Marshall.'

'Who's he?'

'He's a friend of mine. He helped me to find you.'

'A friend?' She smiled knowingly.

'Yes. A friend.'

'A friend that's trying to impress you?'

It was rather nice to see Brontë smile. In her situation I doubted I could have mustered much more than a grimace.

'Maybe.'

'Nice.' There was a lilt to her voice, which made that simple word fall somewhere between a question and a quip.

'Hmm,' I said blankly, as I could see she was about to start on me again. She wriggled up the bed, but a rumpus in the corridor distracted us both.

'She has visitors with her. There are only two allowed per room,' a nurse explained.

'Young lady! You are barring me from my daughter. I will not stand for it! Get the matron.'

The door flew open and our mother sashayed in like an ocean liner under full steam.

'Brontë! My darling! My poor baby!' She waltzed straight past me without a glance and clutched Brontë to her bosom. 'What happened, dear? What did he do to you?'

'Nothing . . . nothing . . . Mum, Max is here,' Brontë gasped.

'What on earth is the child doing here?' My mother swung round in horror.

'Oh,' she exclaimed upon spying me, as if that explained things. 'Couldn't you look after him for even one day?'

'Brontë wanted to see him.'

'After what she's suffered? I don't know what you were thinking.'

I was thinking, *Drop dead, you old bitch*, but Max came and hovered at his granny's side. He tugged at her hand.

'Granny, I've missed you.'

Mother picked him up and kissed him. 'I've missed you too, darling.'

'Don't be cross with Ern. Her two new friends wanted to come here. I met a policewoman and she could draw rabbits and cats with two rounds.'

'Circles,' Brontë corrected.

'And Alex isn't her friend any more,' Max added.

'Yes, well, we know about that. The *whole nation* knows about that.'

'Mother, may I have a word outside?' I asked.

'What, dear?' She dropped evasively into dizzy-old-bat mode.

'A word. Outside.'

'Oh, Erin! There's nothing you can't say in front of

Brontë and Max. Is there now, darling?' She snuggled her nose into Max's neck, making him wriggle.

I smiled threateningly. 'Oh, but there is.'

'Not now, dear. It can wait. It's Brontë we must be thinking about.'

She popped Max back down on the floor.

'Fine,' I sighed. 'I'll come back later, Brontë. Is that OK?'

'Could you take Max with you?' Mother asked.

'No.'

She rallied her fractious forces again. 'What do you mean, "no"?'

'I have work to do.'

'Work? At a time like this? What work?'

'Didn't I mention it to you? I've started my own law firm.'

'You've what?' she shrieked. 'But you can't!'

'Just watch me.' I smiled gaily and swept out of the room.

I loved dramatic exits.

I heard her shout something about my restrictive covenant, but no court in the land would uphold that.

I had been forced out of my partnership and stripped of my ability to earn a living. But they couldn't deny me the right to earn a living. Restrictive covenants were only partially effective. They might be able to restrict me from doing compensation claims for a year or so, and even then only within Glasgow, but they couldn't stop me from being a solicitor.

I sauntered down the corridor, cursing my big mouth. Who was I trying to kid? How on earth was I going to start my own firm? I might be able to call in some favours and join an existing firm, but unfortunately my reputation preceded me. Another firm would only want what I could bring – compensation cases, and then a restrictive covenant really would mean something.

If I wanted to work, I would have to go it alone.

Thank you, Mother, I thought. You have just clarified the situation for me.

I would show the old witch what I was made of.

TWELVE

As I walked back to my car, I noticed something fluttering under the windscreen wiper. A bloody parking ticket was all I needed. But when I got closer I realised it was a note, probably from spineless Paul.

> *Nobody likes me.*
> *Everybody hates me,*
> *I think I'll go eat worms.*

I looked about in sudden panic. Leland! He used to sing that before he really did make me eat worms.

I took a deep breath and yelled at the top of my voice, 'I'M NOT SCARED OF YOU! I'M NOT SCARED! IF YOU WANT ME, COME AND GET ME, YOU PATHETIC FREAK!'

Passers-by stared at me in alarm and body-swerved around me, but I didn't care. My message was loud and clear. If the killer really had assumed my brother's persona, then that would make him mad. Leland had hated it when I defied or challenged him.

I crumpled the note into a ball and chucked it into the gutter.

It was only when I got back to my apartment that I cursed myself for failing to keep it. It might have turned out to be useful evidence. My stupidity seemed to be increasing daily.

I double-locked my front door and put the chain on. As an afterthought, I dragged my colonial-style bureau in front of the door. I kicked off my shoes, flopped down on my *chaise longue* beside the windows, and watched the sky turn cerise and ochre. I was just drifting off when the phone rang.

Why couldn't people leave me in peace for one second?

'Hi, how are you? I'm sorry, did I disturb you?'

'No. I'm tired. Very tired.'

'I understand. This is very hard for you. You must be exhausted,' DS Marshall said. I squirmed.

'I was going to call you, to thank you for the things you brought for Brontë. It was very kind. I also wanted your professional opinion.'

'What about?'

'It's a long story. DSI Kelman, from Lothian and Borders, interviewed Brontë today—'

'Why?' Marshall cut in. 'This isn't his patch.'

'He thought there was a link between Lucy Grant and Brontë because of the message the killer left on my mobile, but now he doesn't seem to think that they are connected.'

'Why not?' He sounded guarded. I supposed it was politically incorrect for one policeman to criticise a fellow officer's handling of a case.

'Because the *modus operandi* doesn't fit exactly. But when I left the hospital, there was a note on my car. It could only have come from someone who knew my late brother—'

'Whoa, Erin. I have no idea what you are talking about,' he interrupted.

'My brother, Leland, died twelve years ago. Kelman suspects that one of Leland's friends is responsible for the murders. But now he doesn't think he attacked Brontë—'

214

'I'm not following any of this. Do you want to meet up somewhere and tell me a bit more about it? When would suit? I'm working until ten.'

Ten was too late. I needed a good night's sleep. 'Tomorrow?'

'Not tonight?'

'I'm wiped out. I'm sorry.'

'Tomorrow it is, then. I'll call you in the morning.'

It was almost six o'clock and I wanted to rest before visiting Brontë again, but there was a gentle tapping from outside.

I groaned, swung my tired legs back off the sofa and wandered over to my front door.

'Who is it?' I had more than a sneaking suspicion.

'Paul.'

'Piss off.'

'Open the door. You were right.'

'What?'

'You were right.'

I thought that was what he had said, so I pushed the bureau out of the way.

'What *are* you doing?' he called.

'Moving the bureau,' I puffed and opened the door.

Paul was holding a bunch of flowers identical to the ones Brontë had received. He looked at the bureau, which was sitting at right angles to the door.

'I need to get the locks changed,' I said.

'Vase?' he asked.

'In the kitchen. Are those for me? Thank you.'

'Yeah. Did Brontë get the other stuff? It was the best I could do in the time.'

That was odd. DS Marshall had just accepted credit for them.

I got a tall crystal vase out of a cupboard and watched

as he cut the stems off the lilies. He filled the vase with water and plant solution and carefully fixed the flowers, pulling them this way and that to achieve the desired effect.

A good-looking, house-trained man, who could cook and flower-arrange?

'Why don't you have a girlfriend?' I asked impulsively.

Paul viewed me with surprise. 'You think I'm boyfriend material?'

'Em, yes . . . I'm sure there are lots of girls that would have . . . you know . . . would go out with you . . .'

Suddenly he looked frosty and I wished I hadn't brought up the subject. In the good old days, I thought before I spoke, I was guarded, erudite. Alienation was fast becoming my specialist subject. I could now confidently alienate for Scotland.

'Coffee?' It was all I could think of to relieve the terse silence.

'Please. Have you eaten yet?' This sounded more like an accusation than a question.

'Em, yes.'

'No you haven't.'

'I'm not hungry. I'm too wound up.'

Paul came over to the sink and rinsed the cups we had used earlier. Never before had I left dirty cups lying around. My ground zero was shifting with every new development.

'Kelman was way out of line at the hospital,' he said.

'I understand his scepticism, but if it really is one of Leland's friends, then there's an obvious connection between Lucy, Brontë and me. I can't grasp why he couldn't see that. And somebody left a note on my car outside the hospital. Only Leland would have known the significance . . .'

'A note? Can I . . .'

I winced. 'I threw it away. Sorry.'

'That was evidence! What did it say?'

'It said, "Nobody likes me, everybody hates me, I think I'll go eat worms."'

Paul looked at me blankly. 'That's it?'

'My brother used to sing that before he, before . . .'

Paul tentatively touched my hand. I didn't snatch it away.

'Erin, please look at me.'

We locked eyes.

'I think he's going to come after me.'

'I'm not going to let him hurt you. I won't let him near you. OK? I'll be right here.'

'I told him to come and get me.'

'YOU DID WHAT? Have you seen him?'

'I didn't see him! I shouted it out when I found the note. I simply stood in the street and yelled that he could come and get me if he dared.'

'I think I should tell Kelman.'

Paul took out his mobile from his trouser pocket, and pressed a programmed number.

It was a brief conversation.

Paul wandered over to the French doors and stared out at the dark, starless sky.

'What did he say?' I finally asked.

'He doesn't believe in any note. He said, and I quote, "If she's such a hot-shot lawyer, how come she threw away the bloody evidence?"'

'Is that what you think?'

Paul swung around to face me. 'I think that if anyone knew how Leland's mind worked, it's you. You and me.

217

There's something I think I should show you. Come on.'

I got up and followed him through to his apartment. For reassurance, I switched my alarm on and double-locked the door.

In silence, we went up to his top floor and to the far bedroom. Paul unlocked it with a key from his key ring and flicked on the light.

On one wall were A4-sized photographs arranged in chronological order, the oldest nearest the door and the newest furthest away. Under each one was a piece of A4 paper with the date, name, location and a coded description of causes of death and injuries. There were eleven altogether.

I slowly walked the length of the room, scanning them all until I came to Abigail Dawes and Lucy Grant. They were pretty girls with confident eyes. A piece of paper with Brontë's name had been added at the end.

I was stunned. Stunned by the number, stunned by the methodical manner in which the collection was presented, and stunned by how heavy my heart felt. The rest of the room was filled with filing cabinets, also carefully labelled with the names of those poor dead girls.

Looking back at the picture of Lucy Grant, I asked myself how could anyone cause this much misery and suffering? How could I be his sibling? Was it by chance of birth that I wasn't contaminated? Or was I? Did I carry the same gene or character flaw?

I prayed to the same God that had watched all this horror. I prayed for my mortal soul.

'Do you need to sit down?' Paul asked gently.

I shook my head for I couldn't trust myself to speak. There was a cry building in my chest.

Paul folded me into his shoulder and held me. I didn't fight it. I had retreated to a terrible place, a place I had inhabited for too long, a place of calculated safety. In those moments, I buried my heart where only I could find it.

We stood silent and still for a time, my forehead resting on his collarbone, my arms limp by my side.

'Is this why you left?' I mumbled into his crisp shirt.

'Yes.'

'Because you couldn't catch him?'

'Yes and . . . he made it personal.'

He released me gently and went over to the wall of lost souls. 'Number five.'

He gazed up at the young woman who looked past the camera and into the distance. I stood beside him and studied her open, smiling face.

'She was my friend.'

'I'm sorry. So sorry.'

'She didn't fit the MO exactly. That's when I realised it was personal. That's when I understood that he knew our every move. He's clever, but I don't have to tell you that. He watches and waits and does his research. He knows forensics, never leaves a print or sample. He uses a condom. He cleans up after himself. He's always one step ahead . . .'

Until now, I thought fearfully. He was only one step behind.

'The first murder came to light in the spring of 1984. Jennifer Longmuir was a third-year student at Edinburgh Art School. She was twenty-one, the same age as Leland at the time, and a typical society student,' Paul began. 'She was reported missing – from the flat her parents had bought her in Edinburgh's prestigious Old Town – within twenty-four hours of her disappearance.'

Irrationally, I wondered if they had experienced as much difficulty as I had when trying to report a loved one missing.

'Her body was found the following day. Minus her right hand.'

Paul glanced through her file.

'She wasn't as badly mutilated as subsequent victims, but there was evidence of sustained sexual assault.'

'Did she have any connection to Leland? Or his group?'

Jennifer Longmuir had long dark hair and very fine features. The resemblance between us was uncanny. I wondered if anyone else had noticed.

'They weren't highlighted in the original investigation. They may have seen her in the usual student haunts, but nothing that was immediately obvious.'

'Don't take this the wrong way, but how do you know she's one of their victims?'

'They were always very well-bred young ladies. Talented, mostly single: they weren't street girls or runaways. They were instantly missed, deeply loved. It was as if that was part of the thrill.'

'When did Leland come into the frame?'

'The third girl, Isabelle Robertson. He was once seen talking to her.'

I looked at the third photograph. I wasn't sure if it was the camera angle, but she seemed tiny. She had a cloud of soft red hair and almond-shaped eyes. She was very beautiful. Underneath, it was dated 6th January, 1985, Glasgow.

'She was a dance and drama student at the Royal Scottish Academy of Music and Drama,' Paul said.

'The sixth of January would be during the Christmas vacation. Leland would have been home.'

'Yes. He spoke to her in a bar, but he had an alibi.'

'From whom?' I prayed he wasn't going to say Brontë or my parents. I couldn't even recall the police questioning him.

'Jonathan Moncreiffe.'

Our eyes met. I wished the police had contacted me sooner, like a decade ago.

'You mentioned photographs of his friends. May I see them?'

Paul went to a separate filing cabinet marked 'Interviews'. I was glad he kept them apart. Even in death, I didn't want to think of those poor young women having to share drawer space with their likely killers.

'I've only got photographs of five of them. There were another two, we believed, on the periphery of the group, but we never found out for sure who they were. But that doesn't mean they were all involved in the murders.'

He handed me a loose-leaf file. Right on top was a photograph of Leland, wearing his young fogey uniform that was so trendy amongst his ilk in the mid-eighties. I remembered the Aquascutum tweed jacket and Abingdon shirt; sometimes he even wore a cravat, much to my amusement. He referred to it as, 'sartorial elegance'.

What I had forgotten, though, was just how handsome he actually was. Seeing his sculptured features and short dark hair brought it all back. My mother had removed all photographs of him from the house.

Lots of my friends had been besotted with him, dropping in on the pretext of visiting me but actually in the hope of catching a glimpse of my brother. He used to say to me that if it weren't for him, I wouldn't have any friends.

221

I turned over the photograph and looked at the next one. I vaguely recognised the face but couldn't put a name to it. I looked at the back.

'Tarquin Grenhem'. Jeez, what a name.

'Where's Tarquin now?'

'Dead. A year after your brother. Fell out of an express train in France.'

'Were you still investigating him?'

'Yes, but we had lost track of him. He came from a wealthy family in Surrey. We were pretty sure they were hiding him. He dipped out of society and the next thing we knew he was dead.'

'Accident?'

'That's what the coroner decided, he had a high blood-alcohol level.'

I muttered, 'Did he fall or was he pushed?' as I gazed at his doleful blue eyes.

'My thoughts exactly.'

I turned over Tarquin's photograph and looked at the next one. I knew him immediately.

'That's Jonathan Moncreiffe. He came to the funeral.'

'Dead.'

'That can't be a coincidence! When?'

'About five months after your brother. A house fire, very suspicious.'

'And you investigated thoroughly?'

'Oh yes, but we couldn't pin it on any of our chief suspects.'

'So, whoever killed Leland might have killed Jonathan too?'

Paul nodded.

I turned the photo over to look at the next one.

'That's, that's . . . Ryan . . . Ryan . . . Donnelly. Irish

git. I remember him, the worst kind of loud-mouthed boor.'

'He had a sheet for breach of the peace, several cautions. Very talkative when drunk.'

Paul was leaning over my shoulder. I could feel the heat from his body; I could smell his faint aftershave. He steadied himself with his hand on my chair, the backs of his fingers pressing against my shoulder blade. Such close proximity unnerved me. It disturbed my concentration.

'Don't tell me he's dead too?'

'He's alive. For the time being. He's been on death row since 1993. Killed a kid in Texas during a drunken brawl.'

Paul crouched down beside me. His head was almost level with mine and I was very aware of it. I pushed the fleeting image of his naked muscular back from my mind.

'Have you been able to get anything useful from him?'

'Not since 1991 when he emigrated. We used to get quite a bit, though. The uniforms would habitually pick him up and give me a buzz. I would pretend to be his big *polis* pal, get him out of trouble, and unofficially probe for info. They were a tight group, looked out for each other. You could pal up with Donnelly because he didn't quite fit in.'

'Because he was Catholic?'

My family had never gone in for any form of religious bigotry. They might have been completely dysfunctional and included a serial killer, but they weren't prejudiced. A hollow comfort.

'I'm Catholic but not practising, so we had some-thing in common.'

'What did he tell you?'

'He told me he was a member of a secret society. That's when we first cottoned on to the idea.'

'OK, a "secret society", but why did they start killing? And why well-bred, eligible women?'

Paul gently pushed the hair from my shoulder. My skin tingled.

'If I could tell you that, we would all sleep easier at night. I think the choice of victim mirrored their own tastes.'

I knew the face on the next photograph but not the name.

'Frederick Blythe-Gordon,' Paul informed me.

'The chinless wonder!' I was surprised by the bits of information that came tiptoeing back. 'How he ever got into university is beyond me.'

'*Daddy* set up a chair in economics.'

'That can help.'

They were PLU, people like us. How had they become so demented and sick? How had Leland managed to collect them all together?

'And he's dead too, right?'

'Wrong actually, but he's not set foot in the UK for ten years. Joined a far right religious community in the US and gave up his British nationality when he married a US citizen. We have checked up on him, but he's not left the commune in a decade.'

'Hiding from his past?'

'That's what Dr Freud might say.'

I was about to look at the next photo, but Paul suddenly tried to take away the folder.

'That's all, I'm afraid.'

I held on to the file tightly.

'Just let me look. You never know, I might spot something.'

Paul wavered, as if he was about to say something but thought better of it.

'I'll make us something to eat,' he said.

It felt strange to be alone in the room with the images of those poor dead girls. I knew it wasn't the same as real cadavers, but it was still creepy. Vacant eyes looked down at me accusingly. Did they know that I shared Leland's genes, that the same blood ran through my veins? Did they will me to lay them to rest, to avenge them?

Inside the folder there were more photographs of Leland and his sect of weirdos, some obviously taken while under surveillance, using a high-powered telephoto lens. I scrutinised each one and scanned the faces in the background, in case the missing two were hovering on the sidelines. There was a slim chance I might recognise them. I was almost through the file when I got a shock – a photograph of me, taken at Leland's funeral.

I was looking far into the distance, past the camera. I didn't look wretched, as one might expect at the burial of an elder brother. My expression was serene – content even. The sun had caught my hair, giving me a golden halo, my eyes were bright and clear. I looked young and rather beautiful. I turned the photograph over, but all it said was 'Erin'.

I wondered if Paul had taken the photograph.

The next one was of Jonathan Moncreiffe and Ryan Donnelly together. There were no more pictures of me in the folder. I closed the file, but – as an afterthought – I removed my photo. I didn't want even my image being anywhere near Leland.

225

Sharp ginger and garlic scents wafted towards me as I crossed Paul's living room. Surreptitiously, I put the photo on the edge of the worktop.

'Paul, I really should go. I promised to go back to the hospital.'

I felt too shattered to go. Shattered and hungry. The prospect of heating up some dreary cauliflower cheese, when I got back to my apartment, held little appeal.

'Actually, I've already arranged for somebody to see her this evening.' Paul turned from his wok and smiled.

'Who?'

'A friend of mine. Dr Shereen Khalil. She's a psychiatrist but she specialises in victim support.'

'That's very kind of you.' I didn't know why, but I blushed.

'Brontë will be offered counselling through the police, but Shereen is super. I hope you don't mind, but I kind of filled her in on the other details.'

He suddenly spied my photo on the worktop. It was his turn to blush.

'I didn't want it in with all those . . .'

'Sociopaths?'

I nodded. 'Where did you get it?'

He shook the wok vigorously. The sesame oil spat and sizzled as he added scallions. The toasted oil danced in the air, a cloud of flavour.

'I took it.'

'Oh . . .'

'We went to the funeral in case the other two turned up and I took your photo. It wasn't anything weird. I just thought you were . . . pretty.'

'Stop using the past tense. You could give a girl a complex.'

Paul grinned. 'Make yourself useful. Grate and juice this.'

I joined him at the worktop and began to plane the zest from a lime. The scent rose like sea spray, fresh and invigorating, cleansing the senses.

'Where do we go from here?' I asked.

'Let's see how things go, naturally.'

'You mean, simply wait until the killer comes a-calling?'

He burst out laughing. 'I'm sorry. I misunderstood you.'

I gave him a nudge. 'Steady on, tiger.'

'You have slept in my bed.'

'But you weren't in it.'

'Story of my life.'

I quickly changed the subject. 'What are we making?'

'A simple stir-fry. The trick is to use only fresh ingredients. Makes anything taste brilliant.' He grabbed a handful of the shiitake mushrooms and threw them in.

'How long were you in the force?'

'Fifteen years. Joined as a graduate, when I was twenty-one.'

'You're a graduate?'

'You don't have to sound so surprised. Not all policemen are thick.'

'Sorry. I didn't mean to . . .'

That was true. I wasn't trying to belittle him. I had so many preconceived ideas about him, about most people, that it was hard to let them go.

'What did you study?'

'English literature and psychology at Strathclyde University. And no jokes about it being a polytechnic, I know what you alumnae from Glasgow are like.'

'So, you were on accelerated promotion? What rank did you reach?'

'Detective Inspector.'

He popped fresh egg noodles into a pot of boiling water.

I smiled pleasantly. 'DI Gabriel? That's got a nice ring to it.'

He raised an eyebrow. 'So I'm eligible now, am I?'

'Did you simply resign?'

He prodded the noodles.

'No, I was pensioned out due to ill health.'

I managed to restrain myself from asking for details. 'Are you OK now?'

'As far as I can tell.'

He became conspicuously busy with the wok.

'When did you retire?'

'Nineteen ninety-two.'

'Five years after Leland died,' I thought aloud. 'Did you reckon that he was murdered?'

He turned to me, his mouth a thin line. 'I always believed the suicide was staged.'

I didn't know what to say. All this time I had believed Leland committed suicide and had nurtured the secret hope that it was due to remorse.

'But if he was murdered, who wrote the suicide note?'

'There's the rub,' Paul said. 'It was most definitely in Leland's handwriting . . .'

'So, you saw it? What did it say? Did it mention Brontë or me?'

He glanced at me.

'It did, didn't it?'

He shook his head.

'It was a vague concoction of trite little phrases about

not being able to go on, about being sorry for any hurt he would cause by taking his own life. It could have been written by anyone, to anyone. That's what was strange. Your brother was flamboyantly eloquent and literary, but the note was full of tired, unoriginal platitudes.'

I knew exactly what he meant. Leland could have been a writer if the notion had interested him. I was competent and brisk in style, never given to poetic turns of phrase.

'Do you think he was coerced into writing it? Threatened in any way?'

'Maybe, or maybe he was writing a transcript for someone else.'

'You mean they were planning on staging a suicide for one of the others and he was double-crossed?'

Paul shrugged. 'Who knows? It's hard to know what made these guys tick.'

I searched my heart for any feelings of pity or compassion for my brother, but none came.

'Were there any signs of force? Blows or a struggle?' I asked.

'No. Suicidal drowning is relatively uncommon and murder by drowning is really rare. But coupled with a suicide note, the coroner had an open-and-shut case. Dinner is ready.'

Paul handed me a rather daunting plateful.

The lime and ginger aromas merged seductively, the glistening mushrooms and scallions invited that first delicious taste, but hunger had deserted me.

Paul handed me some chopsticks and then placed a large glass of white wine at my right hand. I gazed at it and recognised the hopelessness of our situation.

I gently pushed the plate away.

'Back to my original question. What do we do now?'
He pushed the plate back towards me.

'We have some dinner and a glass of wine. Then we wade through what we know.'

And what we don't, I thought bleakly.

THIRTEEN

The moments of light relief we had shared while making dinner quickly dissipated. I toyed with the food and wine, bogged down with my worries.

This conspicuous internal struggle unnerved Paul. The more he tried to bring me out, the further I retreated. It was too difficult to explain to him, to anyone in fact, that it was my own personal formula for remaining outwardly sane. He cleared away the dishes and began to tidy up.

I thanked him and said goodnight, but as I left he gave me an armful of files.

I placed them, unopened, on my coffee table and glared at them. I really didn't want to study the post-mortems or read the reports from the police investigations. I wanted to declare that it had fuck all to do with me, goodnight and goodbye.

My answering machine blinked with six messages, because I hadn't bothered to pick up the earlier ones.

I stood at the rain-streaked French doors and watched the streetlights glimmer in the drizzle. The wind had picked up and blew wet leaves around my terrace.

Something clattered outside and goosebumps immediately appeared on my arms. I checked that the doors were all locked before going to the kitchen to peer out.

Unless the killer had developed Spiderman's skills, I believed I was fairly safe up here, but that didn't stop me from gazing anxiously around my terrace.

I saw the culprit: one of my bay trees had succumbed to the wind and was rolling across the decking.

Cold, wet air blasted me as I went out and dragged the big pot to a corner, where the tree would come to less harm.

I liked symmetry, particularly in gardens, and owned matching pairs of all my plants. I rolled its partner into the opposite corner. This small action was enough to rekindle a spark. A spark of bravery.

I walked over to the edge of my terrace and let the saturated wind whip my hair around my face. I closed my eyes and took several deep breaths. The rain almost deafened me to the sounds of the city below.

If I didn't help catch Leland's killer, then I would forever have his breath at my ear.

I went back into my kitchen, locked the door and made a pot of camomile tea. While it infused, I pushed my bureau up against the front door again. I might have been feeling a bit braver, but not foolhardy.

Sipping at my herbal tea I listened to my messages.

More calls from Liz and Douglas. I would call them back presently, because I couldn't hide for ever. One was from Catriona asking if I was OK and needed a chat, and there was another bizarre message from the surveyor about an office for lease. My mother's voice jolted me.

'ERIN? ARE YOU THERE?' she bellowed. 'What the hell do you think you are doing? Allowing social workers to search our house! What's this all about? You have a lot of explaining to do. You have a damn cheek letting them into Leland's room!' In the background, I could hear the dogs were barking. Then the phone went dead.

The last message was very faint, so faint in fact that it just sounded like somebody whispering nonsense. I pressed play again and turned the sound up.

'Big fat juicy ones, long little squishy ones, see how they wriggle and squirm . . .'

I leapt away from the answering machine as if the voice could reach out and grab me.

After my heart had stopped pounding, I called 1471 to find out where the message had come from.

'Telephone number 0141 649 210 called today at 19.58. To return the call press 3.'

I pressed 3 and concentrated hard on remembering to breathe. The dialling tone rang and rang until a gruff voice answered.

'Hello?'

There was a rhythmic beep-beep in the background, the sign of a call box.

'Hello. Can you tell me where that call box is?' I asked politely.

'Aye. Outside the Victoria Infirmary.'

My heart almost stopped. I managed to mumble a thank you before I hung up.

Was he waiting for me or was he planning on visiting Brontë? Had he actually answered the phone? At least I had evidence this time.

I pushed my barricade aside, ran over to Paul's apartment and banged urgently on his door.

'Paul! It's him!' I ranted. 'He's left a message on my answerphone.'

I grabbed Paul's arm and rushed him across to my apartment.

I skipped the messages forward.

'You need to listen really closely. I dialled 1471 and it came from a call box outside the Victoria. Do you think he was waiting for me? Do you think he'll go after Brontë again?'

'Shereen is there,' he said. But he didn't look as calm as he sounded.

'Should we phone the police?'

I rummaged in my handbag for DS Marshall's number, but when I tried his mobile it was switched off.

Paul took the phone from me.

'Let me try Shereen.' He knew the number by heart.

'Shereen? Where are you? How did it go?'

He made uh-huh noises as she told him at length.

'OK. I'll see what I can do. Thanks, Shereen. I'll see you tomorrow. Yeah? And you. OK. Bye, sweetheart. Bye.'

He hung up and smiled.

'Everything is OK. She was on her way home.'

'But what's security like at the Victoria? Could he get in?' I bleated.

How could he say everything was OK? A psychotic killer was out there.

'I doubt it. Shereen and I did profiling together and we both think that if he wanted to kill her he would have.'

Profiling together? How cosy.

Paul sat down on the sofa and sort of beckoned me to him. I gave him a filthy look and began to pace back and forth.

'Come and sit down,' Paul said.

'No.'

'Why not?'

'Because I can think better when I'm standing.'

'Come and sit beside me.'

'No.'

'Come on, come and sit down. Here.'

'No,' I said, but my resolve was fading. 'I'm not a bloody dog.'

'No, my dear. *You* are a full-grown vixen.'

'Are you always this irritating?' I snapped.

This time he had the audacity to actually laugh.

'Only when I'm around you, it appears. But welcome back, anyway.'

'What the hell do you mean by that?'

He put his feet up on my coffee table and rested his arms behind his head.

'Well, for a moment there, back in my flat, I could have sworn you were quite sensitive. Nice even. It's good to see the real Erin is alive and kicking. I was beginning to get worried.'

'Sarcasm is the lowest form of wit!' I chanted and pushed his feet off my table.

'You, Miss Paterson, ought to learn some manners.'

'Get off my case!'

'For once, would you please calm down.'

I was reminded of the words of that awful song – 'clowns to the left of me, jokers to the right', blah blah, 'stuck in the middle with you'. I had a psycho stalker and a wacko neighbour. All I needed now was an alien abduction.

'Tell me about Leland.'

'No,' I said, although I had to admire Paul's ability to keep his cool.

'Why not?' he asked softly.

I looked down at my hands and considered my answer carefully. Should I tell him the truth, the reason behind my irrational reticence? Or should I palm him off with a pat little excuse? Pat excuse won.

'I can't tell you. It's too painful.'

'The things he did to you and Brontë?'

'Yes.'

'Well, tell me about other stuff. His relationship with your parents, with your younger brother.'

'My parents adored him, particularly my mother. Finlay didn't know him that well, he was only ten or eleven when Leland . . . died.'

'What's Finlay like?'

'He's like Dylan the Rabbit from *The Magic Roundabout*.' I smiled faintly. 'He's so spaced out and laid back, you have to feel for a pulse.'

'You get on well?'

'He's much younger than me and we don't have that much in common, but we don't fight or anything.'

Suddenly, I desperately missed Finlay. I missed his kooky haircuts and wacky clothes, his lopsided grin and easy manner.

'So he's nothing like Leland?'

I gave him a sidelong look. 'Aren't you going home?'

'No. We've still got lots of things to talk about.'

I gave a huge sigh. 'Paul, I'm too tired. Can't it wait until morn—'

My phone rang and made us both start. I froze and stared at it, but Paul jumped to his feet and answered it.

'Hello. Yep. She's here. Can I ask who's calling? Liz. Hi. Me? I'm her bodyguard,' he grinned wickedly and handed me the phone.

'Hi, Erin. I've been leaving messages left, right and centre . . .'

'I know. I'm sorry. It's been a bit hectic here.'

'What's with the bodyguard?'

I shot Paul a sour look.

'He's my loony-tune neighbour. I'm hoping to get him certified.'

'I heard about your sister. I'm so sorry. Is she going to be OK?'

'Yes, she's recovering,' I said, and took a deep breath.

'Liz, I really regret what happened at the firm and I know it was a very noble thing that you did, but you shouldn't have resigned.'

'I wanted to. So did Douglas. And Karen. That's why I'm calling, actually.'

My heart dipped.

'Liz, if it's about reinstatement, I don't think I'll be much help. I'm the last person they'll listen to.'

'Well, it's sort of about that. Would it be possible to meet up? Say, tomorrow?'

'OK. When and where?' I knew that my unwillingness showed itself in my voice.

'It's not as dire as it sounds, Erin,' she reprimanded me gently.

'Sorry. I've been under a lot of pressure.'

'That's OK. I understand. How about meeting us at the corner of St Vincent Street and West Campbell Street?'

'Is there a new place there?' In Glasgow, bars and restaurants opened and closed more quickly than dotcom companies floated and crashed.

'Em, yes,' she faltered.

'What's it called?' I asked suspiciously.

'Don't know. How does noon sound?' Liz was thoroughly vague.

'OK. Noon, at the corner of St Vincent and West Campbell.'

'Great! I can't wait to see you.'

I hung up. Liz was up to something. And I had a raging headache and a collapsed life.

'Paul?' I called irritably.

'In the kitchen,' his disembodied voice replied.

He was opening a bottle of white wine from the fridge.

'What are you doing?' I asked, although it was patently obvious.

'Getting a glass of wine.'

'Why?' I said unpleasantly. I wanted to be left alone to wallow in self-pity.

The cork popped and he poured two glasses.

'I always give *you* a glass of wine.'

'No. You always *offer* me a glass of wine. There is a difference.'

'Get a life, Erin.' Carefully, Paul took both glasses and the bottle back into the living room.

Get a life? Cheeky git. I had a life. Granted, at this precise moment, it had been swapped for a horrible imitation. I followed him through, bristling more with every step.

'That was Liz, your colleague? And she resigned for you?'

He sank into my sofa and sipped his wine. I remained standing.

'No. She resigned for her. I didn't ask her to resign. In fact, I would have advised against it, had she informed me.'

'But she still felt so strongly that she sacrificed her job and her prospects.'

'That is entirely her look-out.'

'You are so defensive,' he said sadly.

'Take a look around you, Paul,' I hissed. 'I'm being stalked by a serial killer, who just happens to be my *dead* brother's murderer. My sister's in hospital minus a toe, my nephew needs a stable family life, my parents sold me out and I've lost my firm! My father is dying. And my boyfriend shagged the *domestic*! I was arrested for assault and my name has been spewed all over the press. The Law Society will probably strike me off. I've got no job, no family, no boyfriend, no friends, nothing! I have nothing . . . nothing . . .'

'Do you want a hug?' he said.

'A hug? Are you mad? Go hug Shereen!'

He took a long slow sip of his wine. He was so cool, it was killing me.

'Why are you doing this? What do you want? Why don't you just leave me alone?'

'I want to talk to you. I want you to tell me the truth. I want you to help me to help you.'

'What pathetic American psychobabble book did you crib that from?'

'I mean it. Erin, you need my help and I need yours, but until you begin to trust me we'll get nowhere.'

'But why does it matter to you? All you want is for me to lead you to the killer. That's why you moved here!'

I rubbed my hands over my face. I felt tired, alone and vulnerable.

Paul held up my untouched glass of wine. 'Here. It'll help you relax.'

I took it sullenly and gulped down half of it in one.

He sat forward on the sofa, his elbows resting on his knees. I fought an urge to reach out and touch his hair.

'Go to bed.' He stood up and took my half-drained glass from me. 'I'm sorry. You've been through too much. Get some rest. We'll talk in the morning. Go to bed.'

I didn't move. What was it with him? One minute it was 'tell me, tell me, tell me', and then 'go to bed' the next?

'Go to bed,' he repeated.

'I need to set the alarm first.'

'I'll set it.'

'Are you staying?'

'Yes. Go to bed. I'll see you in the morning.'

I did as I was told. I didn't have the strength to keep arguing.

I got ready for bed in my own room and then went up to the top floor. Although I had changed my bed-linen, I still couldn't bear to sleep there.

'What are you doing?' Paul called out from the sofa.

'Going to bed.'

He softened slightly. 'You'll have to sleep in your own room eventually.'

'OK. Eventually,' I muttered over my shoulder, and opened the door to Max's room. I had completely forgotten that it was now a pirate ship. I sighed and closed the door again.

I padded back down the stairs.

'How did you know about Alex and Mrs McCaffer?'

Paul thought for a moment.

'She never cleaned my apartment in a leopard-skin dress and fishnet stockings.'

'How long was it going on?'

'A couple of weeks.'

'Would you have told me, if I hadn't caught them?'

'It was none of my business.'

'Where is she? She's disappeared.'

He smirked at me. 'She's gone into hiding. She says you're a head case.'

I was afraid to ask, but now that I had brought up the subject I wanted the whole story.

'Were there others?'

'Not that I know of.'

He was very blasé. I wondered how he would have liked it, if he came home and found his girlfriend in bed with the window-cleaner.

'Where are you going to sleep? Do you want me to make up a bed?' I said politely.

'I'm not. I'm going to get my laptop and do some work. I've got a two a.m. deadline.'

He got up and went to my front door. 'Sometimes insomnia has its uses,' he said, and left.

I looked around my apartment, which seemed messy and disorganised. I could have made up my other spare bedroom, but it all seemed like too much effort.

I waited until I heard Paul coming back and then slipped silently into my own bedroom. I stared at my bed and realised that it all meant nothing to me. It was my pride that hurt, not my heart.

It was hard to explain to Paul or anyone else for that matter. A shadow that contained the very worst of mankind's depravity had been cast over me since childhood. Only by staying in the light could I remain unharmed.

My light held sexual inhibition, emotional detachment, self-sufficiency and defensive arrogance. The source of my light was the law. I had deluded myself into believing that if I kept my head down and didn't draw attention to myself, I could avoid being noticed in the emotional stillness I created.

Everything that had befallen me forced me further into the darkness.

The place of perpetual mist and darkness. The place inhabited by my worst fears. The place near the land of the dead.

FOURTEEN

Paul woke me with a cup of tea.

I had slept badly, waking up every hour with an overwhelming sense of dread. I glanced at my alarm clock. Quarter past seven. He could have let me sleep in.

'I've got to go. I'm doing a report on News 24,' he whispered, as he put the tea on my bedside cabinet.

I yawned. 'What about?'

'A trial that starts in the High Court today.'

'Oh,' I said dully.

I wondered which case it was. Who the lawyers were, which advocates and QCs had been instructed. At this time last week, I probably would have known. How quickly my law life had disintegrated.

'I'll be back by lunchtime. You could have a look through those files,' he commented as he left. It sounded distinctly like an order to me.

I flopped back on to my pillow and yawned. I didn't want to get up. I wanted to go back to sleep, even if it was fitful, because the small breaks from awful reality were merciful. I dutifully drank a mouthful of tea and snuggled back under my duvet. Another fifteen minutes wouldn't do me any harm.

I woke with a start, as if I had heard something in my sleep. Sitting up, I stared around my room. I listened intently for another full minute before I got up. I had that horrible, overslept grogginess and I was shocked to see it was 10.22.

I debated whether to make some coffee or go straight for a shower. The shower won, because I didn't want Paul waltzing in when I hadn't even glanced at the files.

I turned on the shower, letting it warm up while I brushed my teeth. My reflection in the mirror was, at best, depressing. My eyes were baggy and I had developed a rather unattractive frown line. I would need to save for a facelift. I dipped my toothbrush under the cold tap and nearly choked. There were five, tiny, black cockroaches in my sink.

I turned the tap on full blast and watched them swirl in the whirlpool it created. Cockroaches? How the hell had they got into my sink? They must have come up from the plughole. Filthy little beasts.

I gave an involuntary shudder. Was this fate taking the piss?

I turned off the tap and dangled the plug carefully to let it drop in. Irrationally, I couldn't risk putting my hand near them.

I checked that they hadn't come up in the shower or the bath. Even as I washed my hair and tried to enjoy the relief of warm water, I couldn't stop thinking about cockroaches.

I looked down at my body, my small breasts and visible ribcage, my slim hips and long legs. I hated even the most gentle of caresses because they conjured up earwigs and woodlice scuttling across my flesh. Leland had robbed me of my sensuality at age ten.

The thought of bugs in my bathroom, in the shower-head above me, made me dwell on foul memories of Leland's torments.

He would follow me around with a sly look on his face, dropping elusive hints. My mind would race with all the gross possibilities. As a child, it had an almost narcotic effect on me: the anticipatory fear would paralyse me.

Was that his plan? Subdue me with terror. Were the note and phone messages the first steps in the killer's strategy? He would know that I was aware of what he had done to Lucy Grant. He stole my dread and turned it against me, making it his weapon.

Hadn't I come any further in all these years? Was I still the petrified little girl? The answer was yes, but something had changed. He was the weak one, living off his depraved fantasies. And he had left it too long. He should have come after me sooner. Much sooner.

I forced myself to take my time in the shower. A feeble act of defiance, but the alternative was to let my mind run riot with half-formed imaginings.

I wrapped myself in a big fluffy towel and combed my wet hair. I applied body lotion all over my skin. I leisurely pampered myself.

Just as I pulled on my bathrobe I heard a sound, like the dull thud of a footstep outside. I pressed my ear against the door, straining all my senses as I waited and listened. Panic rose in my chest and contracted my throat until I could hardly catch a breath.

I pushed my back against the bathroom door, as I tried to calm myself. Was he in my apartment? Had he put cockroaches in my sink? I had to get out.

There was only one window in the bathroom, high up the wall, and as far as I knew it opened out to nothing. I tried to imagine the exterior of my building, but couldn't focus.

I was on the fifth floor of an ornate warehouse. The two penthouse lofts were the galleried attic, like the final tier on a wedding cake. My terrace sat on the roof of the fourth floor, but what was below the bathroom? A drop to the next floor? I couldn't remember.

I turned my linen basket upside down under the window. It swayed ominously as I climbed up and unlocked the window catch. I grabbed the ledge and heaved myself up, holding my weight on my stomach as I peered over to see what was below.

There was an eighteen-inch-wide ledge about four feet below my window. The roof of the next building was another eight feet lower. A lane ran between the two buildings.

I swallowed. It was just as I had thought. My terrace was where the colonnade ended. I gazed back at the bathroom door.

A fronte praecipitium, a tergo lupi – trapped between a cliff and a wolf.

I lowered myself back into the bathroom and took off my robe. My fingers were clumsy and uncoordinated as I put my pyjamas back on. I almost wet myself when there was a loud thump at the door.

'Erin? Are you in there? It's well past eleven,' Paul shouted.

'Paul!' I cried, but no sound came out.

In one swift action, I unlocked and opened the door and threw myself at him.

'Thank God! Thank God!'

'What were you doing?' He looked past me to the open window and the overturned linen basket below it.

I gulped at air. 'The killer was here! In the apartment! I was going to climb out the window and round to the terrace.'

He grabbed me by the shoulders. 'When was he here? When?'

'This morning. He left bugs in the sink! A noise woke me and then I heard a noise outside the bathroom.'

Paul shook me vigorously. 'When? When did you hear a noise?'

I couldn't understand his anger. Why was he so angry?

'After I came out the shower. There were cockroaches in the sink . . .'

He let me go abruptly and went to the sink. He lifted out the plug and peered down the plughole. The cockroaches were gone.

'They must have been flushed down the drain.'

'There were no roaches.'

'Yes! Yes, there were! There were! I heard a noise and then they were in the sink. Why would I want to climb out the window?'

Paul closed his eyes for a moment.

'I have no idea.'

He turned on his heel and left.

I bit my lip in confusion. It was just like Mother all over again. Why didn't he believe me? Why?

Did Paul think I was delusional? Had I invented it? I peered down the plughole too, but I couldn't see any bugs. Were they a figment of my imagination? Of course the bugs were gone, they scattered and hid once they were released. Just as they scattered and hid in my clothing and hair.

'Hurry up. Aren't you supposed to be meeting Liz at noon.' Paul's voice reached me and it was not kind.

It was nearly a quarter to twelve by the time I dried my hair.

'Ready?' Paul snapped when I came out of my bedroom.

'Yes,' I answered faintly. What had changed? Why was he so aggressive?

'Let's go.' He held the front door open.

'Are you coming with me?' I didn't recall inviting him.

We went down in the lift in terse silence. I didn't understand what had happened. He was so grumpy and unsympathetic. Maybe the killer hadn't been in my apartment, maybe the cockroaches were a trick of plumbing, but it didn't take away from the fact that I had been genuinely terrified.

The tension in my car was equally fraught. He was broody and stared out of the window.

'I thought you were filming this morning?'

'It was cancelled.'

I bit my lip. 'Why don't you believe me?'

He continued to stare out at the grey rain-soaked streets. 'Because your sister had a long talk with Shereen.'

But that didn't throw any light on it.

'Surely that's confidential?'

'It was an informal discussion surrounding Leland's motivation. Brontë agreed for it to be used by the police.'

'But you're not the police,' I commented dryly.

'But I am part of the investigation.'

'And what did Brontë say?'

'She said that you used to make things up – exaggerate. That you were a drama queen and given to histrionics. They're all classic attention-seeking signs.'

'That was nice of her. Did she mention that I still wet my bed when I was thirteen?' I replied.

'Probably. We didn't discuss the finer details.'

'So you and Dr Khalil think it's hunky-dory to

discuss me? Was it pillow talk or merely gossip?'

He gave me a withering look. 'What do you expect? There's no note, no bugs and there's no goddamn evidence!'

I remained icily calm. 'Oh well, then, let's just wait until he murders me. Then you can really start dissecting.'

He rolled his eyes but didn't answer.

I drove aggressively because anger was welling up. How dare they discuss me? How dare they dispute my credibility? Who did they think they were? Huh, a washed-up detective and a trendy psychiatrist. Actually, I didn't know if Shereen Khalil was trendy, but I scathingly imagined her as tie-dyed and lentil-eating.

I drove up St Vincent Street looking for a parking space and spotted Liz, Douglas and Karen accompanied by another man, waiting at the corner of West Campbell. I suddenly realised that Liz and my former assistants had arranged for me to view the mysterious office that was up for lease.

'Oh, great,' I muttered, as I reversed into a metered space, 'a reunion of the dispossessed.'

Paul ignored me, undid his seat belt and got out of the car.

I got a parking chit and placed it on my windscreen. Paul was waiting for me further up the pavement.

'Have you got business to attend to?' I asked as I reached him.

He shook his head and crossed the road with me.

I greeted the assembled company and pointedly didn't introduce him.

They all seemed mildly embarrassed.

Liz introduced me to the other man. 'David Collier, this is Erin Paterson.'

I shook his hand. 'A surveyor with D.M. Hall, if I'm not mistaken.'

Liz grimaced.

'We'll get started, then,' said Mr Collier. He produced some keys from his overcoat pocket and went into the foyer of the building we were standing beside.

I glanced at the entrance vestibule, which was bright, clean and well kept.

On one wall was a directory of who's who for the building. There was a chartered accountant on the first floor, a solicitor's office on the second and some vaguely named property management firm on the third. By this point, Mr Collier had unlocked a door on the left-hand side of the ground floor. Liz, Douglas and Karen trooped inside after him.

I paused for a moment because I wanted to register my initial impression, to capture what a client might think upon their first visit.

I took a critical look around the vestibule. It wasn't as grand as the one in The Paterson Building, but few were. They had retained the elaborate Victorian cornicing and the *faux* marble pillars. It had a polished mahogany balustrade and a tiled floor. It was nice, professional and old-fashioned in a dependable way. Just the sort of image a new firm would need.

Paul hovered at my shoulder. 'Are you still here?' I hissed.

He gave me a condescending look. He was as fickle as an old maid; all over me one minute and a downright pig the next. Men? Who could understand them? Who could be bothered trying?

'Are you scared?' Paul whispered suddenly.

I threw him a haughty look. 'No. I was born to be a lawyer.'

His hand fluttered at my elbow.

'Erin, tell me the truth. Were there really cock-roaches?'

I gazed past him to a point over his left shoulder.

'I don't know. I thought there were, but now I don't know. I don't know . . .'

He grasped me by my elbow, taking me back towards the front door and semi-privacy. 'Do you think you imagined them?'

'I don't know. I was sure they were there and I was sure I heard something. I was going to climb out on to the ledge. Why else would I do that?'

He brought his eyes level with mine. 'Brontë told Shereen that you have been prescribed tranquillisers and antidepressants.'

'That was years ago! I was suffering from stress.'

'She also said you thought you were being followed, that you saw things that weren't there. You were diag-nosed as paranoid.'

Typical. Everything came back to haunt me. One small episode and apparently I was certifiable.

'I wasn't paranoid. There *was* somebody following me. I couldn't prove it but it was true!'

Doubtfully, he nodded his head. I knew he didn't believe me. Bloody Brontë and her big mouth. Imagine telling Shereen about that. The bloody bitch.

'What were you prescribed?'

'None of your business! What were you prescribed when you were kicked off the force?'

He straightened up and thrust his hands into his trouser pockets.

'I had a nervous breakdown,' he said tersely.

'And I'm sorry about that. But I was followed and now I probably know by whom.'

I gesticulated at the front door.

'He's out there, *right now*, watching and waiting. He's going to get me and probably my sister too, so let's forget all this talk of psychosis and get on with the job. I'll tell you one thing – Brontë's injuries are real, and so were Lucy's and Abigail's and Alison's.'

Paul took a step back and I realised that my voice was raised. Liz popped her head round the office door.

'Everything OK?' she asked cautiously.

'Yes,' I said firmly. 'Just clearing the air.'

'Incidentally, Liz, so it doesn't come as an awful surprise later, I was once prescribed tranquillisers and antidepressants. But I'm much better since the lobotomy. Nice building. What's the lease like?'

Liz grinned and went back inside.

Before I followed her, I turned to Paul. 'Are you coming?'

The internal reception area was freshly painted in magnolia and had a nice seating area in front of the double picture window. There was a long, curved desk facing the door, with two more doors set on either side of the far wall. It was bright, simple and functional.

Karen was looking in the desk drawers and Douglas was trying out the leather seats in the waiting area. They reminded me of children, which was just what I needed – a pair of overgrown teenagers.

David Collier came over to me and glanced at his clipboard.

'This is the reception area,' he stated rather obviously. 'The door on the left leads to the boardroom and the door on the right to the rest of the offices.'

I followed him towards the boardroom and viewed it from the doorway. It was a fairly good size, although it had no natural daylight. I wondered about replacing the dividing wall with glass bricks. It also had another door, presumably leading to the inner offices.

We retreated back into the reception area and I followed him through the right-hand door. I was expecting a dreary corridor and was pleasantly surprised when it turned out to be an additional reception area. It could easily hold three or four secretaries.

Off it were eight doors, one leading into the boardroom, one to the toilet suite, one to a kitchen-cum-staffroom, and the others leading to offices. There were four large offices with double windows. The fifth was not as big but led into two smaller rooms.

I wandered around without saying a word. I found myself envisioning assistants and secretaries. It wasn't opulent and would be quite cramped, but it would do as a start. I was conscious of my erstwhile colleagues as they scrutinised my every move.

'Well? What do you think, Miss Paterson?' Collier beamed at me.

I sniffed the air for signs of damp, but the smell of new paint masked everything. 'How much?'

'To lease or purchase?'

'Lease.'

'It's fifteen hundred square feet – one of the largest. Prime location, ground floor—'

I cut in, 'Spare me the sales pitch.'

He smiled faintly. 'We're talking twenty a square foot.'

I quickly calculated that it was £30,000 a year. 'Rent-free period? Parking? Incentives?'

'Two months rent free. Only two parking spaces, I'm afraid, that's why it's such a steal.'

A steal? Stealing our money more like. 'Rates?'

He looked down at his clipboard. 'Standard uniform business rate, 0.48 in the pound.'

That was almost £15,000 in rates. I looked around again, but my mind was already working out the figures. We would need £45,000 just to cover rent and rates, couple that with services – electricity, telephone, office equipment plus stationery – and there would be little change from eighty K. That was a lot of Ks when we had no clients to speak of.

I blew the air out of my cheeks. We would have to sit down and discuss it in absolute seriousness. I had enough available funds to float us for a year, probably including salaries, but I sensed we would be operating as a democracy, which I didn't like one bit. I was more the dictator type.

'OK,' I said slowly. 'Give me the breakdown and a copy of the lease, and I'll see if we can start negotiations.'

Collier raised his eyebrow. 'Negotiations?'

'Yes. Didn't your mother tell you never to accept the first offer?'

He handed me a bundle of papers. 'I see I've got my work cut out here.'

I noticed Liz and Douglas wink at each other.

'You three. A word outside,' I growled.

It was purely show because I wasn't actually angry, but if we were going to work together, we had to get the fundamentals straight. I was the boss, *facile princeps* – the acknowledged leader.

They shuffled outside sheepishly.

'Coffee?' I said.

We walked, in silence, down West Campbell Street towards Leonardo's. We got a good table in the window and ordered cappuccinos, caffe lattes and Danish pastries. I was slightly irked that Paul remained with us. My business life had nothing to do with the tumultuous events surrounding my family.

I gave them a collective grave look.

'First things first. That was rather a shoddy thing to do.'

'We did try to call you but you were . . . We thought it was best to strike while the iron was hot.' Liz shifted in her seat as she spoke.

'Have you had any contact with Paterson, Paterson & Co.?'

'They've merged with Cohen,' Karen said.

'Yes, but it was Paterson's that employed you. What are your severance deals like?'

'Three months' salary,' Liz said for all of them.

'Any restrictions?'

'Not on mine.' Liz looked at Douglas.

Douglas shook his head. Karen was a legal secretary, so they couldn't hold a loaded restrictive covenant to her head.

'I'll tell you straight. I've got no comps for a year.'

Their faces filled with disappointment. If anything could float this venture, it was my reputation in that field.

'We could do other work,' Douglas finally said.

'Like what?'

'General. Liz can still do corporate and I could do compensation.'

I gave him a 'get real' look.

'Douglas is right,' Paul interrupted. 'He could front the compensation side, but with you in the background, everyone would know you were pulling the strings.'

'Thank you, Mr Gabriel. And you got your LLB where?'

'You don't need a law degree to work out a sound business plan. The marketing angle is a dream. Liz is right, strike while the iron's hot. If you announce that you've formed your own firm, the media will pick it up. I'll make sure they do. You're hot right now, you might not be in two months' time.'

I shot him a narrow look. I might be dead in two months.

'But if I can't do compensation—'

Paul cut me off again, 'But nobody knows that! Joe Bloggs with the broken leg doesn't know about your restrictive covenant. He'll still contact your firm, where you will pass him on to Douglas. It's all about impression.'

Liz and Douglas nodded in agreement. I felt railroaded.

'We need to discuss figures, then.'

Karen got her big desk diary, which should have remained at Paterson, Paterson & Co. as company property, out of her bag. I wondered what else had been pilfered. She produced sheaves of stapled papers, distributing one to each of us.

In neatly typed lines were rent, rates, electricity, telephones, stationery, insurance, office equipment, postage, advertising, professional fees and miscellaneous. My own figure was close to the mark, they had it down as £75,000 to keep our doors open for a year.

The salary column had Karen as head receptionist and secretary at £16,000 per annum.

There were two positions for secretaries, two further posts for trainees, and two newly qualified assistants' positions. All in all it came to £180,000, without a client in the book.

Then there was Douglas and Liz. Douglas would become an associate salaried partner at £25,000 a year, the same as he was on at Paterson's but with a title promotion. Liz would be an equity partner at 60 per cent and I would be the senior partner at 100 per cent. It seemed fair enough, but 100 per cent of diddly-squat wouldn't cover many of the finer things in life, like food and mortgages.

'We wouldn't need all those staff at the beginning,' Karen explained, 'but I thought I would budget them in for future reference.'

'I've got a page missing,' I said.

'What page?' Liz and Karen craned over the table to see.

'The page with all our fees and earnings.'

'There isn't one,' Karen said indignantly.

'My point exactly. You've done a very professional job, but as far as I can see we have no earning power.'

'People will come,' Douglas said.

'You've seen *Field of Dreams* too often,' I muttered.

It wouldn't work. It couldn't work. We required fees of at least £200,000, just to break even. I had my trust fund and investments to keep my head above water, but I was pretty sure that the others didn't have much in the way of lifebelts. It wasn't as if we were bringing a huge client base with us: the majority of Paterson's clients would move to Cohen Paterson. We simply didn't have enough to offer; we had no conveyancing, tax, matrimonial, civil or criminal departments, no commercial property and no litigation. We were the one-horse town of law firms. It was a mammoth risk.

'I'm sorry, but my professional opinion is that it's too risky. I'm sorry you resigned and I truly wish I could help, but I have to advise you that it might not be a viable proposition.'

Liz looked away sharply and Douglas lowered his eyes.

Karen flicked through the desk diary. 'You've got your table for twelve at the Sportsmen's Ball on Friday,' she said without looking up.

The Sportsmen's Ball was an annual meeting-and-greeting bash held in both Glasgow and Edinburgh. It was filled with business people and corporate tables, all networking.

'See if you can sell it.'

Karen gave me a defiant look.

'I phoned six of the guests yesterday to tell them it was still on. Four were delighted and two cancelled. Liz and Douglas can take their places. Em, and you've got Alexander's place to fill too.'

I was appalled by Karen's choice of words, but I was interested to know who was giving me a giant body-swerve.

'Who said no?'

'Jim McRae and Joyce Trafford.'

Jim McRae was an ex-councillor and thought he ran the city, and Joyce Trafford was the marketing director of one of the Enterprise companies, but I couldn't remember which.

'We won't miss either of them. Do you have the phone numbers for the others?'

Karen tapped her desk diary. 'It's all in here, boss.'

I signalled to the waiter for the bill.

'OK. We can go and show our faces, but it doesn't mean anything more than that.'

None the less, I could see renewed hope in their eyes.

I stood up to leave as the waiter brought the bill.

'I'll go through the figures again, but it doesn't look promising.'

'I'll get this,' Paul said, as he put a ten-pound note on the plate. 'Incidentally, you do have a client.'

We all looked at him.

'Me.'

When we got back to my car I was silently relieved that there wasn't another note fluttering under the windscreen wiper. During the time I had been concentrating on business, I was lucid and assured. I needed that.

'Do you want me to drop you somewhere?' I asked Paul hopefully.

'No. I want to go through the files at home.'

'When do you do any work?'

'At night. And when there's a story worth doing. I do standard stuff for the Press Association. That covers most bills. I also do News 24.'

'But I've only ever seen your byline in the gutter press.'

'I'm lucky to get a byline. Most of the reporters get no mention. You get paid more with a byline.' He rose beautifully to my baiting.

'And, of course, you'll be writing a novel.'

He mumbled something that sounded suspiciously like 'piss off'.

'So is it about the serial killers? Am I in it?'

'No. It's not about *them* or *you*.'

'Aha! But you *are* writing a novel. Typical! Isn't that what all journalists dream of?'

'I don't see hundreds of law firms beating a path to your door.'

'That's because they know I'll be back in no time.'

'You're quite unbelievably arrogant, aren't you?'

'I'm arrogant about one thing, my abilities as a lawyer.'

'That's not the be-all and end-all of life,' he said quietly.

I didn't respond but I was thinking – at that moment, it was all I had.

At our apartment block somebody had parked in my parking space and I was forced to park in the service space.

'Bloody cheek!' I scowled at the beat-up Volkswagen on my way past.

A very attractive Asian woman, talking on a mobile, and Brontë, sitting on the floor, confronted us as we got out of the lift.

'What are you doing here?' I said.

'I discharged myself. I couldn't stand it any longer. Mother is having a fit. She's threatening to disown you because of the stuff at the house.'

'It's not my fault,' I said.

I stepped over her and unlocked my front door. The Asian woman switched off her mobile and offered me her hand.

'Hi, I'm Shereen Khalil.'

She was stunningly beautiful. Beautiful hair, beautiful skin, beautiful features. I shook her cool slim hand.

'I brought Brontë here. She didn't want to go back to your parents' home.'

I smiled tightly. The last thing I needed was a nine-toed invalid to look after.

Paul gave Shereen a warm kiss on the cheek. 'Thank you. You've been a great help, we really appreciate it.'

'I hope you do!' She winked. 'You remember about Sunday? I do want you to be there.'

None too gently, I grabbed Brontë under her arms and hauled her to her feet.

'You can stand up, can't you?' I belatedly asked.

'Yes. And I thought the nurses were bad.'

She hobbled in and flopped down on my sofa, placing her bandaged foot up on the arm.

'Don't bleed on it.'

'Give it a rest,' she snapped back at me.

I noticed Paul and Shereen exchange a glance. But this was how Brontë and I communicated, in short bursts of abuse or sarcasm. I was concerned for her, but I wasn't going to play nursey-nursey.

I went to remove the files from the coffee table because I didn't want Brontë snooping through them, but they had already gone. Paul had obviously taken them back when I was in the shower. God, was he huffy, or what?

Shereen placed a comforting hand on Brontë's shoulder.

'Brontë, here's a note of all my numbers. If you need me, please call, day or night. OK?'

'Thanks, Shereen. You've no idea how much this has meant to me. I'm very grateful.' Brontë smiled up at her and I could see the bond.

It was fine for the good doctor to bond with Brontë – she hadn't had to put up with her for twenty-eight years. Shereen looked across at me and smiled to show me her perfect white teeth.

'Em, thanks.'

'You're welcome. I would really like to make an appointment with you.'

Her lovely smile stayed in place.

'Sure. I'm slightly overstretched right now, but maybe in a couple of weeks.'

I hoped she would have forgotten by then.

'I'll be popping by to check on Brontë, so maybe we could get a date together then?'

'Great,' I said, with underwhelming enthusiasm.

She gave Paul a huge hug as she left and whispered something to him. He smiled and glanced at me. I wanted to stick a fork in his eye.

Paul sat down on the back of the sofa behind Brontë.

'We've not been introduced – I'm Paul. I live across the hall.'

'Hi. I'm Brontë, Erin's baby sister,' Brontë fluttered her eyes up at him.

I hated when she said 'baby sister' – it made me sound like a hundred and ten. I wondered if I was premenstrual, even though my periods were almost non-existent, because my bad mood bordered on tangible.

'Can I get you anything? Something to eat?' Paul asked her.

'Yes, please. The hospital food was diabolical, almost as bad as Erin's cooking!' Brontë laughed.

I scowled and went into the kitchen, hoping to find strychnine to put in her food. Paul appeared behind me seconds later.

'This is nice.'

'For whom exactly?'

'It's nice for you and Brontë to spend some time together,' he said from inside my fridge.

'We'll not get any work done. She's worse than a toddler for attention-seeking.'

'Family trait?' Paul was holding my cauliflower cheese in one hand and the stir-fry vegetables in the other. 'Not much of a home cooker are you?'

'I wasn't expecting house guests.'

'I'll bring some things across,' he said, as he left the kitchen.

'Could you bring the files back? I'll scan them if you make lunch.'

'They're in the living room.'

261

I went back through to the living room. 'Where? I left them on the coffee table. I thought you'd taken them.'

'I haven't touched them.'

'Neither did I. I was in the shower. Remember?'

'What have you lost?' Brontë asked, while she flicked through Sky TV.

'Nothing,' we said simultaneously.

'Just some legal files I was working on. I must have tidied them up.'

'Mum's furious about you starting your own firm. Dad will croak when he hears.'

'Brontë! Don't say that!'

'Sorry, but she's *really, really* angry. Apparently, the police turned up at the house yesterday. She says she's going to disinherit you.'

'Why were the police at the house?' I asked her.

'I don't know,' she said evasively.

I narrowed my eyes. She knew damn well. It would be something to do with her drugs habit.

'We're going over to Paul's to bring some things across. Will you be OK for five minutes, Brontë?'

'Yep.'

As soon as we were out of earshot, I whispered, 'He's got keys! That's how he got in this morning.'

'How many sets are there?'

'Mine, Alex's, which you've got, and Mrs McCaffer's.'

We were both thinking the same thing. Paul ran his hand through his hair.

'OK, OK. We'll get Brontë across to my flat and then we'll go and see Mrs McCaffer.'

'What are you two whispering about?' Brontë suddenly asked from my front door.

'Em . . . Paul has very kindly invited us to his flat for lunch. It's simpler than carting all the stuff through to here.'

Brontë eyed me suspiciously.

'And I want to get my place tidied up. It's a real tip.'

That swung it.

'You are so Monica,' Brontë jeered.

'Yeah, and you're Phoebe without the hair.'

'That's not funny!' she snapped.

'Girls!' Paul reprimanded us, but I could see a glint in his eye. He was probably hoping we would have a full-blown cat-fight later.

Brontë made a great show of hobbling from my front door, so great, in fact, that Paul carried her through.

I heard her say something like, 'you're so strong', followed by her tinkly giggle. Resentment rolled over me because I wasn't girlie in the slightest. I was horrid and spiky.

We settled Brontë on Paul's sofa with the remote control and said we were seeing the caretaker because the lift was erratic. We took the generally reliable lift to the basement, where Mrs McCaffer had her flat.

I was beginning to feel jittery. I didn't like Mrs McCaffer, but I certainly didn't want to find her dead.

Paul knocked loudly on her front door. There was no reply. He knocked again, but the sound echoed round the car park and back to us. I shrugged and turned away as Paul tried the door handle. The door opened.

'Oh, God,' I breathed. 'You do know who will be the prime suspect if she's dead? It's me they'll arrest.'

Paul gave me a 'shut up' look. I swallowed and suddenly needed to pee. If the murderer was camping out with Mrs McCaffer's corpse, I didn't want to be the one who found them.

Paul slipped through the half-opened door. I stood outside for a moment, considering my options. Run away? Hide? Call for help?

A thud from behind me made me jump two feet in the air, but it was only one of the high-set car-park windows banging in the wind. It was enough, though, to send me through Mrs McCaffer's front door, careering into Paul as he crept along the hall corridor.

Her flat was semi-dark and stank terribly. I had never smelled death before and wondered if this was it – noxious sour milk and rotting vegetables. It made me want to gag. I put my hand over my nose and mouth. I didn't want invisible, airborne particles of her putrefied flesh getting into my lungs.

The corridor had two doors down the right side, one door on the left side and one directly facing us, which was partially open.

Paul cautiously opened the first door on the left. A double bedroom. The bed was unmade and the curtains drawn; the wardrobe doors and the drawers hung open. Either it had been ransacked or she had left in a hurry. It had the same, strange, high-set windows as the car park. It must have been horrible living in this subterranean world.

We tried the doors on the right. The first opened into a box room, which had no window and was filled with junk. Through the wall, I could faintly hear the hum of the lift as the doors closed and it started to move.

Next door was the bathroom, again with no natural daylight. It was tidy, clean and empty apart from the usual paraphernalia of personal hygiene.

My heart was doing aerobics in my chest and my need to pee was bordering on critical. There was only one more door to try.

The rancid smell got stronger as we edged towards it. A vision of bluebottles filled my mind, their maggots feeding on her gutted frame. I listened intently for buzzing.

Paul nudged the door open. He put his head through the gap and took a swift look. I could see him physically relax before he opened it fully and went in.

I followed less than a step behind.

Her living room was also half lit by those excuses for windows and was fairly tidy. It was open plan to a kitchen, separated by a breakfast bar. The heating was on, the air warm and stuffy, saturated with that awful odour.

'Mrs McCaffer?' Paul called quietly.

I glanced at the kitchen and immediately spotted the cause of the stench. The fridge door was half open, its contents rotting in the heat. I left my position of safety behind Paul and went into the kitchen to close the fridge door. As I reached out my hand, Paul screamed.

'DON'T TOUCH IT!'

I leapt away as if scalded.

'We might have been meant to find it,' he hissed.

I looked down at the innocuous door and took a precautionary step back. It was a horrible take on the horse's head in the bed scenario – the cleaner's head could have been in the fridge.

Paul pulled his sleeve down over his hand and carefully nudged the fridge door fully open. The light didn't go on and I realised that it wasn't emitting the usual low rumble that fridges make. Paul bent at the knees and gingerly peered inside. He let out a low sigh and stood back up.

'It's just the food. The fridge isn't working.'

'What did you expect?'

'I don't know,' he said ominously and looked around.

'She must keep all the keys to the apartments somewhere. You search the kitchen.'

I systematically began to open cupboards and drawers.

The contents of her kitchen were pitiable – long-life meals for one, assorted tins of vegetables in brine, Cup a Soups and Pot Noodles. Her drawers contained old mailshots and the basic utensils of a kitchen not much used. I suddenly felt sorry for her, living in the basement of an apartment block filled by professionals with promising futures.

I wondered how she felt about ending up here, looking in from the outside at all those people who had made it. She was one of us purely because she shared our building, but she was excluded by her socioeconomic circumstances.

I could see why she wouldn't think twice about sleeping with Alex. For a brief moment it let her into the inner sanctum and also punished one of the leading purveyors of exclusion. Even I could tell from the sad contents of her kitchen that she was lonely. She must have thought the same about me.

'Found them!' Paul called from outside the living room.

I thought about coming back later to clear out the garbage in her fridge and give it a clean. It would be horrible to return to, and who knew how long she would be gone. It might encourage vermin. I turned down the thermostat for her central heating and went to find Paul.

He was in the little box room furthest down the hall. He was looking in an old-fashioned key cabinet, which had rows of keys and apartment numbers.

He glanced at me. 'Yours are missing.'

'Anyone else's?'

'Not as far as I can see.'

'So, someone broke in here to get my keys and then have access to my apartment? Wouldn't he realise that I'd get the locks changed?'

'It somehow doesn't fit, does it?'

'Do you know where Mrs McCaffer's gone?'

Paul avoided eye contact. 'Em, no.'

I poked him on the arm. 'Yes, you do!'

'Not for certain.'

'She's with Alex, isn't she?'

'I don't know. I heard a rumour.'

'Good luck to her, then,' I said airily, and left her dim little hellhole.

Paul locked her door with the set of master keys he had taken and joined me at the lift.

'You OK?' he asked.

'I was pretty nervous in there. I've never seen a dead body, except in photographs. I thought the smell was her. I felt guilty that she might have been killed to get to me.'

The lift doors opened and we stepped in.

'We *are* getting sensitive in our old age,' he quipped.

'What was in the files? Have you got copies?'

'Of most of it, yes, and it's on computer. There were interview statements from the last people to see the victims and autopsy reports, background reports. The normal sort of thing.'

I didn't admit that I had no idea what was normally in a police murder file.

'Is there anything that could be of use to him?' I asked as we reached our floor.

Paul thought for a moment. 'Maybe.'

It was not the answer I had wanted.

When Paul opened his front door, I took a sharp intake of breath. I could see the back of a man's head, next to Brontë's as she sat on the sofa.

DS Marshall stood up.

'Hello. I hope you don't mind. I tried your flat, but guessed you might be here.'

He offered his hand to Paul, but Paul ignored him.

'Brontë said you were seeing the caretaker about the lift? It seems fine.'

'It's erratic,' I explained.

'I'm starving!' Brontë complained.

'I'm on it.' Paul went into the kitchen.

DS Marshall spoke to me in an undertone. 'There were some things you wanted to discuss?'

'Em, yes,' I faltered. 'I'll be back in a minute.'

Somehow I felt I would be betraying Paul. This was his investigation, unofficial or otherwise. All my information had come from his research and sources. I wanted to clear it with him.

I sidled into the kitchen. Paul was whisking eggs and milk in a large Pyrex bowl.

'Paul, em . . . I, em, told DS Marshall about our suspicions and he wants to talk about them.'

He stopped whisking and gave me a sour look. 'When?'

'The other night.' I couldn't remember if it was last night or the night before. What was happening to me? My memory was a blur.

'What exactly did you tell him?'

'That we thought one of my late brother's friends was a murderer and that maybe the same person had attacked Brontë and killed Lucy Grant.'

'Did you also mention that Leland officially committed suicide?' he sneered.

'No . . .'

Paul gazed out the window. 'What do you want to do?'

His question surprised me.

'I don't know.'

Mildly exasperated Paul said, 'What does your instinct tell you?'

'On one hand it would seem prudent to, and on the other he might think we're barking mad.'

'I wouldn't worry about the mad angle. It comes down to this – do we trust him?'

I gave him a look. He was a police detective, what's not to trust?

Marshall knocked on the doorframe and interrupted our hushed conversation. I wondered how much he had heard.

'If this is a bad time, I could come back later,' he said.

'No,' I replied politely.

'Yes,' Paul said gruffly.

Marshall looked from me to Paul and back again. There was a hint of something in his eyes.

'You don't remember me? I was part of the CID review team that went over some unsolved cases you and DSI Kelman worked on.'

Marshall sauntered into the kitchen and leaned casually against the fridge.

Paul stopped whisking.

'You two know each other?' I asked.

'Yes and no,' said Marshall. 'Paul was long gone when I came on the scene, but we did interview him.'

'Were either of you going to tell me?'

They weighed each other up. It was like *High Noon at the OK Corral*.

'What the hell is going on?' I demanded.

'I don't think DI Gabriel liked some of our conclusions,' Marshall said calmly.

'I'm plain Mr Gabriel now,' Paul growled.

'Yeah, but you're never far from the crime scene.' Marshall threw a glance towards me.

'What's that meant to mean?' I asked Marshall.

'*Mister* Gabriel would probably be able to answer that,' he replied.

'Right! OK! There's obviously some issues between you, but is any of this helpful?'

'Will you tell her, or shall I?' Marshall said.

'Tell me what?'

Paul's shoulders seemed to sag. 'You're under surveillance.'

'What on earth for?'

'It's complicated,' he said lamely.

'Complicated? Neither of you know the meaning of the bloody word!'

'Now don't get angry,' Paul said.

I laughed. A half-crazed, disingenuous laugh.

'I'm under surveillance! In case I do what, exactly? Punch a no-good, lying, spineless git in the jaw?'

'In case you have contact with the killer,' said Marshall.

I blinked once. Alarm twisted in my ribcage.

'You think I know the killer! Am I a suspect?'

'No. But there are certain angles . . . certain issues, that don't quite fit,' Paul said.

'Like what, for God's sake?'

Paul narrowed his eyes at Marshall. 'What the hell is it that you want?'

'Same as you. Some answers.'

Brontë hobbled into the kitchen. 'What's up with you three?' she asked.

'Nothing,' we said in unison.

'Yeah. Right,' she sighed sarcastically.

'DS Marshall was just leaving.' Paul scowled at him.

Marshall smiled smugly. 'Anything you say, boss.'

'I'll show you out.' I threw Paul a nasty look.

As soon as we reached Paul's front door, I rounded on Marshall.

'What the hell is going on?'

'Nice apartment.' DS Marshall casually appraised Paul's flat and then looked directly at my front door. 'Great views.'

I gasped. 'You mean that Paul was watching me?'

'Unofficially. Officially, you now have your own team.'

'Why are you telling me this?' I hissed.

'Because they botched the last ten investigations. Their track record isn't exactly reassuring.'

'But why are they watching me?'

'Because DSI Kelman is like a dog with a bone. He's got a theory and refuses to see the wood for the trees.'

'Lunch is ready,' Paul interrupted from behind me.

'That's my cue.'

Marshall sauntered down the corridor. I watched him go, aware of Paul's eyes on me.

'DS Marshall,' I called.

He turned.

'Thank you.'

He mimicked a salute and pressed the button for the lift.

I didn't want to go into Paul's, I was livid. But Brontë was there.

'What did he tell you?' Paul asked immediately.

'That you were spying on me, but now, apparently, I have my very own team of voyeurs.'

'That's not true! I kept an eye on you, but only for your own protection.'

'Bollocks!'

Paul grabbed me roughly by the arm and swung me round to face him. He was furious.

'Listen to me! For the last bloody time. It's been for your own protection. Whatever anyone else says, or thinks, I was here for you!'

I took a step back. I had never seen Paul so animated.

'OK, OK. Calm down,' I said.

'That's rich, coming from you!'

'What are you two fighting about now?' Brontë called from the kitchen.

'We're not fighting,' I said as I went in. 'We're just disagreeing.'

'About what?'

'About where all the secrets live,' I said lightly.

She looked bemused.

Paul tried to catch my eye but I had retreated into circumspection.

I had missed the big picture entirely.

FIFTEEN

At last the locksmith deigned to turn up and I was grateful of the excuse to get away from Paul. And Brontë.

I wasn't used to constant company and interference. It brought the change in my circumstances sharply into focus. Normally, I would be tucked up safely at my offices dispensing compensation. Respected. Aloof. Not spied upon by all and sundry.

I was methodical, only flying by the seat of my pants in legal matters. Now I felt constantly on my back foot. This was not the way I liked to live.

DS Marshall's shocking disclosure had added to my confusion, giving me even more information and anxiety to process. I had to sift through what was true and what were lies. Or did the lies have their roots in some piece of hard fact?

His reference to DSI Kelman was ominous, but not specific. All three men knew a lot more than they had admitted, and I knew the reason. They distrusted me – to the extent of putting me under surveillance. It did not bode well whichever way I looked at it. The insinuation was that I was either a suspect or in imminent danger.

Thankfully, the locksmith worked quickly and efficiently. I took my little brush and dustpan and swept up the sawdust he had made, but having a new lock didn't dispel my uneasiness. I still didn't know who had taken my keys and removed Paul's files.

With my front door finally closed and locked, silence fell across my loft. I breathed a sigh of relief.

I picked up the lease for the office we had viewed and flicked through it, although I hadn't come to terms with losing Paterson, Paterson & Co. I couldn't actually believe it was over.

All the other events bombarding me had obscured my vision. The dissolution of the firm had apparently been in the offing for some time, but they had never chosen to warn me. Why?

I went to my desk to re-read the lease. If I was going to get my life back on track, I couldn't afford to dwell on the past.

The lease was pretty standard. There were no bizarre clauses about keeping pets or washing the stairs.

As a trainee, I had once acted for a landlord who wished to evict a tenant for keeping a cayman, a small alligator, which under the terms of his lease was a forbidden pet.

Unfortunately, like all baby creatures, it grew – to four feet long – and eventually ate the landlord's chinchilla. The tenant had argued that the cayman was not a pet, *per se*, but a security device. Naturally, I won. Oh, for the high days of the law. That case had been a joy and we had so many unimpressive puns, along the lines of 'get the statements and make it snappy'.

I suddenly realised that I was smiling. The vague reminiscence of a past case had brought back something, a feeling of belonging, of camaraderie. I could see the faces of my co-workers as we sat around the office joking and drinking coffee. The days of being a partner and forging a career hadn't yet dawned. Maybe I hadn't always been this anal and neurotic? I used to be quite fun – tamely fun, but still invited for a drink after work and hill-walking at weekends. Where had all the years gone? Where were all the laughs now?

I gazed at the lease. I could float it for a year, without touching my trust fund. The money I put in could be held on paper in a capital account, which would allow me to get it back when we started to make a profit. Correction, *if* we started to make a profit. I could turn my hand to other areas of the law – compensation wasn't the be-all and end-all of my abilities. I picked up my Mont Blanc fountain pen and signed.

'We're in business,' I told Liz over the phone, a few minutes later.

'What? *What?*' she gasped.

'I've signed, but we'll have to negotiate down to seventeen or eighteen pounds per square foot and three months rent free,' I blithely said.

'Jeezus! This is great! I can't believe it! Wait until Douglas and Karen hear. They're going to go crazy. This is great! What will we call ourselves? I can't believe it!'

Her reaction reminded me of an old Mickey Rooney film, where they were trying to put on a show in a barn. I suddenly felt like the benevolent parent sewing costumes for the cowgirls.

'Calm down. We've got a lot of work to do. We need to have a meeting and get a partnership agreement drawn up. We need to contact the surveyors. We need to draw up a fuller business plan, which focuses on where we can tout for business and whether we can take any clients from Cohen Paterson . . .'

'But it's great! It's so exciting! You sound like your old self.'

I could see it was pointless continuing the conversation until she had calmed down. 'I'll get on to Mr

Collier at D.M. Hall and you can tell Douglas and Karen.'

'Don't you want to tell them?'

'No. You do it. After all, it was your idea in the first place.' In truth, I didn't think I could stand much more exuberant outpourings. 'We could all meet at some point, to get started.'

'Great. Things are really moving. You'll not regret this, Erin. I promise.'

I made an uh-huh noise and hung up. Regret was already biting at my heels, much like the puppy enthusiasm they would all display.

My buzzer sounded and I bristled at the interruption.

'Detective Inspector Stevenson. Could I speak to Miss Erin Paterson?'

My apartment was becoming a regular blue box for police detectives.

I buzzed him in.

I opened the door an inch to check it really was old beefy Stevenson and glowered at his enormous frame. My bad moods had always contained a random element.

'Could I come in?' he enquired.

I opened the door. DI Stevenson lumbered into my apartment and the place appeared to shrink.

'Is there something I can help you with?'

'Paterson, Paterson & Co., as was, have contacted the police. Apparently, all their files were downloaded and copied off the computer system.'

I gaped at him. 'I know nothing about that.'

'Is it true that on Sunday the tenth of October you signed out a full box of disks?'

'No,' I said, but I did know who had asked for a full box of disks.

'But your initials are on the sheet.'

'Anyone could have put my initials on the sheet.'

'So you deny it?'

'Absolutely. I suggest that you check how long I was actually in the office on Sunday and what activity went on at my computer terminal.'

DI Stevenson ambled over to my desk.

'That's not possible. On Tuesday, the twelfth, the computer system crashed. A virus apparently.'

I let out a laugh. 'And you're really trying to pin this on me? I haven't been back to the office since Monday. I hardly know how to work my e-mail, never mind make a virus!'

Stevenson picked up a page of the new property lease.

'You have plenty of resources, Miss Paterson, and a very strong motive.'

'Please refrain from looking at my private correspondence, Detective Inspector Stevenson,' I said sharply.

'Got something to hide, Miss Paterson?'

'Yes. The decomposing body of the last detective who annoyed me.'

He threw me a snide little smile. 'DS Marshall told me about the burglary.'

'If you could call it that. It was petty vandalism, really,' I said nicely. There was little point in rising to his bait. Time spent with Paul was having a useful effect.

'He was here a while ago,' I added.

'The perpetrator?'

'No. DS Marshall.'

'Why?'

'Following up enquiries, I suppose. After what happened to my sister.'

'Sorry? What about your sister?'

'I presumed you knew. She took an overdose and was injured.'

DI Stevenson frowned in confusion and my curiosity twitched.

'Have you worked with DS Marshall for long?'

Stevenson raised a chunky eyebrow. 'A year or so. He worked in CID before. Why d'you ask?'

I gave a coy smile to put him off the scent. 'Married I suppose?'

'Ahh . . . I see. No. He's ambitious. Married to the job.'

I gave a *c'est la vie*-type shrug. 'Well, if there's anything else I can help you with . . .'

'If you happen to come across those missing disks, you could hand them in at any police station,' he remarked sarcastically.

'I have no idea what you mean,' I said, and showed him out.

I now knew two things. DS Marshall was investigating unofficially and he really had been working on Paul's old cases. I awarded myself two points, but deducted them again because I didn't know if it was of any consequence.

I picked up my phone and dialled. He answered in two rings.

'Douglas! What have you done? . . . No, not about that . . . The disks . . . Yes, the police were here . . . Yes . . . Of course not! They think it was me . . . Very funny . . . Jeezus Christ! . . . Can they trace it? No . . . Are you absolutely sure? . . . You're an asshole . . . Yes. OK . . . Good . . . Yes, I'm still angry . . . Yes, I said "asshole." Right . . . Bye.'

278

Douglas was a clever little bugger. And it served the back-stabbing bastards right.

I glanced at my watch. I knew it wouldn't be long before Brontë and the omnipresent Paul would be knocking at my door. I'd spent a year avoiding the man and now he turned up with unerring regularity. Like DS Marshall. And DSI Kelman.

It was time to get proactive.

I phoned Paul and asked him for copies of the files. Within an hour he brought over the reassembled and reprinted files. The downside was he brought Brontë back, too.

'Mum's taken Max to the cottage. Without even asking!' Brontë complained, as soon as she arrived. 'Didn't she realise I would be desperate to see him?'

I could have said: maybe if you hadn't rushed here, she would have had more of an idea, but I didn't.

'She probably thought it was better to let you rest and recover.'

She threw me a look. 'She's punishing me for supporting you.'

I bit my tongue. Supporting me didn't come into it. She was hiding here, for her own selfish reasons.

'Probably,' I said.

Brontë blinked. She hadn't expected that.

'They'll be back at the weekend. It's only a couple of days,' I soothed.

She scowled. 'Why are you being nice?'

'Thanks,' I said, and went into the kitchen.

I hadn't acknowledged Paul, apart from taking the files and putting them safely in my bedroom. The tension was palpable as soon as we were alone together. He was putting a home-made lasagne in my fridge. Nastily, I wondered about his 'mothering' obsession.

'Thank you for looking after Brontë,' I said formally.

'I need to talk to you . . .' he began.

'There is nothing to talk about.' My face was set. Inscrutable.

'There is. About what Marshall told you. You don't know the full story.'

'I have no wish to know,' I lied, and busied myself with the cafetière.

'Erin, please listen. I know you're hurt and upset. I know you're—'

I cut him off. 'Actually, Paul, you know little about me or my emotions. I shall read the files and share any insight I may have, but apart from that, there is nothing further to discuss.'

In exasperation, he threw his hands up. 'God! You are so fucking difficult!'

'After a year of spying, I'd have thought that was obvious.'

He thumped his fist on the table and I jumped, clattering the top of the cafetière into the sink. He slammed the front door as he left.

'What have you said to him now?' Brontë called from the living room.

I ignored her and slumped down at the table. I laid my head on the hard, cold surface. Hard and cold, like me. Paul was kind and special. He was strong and handsome. I could really have felt for a man like him. But I didn't do feelings.

'Erin? Are you OK?'

I rolled my head sideways and glanced towards Brontë.

'No.'

She hobbled in and sat down opposite me. 'What's wrong?'

'Everything.'

'Seriously. What's wrong?'

'God, Brontë. Where do I begin?'

She was silent for a moment.

'Is it . . . is it because of what I said? To the police.'

I rolled my head away and looked at my stainless-steel appliances.

'No. It had already started by then,' I mumbled.

'What had?'

'Everything.'

'But what's everything?' she cried in frustration.

I sat back up and pushed the hair away from my face. I stared into her eyes.

'Brontë, I need to know the truth. About what happened . . .'

'But I've already told you!'

'No, Brontë, you haven't. I need to know, not because I'm angry or anything, but because of Lucy. I need to know because of what happened to Lucy.'

Brontë scowled.

'To be perfectly honest, normally I would prefer not to know. It's your life. But on this one occasion, I must know. There's a lot depending on it.'

Her face tightened and she went sulky.

'Please, Brontë. You have no idea what I'm up against. No idea. I'm barely holding on. Brontë, please.'

I knew by the very fact she hadn't screamed at me or stormed out that I was close.

'Did you score some drugs?' I asked quietly.

She gave the slightest of nods.

'And did you know the guy you bought them from?'

Again the nod.

281

'Did you run out of money?'

She broke eye contact with me, but I had to keep going. I had done this often enough with reticent witnesses, asking them question upon question, until we got a clearer picture of the events. I knew she wouldn't be forthcoming with details, but at least I would get a sketch. If I was lucky, I would get one-word answers.

'Do you know what drug you took initially?'

'Yes,' she breathed.

'OK. Good. Well done. I know this is hard for you. Did you have GHB?'

She nodded.

'But why the coke?'

She bowed her head. I knew I had to be gentle but I wanted to scream at her: *what about Max*?

'Is he your regular dealer?' I ventured.

She gave a little sob.

'And you owe him money. Not just for those drugs?'

Her chin was forced into her chest. Her shoulders had started to shake.

'And you said the other stuff, so that you didn't have to name him?'

She was crying steadily, not a great howling, just terrible, tragic tears.

'How much do you owe?' I whispered.

'Eight . . .'

'Eight thousand?' I gasped.

She glanced up at me, her eyes full of astonishment.

'Hundred . . .'

My mouth hung open.

He had cut off her toe for eight hundred bloody pounds. Jeezus! I could have cut it off for her and got her two grand in compensation!

'Oh, Brontë!' I wailed. 'Why didn't you tell me? Why didn't you come to me?'

She gave a small snort of disbelief. I could see her point. I grabbed some paper tissues and handed them to her.

'What ... what happens now?' she asked.

'What d' you mean?'

'Will ... you tell the police?'

'Of course! And we'll get you a detox programme ...'

'I'm not an addict,' she countered indignantly.

'OK ... well, why do you take drugs?'

'Everybody does.'

'I don't.'

'But you're ... weird.'

I let that pass. 'I know this is difficult, Brontë, but why did you take the coke? On top of the GHB?'

She closed her eyes. Her eyelashes were thick and black from her tears. 'Because ... of the stuff in the papers. I wanted to ... I wanted to blot it out.'

So it was my fault. If I hadn't thumped Alex, none of us would have been mauled in the press. I had caused this.

'I'm sorry,' I whispered.

She gave me a brave smile.

'Do you know where he lives, the dealer?'

Her eyes widened in horror.

'He's a low-life drug dealer. He mutilated you. He has to be brought to—'

'But I don't want to go to the police! He knows where I live. He's got friends!'

'For crying out loud, Brontë. If you don't stand up to these people—'

Again, Brontë didn't let me finish. 'You have no idea

about the real world!' She gesticulated at my kitchen. 'You live in an ivory tower. This is not how ninety-nine per cent of the population lives!'

'You and I had the same chances, the same upbringing and privileges. You could have this, if you tried.'

She tutted angrily. 'Don't preach to me, Erin. You're not exactly the pinnacle of success right now, are you?'

I was stung but wouldn't let go.

'All I can say is you'll have to do something. You can't hide out here for ever. You still owe him money. You either pay him off or go to the police. Those are your only options.'

'How can I pay him off? If I had the fucking money, don't you think I'd have paid him?' she hissed.

'What about Mum and Dad?' I suggested.

'They're furious! Because of the thing with . . . and the police coming round.'

'You don't keep drugs at the house?' I said in alarm.

'No! But Mum's mad. Really mad. I mean, haven't you noticed?'

'She's been mad for years.'

'No, I mean furious! Absolutely furious and mad. What about her disbanding the firm? What's that all about?'

I shook my head.

Noisily, Brontë blew her nose and then asked, 'What did you mean when you mentioned Lucy Grant?'

I was startled by her question. I thought she hadn't caught on.

'Nothing.'

'Oh, give me a break. You and Paul and all these bloody policemen. What does it have to do with Lucy Grant?'

284

I viewed her speculatively. She was my sister, my flesh and blood, but I trusted no one.

'On the day that Lucy Grant was murdered, she left a message on my phone. When you went missing, the police thought there might be a connection. But now we can rule that out.'

Brontë's face visibly darkened. 'The police thought Lucy Grant's killer had attacked me?'

'Em . . . yes and no.' It occurred to me that I was actually the main driving force behind that particular theory.

'Yes and no? What does that mean?' she barked.

I sighed heavily. 'Because of the phone call from Lucy there could have been a link to you, but it was quickly ruled out.'

'Why was it ruled out?'

'Because . . . because he didn't kill you.'

Brontë gaped at me. 'Why did Lucy call you? She was in my year. She hardly knew you.'

'If I knew that, life would be a lot simpler.'

'What did she say?'

I swallowed. 'She said she'd try my mobile.'

'Well, that's no big deal. What are the police on?' she said.

'Would you like a glass of wine?' I stood up and went to the fridge.

'Oh, yes, please.'

I knew that would cheer her up. We still had some serious talking to do, mainly about her cleaning up her act. It was liable to produce fireworks.

I got two wine glasses and placed them on the table. I opened the bottle of chilled Chablis and poured. A slight vanilla scent rose from the wine. I was looking forward to that first gratifying taste.

'So why did the police take your mobile?'

Bloody hell. She wasn't as dumb as she looked.

'Because of the message . . .'

'The message the killer left. I could hear you all arguing at the hospital.'

'Brontë, I'm sorry. You shouldn't have heard that . . .'

'It's all right. I've been called worse. My point is, aren't you worried? Scared that he is coming after you?'

I paused for a moment. I was too wound up by all the other events to be truly scared. It seemed such an obscure threat, attached to an unbelievable scenario, that it floated somewhere beneath fear.

I poured some more wine.

'Well?' she said.

'I don't know if I'm scared. I've lost the very thing I held dearest and I can't quite get my head around that.'

'Alex?' she asked gently.

'No!' I tutted. 'The firm.'

She laughed at me. 'You really are the archetypal career woman.'

'Was, Brontë. Was.'

SIXTEEN

I told Brontë I had paperwork to attend to and left her watching some crap on Sky TV.

I viewed the stack of folders lying on my bed and knew I had to read them. I had made a terrible misjudgement in ignoring the newspapers and wasn't about to repeat the mistake.

I made myself as comfortable as possible on my bed, putting two pillows behind my back, and, with a heavy heart, opened the first file.

It made painful reading.

Each girl had a blossoming life, a loving family and a promising future. I had difficulty keeping up with who was who, for they were so often similar in background and education.

The post-mortem reports were horrific. They were sexually assaulted, tortured and maimed. It was a hollow relief that some of these sweet girls had died before their bodies were desecrated. I couldn't allow myself to dwell on those who were still alive at the time.

The first victim, Jennifer Longmuir, was found in a prominent position in Princes Street Gardens, which are at the foot of Edinburgh Castle. No attempt had been made to conceal her body. She had sustained a prolonged and aggravated sexual assault, but even with intensive analysis of the seminal fluids no useful information as to her assailant was found.

She had severe contusions over her body and face,

and her cheekbone was broken. There was strong evidence of her having put up a fight. The poor soul had struggled for her life. The toxicology report from the urine collected in her bladder showed no drugs or alcohol. Her dismembered right hand was found less than four feet away.

. . . dislocation of all digits on right hand and ruptured ligaments, dorsum of hand was fully degloved of skin. Skin flap remained attached to scaphoid, which suggests injuries to right hand were pre-amputation . . .

My mouth filled with bile and I had to take several deep breaths to stop myself being sick.

All her fingers were broken and the full thickness of skin had been stripped off her hand before it was severed just below the wrist. I prayed it was *post obitum*, but my prayer was not answered. She was still alive while he mutilated her.

I stood up and paced the floor, then got myself a glass of water from my en suite. I ran cold water over my wrists in an effort to eradicate the fainting feeling, before I could read on.

Emily Benson was victim number two, a twenty-three-year-old medical student. She worked as a junior house doctor at Bellsdyke Hospital, on the outskirts of Stenhousemuir. She stabled her horse nearby on a local farm. She had died from asphyxiation caused by ligature strangulation. Her own stethoscope was used.

. . . fracture of humerus, ulna and radius of both arms . . . supracondylar fracture of the femur evident in both legs . . . fractures of tibia and fibula in right leg only, blunt trauma causing severe contusions to left tibia . . .

Both her arms were broken, above and below the elbow, and both thighbones. Her lower right leg had also been broken, but not the left. The attempt, however, had caused shin splints. I ran my hands over my face.

Why did such appalling things happen? Why cause such vicious injuries? From the post-mortem, I gleaned that she had been raped and then her arms and legs were knelt on. The killer – or killers – had used their own body weight to snap her bones. Her broken body was found within the grounds of the hospital.

Isabelle Robertson died in Glasgow, early in January 1985. I tried to recall what I might have been doing then, at the exact moment my brother had possibly destroyed another life.

Had I spoken to him when he came home from his awful deed? Did I look at him and see a glimmer of something so dreadful that I refused to recognise it?

I had no recollection.

It seemed so long ago that I found it hard to imagine myself as that naive young woman, that twenty-two-year-old virgin.

Isabelle was small and fragile, five foot two and fifty kilos. She was last seen leaving Nico's, which had been a trendy city-centre café-bar in those days. Her body was found in the Western Necropolis that lies to the north-west of the city centre. The toxicology report found alcohol but no drugs. She had put up a struggle when she was raped, because there was severe bruising to her genitals and vagina. She had compression contusions on her wrists and throat, but that wasn't what killed her.

. . . comminuted fractures of tibia and fibula, major soft tissue trauma with vascular damage found in both right and left legs . . . fractured patella both knees . . . trimalleolar fractures on both ankles . . . consistent with major crush injury . . .

A huge slab of granite from one of the burial vaults had fallen on her – on her legs, to be precise. She died of multi-organ failure due to trauma, blood loss and shock. It was thought that the perpetrators had visited the site previously to loosen the slab, because it would have taken such strength to dislodge it.

I wanted to weep but all I could do was dryly sob. I ran the cold tap again, this time splashing the water on to my burning face.

I read solidly for another two hours. The phone rang several times, but I let Brontë or the answering machine pick up the calls. I was slightly worried that we might get another nursery rhyme, but I also now harboured an additional concern. How much had Brontë told people about Leland's abuse? Particularly when under the influence of drugs. Conceivably it could be her dealer, turning up the heat to make sure she paid him, who was pestering me. He would know which hospital she was in and it had begun right after her overdose.

I wrote down each girl's name and age, date, place and causes of death, plus occupation and particular talent. The obvious similarities between the victims were their backgrounds: they were all well bred, eligible and privileged.

From what I knew about serial killers, and that was largely gleaned from movies, there came a point where they courted publicity, actively wanted it. But to date, that had not been the case with whoever had committed these murders.

It was clear that the mutilation was ritualistic. The perpetrator took whatever was precious, whatever made those girls stand out from their peers.

Jennifer Longmuir, a talented artist, had her right

hand skinned and severed. Emily Benson, a medic working in orthopaedics, had her arms and legs broken. Isabelle Robertson, a dancer, had her legs crushed. On and on it went until Abigail Dawes, skilled archer and fencer, who had had her bow finger amputated and rapiers plunged into her eyes.

Finally I came to Lucy Grant, kind-hearted horse-lover, who had her throat sliced and tongue cut out. I had come full circle, from the precipitous moment of her death to my own expected demise.

Lucy Grant, Lucy Grant, Lucy Grant. Same school, same background . . . I stopped.

That didn't fit.

She wasn't a talented singer or orator. Why cut out her tongue?

Instantly, I knew. And that chilled me to the bone.

To stop her talking.

I began to shiver as the realisation sunk in. It was *me* she had wanted to talk to.

Naturally, Lucy's file was sparse, so I had very little information to go on. What on earth could Lucy have wanted to tell me? And why kill her for it?

I sat bolt upright. That meant the killer also knew.

Fuck, I thought. Double fuck.

Brontë threw open my bedroom door and startled me.

'Erin! Come and look at this!' she screeched and urgently beckoned me.

I leapt from my bed and raced after her. She was halfway to the kitchen.

'What is it?'

'Yucky!'

She was standing by the sink, peering down. I inched forward and tentatively followed her gaze.

Cockroaches! But only three this time.

Brontë reached towards the tap.

'No! Don't! Leave them. I want Paul to see them.'

I dialled his number and asked him to come over. He sounded hesitant but agreed.

Brontë went to let him in while I stood guard over the tiny beasts, in case they made a bid for freedom.

'Look!' I said triumphantly.

He stared at them for a moment, then shook his head.

'How did they get in here?' he said.

'Who knows? I wonder if other apartments have got them? Is Mrs McCaffer back?' I asked him.

'I've no idea.'

I looked for her phone number, then dialled. I was surprised when she answered. And she was surprised I was calling.

'There are cockroaches coming up from the plug-holes. Has anyone else complained?' I asked.

She snippily said, 'Not as far as I am aware.'

'Well, could you check with them?'

'I'm busy.'

'Pardon?'

'I'm busy,' she snapped again.

'Incidentally, I've had my locks changed. The set of keys you held have mysteriously disappeared.'

'No they've not.'

'Yes they have.'

'No they've not.'

'Oh, great. A pantomime,' I said witheringly.

'That policeman took them.'

'What?'

She turned defensive. 'He said he could get a warrant.'

'What was his name?' I said urgently.

'Can't remember his name. He was here the other day. He said it was legal.'

'What did he look like?'

'I can't remember,' she lied.

'Have you no idea what his name was?'

'Nah, but you shouldn't go around hitting people if you don't want to get into trouble,' she sneered smugly, and then hung up.

Paul was staring at me. The look in his eyes made me shudder.

Too quickly he asked, 'What was that about?'

I shrugged evasively. 'She's a bloody witch. She refuses to check into the plumbing.'

'What temperature do I put the lasagne on at?' Brontë interrupted.

'A hundred and eighty for forty-five minutes,' he replied instinctively, but continued to stare at me. I was momentarily glad of Brontë's witterings.

'Would you like a glass of wine, Paul?' Brontë continued.

I silently cursed. I wanted to sneak down and confront Mrs McCaffer. I wanted to know precisely which policeman had taken my keys. There were two here the other day: Kelman and Marshall.

'If that's OK with you, Erin?' Paul said politely.

I smiled falsely. 'Certainly.'

'Oh, and Erin, Liz somebody or other called about an office. And Karen called about some ball on Friday. She said that everyone is set except for you and you need one more woman. Can I come?'

I glanced at her demented hair.

'No. You wouldn't like it. It'll be full of professionals.'

Brontë's face fell and I cursed my unthinking mouth.

'I didn't mean it like that. It'll be boring. It's a talking shop.'

Brontë poured the glasses of wine and said snidely, 'She also said you had to find yourself a man to go with.'

I raised a threatening eyebrow at her, but I could see the wicked gleam in her eye.

'You could take Paul with you.'

'Take me where?' Paul spoke brightly but his face was tense.

'To the ball, Cinders!' Brontë giggled and nudged him.

I noticed that there were now two empty wine bottles sitting by the bin. Brontë was drunk.

'Paul's probably busy on Friday.'

'I've got nothing planned. Do you need a partner?'

Irritatingly, I blushed. 'Em, yes. No. Sort of.'

'I'll get my tuxedo pressed, then.'

'Oh, goody! This will be fun! Will there be lots of single men?' Brontë took a huge glug of wine. If Brontë was going to join us, I would have to get her to a hairdresser.

'No.'

Brontë pouted huffily. 'Why not?'

'Because there never are,' I muttered, and retired back to my bedroom.

I wanted away from them both, particularly Paul, because I couldn't guarantee that the vitriol bubbling in the pit of my stomach wouldn't come bursting out.

I picked up Lucy Grant's file and read it again. And again.

Poor Lucy Grant. Sixth 'most eligible'.

I leapt off my bed and opened my mahogany blanket chest. It contained six carefully labelled storage boxes:

'Photographs', 'Letters', 'Documents', and three miscellaneous. It would be in 'Misc. 1995–1999'. I took it out and sat on the floor.

The pages from the newspaper were near the top, but underneath them was a Valentine's card from Alex. I glanced inside the ludicrously ornate card and remembered how delighted I had been to receive it. Strange how the first optimistic moments of infatuation cloud our judgement. It was tacky and ridiculous, but at the time it had meant a great deal.

I had been out with a group of friends at Yes, a very fashionable restaurant, to celebrate somebody's fortieth birthday. It was a night of high spirits and champagne. Alexander, whom I knew solely by reputation, quickly made eye contact. After the first course all the men were to move their places, and Alex made a beeline for me. I pointedly ignored him. I spoke to the man on my left.

After the main course the men moved again, and Alex simply shifted to the seat on my left. As he sat down he whispered, 'You can ignore me again, but I'll just sit opposite you.' I arched an eyebrow and ignored him. After dessert, he was true to his word. We started dating about a month later, but only after I let him relentlessly pursue me with flowers and daily phone calls.

We never had a future, but we stuck with each other rather than being alone – left on the shelf. It had been more obvious for me. I was constantly reminded that time was running out. Even if I were to meet somebody tomorrow, it took months to build a relationship, then settle down and try for a baby.

If I were lucky, and didn't discover too late that there was a fundamental problem, I could be nearly forty before I conceived.

I put the Valentine's card back in the box with a small sigh.

I scanned the '100 Most Eligible' and cringed at my description. I doubted I'd make the top ten thousand now. The top twenty had larger photographs and three paragraphs, the lower down the scale one got, the smaller the photo and blurb.

My eyes sprang open. Sophie Holbrook was number sixty-seven.

Sophie was twenty-nine, sat on the fund-raising committees of several charities and had inherited two million from her industrialist father. She was a keen scuba-diver.

I blinked at her smudged photograph and recalled her autopsy.

She had been drowned in her own urine and part of her lung had been removed.

Sophie Holbrook was the third last victim, the one before Abigail Dawes.

I swallowed, but my mouth was dry. My heart was pounding. Had I found a link?

Occasionally, my name appeared in the quality papers, purely in reference to winning large compensation awards. My only other claim to fame was in the '100 Most Eligible'. Lucy and Sophie were also in it. Abigail Dawes had received some press coverage from her Olympic fencing aspirations. Could it hinge on that?

There was a quiet tap at my bedroom door.

'Come in,' I called.

Paul popped his head round the door.

'The lasagne's nearly ready,' he said, but his eyes wandered to the newspaper on my lap. 'Found something?' he asked.

'I don't know. Maybe. Did you know that Sophie Holbrook was in the same eligible list as Lucy?'

'No, I didn't. But so were you. Number ten, I believe.'

I didn't need reminding.

Paul came over to me and I handed him the paper.

'Is Abigail Dawes in it?' he asked, as he scanned the article.

'No, but she had received some media attention as an Olympic hopeful. There are press cuttings in your file.'

'But you're in the list, not Brontë.'

I paused guiltily before I responded. 'Kelman was right when he suggested that Brontë had omitted pertinent facts. Brontë's assailant has nothing to do with this.'

'How do you know?'

'We discussed it.'

'Why did she say that stuff about Leland, then?'

I sighed heavily. 'She was genuinely confused and, well, she was creating a smokescreen.'

'Are you OK with that?' he said.

'It's not up to me.'

'Why don't you come through and have something to eat with us?'

'Later.'

'Erin, about earlier . . .'

'Let's not go there . . .'

'But you don't understand . . .'

'I understand perfectly!' I snapped. 'Neither you nor DSI Kelman trust me.'

'That's not true! I trust you. I've shared all I know with you.'

'Have you, indeed? OK, then tell me what's the deal with DS Marshall?'

Paul's features darkened. 'He caused a lot of grief.'

'He reviewed some of these cases. What did he find that makes you and Kelman so touchy?'

Wearily, Paul sat down on the edge of my bed. He was silent for a full minute, as he tried to find the words.

'DS Marshall and his superiors thought the early cases had been mishandled – to the extent of a formal inquiry. Why do you think Kelman's never made it past Detective Super?'

'And were they mishandled?'

Paul looked up at the ceiling and murmured, 'Probably.'

'In what sense?'

'We botched the first three to begin with. We didn't see the pattern. Oh, in hindsight we did, but it's well known that the first forty-eight hours of any investigation are the most crucial. We weren't thorough enough. Crime scenes were disturbed or overlooked. It's bloody hard to extract usable evidence a year or more after the event.'

'But what about the rest?'

'I wasn't involved in them all. I had left. Remember?'

I wasn't letting him off that easily. 'Well, the ones you did work on?'

He rolled his eyes but said, 'The crime scenes were meticulously clean. Not one shred of forensic evidence was found. It was almost as if they had been sterilised. There was a suspicion of either police ineptitude or collusion. Happy now?'

I certainly was not happy.

'Who did they suspect?' I said quietly.

'Who do you think?' he snapped.

Christ. I blinked and tried to calm my rising fear.

'And that's why you left?'

He scowled at me. 'No. I had a nervous breakdown! I didn't mean me!'

'Oh . . .' I said lamely. 'Kelman?'

'No! Somebody in the force.'

'Sorry. It was the way you said it!' I snapped back.

He closed his eyes and shook his head angrily. I had hit a raw nerve.

'What else was wrong?'

Paul hesitated.

'Never mind,' I grumbled, and slowly got to my feet. I was stiff, age was catching up on me, and I reprimanded myself for not continuing with yoga.

I was almost out the bedroom when Paul spoke.

'The whole group thing – the secret sect – it wasn't a popular theory.'

'Why not?'

'Too vague, too unbelievable, too many inconsistencies. Particularly after Leland was gone. We only had five named suspects; two were then dead. The other three accounted for in one way or another.'

'What about the two on the periphery?' I asked.

'We didn't know who they were. The review team thought we had focused too narrowly on the group, to the exclusion of other possibilities.'

'But the earliest victims, apart from Jennifer Longmuir, were gang-raped. Borne out by of the high degree of damage to the genitals and anus. Also, the varying degrees of force used suggest different strengths. The torture and mutilation don't always appear to be from the same hand. In fact, two of the reports state "left-handed blows". It's quite clear from the autopsies that there was more than one assailant involved with several of the victims.'

He gave a resigned smile. 'That's what we thought, but as I said, it wasn't the most endorsed hypothesis.'

I viewed him speculatively. Something had bothered me while I read the files.

'Why is there no information on Leland and his friends in the files? The reports into each case are comprehensive, but there isn't any reference to your suspects.'

Brontë called from the kitchen, 'The lasagne's ready!'

Paul stood up and came over to me. He rubbed his forehead as if kneading away a pain.

'That information was deemed to be too sensitive and therefore confidential.'

It took me a moment to understand.

'You mean too sensitive for me to see?'

He gave a curt nod and went to squeeze past me as I stood in the doorway.

'Reading post-mortems isn't exactly Mills & Boon. What on earth could be worse than that?'

He looked down at me and, fleetingly, I was aware of his proximity.

'It isn't because you might be upset.'

I gaped at him in horror.

'It wasn't my decision,' he added quickly.

'Whose was it? DSI Kelman?'

His face said it all.

'But I don't understand. Kelman wanted me to help build a profile . . .' I said in disbelief.

Brontë came out of the kitchen, wiping her hands on a tea towel. 'I've made a salad to go with it.'

'That's kind of you, Brontë,' I said, but I was watching Paul. He caught my gaze.

'We'll talk later,' he said, as we joined Brontë in the kitchen.

I couldn't eat. My stomach was twisted in knots of anxiety. I managed three tiny mouthfuls of lasagne and two wisps of lettuce.

'It's not good for you, Erin, eating so little. What do you weigh? Eight stone?' Brontë blithely barged in where angels dared to tread.

'I'm not hungry.'

'You didn't eat any lunch either,' she said. 'Seriously. You're too thin, isn't she, Paul?'

He sort of cleared his throat.

'I'm naturally thin. Why is that a big problem for everyone?'

'Normally, you do look fine, but we had noticed you have lost weight.' Brontë was spooning lasagne into her mouth like there was no tomorrow. Self-control had never been a virtue of hers. In any form.

'And who are *we*?' I enquired tightly.

'Shereen, Paul and me,' Brontë said in all innocence.

My mouth hung open for a moment. Paul looked as though a rabid rat had bitten him. Angrily, I stood up.

'Ah, I didn't mean it like that . . .' Brontë began.

'Leave it,' I barked, and bowled out of the kitchen.

Where did they get off? *Cosy Doctor Khalil and Uncle Paul.* Next they would want to discuss my bowel movements. Nosy gits.

I went into my dressing room and stood in front of my full-length mirror. Brontë was right, I had lost weight. I looked pale, thin and hollow eyed.

I pushed my hair behind my ears and gazed at my reflection. My skin had lost its glow and my hair had lost its shine. My eyes were dull and tired. For the first

301

time in my life, I didn't see myself as utterly attractive. My last refuge of confidence had been wiped away.

I felt vulnerable and scared – feelings that had recurred since childhood. Only by constant action and detachment could I keep them at bay and stop them from swamping me.

I went into my en suite and took tranquillisers out of a drawer. I stared at them. I was loath to do it but felt I was teetering on the edge. I popped one out of its individual foil pocket and slowly put it in my mouth. I swallowed it quickly.

I exfoliated and plastered my face and neck with Clarins self-tanning lotion. I padded back to my dressing room and looked at my evening dresses.

There was only one that would do for the ball, my long black Armani. It had a high halter neck, long sleeves and a plunging back. It was a mix of Lycra and silk, and fitted me like a glove. I took it out of the wardrobe to let it air.

Lethargically, I got my Psion out of my handbag and phoned Liz. We arranged to meet at my penthouse at four o'clock the following afternoon. I asked her to tell Karen and Douglas.

It took me three attempts to summon the courage to call Dr Eunice McKay. When I finally did, I got her answering service telling me to call her mobile if it was an emergency, and to leave a brief message if it was for an appointment. I hesitated for a moment after the beep and then hung up.

She couldn't help me and I knew it. Only I could help. We had been over this ground until it was a well-worn path.

I was frigid and neurotic. But who could blame me?

My brother, only a year older than me, started abusing me – in graphic terms – when I was ten.

But it had begun long before that. Long before.

When I was very small, five or six, I could remember him stroking my hair, as if I was a cat. But when I grew tired of his fawning, he pulled it. Really pulled. A short, sharp yank and a handful of hair was torn clean from my scalp.

That was when I realised, in my childish way, do not cross Leland.

He would terrorise what few little friends I made. Mother would say, 'Boys will be boys,' but soon those friends wouldn't come to play. His presence became a persistent, threatening shadow.

He would start off deferential, but if I was petulant or made a wrong move, expression of utterance, he would turn. Like the crack of a whip. Swift, painful, frightening.

And always the threat. The turn of his head, the gait of his walk, the flick of an eye. I knew I would be punished. Oh, I knew.

And then Brontë came along. Lovely, trusting Brontë, a mop of brown curls atop a bubbling toddler, and another weapon against me.

I tried to protect her by feigning disregard for her, by evasion, through a million little tactics thought up on the spur of a moment. Finally, I negotiated.

But it was never enough.

If I wronged Leland, in terms of his sick, tortured mind, his ultimate revenge became Brontë.

I put my head in my hands and felt the tears on my palms. I had even learnt to cry silently. I would will my presence, my aura, to cease.

Brontë knocked and entered. She looked as if she was spoiling for a fight until she saw me.

'Erin? What is it?' she said, and rushed to my bedside.

I gazed up at her. 'Leland.'

I didn't have to say more than that one word.

We knew the same pain.

SEVENTEEN

It was dark but I wasn't cold – I was sweating profusely and felt along the dirt floor for an exit or the stairs.

It took me several tense moments to realise that I was actually in my own bed, in my own room, and I was dreaming.

I had disturbed Brontë and she gave a little mumble. We had fallen asleep together, exhausted from crying and talking.

I had told her everything I could remember about Leland.

Now she knew that when he had hurt her, it was my fault. I hadn't been quick enough or sly enough to dissuade him, distract him – to protect her. She also knew it had been worse for me.

Brontë had shrunk in on herself and I had put my arm around her shoulders, but her body was rigid and strained. All her softness, her amiability, had gone.

I slipped out of bed and went to my en suite. My pyjamas were drenched with cold sweat. I removed them and washed my face. I couldn't recall the nightmare, but I could feel the fear that had accompanied it.

I had asked Brontë if she had told anyone about the nursery rhymes Leland sang or the injuries he caused, but she said she hadn't.

The only logical conclusion was that the killer had left the messages and that frightened me to the core. I dwelt, rather unkindly, on the fact that if Lucy Grant hadn't damned well called me in the first place, then this wouldn't have happened. I knew it wasn't true, but it gave me a psychological buffer. The killer wasn't really after me, but had stumbled upon me by accident.

But it was useless. He knew one of Leland's torments. How could that be possible? It had to have come from Leland. I felt my empty stomach tighten and heave.

In my fevered imagination, I could see them laughing and reliving the moments. The eyes of his cohorts gleaming with pleasure and envy.

I gave a dry wretch. Acid burned my throat, but nothing came up.

I got fresh pyjamas and went back to bed, but my thoughts lingered – no matter how I tried to push them away, they lingered.

The smell of burning woke me just after eight. I leapt from my bed and, in my haste, stubbed my toe. I shrieked in pain.

A billow of smoke, closely followed by Brontë, came from the kitchen.

'What the hell are you cremating?'

'The toaster's incinerating everything!' she said indignantly.

'Put the extractor fan on! And open the bloody doors,' I snapped.

'Somebody got out of bed on the wrong side,' Brontë tutted.

I threw her a filthy look and realised she was wearing my Polo USA-flag sweater and Ralph Lauren chinos. Was nothing sacred?

'Where did you get those?' I demanded.

'Your wardrobe.'

'Why didn't you take some of my other stuff?

Why did you have to take my favourite sweater?'

She gave a shrug and sauntered back towards the kitchen. 'I liked these best.'

Liked those best did she? The cheeky, marauding cow. I grumbled all the way back to my room. They would stink of cooking now and the chinos looked too tight on her – they hung perfectly on me. And *I* had hair. She should keep off the bacon for a while. It was the trivial things that sent me over the edge when I was in martyr-mood.

I stood under a hot shower and tried to wash away my black mood, but no amount of Jo Malone products could activate my calm, happy gene. I stepped out of the shower in a marginally worse mood than when I had stepped in.

I had planned to wear that ensemble today, the casual-chic look. I stared meanly into my wardrobe and hated everything I saw. I grabbed a sweater and a pair of jeans, but they weren't how I wanted to look. I had a thing about dressing how I wanted to be perceived – it was part of my defence.

I ventured into the living room and began to shuffle papers around my desk. I found it hard to concentrate with others lurking in the background, particularly others who were having a rare old giggle in my kitchen. Paul had joined us, yet again. My, my, he was keen.

'Would you like some coffee, Erin?' he asked, from the kitchen doorway.

'Please,' I murmured.

'Brontë said you had signed the lease for that office. Congratulations. It takes a lot of guts to do what you're doing,' he said conversationally.

'Sadly, guts have nothing to do with it. It's all about necessity and requital.'

'How do you mean?'

Paul came over to my desk and I noticed, not for the first time, how much presence he had.

'I can't exactly leave them out on a limb. I'm morally obliged to stand by them. They stood by me. And, if I'm brutally honest, it's my only way back into the law.'

Paul seemed taken aback by my candour.

'I didn't think you'd see it like that.'

'I'm not completely insensitive. Only selectively.'

'I think you're doing the right thing. Well done,' he said, like a schoolteacher.

'Thank you, sir,' I sneered. 'How very reassuring.'

I hadn't forgiven him for spying, lying and withholding. I wanted to make sure he knew that, but he hit right back at me.

'Just some coffee? Nothing to eat?'

I smiled up at him. 'Just coffee, thanks. Strong. Black. No milk. No sugar.'

He hesitated for a moment before he said, 'I thought you took lots of milk. Baby coffee?'

'Not any more,' I lied. I hated black coffee, but if it got Paul's goat then it was worth it.

He narrowed his eyes but said nothing and went to get my coffee.

For all my skills in legal bartering, I was at a loss as to how to handle Paul. He knew things, which he wasn't about to tell me, and that irked me. Actually, it infuriated me.

The mention of 'baby coffee' brought my thoughts back to DS Marshall and my missing keys. I would have to inveigle Mrs McCaffer into telling me who had taken them.

'Your coffee, ma'am.' Paul made a big show of placing a tall mug of steaming black coffee on my desk.

'Thanks. Why are you here?' I asked, not unkindly.

'Brontë asked me over. Didn't she tell you?'

'No. Why did she ask you over?'

'She said there were some things you had to tell me. About Leland.' Paul looked genuinely confused.

I looked genuinely annoyed.

'Oh dear. I've landed her in it, haven't I?'

'Yep.'

He shrugged guiltily.

'Here's the deal, Paul. I'll show you mine, if you show me yours, as they say.'

'It's not my decision . . .' he started to say.

'That's the deal. Take it or leave it.'

He viewed me speculatively.

'All right, all right,' he agreed grudgingly.

'I've some phone calls to make, but I'm free until four this afternoon.'

'I've an article to finish. Shall we say my place at noon and then we can have a spot of lunch too.'

'How come you don't get fat?' I blurted out.

He gave me a wry smile. 'I work out. You should try it.'

'Bugger off. I prefer starvation to exercise.'

'Very healthy,' he tutted and left.

I called Mr Collier at D.M. Hall. He was pleased to hear from me, and then not so pleased by my demand of three months rent free and seventeen pounds per square foot. We managed to settle on eighteen. I hung up the phone and felt mildly encouraged. I had kick-started my life.

Brontë was still in the kitchen, most likely hiding from me. I had to admit that she'd probably done the best thing by calling Paul, but I wondered how much she had told him.

I went into the kitchen to put milk in my coffee and spied Brontë out on my terrace. She looked strangely serene as she stared out over the rooftops. The sun broke through the clouds and danced off the wet decking.

She saw me through the doors and grimaced. A burst of cold air came in with her. She did look better – apart from her hair.

'Sorry,' she said.

'Never mind. What did you tell him?'

'I just said that you remembered a lot more about Leland than I did.'

'You didn't give him any details, did you?' I asked quickly.

'No. That's private. I mean, if you want to tell him, that's OK, but I thought I'd better leave it up to you.'

'Thanks.'

She ran her fingers through her ravaged hair.

'Do you want me to make an appointment at my hairdresser for you?' I asked casually, hoping she wouldn't take offence.

'Yes, please. That would be great.'

I phoned my hairdresser and managed to persuade them to squeeze Brontë in at eleven thirty that morning.

It's just a couple of blocks from here. Are you able to walk OK?'

Brontë stood up and walked across the kitchen. 'It's a bit sore and feels weird, but the consultant said to keep active.'

'We need to sort out the other . . . thing,' I said tentatively.

'You mean, with the dealer?'

'Or the police,' I said hopefully.

Brontë sat back down and rubbed her hands over and over her face.

'I don't think I can face the police. I just want it all to go away. Be over and done with.'

'Are you sure?'

'Yes,' she said resolutely.

'But . . . what if,' I struggled to find the kindest words. 'What if . . . it, well, it . . . happens again?'

She was horrified by the suggestion.

'It won't happen again!'

'Promise me. Promise me, you won't take any more drugs.'

She gave me a scathing look. 'You despise me, don't you?'

'Of course not! How can you say that?'

'Because you're always so angry at me, you're always so . . . distant.'

'I'm not angry with you. I'm concerned and sometimes it comes over as anger, but it isn't. I find it difficult to verbalise how I feel. I'm very—'

She cut in. 'Cold?'

'That wasn't the word I was going to use, but, yes, I suppose I'm not very demonstrative.'

She struggled to smile. 'You and your big words. I'm surprised you haven't quoted Latin at me.'

'Potius sero quam nunquam.'

'What does that mean? That I'm a bitch?'

'No, dear, it means better late than never. But Brontë, promise me about the drugs. I'll pay off the debt, but you must promise me.'

She stood up and came over to me. I knew I looked confused. Then she did something extraordinary. She gave me a hug.

'I promise,' she whispered.

311

Brontë went to get ready for the hairdresser's and I began to tidy up my apartment. All the 'through traffic' of the last few days had left it slightly disordered. Not that anyone else would have noticed, but it bothered me. A tidy home meant a tidy life. Some hope, I thought bitterly.

As Brontë was leaving, I gave her a signed blank cheque and my cheque card. I also handed over some cash and a set of the new keys. She seemed mildly uncomfortable.

'I'll pay you back,' she said.

'No worries. I'm going out for a while, but I've a meeting here at four, with the people I'm going into business with.'

She looked enthusiastic. 'Can I meet them?'

'I suppose so. They're not very exciting.'

'But they must be OK. They gave up their jobs, so they must think a lot of you. I want to meet your friends.'

My sister had flummoxed me, just as they had.

With Brontë gone, I got out the vacuum cleaner and went round the whole apartment. I flung bleach down the toilets and cleaned the bathrooms. There was something therapeutic about housework. But only if you did it occasionally.

I aimlessly began to sort through the dross on my coffee table. I neatly piled up magazines, remote controls and newspapers until I came across Alex's letter – which I hadn't bothered to read.

I didn't know if I wanted to rake over the coals of our relationship.

I sat down on the sofa and weighed the envelope in my hands. It felt heavy and I wondered what on earth he'd written about at such length.

I heaved a sigh as I opened it – I could sense a person-ality assassination heading my way. I was surprised to find another letter addressed to me wrapped inside Alex's. It was postmarked Edinburgh and had already been opened. How charming to discover that Alex had been going through my mail.

I read Alex's note first. It was much as I had expected – a self-pitying, reconciliatory ramble. He didn't mention Mrs McCaffer or selling me out to the news-papers. Very convenient of him to forget all that. I impa-tiently turned the page over and got a shock.

. . . I'm sorry I didn't tell you, but I had no idea what was going to happen. When Lucy Grant rang and asked for you, I just thought she was going to stir up trouble. She called again the next day and said it was important, but I gave her the runaround. She must have realised that I hadn't mentioned she'd rung because this arrived for you. I should have given it to you but, as you know, things got out of hand . . .

What did Alex mean by trouble? Had he been seeing her behind my back? The newspapers had said they had had a relationship.

I let his letter flutter to the floor and stared grimly at the envelope from Edinburgh.

Gingerly, I opened Lucy's letter, carefully tearing away the tape that Alex had used to reseal it.

Dear Erin
I have been trying to contact you for several days. I know this will seem very strange to you and I'm not really sure how to put any of this,

313

*but it has been preying on my mind. I remem-
bered you and your sister from school and I was
trying to contact Brontë to tell her about a class
reunion, but I spoke to your mother instead.*

*I happened to remark that I had seen her in
Edinburgh several days earlier with a man I
presumed to be your brother, Leland. She got very
annoyed and said some pretty odd things before
slamming the phone down. Frankly, I was quite
offended.*

*It was only when I mentioned the phone call
to my own mother that I realised the awful faux
pas I had made. I have since tried to speak to
your mother to apologise for any upset I may have
caused. I am truly sorry.*

*I have written to you in the hope that you could
apologise on my behalf. I realise that you have
not been taking my calls and therefore there is a
good chance that she has already told you of my
terrible blunder.*

*I am deeply sorry, but it truly was a genuine
mistake. I would be very grateful if you would
contact me so that I may correct my error.*

*Yours sincerely
Lucy Granville-Grant*

Lucy must have seen Finlay, thought he was Leland,
and by a quirk of fate mentioned it to Mother.

I wondered if this was the very last letter Lucy had
written.

Bloody Mother and her histrionics. I hoped she felt
bloody awful for not accepting Lucy's apology.

But a peculiar thought popped into my mind.

Mother had said she knew nothing about any recent

314

contact with Lucy. Why would she deliberately not mention such an innocent thing? I understood that anything to do with Leland was a sensitive subject for her, but why the deception? Even after knowing the poor girl was dead!

Mother was a stupid old bitch.

I felt like phoning her, there and then, to give her a mouthful.

I glanced at my watch and realised I was ten minutes late. My usual punctuality had gone out the window, like everything else.

I brushed my hair, applied lipgloss, grabbed my keys and went over to Paul's apartment.

He didn't look particularly pleased to see me.

'What's up?' I asked.

'Kelman's been taken off the case.'

I followed him into the kitchen.

'Why?'

'Who knows! Probably that little bastard Marshall.'

'Surely he's not senior enough to do that?' I said stupidly.

'That has nothing to do with it! He's fast-tracking. He has the ear of the chief. He's about to be made a DI.'

'Calm down, Paul. There's probably a logical explanation . . .'

He rounded on me. 'And apparently there's been an official complaint.'

'Well, don't look at me!' I snapped. Bloody cheek. But if only I had thought of that.

Paul scowled.

'I can't be bothered with this. I'll come back later,' I grumbled, and went to leave, but he put his arm out to bar my way.

'Shit, Erin. I'm sorry. I'm wound up.'

'You're telling me. Let's get this straight. I haven't complained.'

'Just when it looked like we might get somewhere, this bloody happens.'

'We might have got somewhere anyway. I have a letter from Lucy Grant and it explains why she called me.'

'She wrote to you? And you've only just mentioned it?' he thundered.

'It was in the letter that Alex left. I only *just* opened it.'

'What does it say?' he demanded.

'It says she was only trying to contact me because she had an altercation with my mother and she wanted to apologise. It's that simple.'

'Did you bring it?'

'No . . .'

'What exactly does it say?'

'Lucy said she was sorry for upsetting my mother and could I apologise on her behalf—'

He didn't let me finish.

'You've still got the letter. Right?'

'Of course.'

'Come on,' he barked, and herded me back across to my apartment.

I handed Paul Lucy's letter as soon as we went in. He read it twice.

'So, you only opened this today?'

'As I said. It was in the letter from Alex. Which you only gave me on . . . Tuesday.'

'Don't you find it strange that Lucy mistook Finlay for Leland? What's the age difference?'

'Ten years. They do . . . he did . . . Finlay does look

like Leland did. There *is* a family resemblance. There's a good chance that Lucy didn't even know Finlay. Anyway, the point is that it explains why Lucy called me.'

'But it doesn't explain why your mother didn't tell you about it and why Lucy thought she had seen Leland.'

I rolled my eyes. 'My mother didn't mention it because she was upset. Lucy couldn't possibly have seen Leland.'

'But why would that innocent mistake upset her so much?'

'Because any reference to the dear, departed Leland sends her into a tizz of epic proportions.'

Paul shifted uncomfortably. I could feel my hackles rising.

'What? What is it now?' I snapped.

'A bit agitated, aren't we?'

'No. A bit tired and suffering from a thumping headache.' I felt under hostile scrutiny.

'Let's go over what we know, shall we?'

'Spare me,' I muttered.

'Just bear with me, Erin. Indulge me. Lucy Grant contacted you to apologise for accidentally upsetting your mother, because she thought she had seen Leland. However, she had already tried to apologise to your mother personally. Then Lucy is murdered and we hear a graphic account of the rape on your mobile phone.'

He thrust his hands in his pockets and began to pace the floor. Obviously, it was a common idiosyncrasy. He waited for me to say something, but he would have to wait until hell froze over. What could I say?

'OK. Furthermore, you say that you were left a note,

a note so personal to you and your dead brother that it could only come from him . . .'

I wanted to butt in, but he continued before I could.

'Or . . . or somebody who knew him well. There was also a strange message on your answering machine.'

I nodded impatiently.

'So, this killer is singling you out. Why would that be? Why would he contact you from his last kill and then terrorise you?'

I took a deep breath. 'One – Lucy's mobile phone could have accidentally been activated to ring the last number dialled. Two – it was *your* theory that my brother was part of a secret sect that probably, possibly, *shared* their atrocities. And three . . .' I stopped because I couldn't think of a three.

'What did your mother say when Kelman asked her about Lucy?'

'Nothing. She said she hadn't heard from her.'

Abruptly, he sat down beside me and leaned towards me. Feeling interrogated, I leant away from him.

'Erin, think! It's staring you straight in the face.'

'What is?'

'She lied! She lied about Lucy because she didn't want anyone to know.'

I frowned at him in confusion.

'What *exactly* didn't she want people to find out?' he yelled.

'For God's sake! That Lucy thought she had seen Leland!'

Paul nodded wildly.

My mouth opened but no sound came out. He was insane. He thought a ghost was killing people. This I had not foreseen.

My mind went into grasshopper mode. Insane man.

What does one do? Scream? No hope of anyone hearing. Distract him? Humour him? No. Think! Bloody well, think! Run away.

'Can I . . . can I go to the bathroom?' I asked meekly.

'Of course.'

I darted into my bedroom, grabbed my bedside phone and tried to wrench it into the en suite. The cord wasn't long enough and my shaking fingers dropped the bloody thing.

Paul appeared at the bedroom doorway. Involuntarily, I was reminded of *The Shining*. In an instant, he spied the phone that I had hauled across the carpet.

I made a dash for the en suite, but he was fast and caught me before my hand had touched the bathroom door. He grabbed my arm and jerked me round.

'What were you doing?'

'I was phoning—'

'Who? Who were you phoning? Leland? Were you phoning Leland to warn him?'

He had confirmed my worst fears. He was totally insane. Mad as a hatter.

He ushered me back through to the living room and made me sit on the sofa. I could see the headline: MAD NEIGHBOUR KILLS TOP LAWYER. Correction: MAD EX-POLICEMAN KILLS EX-TOP LAWYER.

He paced round and round the coffee table, stopping intermittently as if he was about to say something, then round and round again.

'Were you trying to phone Leland?'

I blinked at him and willed Brontë to come home. Help me, Brontë, I willed. Help me.

'Were you?'

I cleared my throat. 'Em, no.'

'No? Are you sure?'

He looked furious. Furious and crazy. Humour him.

'I don't know how to tell you this, Paul . . .'

He leaned towards me, his eyes gleaming. 'Yes? Tell me.'

'Em, well, em, Leland's dead.'

Darkness passed across his face. He straightened up and began to pace again. 'So you say.'

Answer him or keep quiet? Quick! Which? Keep quiet.

'Well, actually, I don't say—'

'Aha! So you—'

'Leland's dead! I went to his funeral. So did you. His body was identified by my mother. I think you've gone mad!'

'What?'

'I think you've gone mad and you're scaring me!'

He stopped in his tracks. I was visibly shaking.

'Oh, God. I'm sorry. We thought, we thought that you knew. I'm sorry.'

'Paul, please go home. Please.'

'We thought that you knew. We thought that somebody did. We thought it might be you.'

I was trembling. He thought the ghost of my brother was killing women.

He sat opposite me on the coffee table and sighed.

'We thought you were protecting him.'

'Leland's dead. He's *dead*.'

He didn't respond. He stared into the distance, angry turmoil twisting his features.

I swallowed. In for a penny . . .

'Who thought I was "protecting" him?'

He gave me a sidelong glance and leaned forward, putting his head in his hands. I almost felt I should comfort him but it galled me to do so. His accusations were thoroughly insulting, downright offensive.

320

And how dare he scare me like that? He had some explaining to do. I cleared my throat assertively.

'Correct me if I am wrong, but from what I understand of our little discussion, you either think Leland's ghost is killing people – perhaps not the most plausible of theories – or that Leland isn't actually dead.'

He threw me a harried nod.

'Sorry? Which is it? The ghost or the resurrected?'

'We don't think he's dead,' he muttered wearily.

'And how long have you been of that opinion?'

'About a year.'

'A year! What was all that about – he's got a disciple, it's somebody pretending to be him – then?'

'We genuinely thought someone was protecting him!' he shot back. 'Until, well, until another agenda was indicated.'

'What agenda?'

He didn't answer.

'How does that imply Leland's alive?'

Silence.

'You think somebody in the family is shielding him and now you're trying to narrow it down.'

He closed his eyes for the briefest moment before he agreed.

'Charming. Well, I think Leland is dead and you're clutching at straws.'

'But your mother lied!'

'But if you knew her, then it wouldn't seem out of character. If there is something unsavoury in the offing, she will quite blatantly deny its existence. I was annoyed that she had deliberately not mentioned such a seemingly small occurrence. However, she had no way of knowing that subsequently it would grow out of all proportion. But it didn't surprise me.'

321

'Honestly?'

'Cross my heart.'

'You know, for a time after his suicide, we thought he was still alive,' he said, almost conversationally.

'Good God! Are you all mad? My mother, Lady Georgina Maxwell, identified his body!'

'She could have been . . . mistaken.'

I eyed him suspiciously. 'Why don't you have the body exhumed?'

'What? An urn of ashes?'

'He was buried, Paul. You were at the funeral. You took a photograph of me.' The truth hit me. He hadn't thought I was pretty, he had thought I was part of it.

'Yes, he was buried, but in 1997 the body was exhumed and cremated. Don't tell me you didn't know?'

Again, I opened my mouth in horror.

I had no idea that she had him dug up and cremated. What on earth for? But I didn't want to go there – to the rational explanation.

'You had no idea,' he said quietly.

I racked my brain for such a case. My expertise in Scottish law didn't cover this area. Normally, a body could be exhumed due to fresh evidence of suspicious circumstances and, after a further post-mortem, reburied or cremated, but only by petition to the Sheriff Court.

If what Paul said was true, in 1997, there were no new, suspicious circumstances.

'What reason did she give for his exhumation? I mean, surely it would require a court order? Did she have a second post-mortem? Did she suspect he had been murdered?'

He smiled faintly. 'Erin Paterson, lawyer, is back in the building.'

'Oh, fuck off patronising me. Back to my point, did she have another autopsy?'

'No.'

I was afraid he'd say that. If she had, then I could have argued that she suspected foul play, but without a second autopsy she was more probably eradicating any evidence. DNA evidence. No matter how I wished to disguise that fact.

'Oh, God,' I sighed.

I couldn't go on. I was exhausted and teetering on the edge of massive depression. Was anyone trustworthy or honest?

'Are you OK?' Paul asked.

'Get real. What about the first autopsy? There must be something from it.'

'Nothing to prove he wasn't who your mother said he was. Mid-twenties, Caucasian male. Nobody was looking for a body double.'

'Nothing else? Distinguishing marks? Would they keep any samples?'

Paul shook his head.

'Do you have the post-mortem report?' I asked.

'Yes, but I don't think you . . .'

'Paul! If Leland's alive . . . God, it doesn't bear thinking about! Reading the details of his death would be a relief.'

If there were anything unusual in his autopsy, I would spot it.

I knew Leland's body. It had been seared into my soul and had robbed me of my life.

EIGHTEEN

The actual cause of death was suffocation by asphyxiation. It was noted as 'wet drowning' from aspiration of water into the lungs.

Previously, I had worked on a compensation claim that involved 'dry drowning'. That referred to laryngospasm, the sudden constriction and closure of the airways, caused by liquid in the throat. It wasn't strictly an accurate description of what most people thought of as drowning because no liquid entered the lungs.

Drowning of either sort was a diagnosis of exclusion, based on the circumstances of death. It was difficult to determine the manner of death, be it accident, murder or suicide. All victims died from suffocation, but exactly how it had occurred was not easily identified by an autopsy.

I skimmed through his autopsy looking for anything unusual, a recently received injury or an unexplained one. Nothing struck me.

. . . *cerebral anoxia* . . . lack of oxygen to the brain.
. . . *pulmonary edema* . . . waterlogged lungs.

When he began to decompose, gas had formed within the tissues which gradually caused his body to rise to the surface. He had been in the water a long time, two months, I recalled.

Even after the suicide note, Mother had hoped against hope that he would turn up, safe and well. Was karma repaying me for not sharing that hope?

In the cold water off the Scottish coast, the gas had

formed slowly and his body had remained submerged, although rigor mortis had set in relatively quickly, caused by the depletion of adenosine triphosphate (ATP) from his muscles. That was common in drowning due to the violent struggle victims could not suppress, even if they wished. They would fight for air, taking in more water, gasping and striving in a vicious cycle until respiration stopped. A slow and agonising death.

Leland was a strong swimmer, athletic, and the skiff was seen over a mile offshore around the time he went missing. In the icy, deep water he wouldn't have stood a chance.

His toenails and fingernails had loosened and some had come away completely. All standard, until I turned the page.

. . . perianal abrasions and contusions . . . penetration of the anal sphincters . . . lacerations of the rectum, recent and healed . . . presence of acid phosphatase in rectum . . .

I read it again. And again.

He had been sodomised. And not just that day. I didn't know what acid phosphatase was.

Paul was in the kitchen and looked expectantly at me as I entered.

'Do you know what acid phosphatase is? What does it indicate?'

'It's an enzyme the prostate produces. In sexual terms, it pinpoints ejaculation that has occurred within the last twenty-four hours.'

'Have you read this?' I said sharply.

'Of course.'

'This says . . . it appears that he was sodomised . . .'

'Regularly, from what I read.'

I sat down at Paul's kitchen table and struggled for words.

'But that's . . . just . . . so . . . it's just not . . . Leland. Leland was a raging homophobe!'

'Not according to that.'

'I know you'll think I'm being . . . but honestly. He was absolutely anti-gay. It simply doesn't feel . . . true.'

'What about the physical descriptions? Did you find anything in them?'

'No. He was decomposing. He was approximately the same height, build, weight, age. There were no distinguishing features in the report that would lead me to question its veracity.'

'So, it was probably Leland's body?' Paul asked.

I reached across the table and took Paul's hand. He looked as surprised as I was, but it was the only way to make him see how strongly I felt.

'Paul. I knew him. I knew his tastes. Penetration was not high on the list and most certainly was not anal. Anything to do with that disgusted him. I can only tell you that something says to me that this might be a breakthrough. I know it's not much to go on. Jennifer Longmuir, who you were pretty certain was his first and his alone, was not sodomised. That came later.'

'OK, but wasn't Sophie Holbrook . . . ?'

'Yes. But Abigail and Lucy weren't,' I sighed and released his hand. Damn, I thought. Damn, damn, damn.

'But with Abigail we reckoned he was disturbed. Remember? Only the one finger was severed? Maybe he hadn't got round to it,' Paul argued.

'What about Lucy?' I said.

Paul lowered his eyes.

'Paul?' I could feel myself tensing. Not another body blow. Please, God, I prayed, give me a break.

'Lucy's different. You and I both know it.'

I hesitated before I said the words.

'She's another Alison. He's made it personal again. Another reason I don't think this is Leland's autopsy.'

'Would you swear to that?' he asked.

'Swear to what? Everything in the autopsy is correct. I could only swear to my particular prior knowledge.'

'There're some things that I should tell you, things we gleaned from interviews and surveillance. The problem is they throw doubt on your theory.'

'But it isn't my theory, it was yours and Kelman's. All I've said is that one angle of the autopsy doesn't seem true, but people change, their sexual appetites change. I could be wrong.'

He weighed me up but I was already miles ahead.

'What is it you and Kelman want from me? To officially cast doubt on Leland's death, so that you can repair your own reputations?'

'What do you mean by that?' he asked.

'You've already admitted that the secret-sect hypothesis was treated with derision. And DS Marshall mentioned that Kelman refused to let it go. Are you hoping my intervention will give it some validity?'

'DSI Kelman is a professional detective. I doubt your endorsement would mean much,' he sneered.

I gave him a little smile. Paul looked huffy, but he was lucky. Five days ago I would have made him squirm endlessly.

'So, you do need my corroboration. OK. What else did you want to tell me?'

'Jonathan Moncreiffe frequented gay clubs and bars. He was most probably a closet homosexual. We think he had a serious crush on Leland. He followed Leland everywhere. Rarely would you find Leland without Jonathan close by.'

'Were any of the others gay?' I asked.

'Certainly not openly. Although Frederick Blythe-Gordon was hauled up for buggery at boarding school.'

If that wasn't Leland they fished out of the North Sea, then who was it? Why fake your death? The answer to that was simple: Leland had gone underground. You can't be the chief suspect in serial murders when you are officially dead. But whose body was it?

'Paul, do you remember telling me you thought there might have been a power struggle? Let's take that one step further. Leland could have murdered our John Doe because of his homosexuality. The group disintegrates and then there are scores to be settled.'

'But only one person was seen in the skiff. And how did he get back to shore?'

'It's a long shot, but we were all taught to scuba-dive. He had his own wet and dry suits. He could have swum. Also, the victim could have been trussed up, incapacitated somehow, on the floor of the skiff.'

'There were no indications of that. No ligature marks, no drugs in the toxicology.'

I thought of the fascination Leland aroused in people. The infatuations he generated in countless girlfriends of mine.

I could almost see him seducing the poor sap with a kind word – significant eye contact, a suggestive invitation.

'Whose sperm was found in the body?' I asked Paul.

'Nobody that we had a DNA record of, and none of our suspects. Why?'

'I'm not sure. It's just an . . . image I get. I spent the best part of my younger life scrutinising Leland's

328

every move. Watching for the signs. It was how I survived. My only defence was pre-emption.'

'An image? Do you remember one of the guys?'

'No. It's just I can see . . . I could see how Leland could beguile an admirer, with an implicate promise, into lying still, hidden, on the bottom of a boat. He would make them excited about their clandestine actions.'

'Was that what it was like?' he whispered.

'Not for me . . . for Brontë. She was so young, so easily manipulated, but it wasn't her fault . . .'

'Oh, God, Erin. I'm so sorry,' he breathed.

'So am I,' I said.

NINETEEN

Although I was slightly uneasy with Brontë present, I made the introductions. I knew it was mean, but I didn't trust her entirely, and she kept interrupting with daft questions. At least her hair was nice now.

We sat at my dining table, in the recess of my living room, and went over the lease, partnership agreement, proposals and finances. Everything went smoothly apart from Brontë's witterings and Douglas's distraction. He was very distracted by her. I wished I had some bromide to slip in their tea.

By six o'clock we were discussing staff recruitment and smaller details.

'We can either use a recruitment firm or do direct advertising,' Liz suggested.

'Direct advertising will be cheaper. There's bound to be a few graduates out there who've had re-sits, or those who passed last summer and haven't yet found a traineeship,' I agreed.

'What about NQs?' Douglas said.

'What's an NQ?' Brontë asked.

'Newly qualified. We could go for direct advertising and, if nothing turns up, then go to recruitment,' I proposed.

'What does newly qualified mean?' Brontë asked.

How had Brontë managed to spend her entire life around a family of lawyers and not pick up any of the lingo?

'It means that they have finished their traineeship.'

'What's a traineeship?'

'Give me strength! When you graduate, you spend two years as a trainee, then you become newly qualified.'

Karen was quick to avert a fight. 'We can easily get secretaries through the newspapers.'

Brontë's eyes lit up. 'You need secretaries? What do they have to do?'

'The normal things secretaries do!' I screeched.

'I can type! And I can file.'

My heart sank. I knew what was coming next.

'I could be your secretary.'

'That's a brilliant idea!' Douglas said, until he saw my expression.

Brontë stood up triumphantly and dashed over to my computer.

'I'll show you! I can do sixty words a minute.'

I put my head in my hands and muttered under my breath. Brontë working for me? It didn't bear thinking about.

Liz piped up, 'What about a name?'

'I've thought of one,' Douglas said. 'Paterson, Miller and Thomson.'

I sneered at him, 'Great, Douglas. It would be shortened to PMT.'

'Erin!' Brontë called. 'There's something wrong with your computer.'

Irritated, I stood up and went over to Brontë. She was ineffectually wiggling the mouse.

'What did you do?'

'Nothing. I just switched it on and nothing happened. I heard it boot up.'

I stuck my head under the desk and could see the little green light was on. I wiggled the mouse too, but

331

nothing happened. Douglas came over and looked under the desk, just as I spotted the fault. I pressed the button for the monitor and the screen came to life.

I winked at Douglas. 'Proof that artificial intelligence is no match for natural stupidity?'

If we employed Brontë, we could legitimately register as a charity.

'We've thought of a name,' Karen said, as Douglas and I sat back down.

'Paterson Associates.'

'Paterson's might object,' I said. It was a huge compliment, but I wasn't sure if Companies House would allow it.

Liz shook her head. 'But they don't exist any more. It's now Cohen Paterson. I don't see a conflict.'

'Are you sure you're OK with that? Just having my name?'

'Yes. You're the player. It's confident and it shows you're not shrinking away into obscurity. Punters will recognise the name, know where you are and instruct you.'

'Let's take a vote,' Karen said. 'Those in favour.'

They all raised their hands. A smile forced itself across my face.

'We're in business!' Douglas exclaimed, and did a high five with Liz. 'To Paterson Associates!'

'You're all mad,' I sighed.

Champagne was called for. I always kept a couple of bottles chilled. I went to the kitchen and collected a bottle and champagne flutes.

We clinked glasses and sipped champagne, congratulating ourselves on our ability to rise to the occasion. My little nagging voice muttered in the background, 'no clients, no fees, ultimate failure', but dutifully I smiled. It was nearly seven thirty before they left, high on champagne and optimism.

I shut the door and flopped down on the sofa. Brontë crashed down beside me.

'Can I come and work with you?' she whined.

'Work *for* me. There is a difference.'

I yawned and flicked on the TV.

'Well, can I? Please?' Brontë snuggled into my neck like a gigantic cat.

With pained resignation, I let her snuggle.

'Only if you behave yourself. If you're late, sloppy, difficult, or anything, and I mean anything that I don't like, then I'll sack you.'

'I promise, I'll be brilliant. I swear.' She gave me a big soppy kiss on the cheek. I knew I shouldn't have let her have any champagne.

'OK, you'll be brilliant. Now shut up so I can hear the news,' I grumped half-heartedly.

I flicked through the channels until I got to the news. It was a dull report on GM food crops.

'This is boring,' Brontë moaned and raised her head off my shoulder.

We watched for another fifteen minutes, until Brontë's huffing and puffing became unbearable and I switched channels.

'Can we watch *Mad About You*?'

I tossed the remote control at her.

'Do you want something to eat?'

'Yes. What have you got?'

I thought about it. 'Nothing. Shall I get a Chinese?'

'Yes. Can I have a glass of wine?'

'No. You've had more than enough.'

'Oh, come on! We're celebrating.'

I pulled a face and traipsed through to the kitchen.

I opened a bottle of white wine and then I called for a home delivery from the local Chinese restaurant. I realised that we hadn't done this for years.

My sister and I hadn't chosen to be in each other's company, watching TV, drinking wine and waiting for food, for such a long time that I couldn't remember when it had last occurred. I wondered if Brontë realised it too.

She was sprawled on the sofa, so I sat down with her legs across me.

I stared vacantly at the TV, but didn't take any of it in. I had drunk only one glass of champagne but I felt jittery and nervous. I had so many monumental betrayals to process.

Brontë squinted at me. 'You've gone all brownish.'

'Self-tanning lotion.'

'Can I use some?' Brontë swung her feet off me and sat up expectantly.

We went through to my en suite where Brontë rifled nosily in my cosmetics drawer. I passed her a fresh hand towel.

'You need to exfoliate first.'

'What are you wearing to the ball?' she asked, as she rubbed the exfoliating cream into her face.

'The black Armani. Have you seen it?'

'Yeah. Backless? Very sexy.' She splashed water everywhere as she cleaned off the scrub. I subtly wiped it up.

'Have you put self-tanner on your back?' she mumbled, as she vigorously dried her face.

'No.'

'You'll have to, or you'll look really odd with a brown face.'

'OK. When I've done your face, you can do my back,' I said bravely.

I hadn't been undressed in front of Brontë since we were small.

Brontë smiled and perched on the edge of the sink unit, her face held up expectantly. I carefully rubbed the lotion into her skin, making sure that there would be no streaks.

'Now you,' she said.

I pulled my sweater over my head and slipped it off, turning my back to her as I did so.

'You'll need to take your bra off too,' she said lightly.

I hesitated and then undid it.

'Lift up your hair. Wait. Hold on. Here.' She passed a scrunchie over my shoulder. I tied up my hair as she began to rub the lotion into my neck, shoulders, back and arms.

'You're a walking skeleton,' she muttered. 'I never knew you had a birthmark on your shoulder blade. It's shaped like a strawberry.'

'I think it's called a strawberry birthmark.'

'It's faint but really cute. You should have it tattooed.'

'Yeah, right.'

'I've got a tattoo,' she giggled.

I was appalled. 'You have not!'

'I do! I'll show you in a minute. We're nearly done. There.'

She passed me the hand towel over my shoulder. 'Hide your modesty until it dries. The label says not to get it on clothing.'

I tucked the towel under my arms while Brontë washed her hands.

'Let's see your tattoo, then?' I said, but the sound of the buzzer interrupted me.

'Food!' Brontë whooped, and dived out of the en suite.

'You'll have to go down for it,' I called after her.

Her disembodied voice called back, 'OK. Where's your wallet?'

'Handbag!'

I heard her buzz them into the building and tell them she was on her way down. I wandered through to the kitchen to get plates and cutlery, still clasping the little towel to my bosom. It felt very strange to be in such a state of undress.

Less than thirty seconds later, there was a knock at the door. I rolled my eyes – Brontë had forgotten the money.

'You're a halfwit!' I joked, as I opened the door.

Paul looked me up and down. 'Thanks.'

I hugged the towel closer. 'I thought you were Brontë.'

'She got out the lift as I got in. She said to knock.' Paul looked faintly wicked. 'A promise of Chinese food?'

'Oh. Come in.'

I stood aside to let him past and then shuffled back towards my bedroom.

'Why are you wearing a towel?' he asked.

'Em, Brontë was putting some lotion on my back.'

He was all false concern. 'Have you hurt it? Let me take a look.'

'No!' I squeaked, and dived away.

I found a black cotton shirt to put on. Brontë was back with the Chinese takeaway by the time I resurfaced.

'Can I eat in the living room? I want to watch *ER*,' Brontë said.

'As long as you don't spill anything,' I warned.

'Yes, Mum,' she grumbled, and took a tray through.

Paul sat down at the kitchen table. 'I hate eating off my knees.'

I sat down. 'So do I.'

He piled rice on to my plate.

'Did you speak to Kelman?'

'Yes. I told him what you thought of the autopsy. He seemed a bit put out. I don't know . . . He said he would call tomorrow to go over it. Is that OK?'

'I've got to take Brontë to the hospital for twelve and do some other things, but I'm free the rest of the time.'

Paul passed me a carton of chicken in black-bean sauce.

I stared at it and felt sick.

Leland was out there, somewhere. Watching. Waiting.

Lucy was a warning. But not just to me.

I tried not to dwell on the thought that fought its way to the surface every time I was stationary. I tried to force it back into its allotted space, as I had done with so many of my fears. But no amount of pushing or distraction could dislodge it.

Prior to Lucy's murder, only three people knew she had seen Leland.

Lucy, Lucy's mother and my own mother.

I ached for reprieve from my insight, my perception of her death.

TWENTY

Brontë shook me.

'Erin, wake up.'

'What is it?' I groaned, turned over, and felt like a truck had hit me.

'It's half past ten. You've got to take me to the hospital.'

Meanly, she pulled back my duvet and let out all the warmth.

'Get a taxi,' I muttered, and curled into a ball.

I felt rotten, as if I was incubating something, but she tugged at my arm and managed to pull me right off the bed.

'Fuck off!' I barked, and struggled to my feet. My legs were jelly. I lurched in the direction of my en suite.

'You look like crap,' Brontë commented. Never a truer word.

I had a shower and staggered back out at eleven. Brontë was now wearing my black leather trousers, black crew neck and one black boot.

I glared at her and flopped down on the bed. 'I think I've got flu coming on.'

Brontë pulled me into a sitting position. 'Hurry up!'

Grumpily, I went into my dressing room. Evidently, a mini tornado had passed through.

'Brontë, if you're going to stay here, you'll have to be tidier,' I snapped.

'I'm not staying after tonight.'

She lounged against the doorframe and watched as

I put all the clothes she had raked through back into the wardrobes.

'I phoned Mum last night. They're coming back today. They've asked me to come home on Saturday, because they want to go back to the cottage. Max is staying the night at Martha's, so I can still come to the ball.'

I saw one of my other evening dresses hanging over my Armani. I indicated it with my head. 'Are you planning on wearing that?'

'Yeah. I tried on some of the others, but . . . what size are you?'

'Eight to ten,' I said airily.

'That explains it. I'm a ten,' she sighed, and left me to clear up her mess.

Throughout the time I was getting dressed and drying my hair, my stomach made terrible noises. If the psycho didn't kill me, circumstances beyond my control were lining up to do it.

Impatiently, Brontë was waiting for me in the living room.

'Hurry up,' she urged again.

I drove like a lunatic to the South Side. It was typical that I – who hardly ever drank and who ate so carefully – should catch something, and Brontë, who abused her system at every conceivable opportunity, wasn't affected.

I was determined not to park in the street and tempt fate by getting another note, so I drove round and round the pathetic car park at the Victoria Infirmary for ten minutes before we snatched a space. Brontë rolled her eyes at me in irritation. I told her that I was afraid my car, which was still full of boxes, would be broken into. I thought it politic not to mention that the killer could be shadowing us.

I sat in the waiting area while Brontë was examined. I flicked through an old *Golf Monthly* because it was the only magazine that didn't look like it had been mauled by a Rottweiler. I tried to concentrate on an article about American golfing holidays to take my mind off my grumbling stomach. Mount Vesuvius in miniature.

'Miss Paterson?'

I looked up and saw the young doctor that had originally treated Brontë.

'How's your sister doing? She shouldn't have discharged herself so quickly.'

I smiled pleasantly and he perched on the seat beside me. 'She's remarkably well. Her foot seems to be on the mend.'

'How's she coping with . . . the other things?'

'She seems fine, but maybe she's *too* fine,' I added significantly.

'Are they any further forward with catching him? A detective came by yesterday to copy her files.'

'She's quite reluctant about getting the police . . . Surely they already have copies?'

'Yes, but he said it may be linked to another case.'

'Were you on duty? Can you remember his name?'

Leaning away from me slightly, he viewed me speculatively.

'Please, it's very important,' I said.

'A detective Kelman – I can't remember his rank – but you didn't hear that from me.'

After he left, I sat with the open *Golf Monthly* on my lap and asked myself again and again, why would Kelman want Brontë's file?

Brontë came back to the waiting area half an hour later and startled me out of my daze.

'I have to come back next week,' she commented casually.

We wandered back towards my car in silence. I wasn't able to engage in conversation because I couldn't stop my mind from racing.

Why would Kelman want Brontë's file? What was he up to? What did he suspect?

'You OK?' Brontë asked.

I shrugged lamely. 'Mm. Just thinking.'

'What about?'

'Nothing.'

'Oh.' There was a tiny bleat in her voice.

'I'm sorry. I was miles away.'

'Wish I was.'

'Personally, I think you're remarkable. I'd have gone to pieces after what you've been through. I would be locked in my room, frightened to ever come out.'

'I am frightened,' she said quietly. 'But I can only remain OK if I ignore it. When I think about it, I just want to ... to die ...'

'Don't say that. I couldn't stand it if anything happened to you. You're all I've got.'

When we arrived back at my building, Paul's car wasn't in the car park.

Inside my apartment the air was stale. It reminded me of that fateful morning only one week before.

I opened all the doors on to the terrace and let the brisk October air circulate throughout the loft. Brontë grumbled and bickered about it being cold, but I was blowing away the cobwebs.

She sat on the sofa, wrapped in a duvet, aimlessly watching a series of dreadful American chat shows. I found myself fascinated by the appalling people who were so thrilled to air their dirty laundry in such a public manner. Our warped family situation would have been manna from heaven to these pedlars of inanity.

We had been back for over an hour before I noticed that my answering machine was blinking with new messages. I could hardly be bothered to retrieve them, for a stifling cloud of lethargy had enveloped me. It was that rainy Sunday afternoon feeling, when all one wanted to do was eat rubbish and watch old movies. I hadn't felt like this for years, since Christmas holidays when I still lived at home. I wondered if living with Brontë had a contagious side effect.

There was a message from Liz, arranging a lease-signing meeting at the surveyors for Monday and also firming up the details for the ball.

Paul's voice was hoarse and tired.

'Erin, I've spoken to Kelman again and he wants to arrange a meeting. I told him to call you direct. Hope that's OK. I'll see you later. Bye.'

Kelman's message was next. 'It's Detective Superintendent Kelman. Paul asked me to ring. I'll call round later, maybe around six. Bye.'

I glanced at my watch. It was knocking on four. Six o'clock was cutting it fine. We were due to be at the ball at seven. I would have to be dressed and ready before he came.

'Tell tale tit, throat got slit, can't hear her shout, cause her tongue's cut out!'

Brontë twisted around on the sofa and stared at me. 'What was that?'

'A message. It's all distorted.' I shrugged, but my heart was racing.

Lucy Grant's injuries weren't common knowledge; he could only be referring to her.

Brontë came and me stood beside me.

'It sounded like a nursery rhyme. Play it again.'

I pressed play and we simultaneously bent closer to the answerphone.

'Tell tale tit, throat got slit, can't hear her shout, cause her tongue's cut out!'

'He said "throat got slit" . . .' Fear strangled Brontë's voice. 'He said "tongue cut out!"'

'It's just a prank. It'll be a kid playing a prank,' I said, but Brontë grabbed both my arms and squeezed tightly.

'It's not. It's him! It's the killer!' She looked about wildly as if she half expected him to be with us. 'He's coming after us! What will we do? What will we do?'

I was shocked. How did Brontë know about the killer? Who had told her?

'How do you know about that?'

'I read the files. The ones in your room.'

'Oh, Brontë, you shouldn't have. Not in your state. You've only just come out of hospital. . .'

'For God's sake, Erin! You should phone the police and tell them. He phoned you from Lucy's mobile. He's not some random guy! He's a fucking serial killer!'

I sighed heavily. Should I tell her the truth? Tell her it might actually be Leland? That would scare the wits out of her. It did me.

'We'll wait,' I said eventually.

'Wait until he comes? Are you mad? He'll kill us!'

I went to the open terrace doors, letting the wind whip my hair. 'There's nothing else we can do.'

'What?' she wailed. 'What is going on? All these detectives? There's something else, isn't there?'

I stared across the city, which was dappled in golden sunlight that flickered and plunged into shadow with each rolling cloud.

'It's about things that happen and however much they don't seem to be connected, they are. Invisible tentacles creep across apparently random lives, binding them together and crushing them.'

'I don't understand you,' she whispered.

'Neither do I.'

I closed the terrace doors and went back to the answering machine. I turned the volume up full and played the message again. Brontë looked aghast.

I played it again and again and again, until it sounded pathetically comical, until it held no threat.

'Do you recognise the voice?' I asked her.

'No. Do you?'

'He's a right prick, though, isn't he?' I said recklessly.

'We have an A-class dickhead on our hands,' Brontë said.

I was blasée. 'We've been surrounded by dickheads all our lives, what's so special about this one?'

She pulled a scary face. 'Apparently, he's coming to get us.'

I giggled and nudged her. 'Why don't you go and have a long, hot, foam bath and get ready for the ball?'

'Are you sure? Don't you want me to stay down here with you?'

'No, we're safe here. Go and get ready.'

She shuffled across my living room and went upstairs. We both knew it was naive bravado, but the alternative was worse. Terror and paralysis.

We had reached an unspoken agreement. If we could inspire belief in each other, however unfounded and transparent, then we still had a fighting chance.

One could only remain terrified for so long before the fear ran out and was replaced by something else. In my case, it was replaced with a sneering superiority, which had been instilled in me from the cradle. He was a creep and therefore beneath my contempt. I locked all the doors, though. I had run out of fear but I wasn't stupid.

I went to my own en suite and had a long shower, super-conditioning my hair so that it would be malleable enough for me to put it up in a French roll. Normally, for a ball I would have booked a hairdresser, but normality had gone out the window. I rubbed scented body lotion into my skin, then dried my hair and set it in big heated rollers.

Purposely, I hadn't focused on the night ahead because I realised it could be quite stressful. Former colleagues from the now defunct Paterson's might be less than gracious, and my recent brush with the law and media-driven notoriety would titillate many others. I needed to look as beautiful as possible. That single confidence would offer me superficial support.

I went into my bedroom and sat on the bed, wrapped in my fluffy towelling robe.

I toyed with the phone and finally dialled his mobile. He answered quickly.

'Paul Gabriel.'

'It's Erin. I just thought I would give you an update. Can you speak for a minute?'

'Of course. What's up?'

'Kelman got copies of Brontë's files from the hospital yesterday and our mystery caller left another weird nursery rhyme on my answering machine.'

'*Jeezus*. Hold on a sec'.' I could hear him speaking to someone in the background.

'Kelman's here. He's going to come over. I'll be stuck here for a while, so I might have to meet you at the ball. I'll be there by seven thirty, at the latest.'

'Will you have time to change?'

'Yep. I've got my tux here. I'll grab a shower in the newsroom if it's getting late. Don't worry, I won't let you down.'

'OK. When will Kelman be here?'

What was Kelman doing in the newsroom with Paul? There was more talking in the background.

'At about six-thirty. Bye.' He rang off before I had a chance to say that six thirty would be too late.

I glanced at my reflection in my dressing-table mirror. I looked tired and middle-aged.

I padded through to the living room and called Brontë, telling her that Kelman would be here in less than an hour. Then I booked a black cab for six forty-five. As the hostess of the table, it was *de rigueur* to arrive early in order to greet my guests.

Brontë came down from the top floor swathed in her duvet.

'I wish you hadn't left the doors open. It's freezing up there. I need a medicinal drink to warm up.'

'Some excuse,' I jeered, and followed her into the kitchen. 'Have some hot tea.'

'Get real.' She flung open my fridge. 'You've only got champagne.'

She hauled out one of the bottles I had put in earlier.

'Brontë! You'll be drunk.'

'Not if you share it.'

She tore off the foil, removed the wire and popped the cork in five seconds flat. Obviously, a practised hand.

She passed me a glass of fizz and clinked it against hers.

'Here's to you and your new firm.'

I knew I shouldn't drink it, particularly since I'd had

an upset stomach earlier and still hadn't eaten anything, but regardless I took a sip.

'Let's get dressed together,' she said happily and went through to my bedroom. There was a reckless feeling of freaky holiday.

I slipped on my dress, which clung like a second skin. I sorted the long sleeves, fixed the halter neck and put on my black slingbacks before I allowed myself a peek in the dressing-room mirror. I gave a little gasp.

My hip bones protruded. Maybe I was too thin? I examined myself from every angle, while listening to Brontë huffing and puffing her way into her dress.

'Erin! Can you come and help me?' she called from the bedroom. I glided through with careful steps.

'Wow,' she breathed. 'You look stunning. Apart from the rollers.'

I smiled and zipped her up with difficulty. She was wearing my black, fitted, silk number with the fishtail skirt. It was tight. Very tight.

'I don't know if I can sit down!' she giggled wildly, finished her champagne in one and then wiggled back to the kitchen for a refill.

There was only one way to stop Brontë drinking the whole bottle, short of duct-taping her mouth: drink some more of it myself. I sashayed after her like her geisha twin.

We had another glass each and then she downed the rest. I felt high and courageous. I would wow them tonight. I would be the life and soul. I would rise triumphant. Paterson's without the Paterson – what use was that? There was a new Paterson's in town.

We giggled girlishly and Brontë put my hair up into a seductive, tousled French roll. She left little wispy strands at the nape of my neck and my hairline, softening my face sexily. Then she started on my make-up. I was transformed. My eyes were glittering, from both the champagne and the renewed delight in my sister's company.

We didn't hear the door buzzer until it buzzed relentlessly.

'That must be Kelman!' I gasped, and rushed through to let him in.

'Taxi for Paterson,' a voice said.

I told him we would be down in a moment. Time had run away with me and Kelman was late.

'Brontë, the taxi's here. You'll have to go ahead without me. Kelman's late but he's due at any minute. I'll try not to keep everyone waiting. But make sure all our guests know who you are and which table is ours, buy them champagne or whatever they want . . .' I gushed anxiously, as I pressed my credit card into her hand.

She gave me a reassuring squeeze on my arm. 'Don't worry, Erin. We'll hold the fort.'

As she left I told her she looked lovely, which she did, in a blonde punk-rocker kind of way.

I paced around my apartment, glancing at my watch every two seconds.

Where was he? I couldn't wait for ever and I didn't have a contact number for him. I rang Paul's mobile again, only to be told to leave a message. I left a brief one, explaining that Kelman was late and I couldn't wait much longer.

I sat for twenty minutes considering what to do. I wanted to give Kelman Lucy's letter and I wanted to make him squirm. I was pretty sure he was the policeman who had purloined my keys and taken Paul's files. It was transparent that he didn't trust me because he had put me under surveillance. And Paul had admitted that they thought I was involved.

I tried Paul's mobile again but got the answering service. Where were they?

It was past seven-thirty and I had a difficult decision to make. Go to the ball to support the new firm or wait for Kelman?

In a moment of utmost vanity, I decided to go. When would I get another chance to show my critics what I was made of? When would I get such an opportunity to show Paul how attractive I was?

I called another cab and scrawled a brief note to stick on my door, telling Kelman he could find me at the Hilton and that I had changed my locks.

TWENTY-ONE

It was well past eight by the time I got to the hotel. I couldn't have arrived at a worse moment.

The toastmaster for the evening was a Scottish TV comic and my sad attempt at sneaking in unnoticed was the type of thing he thrived on.

'Delighted you're able to join us, Miss Paterson.' His mike hissed a little as he spoke. 'Did they let you out early for good behaviour?'

Laughter.

'No. For decking the warden,' I shot back blithely, while frantically searching the ballroom for our table and relative anonymity.

'Glad to see you've still got a sense of humour!'

'That's something I've never been accused of before,' I twinkled back girlishly.

I was hardy aware of the ripples of laughter my reply received, because my heart lurched when Paul stood up and beckoned me to our table. He looked dashingly handsome in his tuxedo.

'A hand for Erin Paterson, ladies and gentlemen. A truly unique talent!'

The round of applause surprised me, and I was glad to find my chair and at least five pairs of welcoming eyes.

'I am so sorry I'm late,' I gushed to the corporate guests. 'I really was helping the police with their enquiries. Again!'

There was a murmur of laughter amongst them, and

I thought, this could be OK. I had 'mentioned the war'. The taboo wouldn't hang over us for the rest of the evening.

There was a round of quiet introductions and re-introductions. The comic talked up the charity side of the evening, encouraging us to 'dig deep'. I used those moments to get both my breath and equilibrium back.

Paul was seated beside me. He wore that suppressed anxious expression I was becoming so familiar with.

'How did it go?' he whispered.

'He didn't turn up. I've left two messages on your answering service to say so. I really don't know what's happened.'

'That's odd.'

'I waited for as long as I could. I did leave him a note saying that we were here.'

Paul frowned and poured me some champagne, while I made apologetic eye contact with Liz and Douglas.

Bruce Lindsey, a director with one of the big energy companies, was on my left. I was mortified when I couldn't remember which one.

'So, Erin, tell me about this BBC profile thing?' he asked.

I blinked and smiled demurely, while thinking, What?

'Oh, come on, don't be bashful! Paul was telling me all about it. How they're going to follow the setting-up and teething problems of the new firm. Paterson Associates, eh? That's one in the eye for the old man. Sort of like that airport fly-on-the-wall thing they do. Fantastic free advertising. You're a smart cookie getting the Beeb on board.'

I smiled fixedly and gave Paul's ankle a swift kick under the table.

'Is there a film crew here tonight?' Bruce swivelled round in his chair to check behind him.

Paul leaned over me slightly and said in a stage whisper, 'Unfortunately, not. Couldn't get all the parties to agree. I think they thought it would be bad publicity for them. You know, the underhanded manner in which it was all arranged.' He sat back up and fixed his napkin. 'Personally, I thought it would give them the chance to air their side, but Bruce, I'm sure I don't have to tell someone in your line of business, that there are always people who refuse to recognise the bigger picture.'

It was Bruce's turn to do the mock secrecy. 'You are so right. Sometimes the old guard simply won't move with the times. It's all about media image these days, and that costs. Paul, if you don't mind, I'll give you my card and if you fancy doing some brainstorming about a profile on the nuclear industry, give me a buzz.'

I was astounded. Paul was schmoozing like an old pro, he was a natural.

'Erin, Liz says you're turning your hand to corporate. How do you think that will sit with all your compensation work?' asked Bajit Singh.

'Well, Bajit, I've been training Douglas here for four years now. In fact, before all the nastiness at the old firm, he was about to be let loose on the clients. What Douglas doesn't know about compensation, you could write on a postage stamp. I'll still offer him my advice, purely as a consultant, but I won't be hands on.

'I'm planning to become a solicitor advocate, which will allow the firm to take on high-profile corporate work, High Court and all that, but also keep a tight

352

lid on the client's costs. We should be able to keep it predominately in-house, and therefore reduce the fees on counsel. We also have an A-class corporate lawyer in Liz.'

'Yes. Liz and I have worked together before. Does that mean you will offer cheaper rates?'

'Let's say, better value for money. The overheads will be lower. I think that very large professional firms reach a plateau, where any savings from economies of scale are effectively lost. Obviously, that doesn't apply to the retail sector.' I alluded to Mr Singh's very successful sports-equipment business.

The first course arrived. He nodded in agreement and began to discuss out-of-town retail parks with Liz.

'I took the liberty of ordering for you,' Paul whispered. 'I hope you don't mind. I ordered wine as well.'

'Not at all. Thanks.' I was more than happy to let him take command.

Melon and Parma ham were placed before me. I was relieved he hadn't ordered the pea and mint soup. It looked a very lurid green.

I caught Brontë's attention and gave her a little half-smile.

She gaped back at me and started pointing with her left index finger.

I followed the finger and nearly choked on my melon. Mother and Father were at a top table, right on the other side of the dance floor.

Father hadn't been to one of these balls for at least five years. I surreptitiously scanned their table. They were sitting with Michael McCabe, Matthew Stuart and Mat Cohen, two Members of the Scottish Parliament and the chairman of Scottish Enterprise. A high-powered table indeed.

I mouthed at Brontë, 'Have you spoken to them?'

She shook her head.

Irritatingly, as I glanced back at their table I caught Michael's eye, but he didn't acknowledge me. I knew, without a doubt, he had not expected to see me.

'Are you OK?' Paul whispered. He had followed my gaze.

'Yes,' I croaked, but I wasn't.

I was upset and furious in equal measure. I sipped my champagne and felt the cold bubbles dance rapidly towards my brain.

A wall had been built between my dearest mentor and me. And I was furious with my mother. How could she live with herself? Lucy was murdered because she had warned Leland. Her hands were as bloodied as his.

'Is the melon hard?'

I glanced at Paul and shook my head.

'You've only taken one bite.'

I gently touched his arm. 'Paul, I really can't take a lecture right now. You're right. I know you are right, but please, just leave it. Just leave it, for tonight.'

Our dishes were cleared and the next course appeared briskly.

I exchanged small talk and business talk with our guests, but had to make a conscious effort not to let my gaze wander. I thought I could feel one hundred pairs of hostile eyes burning into my naked back.

I drank another glass of champagne and castigated myself for being paranoid. Nobody was looking at me; they were wrapped up in their own tables, their own conversations, their own worlds. Why did I imagine they were interested in me? Was it vanity? Delusions of grandeur? Or was it more sinister than that?

The meal was over too quickly. Everyone was there for the same reason – networking. Our table would disperse promptly after the speeches and charity auction. Then I would be at my most vulnerable.

I drank another glass of champagne without tasting it. I needed the rush, the false stole of courage it draped effortlessly across my shoulders.

I was charming and vivacious. I made self-deprecating jokes. My newly animated persona received peculiar glances from those who knew me well. I wanted to tell them that only by re-inventing myself could we pull this off.

If my reputation as a cold and distant person continued unabated, then clients were unlikely to instruct us. It didn't matter how competent or professional I was, at the end of the day it came down to having an amicable personality, for which I wasn't renowned.

The speeches began and were full of parochial references, intermittently dull or raucous. My champagne-induced boldness allowed me to cast glances around the room. I managed to make eye contact and smile at several acquaintances. I had chosen to come, so I couldn't exactly bow my head and hope for anonymity.

'I would also like to extend a special welcome to some of our illustrious guests,' the master of ceremonies began. 'Ladies and gentlemen, Sir Maxwell and Lady Paterson, MBE.'

There was a round of applause.

I went rigid in my seat as some idiot shouted, 'Speech! Speech!'

The emcee looked unsure of what to do, hesitating with the mike, but ready to take it to my father's table. My heart sank. I couldn't let him be humiliated.

Mother was hissing something in his ear. Instinctively,

I had half risen out of my seat, but Paul placed his hand on my arm, gently pulling me back down.

Mercifully, Michael McCabe rose and offered his thanks on behalf of Sir Maxwell and Lady Georgina, and also the newly merged firm of Cohen Paterson. I was aware of several heads turning in my direction to gauge my reaction, but it was Michael's attention I wanted to attract. Fortunately, he did glance across at me as he retook his seat.

'Thank you,' I mouthed. He nodded his acknowledgement.

The auction began immediately. I continued to drink too much champagne and laugh too loudly. Brontë kept bidding for things she couldn't possibly afford and drawing unwanted attention to our table. What had started so well, seemed in danger of careering out of control.

I was grateful when the auction finally finished, but not so delighted to have to sign for the dreadful oil painting of *The Isle of Mull and A Night at Skibo Castle*, which Brontë had managed to buy on my behalf.

I glowered at her across the table.

'But Madonna got married there,' she said.

'It's for a good cause,' added Bajit.

'I'll sell it to you for half of what it cost me,' I offered in earnest.

'Give me a call when Paterson Associates are up and running. I'll see what I can put your way.' With that Bajit Singh stood up, offered his thanks and left the table.

The other guests took the opportunity to stretch their legs. I was quietly delighted that they had all come. Not everybody had the gumption to sit at such a condemned table.

Liz was beside herself and moved swiftly round to Bruce Lindsey's vacated seat.

'Bajit's talking of moving into out-of-town retail parks, not just high street! He wants us to help him build the business and their profile.'

'Fantastic,' I managed to say, but I really wanted to ask why.

Liz answered me before I got the chance.

'He thought it was really impressive how we dusted ourselves off and got back on our feet so quickly. He said he wanted to work with a young, hungry firm!'

'Ah, to negotiate lower fees.'

'He didn't say that,' Liz countered defensively.

'It doesn't matter, we have a potential client! Make sure you mention it to anyone you speak to.'

I looked over at Douglas, who was involved in a very intimate conversation with Brontë. I didn't want to consider the ramifications.

'Douglas,' I said loudly.

He looked up.

'You should start networking. See if you can find NQs or trainees that we can poach. You'll know most of them. Oh, and talk it up.'

'OK boss,' he smirked, and stood up unsteadily.

Huffily Brontë asked, 'What should Karen and I do?'

I smiled wickedly. 'You're part of the firm, go and see if you can find any disgruntled secretaries.'

Brontë giggled and nudged Karen.

'Thanks a lot,' Karen hissed at me on her way past.

'It's like a military operation,' Paul commented.

I poured myself another glass of champagne. 'It has to be. There are only five of us.'

'Six.'

'Six? You? I don't think we can afford you.'

'Let's call it care in the community,' he smiled. 'Shouldn't you be doing your stuff, too?'

'Yes, but I need a couple of minutes to recharge my charming streak.'

'That was rather a rabbit out the hat.'

'I'm not horrid all the time!' I laughed. 'Only when under unremitting and severe pressure.'

Michael McCabe had approached our table, 'Would you like to dance?'

'Em,' I hesitated. 'Yes.'

I was aware that Michael's hand never left the small of my back as he guided me through the throng of people.

He held me close, too close.

'So how are you?' he asked into the top of my head.

'Apart from being ousted from *my* firm, vilified in the press and arrested? I'm fine.'

'Is it true about the BBC profile? It's the talk of the town.'

'Is that why you asked me to dance?'

'No. I asked you to dance because I want to offer a truce.'

I flung my head back and laughed.

'This truce, it couldn't have anything to do with the BBC profile and my new firm?'

'Maybe,' he smiled. 'That's Paul Gabriel from the Beeb, isn't it? I've seen him on News 24.'

I nodded. He swung me around enthusiastically. My stomach sloshed with champagne.

'Stop!' I gasped. 'I'm dizzy.'

'Sorry.' Michael pulled me close again and we gently swayed for a minute as the music slowed.

'I wanted to thank you for earlier with Dad and the

speech. I couldn't have stood it if . . .' I gushed before he left the dance floor.

'Shush. I know. Neither could I. Good luck, Erin.'

'Luck has nothing to do with it. I'm a damn good lawyer!'

Michael gave me a wet kiss on the cheek. 'I know. You never stopped telling me.'

I dashed off the dance floor before anyone else could accost me, because I was desperate to pee.

Gliding through the press of guests I noticed Paul at the bar, but I headed straight for the ladies'. Naturally there was a queue. I had been to hundreds of dos at the Hilton – the ladies' in reception would be quicker.

It was busy but not mobbed. I sat in my cubicle for a full five minutes pondering my next move.

I needed to confront my mother. If I had figured out she had told Leland about Lucy seeing him, then surely the police wouldn't be far behind. I needed to know why she had done it, why she was protecting him. But mostly I wanted to know where he was.

I wound myself into a knot of anger and hurt. I knew what I had to do, but garnering the courage was the problem.

I reapplied my lipstick and tidied my hair before I ran cold water over my wrists. I walked straight into Paul as I left the ladies'.

'I'm leaving,' he snapped.

I was taken aback. 'Oh?'

'I'm sure you'll be fine with your old beau.'

I arched an eyebrow. 'Is that jealousy I detect?'

'Of that lanky piece of piss? Yeah. Right.'

Just then I spotted my father's wheelchair disappearing out the front entrance. 'Shit,' I muttered.

'Pardon? Why on earth would you imagine I'm jealous?'

'I wasn't saying shit to that.'

I scanned the reception area for signs of my mother.

'Who are you looking for? Michael?'

'No. My mother. I want to speak to her, but Dad has just left . . .' I cast about the swarm of tuxedos and ball gowns but couldn't spot her.

'She's still inside. I've just come from the ballroom. One of the gentlemen from their table took your father out.'

'Are you sure?'

'Absolutely.'

'Thanks,' I said, and went back towards the ballroom. Paul followed me.

'Are you coming with me?'

'Yes.'

'Why?'

'Because you're up to something.'

He began to guide me through the milling guests and on to the dance floor.

'Paul, I'd love to dance but I need to speak to my mother . . .'

'She's not going anywhere and you owe me.'

I conceded ungraciously and said a prayer of thanks that it was not a slow number. The Goddess of Mockery must have heard me because within a minute the music changed tempo to a leisurely waltz.

We danced, cheek to cheek. His arm enfolding my waist. My hand, held tightly in his, against his chest. His breath in my hair and ear.

I closed my eyes and let myself drift. We were hardly dancing, we were swaying – holding on. I wanted to kiss him. I swallowed and bowed my head to put another few centimetres between temptation and me.

'You look so beautiful tonight,' he whispered.

'Thank you.'

'There isn't a man here that wouldn't swap places with me.'

'Does that scare you?' I said timidly into his chest.

'No. Not at all. They might want to dance with you, but . . .'

'But what?' I breathed.

He thought for a moment.

'But I don't think they'd want to take you home.'

He might as well have slapped me. My head sprung up and I glared at him.

'What the hell is that supposed to mean?'

He smiled endearingly and crushed me into him. 'You are quite, quite lovely, but you've got a lot to learn.'

I pulled away from him but he sort of bear-hugged me.

'I hate you,' I hissed. 'Get off.'

'I know,' he laughed, and then let me go.

I gave him another caustic glare and lurched in the direction of my parents' table. He swiftly caught my elbow.

'Careful now. You're a bit wobbly.'

I wanted to say get stuffed, but he was right. The combination of champagne and no food had left me unsteady.

I noticed Michael, Mother and Mat Cohen had their heads crowded together. Probably plotting their next stitch-up.

'Hi,' I said nicely.

Mat looked disconcerted. 'Oh, em, hi, Erin.'

'Congratulations on the merger.'

'Thanks.' Mat looked at Michael and my mother in bewilderment.

'Mother, would it be possible to have a quick word?' I was utterly pleasant in the hope of lulling her into a false sense of security, but she viewed me sourly.

'Now?'

'Yes, please. It is quite pressing.' My smile remained intact.

She sighed heavily and slowly got to her feet.

'I hope it's not about the merger,' she hissed.

'If only,' I muttered.

With Paul in tow, we found a quiet corner of the vestibule outside the ballroom. She folded her arms defensively across her chest.

'I don't think we've been introduced,' she said rather curtly to Paul. He shook her hand firmly.

'Paul Gabriel.'

She narrowed her eyes. 'Don't I know you?'

'We have met before.'

She nodded suspiciously, obviously trying to place him. It occurred to me that Paul could have interviewed her when he was still a detective.

'Well? What have you got to say for yourself?' she snapped.

'It's about Lucy Grant.'

Her face visibly darkened. 'And?'

'She wrote to me. She told me what happened.' I was icily calm. I wanted to see if she would continue to deny their contact.

'Happened when, dear?'

I could have bet money that she would drop into dizzy-old-bat mode.

'Cut it out, Mother! She wrote to me! About thinking

she had seen Leland. And she wrote that she spoke to you about it . . .'

'Oh, that! That was just a little misunderstanding,' she said too gaily.

I rocked my foot from side to side and loosely folded my arms across my chest. It was my courtroom stance, prior to tearing a witness apart.

'If it was such a "little misunderstanding", why didn't you tell the police?'

'It was of no relevance!'

'No relevance? Exactly how did you come to that conclusion? Have you no comprehension of how that reflects on you? Have you lost your senses?'

'How dare you speak to me like that! I'm not one of your staff.'

'You most certainly are not! My staff have integrity. I will be handing Lucy's letter to the police. You . . .'

She looked genuinely alarmed.

'Erin! What does it matter now? They know you had nothing to do with it! They don't need to know about—'

'Yes they do! The man who killed Lucy, then called me! Don't you understand? Because my number was on her phone, he called *me*.'

She took two steps back and seemed to gasp for air.

Paul and I both grabbed her elbows and steadied her between us. We helped her to a chair and made her sit down. It was my turn to be alarmed.

'Are you OK?'

She stared up at me and something flashed across her eyes.

'You'll only make things worse. Don't do it. For your father's sake. For Brontë's sake.'

363

I crouched down beside her. 'I have to. I'm morally bound.'

'I was only trying to protect you,' she said.

'Protect me from what?'

I wanted her to say it. I wanted her to admit that Leland was alive.

She shook her head. 'Are you sure he called you? Couldn't it have been a mistake?'

'He's left notes. He's left messages on my answerphone. He's coming after me,' I stated calmly.

'That's ridiculous! He's not coming after you at all.'

'How do you know? Did he tell you? Is he just trying to scare me?'

She glanced up at Paul. 'Detective Inspector Gabriel, isn't it?'

'Not any more. I've retired.'

'What have you told her, Mr Gabriel?'

'Everything and nothing,' he said solemnly.

'Well, that's it, then. That will be the end of it.'

'The end of what?'

Say it, I willed. Say, he's alive.

'Everything. The end of everything.'

She was giving an Oscar-winning performance.

'The end of what "everything"? Don't be so melodramatic, Mother. Cut the riddles and just tell me!'

She shook her head. Mother had made up her mind. I knew from bitter experience that it was hopeless to badger her.

I stood up. Bloody confrontations. That was why I avoided them. They never worked out as one planned.

'Has Dad gone home?' I asked quietly.

'Yes. Martha's there,' she said dully.

'I'm so . . . disappointed,' I said more to myself than to her.

She shook her head and gazed down at her hands. A pianist's hands – long-fingered, tortured, compliant.

'Shall I take you to the police?' I said softly.

That got her attention.

'What on earth do you mean?'

'Mother, they are closing in on him. And you. You would be better off telling them everything you know, trying to repair some of the horrific damage you've caused.'

'I don't know anything!' she snapped.

'Yes you do. I know you do. You either go to the police of your own accord or I shall. Do you understand? I shall.'

She gave a slight snort of derision. 'Oh, I know you would. You'd do anything to hurt me. Anything!'

'Mother, I have never hurt you.'

She stood up and hissed at me, 'You were always trouble! Always trying to get your own way. Mark my words, young lady, I won't let you.'

'Mother! He's a bloody murderer! He killed Lucy!' I shrieked.

People around us turned to stare.

'No he didn't! He didn't! He's dead!'

My mouth hung open. She had finally lost it.

She reached out and gently tried to push a strand of hair from my cheek, but I jerked away. It was the fondest gesture I had received in years. Her eyes wandered over my face. Sad, old, remorseful eyes. A lump caught in my throat.

'Everything OK out here?' Michael said crisply. He immediately stood at my mother's shoulder, but I couldn't tear my eyes from her.

'Yes, dear. Just clearing the air. Much better for that, I always think.'

I blinked at her in astonishment.

'Mother?' I whispered.

She held up her hand to silence me and walked away.

'Goodnight, Erin. Goodnight.'

'Mother! Don't go. Stay and talk to me!' I pleaded.

She ignored me, and Michael guided her back into the ballroom.

'Do you want me to call Kelman?' Paul said.

'Fuck! I don't know. Fuck!' I snapped, and stormed towards reception.

'Wait a minute.' Paul caught up with me, grabbed my arm and swung me around to face him. Suddenly, a flashbulb blinded us.

'Piss off!' we growled simultaneously.

The photographer cursed back at us and took another shot before he stalked off.

'Do you want me to call Kelman?' Paul repeated tersely.

I anxiously glanced back towards the ballroom.

'I don't know. She's lost her marbles!'

'You're telling me,' Paul said in an undertone.

'Let's get Brontë and then call Kelman. And DS Marshall,' I said, and hurried towards the bar.

Brontë refused to come home with us and I understood why.

I also wanted to stay and flirt and pretend there was nothing wrong. Pretend that a huge vortex of lies, half-truths and fear wasn't swelling around me.

We didn't manage to get hold of either DS Marshall or DSI Kelman, although we tried for over an hour, leaving several messages. Finally, Paul agreed to wait until morning. I showed him out of my apartment courteously, but bitter recriminations lingered like smoke.

I didn't want to be here in the morning. I wanted to be somewhere else entirely, or have skipped back in time to last Friday. I wouldn't hit Alex. I would take Lucy's call. Was that all that separated me from this quagmire of deceit and death?

And I couldn't set the alarm because Brontë hadn't come back. Meanly, I hoped she would behave herself.

TWENTY-TWO

Martha woke me the next morning.

'Sorry to phone you so early on a Saturday, Erin, but your mother wants you to send Brontë home right away. They're off to the cottage and, well, I've got something on today so . . . em, she needs to come home and collect Max,' she explained apologetically.

'It's OK, Martha. I'll go and tell her ladyship.' I yawned and cursed my raging hangover in unison.

Slowly, I levered myself out of bed and shuffled up the stairs to the top floor. Before I knocked on the door, I prayed I didn't find a large, hairy man in bed with her. Brontë was a notoriously heavy sleeper, so I wasn't surprised by the lack of response.

'Brontë,' I said, as I opened the door. 'You've got to get up and collect Max.'

The bed didn't look as though it had been slept in. I checked the other bedroom, cursed, went back downstairs and looked in the kitchen. It was conceivable that she had fallen into a drunken slumber elsewhere, so I checked the bathrooms, but there was no sign that Brontë had come home.

I cursed again. The image of her listless frame in that hospital bed flashed before my eyes. If she had gone back to the drug dealer, I would personally strangle her.

I dialled Douglas, cradling the phone at my neck, and began to make coffee.

His mother answered.

'Hi, Mrs Thomson, it's Erin Paterson here. Could I have a word with Douglas?'

'He's still in bed, dear.'

I desperately wanted to ask if he was alone, but thought Mrs Thomson might faint.

'Would you mind waking him? It's rather important.'

'Not at all, dear,' she said sweetly, then yelled 'DOUGLAS! PHONE!' at the top of her voice. I dropped a whole sachet of fresh coffee into the sink.

'Bugger,' I hissed.

'Sorry, dear?' Mrs Thomson replied.

'Nothing. I was just talking to myself.'

'First sign of madness,' she commented helpfully.

'Here he is now, dear,' she said, and handed the phone to Douglas.

'What's up?' he yawned.

'Em, Brontë doesn't happen to be with you, does she?'

'No,' he snorted scornfully.

'When did you last see her?'

'Last night.'

I rolled my eyes. 'Yes, I know you saw her last night, but when was the last time? Did she leave with somebody?'

I could hear Douglas scratching his head. His ginger hair was a fright in the morning. It sometimes took until midday to calm down.

'Er, I think she left about two o'clock. She was going to get a taxi. She wasn't with anyone but she was fairly gished.'

'Was she coming back to my place?'

'I don't know. I think so . . . is something wrong?'

'She didn't come back here and she's not at my parents'. If you think of something, Douglas, anything, give me a call.'

I hung up and stared at the phone. Panic hadn't quite taken hold, but it was dancing around the periphery.

I rang my parents' house. Mother answered.

'Don't hang up! Brontë's not here and I don't know where she spent the night,' I gushed.

'Probably at a friend's,' she replied coolly.

'Could you check the house just to make sure she's not there?'

'For goodness' sake, Erin! We would know if she was here.'

'Mother, please just check!' I said into the dead receiver.

Bloody bitch. She could hide a murderous son, but check on her daughter? Don't be ridiculous.

An icy blast froze my whole body. I almost expected the terrace doors to have burst open.

If he couldn't get to me, where had he always gone next?

I was dressed and thumping on Paul's door within five minutes.

He was only wearing a pair of grey Calvin Klein trunks when he answered. I could feel the warmth from his skin.

'Brontë's missing,' I said, and brushed past him, eyes averted.

He blinked a couple of times before he said, 'Missing? How come?'

'I don't know. She didn't come back to my place or go home. I'm worried.'

'Come and have a coffee,' he yawned.

I hesitated and watched him wander towards the kitchen. He did work out.

'Em, would you like me to get you a robe?' I called as he disappeared.

He popped his head back round the entrance to his kitchen.

'Am I making you uncomfortable?'

I gave a pathetic shrug.

'I don't own a robe. Grab a shirt and jeans,' he mumbled.

I spotted his jeans and a shirt slung over a chair as soon as I entered, but I was drawn to his bed. Gingerly, I touched the space his body had left. It was warm and dry. No cold sweats disturbed his dreams. I caressed the indent on his pillow. Out the corner of my eye I noticed the foil sheet of six capsules. Four were empty.

'Sleeping pills,' Paul said from behind me.

I jumped in horror. He was leaning against the doorframe, in that same, sexy, casual way I had witnessed only eight days previously.

'I'm sorry . . . I mean . . . I didn't mean to snoop . . . I was . . .'

'Did you check in the drawers too?' he said sarcastically.

'No! I really am sorry. I simply came in and . . . spotted them . . .'

'As you were about to make the bed?' he said knowingly.

Oh, God! He had seen me. He had seen me stroking his bed! Was there no end to my humiliation?

'Em . . . yes . . .' I agreed lamely. I could feel my face burning.

'Let me help,' he grinned.

Let me die now, I prayed, before I spontaneously combust from embarrassment.

He took one end of the duvet and handed the other to me. We shook the duvet and let it parachute to the mattress.

'I think you've already plumped up the pillows, right?'

'Right,' I squeaked, and hared out the door.

I could hear him laughing.

I sat in the kitchen and continued to squirm. I really needed to see a psychiatrist or a sex therapist, or someone. I really needed to get a handle on my neurosis. Otherwise, I was destined to be a spinster of this parish.

'OK. Have we all calmed down now?' he said, when he came through.

'No. If it's Leland . . . if he can't get to me, then Brontë could be next. I have an awful feeling. I can't explain it.'

'Before we jump the gun, let's try her usual haunts.'

'Mother has a note of all her friends.'

'After last night, will she be forthcoming?' asked Paul astutely.

'No. She's already hung up on me this morning.'

Paul studied me for a few moments before he said, 'Time to call in some favours. You make coffee, I'll round up a posse.'

I listened quietly as he called round. I was pretty sure some of the people were police officers and some were snouts. Not once did he sound anxious, not once did he drop his guard. His explanation to them was simply, 'a big story'.

By noon we had heard nothing, not one word, and I had worn a groove around Paul's kitchen table.

'Has Kelman or Marshall called you back yet?' I asked.

'No,' he sighed, and poured us both more coffee.

'Isn't that a bit odd? Considering my mother almost confirmed Leland was alive?'

'Very odd, but there are some things I didn't tell you, about Kelman and his—'

'Like stealing keys?' I interrupted.

'How do you know?'

'Process of deduction. He thought I was involved and wanted to make damn sure I didn't read anything in your files that might be of use to Leland. I'll bet he told you to remove all the stuff on the suspects.'

'Yep.'

'What else did he want kept from me?'

Paul's face clouded slightly.

'Paul? What else?'

'Personal stuff,' he said, and stood up abruptly. 'I've got to do a news report in a couple of hours. I'll get my calls forwarded to my mobile. Will you be OK?'

I stood up too. 'I just wish I knew she was safe and sound. I wish I had pressed her for the name of her dealer. That would be somewhere to start.'

'I've already got someone on that,' Paul said.

'Do you know who he is?'

'No, but I know people who do. They'll check it out.'

'Thank you, Paul. For everything,' I said as I left.

When I entered my apartment, I hoped against hope that Sky TV would be blaring and Brontë would be sprawled on the sofa, moaning about her hangover.

But the apartment was silent.

Where are you, Brontë? I thought over and over.

I checked my messages, but only Marshall had returned my calls. I cursed myself for not having been at home. Marshall explained that he was 'up north' for the weekend and mobile reception was patchy. I was confused. We were handing Kelman Leland on a plate, but he was being evasive. Why?

I tried Douglas again, but he didn't come up with anything new. I felt helpless and useless. Brontë was missing and all I could do was aimlessly pace and re-dial the same people.

I wanted to be proactive, scouring the streets, looking in bars, shouting out her name.

I called my parents' house again, but got the answering machine. Maybe Brontë had gone home. Martha hadn't called me back about Max. I clung to false hope for a full two minutes.

My phone rang and I snatched it up after one ring. 'Hello!'

'This little piggy went to market, this little piggy stayed at home . . .'

'Leland! You sick fuck! Have you got Brontë?' I shouted.

'This little piggy had roast beef. And this little piggy's all gone! That must have hurt.'

'Leave her alone, you bastard! Where are you? Let me speak to Brontë!'

The receiver thrummed dully. He had hung up.

I immediately dialled 1471, but was told 'the caller withheld their number'.

Jeezus Christ! Where were they?

I rang Paul's mobile first and left a garbled message. I tried DS Marshall and DSI Kelman. Again, I left messages. There was only one place left to try.

'My sister has been kidnapped by a serial killer, who is actually our brother, but he was presumed dead,' I stated calmly.

The desk sergeant sighed heavily. 'Take a seat.'

'But I need to speak to somebody. My sister is in danger!'

'Take a seat, miss, someone will be right with you,' he drawled.

'DSI Kelman of Lothian and Borders was working on the Lucy Grant and Abigail Dawes murders. He can confirm I'm not making this up!'

The desk sergeant looked blankly at me for several seconds.

'Please take a seat, miss.'

'Jeezus!' I shrieked. 'Write this down! Brontë Paterson has been abducted by Leland Paterson! She may already be dead! Can someone please help?'

'There's no need for that, miss,' he barked.

I scrawled various phone numbers and names on a piece of paper and thrust it towards him.

'The name is Brontë Paterson – abducted by her brother, Leland Paterson. I suggest that you pass this information on as quickly as possible.' I turned on my heel and left.

Bloody policemen.

I almost laughed at my stupidity. I had my own surveillance team. Surely they could help?

I stood at the top of the police station steps and scoured the car park for a suitable candidate. But I couldn't see anyone that fitted the bill. There was no car with the motor idling. Had surveillance been cancelled? Just when I needed it.

My nerves were in tatters. My hands shook, pins and needles of apprehension shot up and down my arms. I fumbled with the keys trying to start my car.

Where was Leland? Where would he go? I had no idea. Where had he been hiding for all these years?

Mother would know, but she was on her way to Crail. Damn you, I thought. Damn you.

Leland's jeering rhyme haunted me.

'This little piggy went to market, this little piggy stayed at home . . .'

I screeched out of the car park to a burst of irate horns.

Like a bat out of hell I drove towards the South Side, weaving in and out of traffic, full beams glaring, and hoped a cop car would pick me up and follow me. Naturally, none did.

As I turned into the cul-de-sac I realised that alerting Leland to my arrival was not the brightest idea, so I swung a tight U-turn and parked around the corner.

I dropped my keys twice before I managed to centrally lock my car. Fear made me clumsy. It made me hyperventilate and panicky.

Keeping close to the hedges, I darted along the avenue to the gates. Anxiously, I glanced up at the windows for any sign of occupation. The house was dark in the twilight gloom. The orange street lamps buzzed and flickered to life overhead.

The most obvious route for entry was the garden/basement door, but I had seen enough movies to know that was folly. The back door was my only other option.

In order not to step on the gravel, I slipped down the driveway via the herbaceous border. I hared across the parking bay and on to the steps that led up to the back door. With my back against the damp sandstone, I tried to regulate my breathing. I felt in my pocket for the keys. The sound seemed to echo around the quiet street. Even the birds had fallen silent.

Hands trembling, I put the key in the lock.

The deadbolt turned and the door sprang open half an inch. There were no dogs to greet me.

I was inside and leaning against the door before I had figured out what on earth I planned to do. I swallowed hard and listened intently for any noise, but my own thundering heart was deafening.

I didn't need to switch on the lights – I knew this house like the back of my hand. Tentatively, I moved further along the back hall to the kitchen.

The door was open and I cast a quick glance inside. The Aga spilled warmth into the empty room. I went in and pressed re-dial on the phone. It rang six times before my answering machine picked up.

He was here! My hollow triumph was quickly swamped by suffocating terror.

Silently, I closed the kitchen door and crouched down on the floor. Then I dialled 999.

'Police,' I whispered, when asked which service I required.

'There's a man in the house. He's got a knife,' I breathed.

'Where are you?'

I told them the address.

'Where is the man?'

'I don't know. Somewhere in the house!'

'Did you see him? Did you see the weapon?'

'No . . . I just know he is here!'

'OK . . . well, you just stay put and we'll send somebody round.'

Stay put? They had to be joking. I had done my bit. I would wait outside until they got here.

I heard footsteps somewhere in the house and my heart nearly stopped.

'Miss . . . ?'

I carefully replaced the receiver, and shuffled backwards, as far away from the door as I could get.

I was ten years old. I was in the dark searching for a place to hide. Leland was coming.

I crawled across the flagstone floor. Leland was coming. I needed to pee. I needed a place to hide. I scurried like an animal towards the far end of the room. Leland was coming.

I felt along the fitments for a large cupboard in which to cower. Leland was coming.

I had to be quick. I could feel the tears as they struggled to the surface. Must be quiet. Must be still. Quiet, Erin. Quiet. Still. Be still.

Frantically, I searched the cupboards with my shaking hands. Iron straps gripped my chest and crushed my lungs. Leland was coming.

Under the table!

I slid under the kitchen table. But he could still see me! I pulled two of the chairs tightly in.

The light blinded me. I blinked a couple of times and pulled my knees up under my chin. I watched a pair of legs circle the table.

'Mum?'

She gave a small shriek as I popped my head out.

'Erin! What on earth are you doing?'

I scrambled to my feet.

'Where's Brontë?'

'Certainly not under there,' she tutted.

'For God's sake! Where is she?'

'She drove your father and Max up to the cottage. Why are you suddenly so interested in Brontë?'

'Did you phone me?'

She arched an eyebrow. Ask a stupid question.

'Did you phone me from here earlier?' I repeated.

'No. Martha phoned.'

'Bugger!' I screeched. But then I heard the sirens.

The look my mother threw me could have killed a herd of wildebeest.

I explained as best I could, but, with Mother rolling her eyes at every statement I made, I could see the two police officers thinking, we've got a right one here.

The senior officer glanced at his notebook.

'Are you the same lady that reported Brontë Paterson's abduction at Pitt Street Police Office earlier today?'

'Yes.'

'But your mother has since confirmed she is safe and well?'

'Well, yes, but at the time I thought she had been abducted . . .'

'So, there is no man with a knife in this house?'

'No.'

'Where is your brother, Miss Paterson?'

'I don't know! He's hiding. Ask her!'

Mother tenderly placed her hand on my shoulder and said, 'Erin, your brother is dead.'

The officer gaped at her. 'What do you mean?'

'Erin's brother drowned over a decade ago. She hasn't been able to . . . come to terms with it.'

'But he's not really dead! Ask Detective Superintendent Kelman of Lothian and Borders. He'll tell you.'

The officer frowned. 'He's been suspended from duty, miss.'

'What on earth for?'

'I'm not at liberty to say,' he sighed, and stood up. The other officer followed suit.

'Are you leaving? Aren't you going to do anything?'

'Miss, I think you may need some help. You've wasted police time, but, given the circumstances, we'll leave it at that.'

I heard Mother whisper, 'She's under a lot of stress,' as she showed them out.

I had well and truly blown it.

'What on earth are you trying to do?' she shrieked as soon as they'd gone.

'I'm trying to flush out Leland before he gets to me or Brontë!'

'Don't be ridiculous!'

'Mother, you told Leland about Lucy Grant. Lo and behold, she's murdered!'

'Leland's dead.'

'But at the ball you said . . .' I was at a loss. What had she actually said? Nothing really.

'What the fuck is going on?' I snapped.

'Erin Georgina Paterson! Mind your language!'

I put my head in my hands. 'Are you mentally ill?'

She gave me a superior look. 'It appears to me that you've staked a claim on that.'

'I'm going home,' I said wearily.

'Fine, dear. Could you take out the bin for me?'

Dutifully, I went into the kitchen.

I hauled the bin bag outside and threw it in the trash. Did insanity run in families? I couldn't believe what was happening to me. The police thought I was barking. Perhaps I was? Had I succumbed to the damaged gene that seemed prolific in my family?

I was halfway down the avenue when I remembered my car keys were on the kitchen table. Add: premature senility.

This time I let myself in through the front door. I was almost at the kitchen when I heard her.

'I've told you before. This can't go on. For everyone's sake!'

Silence.

I hesitated. Was she on the phone?

'Don't give me that look. If what you say is true, then we must sort it out! Things are only going to get worse.'

There was somebody with her and I didn't need to guess who. My legs turned to jelly. Gripping the wall for support, I sidled backwards and into the plant stand. It rocked once and tipped over. The ceramic pot smashed to the ground. In slow motion, I stared at it and back at the kitchen door. I could hear a chair scrape across the floor.

I dived along the corridor and fell over the upturned stand. I was bathed in light from the kitchen, but I didn't look back. I scrambled to my feet and lunged at the basement door on my left. I had hauled it open as he closed in on me. I felt his hand on my back, in between my shoulder blades. I stumbled forward and lost my footing.

I heard my leg break before I registered the pain.

I wanted to scream but couldn't. I lay, winded, in an awkward position at the bottom of the stairs and tried to breathe through the shock. I sucked in deep gulps of air and blew them out slowly. I thought I would pass out.

The door above me closed and panic rose in my chest.

Only one thing stood between him and me – the dark.

I dragged myself across the dirt floor, hauling my body towards the garden door. I could hear them above me and strained to catch what they said, but fear thundered in my ears.

I put my hand down on a nail and winced, but continued along the floor until I reached the garden door.

I rattled the doorknob but it was locked. Locked by me that fateful night. My hands were clammy and uncoordinated as I felt around the floor and window sill for the key.

In the faint light from the window, I peered down at my left leg. Cautiously, I moved my hand over it and felt a sickening dent in my femur just above the knee. A supracondylar fracture. My lower leg and knee stuck out at a fearful thirty-degree angle.

I knew the artery would be disrupted. I had about twenty minutes' grace before the pain really kicked in and I would go into shock. I wished I didn't know quite so much about medical things. The expectation of agony was akin to the fear Leland instilled in me.

A ruckus above me focused my attention away from my thigh. There were heavy footsteps and something crashed to the floor. What were they doing? Fighting?

I was a sitting duck.

Dragging my twisted leg, I struggled towards the tool cupboard on my right. Backing into the room, I collided with hedge-trimmers. The serrated edge caught my clothing and tore my skin. I wanted to find a space under the shelf, a hiding place of old, but my hands stretched out into blackness, as I gingerly felt various sharp gardening tools.

The door to the basement slammed shut again and I heard footsteps on the stairs.

I held my breath and listened.

Silence.

He was listening too.

Our childhood hierarchy replayed.

Cat and mouse. Hunt the thimble. Hide and seek. Fee, fie, foe, fum.

I never searched for him, though.

My lungs were bursting. I almost cried out when I heard him curse under his breath. I was sure he would hear my desperate swallow of air.

He shuffled around the basement, the sound rising and falling as he ducked in and out of different rooms.

Where was Mother? Why didn't she come down? I need you, Mum, I thought. I need you. Where are you? Help me.

The pain in my leg was burning, a hot searing pain, sending waves of nausea up through my chest.

I heard a dull thud. My throat contracted. Was that the door again? What was he doing?

A patch of warmth spread beneath me. Blood oozing from my fracture.

I saw Leland's delighted, demented face leering down at me and jerked my head backwards, forcing the image away.

I had peed myself. I was slipping into shock. Why so quickly? Starvation and fear . . .

It gripped me like a fist. I had to get out before the adrenalin in my system dried up. I tried to make the tiniest of moves, but my muscles were rigid and in spasm.

I glimpsed a flash of dim torch-light. My lips and tongue went numb.

I wanted to cringe away, hide, but I couldn't move. The smell of urine was overpowering. He would sniff me out like the giant. *Fee, fie, foe, fum . . . I smell the blood of an . . .*

Light blinded me. I turned my head away.

'Erin?' he whispered.

I recognised his voice.

'Kelman?'

383

He crouched down in front of me. 'Where is he?' he mouthed almost silently.

'Somewhere down here . . .'

'Are you hurt?'

'My leg's broken . . .'

'OK. I'll get some help,' he murmured, and went to stand.

'Don't leave me!' I gasped and made a grab for him.

'Shush!' he hissed. 'I need to get help. Stay here!'

Where the hell did he think I was going?

I listened as he crept across the basement. He had bloody well given away my hiding place. Just like Brontë!

I didn't want to play any more. I wanted to go back upstairs. Into the light. There were spiders down here. And earwigs.

And Leland.

I would never make it across the basement. I felt around me again and thought I could feel a little gap. I wrestled my way further into the corner. My leg didn't seem to hurt as much, but I was cold. Very cold.

My eyes snapped open. The shock had taken hold. I had dozed off. How long for? A minute? A few seconds? It seemed eerily quiet.

Maybe they had gone home. Maybe they had become bored and gone home. Maybe I could come out of my hidey-hole and go up to bed. Warm bed.

Sleep was engulfing me. Must stay awake.

What was that smell? It was sweet and familiar.

I saw a light dipping in and out of the shadows. I opened my mouth, but nothing happened. Was I still asleep? In one of those nightmares where you can't run, where you can't cry out, no matter how hard you try.

384

Help me! I willed. Help me!

'Leland Paterson! I am arresting you for . . .'

There was a muffled whack and somebody groaned, a deep, arching moan, and a loud thump as a body hit the floor.

Had he said Leland?

My skin was clammy, beads of cold sweat had collected on my forehead and lip. Who was out there, in the dark, creeping around? Something tugged at my memory. Why was I down here?

I wedged myself further into the corner. Something prodded my lower back. I felt it briefly. It was warm and wet. I touched my finger to my lips. Blood. I was impaled on something.

Why hadn't I felt it? Shock. Yes . . . yes . . . shock . . . broken leg. Which one? That one. The one that was twisted and cold.

'What have you done?' Mother screeched. 'You must go. Right now!'

'I need to see Erin!' he snapped.

See me? Ha! Torture me, more like. Well, he'd have to find me first. And I was safe in my hidey-hole. Na, na-na na, na.

A shadow appeared before me. This time I screamed.

'There you are! I've been looking for you.'

I couldn't make out his features, only the form of his looming blackness against the dark. Satan.

He was whispering to himself. His voice seemed strange, different. Did he have an accent?

I tried to make myself even smaller, but he crouched down between my twisted leg and the other one that was crushed tight against my chest.

I watched his arm reach out and touch my ankle, but I couldn't feel it.

385

'What have you done to yourself?' he whispered.

I was mute with fear. Was this Leland? Or a grotesque dream?

'Cat got your tongue?'

I wanted to gag.

'Remember, Pushkin, the cat? That's what you called her, wasn't it?'

'You killed her . . .' I breathed, and thought I felt a tear roll down my cheek. Was I crying? I hadn't realised. It didn't smell like Leland.

'She was a naughty kitty . . .'

'Leave me alone . . .' I hissed. *Mummy, help me! Leland's here! He's going to hurt me. He's going to touch me. Mum! Help!*

'That's not very nice. I've come all this way for you and this is how you . . .'

He lunged forward suddenly, right on top of me, and I shrieked.

His forehead smacked into my front teeth. I could taste blood from my split lip. His shoulder crashed into my chest, his jaw smacked into my collarbone. I felt his teeth make contact. Was he going to bite me? What was he doing?

'Get off, get off!' I cried, and shoved at his dead weight.

Suddenly, he was hauled away from me.

Kelman leaned forward, having thrown down the garden spade he had used to hit Leland.

'We've got to get out of here,' he said.

'I can't walk.'

'I'll help you. Give me your arm.'

'Where's my mother? She's here. I heard her.'

'I don't know! We've got to move. Now!'

'I can't! I'm impaled!' I cried.

'Jeezus! Let me see. Let me see.'

Kelman knelt down and tried to pull a lifetime of gardening junk out from under the shelf.

'Have you called for help?' I asked, but he didn't respond.

He sort of slumped forward, half on top of me. Angrily, I tried to push him off, but he only made a gurgling sound.

I let him rest there for a moment. He was heavy but warm. I wasn't pleased, but it was better than Leland lying on top of me.

Tentatively, I put my arm around his back and gave him a comforting pat. It must have been raining outside. His jacket was soaking.

I waited for ages for him to get up, but he just lay there, his head on my shoulder, his breath laboured. An eerie calm settled.

'Kelman?' I whispered. 'Can we go now?'

Nothing.

'Kelman? Wake up!'

'Erin?' A muted voice called.

'Mum?'

'Where are you?' she whispered.

'In the tool cupboard.'

'I can't see you . . .'

What was that smell? It reminded me of something. It smelled like my Jeep when I put petrol in it.

A vision of my flame-charred skeleton flashed before my eyes.

'Mum? Help me . . . I'm stuck.'

'Can you crawl?' she whispered.

'No. I'm really stuck. Mum, go and get help. Call the police . . .'

Her voice trembled. 'Shush. He's gone. Can you crawl? I didn't know you'd fallen . . .'

'Mum, listen to me! Go and get help. Get out of here and get help.'

The pain rolled like a wave, leaving me faint and dizzy, and a whooshing filled my ears.

'I can't. You have to be brave and crawl like that little girl, remember? What was her name? Jessica? Yes, that was it. Jessica. She got stuck. It was on TV. She was much younger than you and she got out. Come on. Try. Crawl . . . crawl . . .'

I listened to my mother as she coaxed me in a tone that I hadn't heard for decades. My eyes filled with tears.

I prodded DSI Kelman several times, but he didn't stir.

'Mum? Are you still there? Mum? Mum?

'Mum, help me,' I whispered, but sorrow choked me.

I closed my eyes and prayed. I prayed for forgiveness for not protecting Brontë all those years ago. For not stopping Leland before it was too late. I prayed for my mother and father and all those young women. I could hear singing.

'. . . Hush, little baby, don't say a word, Mummy's going to buy you a mocking bird. If that mocking bird can't sing, Mummy's going to buy you a diamond ring . . .'

I squinted at Kelman, but he definitely seemed asleep. Imagine that! A DSI falling asleep on top of me. The press would have a field day.

Nausea swept over me. I wanted the singing to stop.

'. . . is brass, Mummy's going to buy you a looking glass. If that looking glass gets broke, Mummy's going to buy you a billy goat . . .'

'Mum? Are you singing?' I asked.

'. . . if that billy goat runs away, Mummy's going to buy you a sunny day . . .'

'Mum! Stop singing and get help.'

She was barking mad, singing at a time like this.

I took a deep breath and rasped, 'Stop singing and get help.'

'Erin? Is that you? Are you OK?'

Who the hell did she think was down here?

'No, I am not OK. I have a broken leg. Get some bloody help!'

'I can't . . . I can't . . .'

'Mum, PLEASE! I'll explain everything to the police. Don't worry. Just get some help. Please, Mum. Please.'

'I can't, Erin . . . I can't . . .'

'Mum, are you hurt? Are you injured?'

'No. Yes. He hit me.'

'OK.' I breathed deeply in an effort to remain lucid. 'Where did he hit you? Can you walk?'

'He hit me, Erin . . . I'm sorry, Erin. I'm so sorry,' she bleated.

'It's OK, Mum. It's not your fault. Can you walk?'

She started to cry.

I prayed for strength. The air was thick with petrol fumes and I was exhausted and nauseous.

I squinted sideways at Kelman's balding head.

'Mum listen to me. You get some help. Please. I'm dying down here. I'm impaled . . .'

Was she going to leave me here to die? *Don't leave me here, Mum! Don't leave me!*

I could hear voices. Were they angels?

No. Deep voices, men's voices, urgent voices.

'Help me,' I cried soundlessly, 'help me. She's going to leave.'

I could hear footsteps and snatches of conversations.

'. . . There's petrol everywhere . . . don't bring that

in . . . Shit, this place could go up . . . Jesus! . . . Can we turn off the boiler? . . . Who called it in? . . . Weren't they here earlier? . . . Something about a man with a knife? . . . Yeah, some fruitcake lawyer . . .'

I wondered if it was any lawyer that I knew.

'Over here, quick! . . . we've got a casualty . . . somebody see to her . . . No! Take her out . . . all we need is oxygen in here! . . . Watch out for the blood . . .'

Help me. Help me.

A light swung past Kelman's feet.

'. . . Don't even think of switching that on! . . . It could go up . . . Turn off that fucking radio . . . Who's he? . . . What's he doing here? . . . Oh, right . . .'

'. . . A neighbour reported a man breaking in? . . . after that fruitcake called . . . Yeah, bloody lucky we came . . .'

'What the fuck is that? Who's down there?'

I woke with a start and a light blinded me.

Where was I? What was DSI Kelman doing here? Why was he lying on top of me?

'Help . . .' I mouthed.

'It's OK, miss, we'll have you out in a jiffy,' a man said, as he crouched down beside me.

I mouthed, 'Impaled.'

'What? What did you say?'

The man held his ear right up to my mouth. I could feel the weight of Kelman being lifted off me.

'I'm impaled . . .'

I could vaguely hear commands being issued as objects were dragged across the floor.

'Get the cutting gear! And oxygen . . . I don't give a fuck what I said earlier! . . . She's going . . . What have you got? . . . How many units? . . . Call ahead . . .'

I dipped into delicious sleep.

'What's your name, luv? We'll have you out in a minute. All right? OK? Miss? Miss?'

I ignored him.

'What's your name, luv? Talk to me. Stay with me . . .'

Go away. I want to sleep.

'. . . Erin? . . . Her name's Erin? . . . OK . . .'

'Erin! Erin. D'you know how long you've been down here?'

'I've broken . . . leg . . .' I murmured.

'OK, Erin. You just sit tight and we'll have you out in a minute. OK, Erin? Can you hear me, Erin?

'Erin! Answer me. Can you hear me?'

Go away! Let me sleep.

The adrenalin had dried up. I wanted to be nursed and comforted. I wanted strong arms around me, soothing away the pain and hurt. I wanted my mother. I thought of Paul holding Shereen in his arms, caressing her hair and murmuring love to her, and wished it could be me.

'How we doing, Erin? Can you answer me, luv?'

'I . . . want . . . sister.'

'OK. Where's your sister?'

'She's in shock. She wants her sister. How long has she been down there? Christ . . . she's in a bad way . . .'

'Who's your sister, Erin? Where will we find her?'

Shock? What did he know about shock? Shock was finding out your brother was a sadistic serial killer. Shock was your mother leaving you to die. Shock was being jammed in a corner by a sleeping policeman. What was I doing here, anyway?

'Who's your sister, Erin? Speak to me.'

His voice was a long way off and I wondered who he was. Was he outside? Why was he asking about my sister? Couldn't he just let me sleep? If I had a little nap I would feel much better.

'She lost . . . toe,' I whispered.

'She lost her toe? How come, Erin? Erin?'

'We're losing her! Get her out of there. She's going!'

I snorted with delirium . . . *this little piggy went to market* . . .

'Was it an accident, Erin, when she lost her toe?'

His voice drifted in and out of my head . . . *this little piggy stayed at home* . . . Where was I? Who was the man that kept waking me up? Was it a radio?

'Where's your sister, Erin? Can you hear me? Answer me, Erin! Hold on, Erin! Erin? Erin?'

TWENTY-THREE

An awful chemical-cum-rubber smell woke me.

The first thing I saw was my leg, carefully bound in a Thomas splint, suspended in front of me. I stared at the steel frame and leather bindings that ran from the top of my thigh to my ankle.

'Nurse!' I called weakly as I looked for a kidney bowl. 'Nurse!'

She was by my side in an instant.

'Feeling sick?'

She thrust the papier-mâché bowl under my chin. I gave several, painful, dry retches but my stomach was empty.

'Don't worry. People often feel sick after a nasty break and shock.'

She took my pulse and blood pressure. I felt dazed as she fussed around me.

'The consultant will be along in a minute to talk to you. And the anaesthetist.'

The anaesthetist meant only one thing, a general anaesthetic and surgery.

'Is my mother here? Is she OK?'

The nurse shrugged. 'Oh dear, I don't know. Was she injured?'

'I don't know. I . . . I . . .' What could I say? 'It doesn't matter. What time is it?'

'It's just past nine. Don't worry. You just rest until the consultant comes.'

'Is my sister here?'

'Not as far as I know. You came in by ambulance with two policemen. Tell you what, I'll check in the waiting room for your family. Okey-dokey?'

She smiled pleasantly and closed the door.

The consultant and anaesthetist appeared ten minutes later. They both asked questions about my general health, which I answered as best I could. The consultant commented that I was underweight.

'You have a supracondylar fracture to the left femur, which unfortunately caused disruption to the artery. I'll make small incisions here, and here, and a larger one, maybe three inches or so, vertically over your knee.

'I'm afraid we'll have to put an intra-medullary through the centre of the bone. It's like a twelve-inch nail with pins to hold it all together. The upside is that you should be mobile with the help of crutches in three or four days.'

'Great,' I smiled faintly.

'You'll be taken down shortly for pre-med. OK? Anything you want to ask?'

I shook my head.

The consultant looked down at me. 'Cheer up. It could be worse.'

Not from where I was lying.

After surgery I woke up feeling shaky and unwell. The Thomas splint had gone and my leg was nestled in a comfortable open splint, with strapping across my knee. I had one gigantic, swollen, elephant leg. I prayed that it wasn't permanent.

'You're awake,' a different nurse said, as she entered my room.

'I'll just take your blood pressure and then you can have a nice cup of tea.'

'Any brandy?' I asked hopefully.

'Afraid not, but you see this?' she pointed to the intravenous drip I was attached to. 'It's better than brandy. It's morphine for the pain. You administer it yourself.'

'This,' she held up a little button, 'works this.'

She pointed to the Venflon taped to the back of my hand. 'It's a syringe-driver.'

'Couldn't one overdose?' I asked, mildly perturbed.

'Nah, we don't give you enough for that, and you can only get a regulated dose. You ready for some tea and toast? D'you take milk?'

'Yes. Thanks.' I would have preferred brandy.

She came back a while later with a meagre one slice and a cup of watery tea.

'Is my sister here?'

'I don't know. Do you want me to check?'

'Yes, please. Is there a phone I could use?'

'We've got a call box on wheels. I'll bring it along when it's free. Now, I've just got to check the stitches in your back. Can you lean forward a bit? I know it's difficult.'

'What happened?' I asked.

'To your back? I'm not really sure, but you needed eight stitches. Were you in a car accident?'

'No . . . I fell down some stairs . . .'

Slowly, it came back to me. I was hiding in a corner, under a shelf, and managed to stab myself in the back. The irony was not lost.

'Oh, nasty! You must have fallen on something sharp. Your stitches are fine, though. That's the girl. You can sit back now. Careful. Well done.'

I ate my toast, drank my tea and waited. I waited for what seemed like ages, feeling isolated and vulnerable, until I dozed off.

Thumping pain from my leg woke me. I pressed the button and within seconds I felt warm and fuzzy.

I wanted to get up and wash my face, brush my teeth and have a pee. I sat there for a moment and wondered how to go about it, before I realised that I was attached to a urethral catheter. How lovely.

The nurse came back and smiled apologetically as she ushered in two men. I recognised them instantly because I was an expert at this now. They were police detectives. They introduced themselves, but I didn't really take in their names.

'May we have a word about the incident yesterday?' the senior one asked.

'But I've just had surgery . . . maybe you could come back later when I'm feeling a bit better?'

'You seem quite coherent to me,' the younger one commented, and took my chart from the bed-end. He scanned it wearily, then pointedly replaced it.

Their whole demeanour screamed hostility.

'We would be grateful if you could answer some questions about what happened to Detective Superintendent Kelman.'

'I'm not really sure what happened . . . he had come to help me and then he just kind of slumped on top of me.'

The senior officer made a big show of examining my morphine machine. 'What were you doing in the basement?'

'I was hiding.'

'Hiding? From whom?'

'My brother. It's very complicated. You see my brother, Leland, is meant to be dead, but he's not. He was in the house and I fell down the stairs when I was running away from him.'

He gave a contemptuous laugh, which surprised me.

'This is the "dead" brother you claimed abducted your sister yesterday? The dead brother you claimed was in the house, wielding a knife, not an hour before?'

I nodded. I felt woozy and dehydrated, and scared.

'You left several messages for DSI Kelman yesterday, asking him to call you, claiming Lucy Grant had seen this dead brother of yours. Can you explain that, Miss Paterson?'

'Lucy wrote to me and said she had seen Leland. It was the proof that DSI Kelman was looking for, because he thought that Leland was alive.'

'You were aware that DSI Kelman had been suspended from duty?'

'Yes, but I only found that out when the other police—'

He didn't let me finish.

'The officers that spoke to you yesterday? Your mother told them that you were having some sort of mental breakdown.'

Oh, my God! They didn't believe me!

'But she was lying! She knows he's alive. And Leland was there! I spoke to him!'

He rolled his eyes. 'When was he there? When did you speak to him?'

'When I was hiding . . . and DSI Kelman said he'd get help and . . . Leland was there! DSI Kelman tried to arrest him and he fell forward and . . . and Kelman came back and tried to help me up and then he fell . . . and . . .'

I wished that I hadn't taken the painkiller because my brain seemed to have a ten-second time lag.

'Did you or did you not stab DSI Kelman?'

'What? No! Of course not!'

Kelman was stabbed? When did that happen?

'Miss Paterson, you were lying injured in a tight cupboard space. While DSI Kelman was trying to reach you, he was stabbed in the back – with garden shears!' he hissed angrily.

Garden shears? How truly awful.

'I thought he was having a nap . . .'

'A nap?' he roared in disbelief.

'Yes, but I was in shock.'

'Miss Paterson, there were only three people in that basement. You. Your mother and DSI Kelman. DSI Kelman was murdered. Either by you or your mother.'

'No! Leland was there! I spoke to him. It must have been Leland!'

'For goodness' sake, Miss Paterson! He was not there. He couldn't possibly have been there.'

Great fearful sobs caught in my throat. 'But he was. He was! Ask her! Ask my mother.'

They exchanged evasive glances.

'What's happened to my mother?'

He paused dramatically before he said, 'She's having a psychiatric evaluation.'

'Why?'

'She's incoherent,' the junior officer muttered.

I frowned at him. Incoherent or wouldn't capitulate?

'She said Leland was there. Didn't she?'

'No, Miss Paterson. She denies being there at all.'

'But . . . but how could that be? I spoke to her.'

Had I imagined it?

'Miss Paterson, we know that she was there. She was found at the scene.'

I breathed a silent sigh of relief. Why had she denied being present when I needed her to back me up? Stupid cow. I, for one, wasn't going to lie, however unbelievable the truth.

'Did your mother stab DSI Kelman?'

I gaped at him. 'Don't be ridiculous! Leland stabbed him. He must have done.'

The officer sighed irritably. 'That's your statement, is it? The ghost of your dead brother stabbed a senior detective?'

'No. My statement is that my brother, Leland, is alive and well, and in his living form killed DSI Kelman. Check the forensics. There's no way I could have stabbed Kelman from the position I was in.'

Ominously, he was silent.

'My father. Does he know?' I asked.

'Has nobody been to see you, Miss Paterson?'

I shook my head.

'I'm sorry but . . . he had a stroke last night.'

'Don't say that! That's not true. That's a lie!'

'We thought that you would have been informed by now.'

'Do you know how he is? Do you know how bad it was?'

'I'm afraid I don't.'

'I need to get out of here. I need to see him,' I said more to myself than to them.

I rang the bell for the nurse and shifted uncomfortably in my bed. I could hardly move, never mind walk.

I clawed at the Venflon. The needle stung and blood spurted over my hand.

'Stop that. You'll hurt yourself!' the nurse shouted, as soon as she entered.

I ignored her and levered my body upright.

'I have to leave. I have to go to my father. He's had

a stroke. He needs me. How do I stand up? I need crutches or a wheelchair.'

'You can't get up!'

'My father needs me. I'm discharging myself. Get me some bloody crutches!'

My father, my poor father. What if he died, what if I never spoke to him again? It was too awful to imagine. My heart shattered with the very thought.

'Sir, could you hold her?' the nurse said.

The young detective forced me back against the pillows and the nurse raced from the room.

'Get off me! I'm discharging myself.'

I writhed under his grip but he pushed me back against the pillows.

'Calm down! Calm down.'

'Get off me! I can't stay here! He needs me! Don't you understand? He needs me.'

A doctor, syringe in hand, appeared within seconds with the nurse.

'All right, miss, that's enough. This is just a mild sedative. It will help you relax. OK? Nurse! Hold her. Get her arm.'

I tried to wrestle away but the doctor stuck the needle in my arm.

'I don't want you to do that! I don't want to relax. I need to get out of here ... I need ... to get ... my father ... I need ...'

The room was quiet and dim when I woke.

I tried to sit up but couldn't. For a sickening moment I imagined I was paralysed. I gazed down at my deadened leg and gasped when I saw the restraints.

Straps lay across my abdomen, across my thighs and over my ankles.

How had I come to this? How could they treat me so appallingly?

I lay prostrate, silently fuming. I would bloody sue them.

The nurse hesitated before she entered.

'How are you feeling now? A bit better?'

I glared at her. 'No, actually. Being bound up like a Christmas turkey isn't exactly my idea of recuperation.'

'Now, now,' she tutted, 'it was for your own good, to stop you from hurting your leg. You need to rest your leg.'

'My father? Is he OK? How is he?'

'He's stable.'

'I need to see him.'

I saw a glimmer of sympathy. 'That's not possible right now.'

'Can you untie me?'

'Only if you promise to behave yourself. No trying to get out of bed or moving that leg of yours,' she said reproachfully, as she took my blood pressure and pulse.

They were both racing. She raised her eyebrows and began to fill in my chart.

'This is ridiculous! Do you have any idea what I've been through?'

'Now don't get in a tizz. You'll only make yourself upset again. I won't undo these if you're going to be difficult.' She gave me a stern look.

'OK. I promise.'

As she undid the restraints she asked, 'How does your leg feel? Are you in any pain?'

There was a dull pain but not excruciating. I didn't want more morphine because it messed with my brain. If I was going to get out of this place, I needed my wits about me.

401

'It's OK just now,' I lied.

'Good. Are you up to seeing your visitor? Your partner's here,' she commented, as she left my room.

My partner? The last person I wanted to see was Douglas. I didn't want him to witness my pathetic state, my vulnerability. It would change how he viewed me.

There was a quiet knock at the door, but I feigned sleep. I wasn't up to sympathy and concern. I wanted solitude and self-pity.

'Erin?' he whispered.

'Paul?' I opened my eyes. He looked crumpled and exhausted, with dark shadows under his eyes. 'I thought it was . . .'

'I lied. It's family only, but we've got the same address, so I said that I was your partner. How are you?'

'Crap . . .'

He peered at my elephantine leg.

'It's a bad break, but with the big pin in it I should be up and about on crutches in a few days.'

'Good, good . . .' he said vaguely.

There was a distinct atmosphere.

'The nurse said they had to sedate you.'

'I was upset when they told me about my father, I overreacted.'

Why did I feel so awkward?

'He's OK. Brontë's with him.'

'Brontë! Jeezus! She doesn't understand him. It's me he needs.'

He gave me a sharp look. 'Brontë's doing fine in the circumstances.'

I felt chastised.

'I'm sorry. It's been such a . . . I'm sure she's . . . Is Max OK?'

'Yeah. He's a super wee guy. I've looked after him today. He was asking for you.'

I didn't want to recognise the feeling that came over me, a destructive mixture of jealousy and fear. I could see them in my mind's eye, cosy and happy, the potential family in the making.

Paul shifted uneasily. 'Is there anything I can get you? Magazines? Fruit?'

'No. I'm OK. Thanks.'

We were like strangers. He had difficulty making eye contact. A shiver ran through me.

'Paul? What is it?'

He put his hands in his pockets. That familiar feeling of dread swept over me.

'You think I'm involved, don't you? You think I had something to do with this!'

'Kelman died trying to save you. Even though he knew a fucking psycho was there and the place could go up at any second! He left three kids and a wife, and for what? A lying, stuck-up bitch! My best friend died for you.'

'But . . . I don't understand!' I wailed.

'You lured him there.'

'How did I lure him? I didn't even know he was . . .'

'You knew he was following you. I told you myself. He warned me not to trust you.'

'Listen to me, Paul,' I begged. 'I didn't know. I went to find Brontë. Leland left a message and I realised he was at the house. I tried to tell the police but no one would listen to me.'

'Kelman was suspended because of you!'

'How?'

'Did you or did you not report him?'

'Of course I didn't!'

'You honestly didn't write to the chief constable complaining about DSI Kelman?'

'No.' I rubbed my hands over my face. My lip hurt and I gingerly felt it. It was swollen and bruised.

Paul perched on the far edge of my bed.

'It was supposed to have come from you. That's why Kelman wouldn't return our calls. He thought you'd had him kicked off the case.'

'But why was he there? At the house?'

'He called me, after you parked around the corner and sneaked into the house. He wanted to know what you were up to, if you were meeting Leland.'

'But I called the bloody police!' I exclaimed.

'Kelman thought you were trying to get him arrested for unlawful entry.'

'Oh, Christ . . . what have we done?' I whispered.

Paul frowned.

'The police won't believe a word of it! With Kelman gone, there's nobody. Leland will disappear back into the shadows.'

'Was Leland definitely there?' Paul asked quietly.

I glared at him. 'Not you as well. Of all people!'

'Sorry! It's just so—'

'Fucking unbelievable,' I hissed.

The next six days were spent being browbeaten by physiotherapists into using my crutches. But it was wonderful to have the disgusting catheter removed.

They seemed like the longest six days of my life.

Neither my mother nor I were formally charged with DSI Kelman's murder, although details of the incident were widely reported in the press. There was no mention of Leland. And I knew what that implied.

404

Dutifully, Brontë had allowed the police investigators full access to our parents' files and personal papers. My mother, it seemed, had been withdrawing large sums of cash.

The two detectives came to see me several times, relentlessly going over my statement. They tried to be polite, but it was clear they suspected that I might be an accomplice to a police officer's murder.

Stuck there in my dismal room, hopelessness and despair threatened to sink me. I couldn't imagine picking up the pieces of my broken life.

And Leland's spectre haunted me.

A footstep outside my hospital-room door was enough to make me catch my breath. He could be lurking anywhere, seeking his chance. A passing shadow would make my skin tingle in terror.

I expected to see his face every time the door opened. I knew I couldn't live like this for much longer. My nerves were in shreds.

Only after false assurances that my sister would look after me was I finally allowed to leave. Liz drove me home, but I didn't invite her up to my apartment. I ached to be alone.

I had hobbled inside and groaned.

Paul's lilies were dead in a dry vase.

We had decided to postpone the opening of the new firm until December. We made the excuse that this would give me more time to recover, but the real reason was somewhat darker. Things had changed.

No longer was I viewed as a mildly eccentric, comical figure. Now I was seen as the inbred daughter of a crazed police killer. My previous bout of adverse publicity was innocuous, almost benign, compared to my present state of disrepute. We hoped my family notoriety would fade sufficiently for the new firm to open without lurid headlines.

I limped around my apartment, but doing anything was nigh on impossible. I needed both hands for my crutches, and my leg was so swollen and painful that I could only stand for a few minutes at a time. I wasn't even able to make a cup of coffee on my own, which heightened my sense of vulnerability.

I lolled around on my sofa, flicking channels, but his words tormented me, over and over. *I've come all this way for you . . .*

I hadn't spoken to my mother and she, in turn, had refused to speak to the police or her QC. Her silence left so many questions unanswered. Kelman was dead and, contrary to contrived post-mortem dramas, the dead do not speak.

Had I unwittingly given Leland the opportunity to murder him?

TWENTY-FOUR

The sky was charcoal-grey, threatening rain. Through the sunroof I watched the clouds roll overhead and felt time stand still.

I longed to see my father and dreaded it. I felt compelled to seek comfort from him, but feared the strain it could cause. I was afraid of tainting his precious memories.

I watched Paul's hands as he drove. Smooth hands, strong hands, hands that I had longed to hold. His wife had left him because of his nervous breakdown. They were another set of victims.

Paul and I had talked into the small hours the previous night.

Dissension had followed theory. Plausibility followed doubt. Argument followed consensus.

Fearful realisation was the outcome.

Leland was alive.

The shattered fragments knitted together, but dark and hideous thoughts flashed through my head. Thoughts I could not share.

Lucy's simple act of apology had sealed her fate. Her throat was cut and her tongue was removed in castigation. He had chosen her for no other reason than his own concealment. My mother, by telling him, might have wielded the knife herself.

As we parked outside my family home, I looked up at the house and felt thoroughly beaten. I was a fully paid-up fatalist now.

Max came bounding out to greet us, followed by Smith and Jones. Paul picked Max up and swung him in the air.

The dogs sniffed me enthusiastically, but Max stood three steps away, viewing my leg and crutches with apprehension.

'It's OK, Max. I'll be better in no time,' I coaxed, but that wasn't enough. He darted back to Paul.

'Max will get used to it. He's got a lot of things to adjust to right now,' Paul said, as he helped me up the steps and into the house.

'God, Erin!' Brontë sang as she greeted me. 'You look a fright.'

She had a point. I could barely take a shower or bath. I needed somebody to help me.

'Is Dad downstairs?' I asked hopefully.

Without a stairlift I would never make it up to his room. I had become a geriatric in the space of a week.

'Yes. We've made up the study as a bedroom. I was going to use the dining room, so he could see the pond, but it was too complicated to move the table and sideboards.'

'Paul. Come and see my Lego castle!' Max hollered from the den.

Paul smiled warmly at Brontë and ran up the stairs. My heart lurched. They were special friends. I was the outsider.

'How much does Dad know?' I asked, as I hobbled down the hall towards the study.

'Not much. But, Erin, prepare yourself. He dips in and out, you know. He seems quite switched on and then suddenly he's away with the fairies again.'

I always liked Brontë's choice of words.

'And Mother? What does he know about that?'

'I'm not telling him. You're the oldest. It's up to you.'

'Cheers,' I muttered, and entered his room.

It was dim and stank of old people and stale breath. I was shocked by how small he seemed in the large bed. Small, thin and old.

I sat down with difficulty and carefully placed my crutches on the floor. He didn't need to know about my fall.

I took his hand in mine and gave a gentle squeeze.

'Dad? Are you awake?' I whispered.

I felt a little pressure from his hand.

'It's me. Erin.'

The pressure was slightly stronger this time.

'How are you feeling? Any better?'

He half opened his eyes and peered down his nose at me.

'Mmm.' It sounded like 'Mum'.

'Mum? Do you want Mum? She's not here. She's away.'

'No,' he breathed.

'No? You don't want Mum?'

'I know . . .'

'Oh, good . . .' I faltered clumsily. 'You know she's away.'

He squeezed my hand quite fiercely.

'About him . . .'

I almost swore. What did he know? I hauled myself up to get closer to his quiet, laboured words.

'About who, Dad? Who do you know about?'

Saliva trickled from the paralysed side of his mouth, '. . . boy . . .'

He sort of tugged my hand towards him and gazed into my eyes.

'. . . careful, don't let him . . .'

409

'Leland? Do you mean Leland?' My heart was racing with fear.

He blinked at me, confusion slipping into his eyes. 'He's dead . . . be a brave girl . . . it's a long time ago . . . don't fret . . .'

I let out a breath of relief.

'What boy do you mean?'

He gave a tiny twitch of a smile. 'Boyfriend . . . he's a good man . . . careful, you don't freeze him out . . .'

'Paul?' I whispered.

He closed his eyes, but the tiny scrap of a smile remained.

'Paul's a good . . . Erin . . . you must try . . . be happy . . .' His words trailed away and his jaw hung slack.

Dad! Don't leave me! Please don't leave me alone!

'Brontë!' I screamed. 'Brontë! Get the nurse!'

I pushed my head across his chest and listened for his breathing. My fingers were still entwined with his, but his hand seemed limp.

Brontë and the nurse burst into the room together.

The nurse hauled me off him, none too gently, and took his pulse. Her eyes scanned the monitor he was attached to.

'He's fine. He was only falling asleep.'

'I thought . . . I didn't realise he would just . . . drop off like that.'

'I did warn you,' Brontë muttered.

'I didn't mean to alarm you. I'm sorry.'

Brontë rolled her eyes and helped me out of his room. 'What did he say? Did he ask about Mum?'

'Nothing, really. He mumbled something about knowing she was away.'

'So you didn't tell him?'

I hobbled away from her towards the kitchen.

'It wasn't necessary.'

I sat down at the kitchen table and let my pent-up emotions go.

Oh, Dad, don't leave me. You're my last hope. My last refuge. You're innocent. You didn't know. You believed Leland was dead. Don't leave me. I love you. I need you. Don't go.

My heart was breaking because I knew it would be soon.

Brontë came bustling in.

'Erin? Are you OK?'

I sniffed, wiped away the tears with the back of my hand and cleared my throat.

'No.'

She draped a comforting arm around my shoulders. 'I know. I was worried about how you'd take it.'

'Where does he think Mother is?'

Brontë looked slightly sheepish. 'At a bridge tournament. It was the best I could think of.'

'Well done. What about money? Do you have enough for the nurse and things?'

'Yeah. The firm's paying for it all.'

'Good. And you? What about the other problem?'

Brontë gave a little shrug. 'That's sorted. I mean, I've paid it off.'

I gave her a look. 'What with?'

'Would you like some coffee?' she said evasively.

'Yes, please. But what with?'

'I asked Dad, when I drove him to Crail. He was fine about it.'

For an awful moment I imagined Brontë had caused his stroke. 'My God, Brontë! You didn't tell him what it was for, did you?'

'No! I said I had overspent on credit cards.'

'OK, OK. Sorry.'

She busied herself making coffee.

'Paul's been a great help, I hear.' I tried to sound nonchalant but didn't quite manage it.

'Yeah, he's been super and he's a natural with Max.'

'Dad seems to think he's my boyfriend,' I said lightly.

'That's probably my fault.' Brontë poured me some coffee. 'Dad wanted to know who Paul was and I said he was your friend. He's just a bit confused.'

'So Dad has met Paul?'

'Yeah, he's been reading to him and stuff. They seem to have hit it off, as much as they can in Dad's state.'

'And . . . what about you?'

Brontë sat down opposite me and grinned. My stomach somersaulted.

'He's great. I mean, really chilled and thoughtful. But he's not my type.'

'That's not what I meant.'

'Oh?' She arched an eyebrow. 'I got the impression you had a soft spot.'

'To be perfectly honest I'm past caring now,' I lied.

'Do you want to talk?'

'No. Not about that. I need a favour from you.'

'Sure.'

'I need you to drive me to Leverndale.'

'You're going to see Mum?'

'Yes. Without her, none of this makes sense. And I can't go on like this. I simply can't.'

'OK,' she said, and quickly finished her coffee.

I stared out of the window and felt the emptiness inside me grow. There would soon be nothing left of me, only the faintest trace of my existence.

How can you mend a broken heart?

TWENTY-FIVE

Leverndale Psychiatric Hospital was on the outskirts of Glasgow. Majestic, Victorian buildings set high on a hill, with rooks and doves fluttering in and out of paneless windows.

The buildings were A-listed, but they had been abandoned to the elements. A relic of a bygone era, they sat imposing and resonant.

Leverndale had been rebuilt within its own grounds – neat modern bungalows in the shadow of the noble original. Foreboding engulfed me as I gazed up at its empty, lifeless shell.

Brontë parked and then helped me out of the car, but did not accompany me.

'Aren't you coming?' I asked.

'I can't,' she said. 'I just don't ... want to. After what has happened.'

'OK ... but ...'

'Sorry, Erin. But I can't.'

I understood her reluctance but was irritated just the same. For once, I had thought I wouldn't have to go it alone.

With polite efficiency, I was signed in and escorted to Secure Ward 2. My stomach knotted with anxiety.

She was waiting for me in a small anteroom. She looked ten years older.

'Oh, my! What have you done to yourself, dear?' she exclaimed.

'I broke my leg. Don't you remember? You were there.'

She wrinkled her forehead. 'No . . . when was that, dear? Were you skiing?'

'About eight days ago! In the basement,' I said impatiently.

'Goodness! What were you doing down there? Does your father know? I hope the firm is paying for the best orthopaedics.'

With difficulty, I sat down opposite her on a hard wooden chair. Subtly, the nurse sat on a chair beside the closed door. And the panic button.

'Mum, the firm is . . . gone.'

She gasped in horror. 'What do you mean, gone?'

Either she was completely gaga or a world-class actress.

'You and Michael McCabe dissolved the firm and went into partnership with Cohen Freidmann.'

She looked utterly bewildered.

'When?'

I glanced over my shoulder at the nurse, who smiled back sympathetically.

'A couple of weeks ago, before Detective Superintendent Kelman died . . .'

'Oh? Who was he, dear? Did you know him?'

'Yes, Mother. So did you. You were there.'

'At the funeral? When was that?'

'Not at the funeral. When he died!'

'Oh, no, dear. You must be mistaken. Was he one of your lot?'

By that, she meant had he attended an upmarket independent school, had he been in The Pony Club?

'No, he was . . . he interviewed me after Lucy Grant died . . .'

'Lucy Grant? Of the Granville-Grants? How awful!'

414

I blinked at her in absolute disbelief. Was she going to feign memory-loss about everything I said?

'Leland murdered Lucy. DSI Kelman was investigating him.'

'That's not a very nice thing to joke about, Erin. Not about people we know. Colonel Mustard in the kitchen with a candlestick is funny. Manners make the man, dear. Remember?'

'Mum, stop! Please. Tell me what happened?'

'Happened – when?'

'The day DSI Kelman was murdered!'

'But you said he died.'

'Yes. But he was murdered!'

She pursed her lips.

'Is this some sort of word game, Erin? You know I can't abide those. Don't like crosswords much, either. Can't we play cards instead? Or Monopoly?'

The insanity plea might just work. We used to have this argument on rainy Saturdays at the cottage. I was never allowed Scrabble or anything vaguely cerebral; it always had to be cards or snakes and ladders. We had regressed two decades.

'I didn't bring any cards,' I said lamely.

She smiled. 'That's all right. They'll have some in the drawing room.'

'It doesn't matter. How are you? Are you OK?'

'Oh, yes. It's quite nice here. We should have come on holiday here before.'

I closed my eyes for a brief moment. It was true. She was barking.

'Can I bring you anything? Some books? Anything?'

'No, dear. I'm fine. They've got a nice library. Would you like to stay for tea?'

Stay for tea? Where on earth did she think she was?

'Yes. Thank you. I'd love to,' I stammered.

'How lovely! Sometimes they have angel cake.'

'Oh, goody. How nice.'

I was dumbfounded.

We sat in hushed composure for one more life-draining minute. Mother would smile at me every now and then, and I would smile back. Jane Austen revisited.

'Well, then,' she said eventually, 'shall I ring for tea?'

The nurse stood up and opened the door. Mother smiled at us both and ambled out. I remained seated in stunned silence.

Eventually, I levered myself out of the low chair and went in search of her doctor.

He was portly and avuncular. Somehow, that was strangely reassuring.

'Lady Paterson', he sighed, after ten minutes of interrogation, 'is exhibiting classic signs of psychiatric illness, psychosis and denial.'

'But how can she think she's on holiday in a country house hotel?'

'She's displacing. If she admits to herself she's in a secure psychiatric unit, then she has to admit the reason why she is here.'

'Will she . . . ever get better?' My voice quivered.

He gave me a supportive pat on the hand.

'Perhaps.'

That meant, no.

Before I left, I peered through the little window into her room.

She was sitting in an easy chair, humming to herself while reading a magazine. My eyes filled.

I faced losing both my parents and couldn't find the strength to be stoical.

TWENTY-SIX

'Why are there two goldfish in a bowl on my desk?' I asked Karen, on my way through reception. 'Have you been to a fair?'

'Suzi said it's good feng shui. I think they're cute. She's getting me some too,' Karen said, before she answered the phone.

I rolled my eyes skyward. Suzi Lu was our newly qualified assistant. I had to admit she was good at her job, but from one day to the next I didn't know which way my desk would be facing.

I went back to my office and glanced at the fish. Admittedly they were cute, but would they smell? I opened my sandwich and watched them do a couple of circuits.

Douglas knocked and came in.

'Neat fish. What are they called?'

'Fang and Huey?'

He put a file on my desk and hovered. I glanced at him, sighed facetiously, and opened the file.

'Before you say anything, I think it's worth a review.'

'Douglas, I do compensation. This is a civil action to prove . . .'

'Yes, but if we won, we could sue for compensation.'

'The guy was tried in the High Court, the verdict was "not proven". What makes you think I could conduct a pseudo-criminal-cum-civil action to prove his guilt? The advocate deputy couldn't make it stick.'

'But it's obvious he's guilty. The jury were just too intimidated to find him guilty.'

'Why is this so important to you?'

He shuffled uncomfortably.

'Her parents. They're devastated that he got off. They think it's because he is wealthy and powerful, and well connected. I looked at the evidence and it's all there.'

'Douglas, he had one of the best QCs in the country. I'm only a solicitor. I would be a lamb to the slaughter.'

'Like she was,' he muttered. 'Anyway, I thought you were going to take the Bar exams?'

'Eventually, not tomorrow.'

I watched his face fall.

'OK, OK. I'll look at it. How are they going to pay?'

'Well, I thought that we could cover the costs and recoup from any compensation award made.'

I put my head in my hands. '*If* we won an award. This is a business. Remember? It may resemble a charity, but it's still a capitalist venture, however heavily disguised.'

'You'll consider it, though?' he asked. He knew he had me.

'On one condition. You find a new cleaner,' I said quickly.

How difficult was it to get someone to come in each morning or evening to vaccum and dust? Nigh on impossible, we had discovered. They either didn't turn up or spent all their time smoking and drinking tea.

'It's a deal,' he said cheerfully.

The victim was a seventeen-year-old girl called Morag McCallum, who lived quite near to the alleged killer. He was a forty-one-year-old divorcé, George Kemp, who had inherited a small engineering firm that he had turned into a major success. He lived in

Bothwell, a town outside Glasgow, home to footballers, motor-trade and confectionery millionaires.

I read through the precognitions from the failed criminal trial and was surprised by the not proven verdict. Maybe Douglas had a point?

Her body was found face down in a wooded area close to the River Clyde. It was popular with dog-walkers and the path eventually led to the ruins of Bothwell Castle. She had been dead for approximately thirty hours before she was found. I skipped to the post-mortem.

. . . rigor mortis resolved, body flaccid . . . livor mortis settlement and fixed lividity evident in the dorsal aspect . . . face and neck congested and dark red . . . jugular vein and carotid artery occluded . . . petechiae present in the conjunctiva and the mucosa of the lips . . . Blunt trauma to throat consistent with compressive force by hands . . . fracture of hyoid bone and severe contusions to the neck . . .

She had been strangled – manually, it would appear, because there were no ligature marks – but not sexually assaulted. She had also been moved. She had been found face down, but the autopsy showed that immediately after she had died she had lain on her back for at least six hours.

Lividity was caused by the stagnation of blood in the blood vessels, which then settled into parts of the body. If a corpse lay undisturbed for six hours or more, the blood collected in the body parts closest to the ground. Morag had been turned over.

Did I want any part of this new nightmare? In absolute honesty, no. Why had they brought it to me? I wasn't known for these types of cases. Did they somehow imagine that it would strike a chord? I gave an involuntary shudder.

A strand of the web from a stranger's life had attached itself to mine. The mere act of acknowledging her trauma and reading her file was enough to connect us.

Was this really how the world worked? A chaos of lives that intertwined and then ran parallel from one moment to the next. If that were true, then one's own decisions were meaningless. Destiny laid out a plan and would have its way, no matter how anyone tried to resist.

I closed my eyes and thought for a moment before I opened the forensic entomology report. From the insect activity we would know whether she had been murdered where she was found, or had been dumped there.

Brontë knocked on my door before she entered. I shut the file quickly.

Finlay sauntered in behind her. 'So, this is the nerve centre? Cute fish, man.'

'No, this is just my office. Centre of operations appears to be reception.'

Everybody seemed to have a rare old time out there, while Liz and I worked in the back recesses.

'Finn wants to know what we're doing for Christmas. Do you think they'll let Mum out for the day?' Brontë said.

'I don't know. It would probably have to be supervised.'

'It would be nice for Dad if she was home,' Brontë added.

'I'll speak to them and see if they'll consider it.' Privately, I thought it might throw up another problem – what we would tell Dad when she left again.

'Do you want us to come with you?' Finlay suggested.

'No, I'll be OK.'

Finlay dipped his finger into my fishbowl and frightened the fish. 'Have the police got any further with their investigation?'

We had been oddly thrilled when the police had asked permission to carry out DNA tests on Brontë, Finlay and me. It indicated that unidentified forensic evidence had been discovered. I hoped it was close enough to our DNA samples, but not an exact match. I prayed it suggested Leland.

'I don't know, but maybe with the DNA they might conclude that he really was there and not a figment of my imagination.'

Finlay dried his fingers on his cargo pants.

'If they caught him, would they let Mum out?'

'Well, she hasn't been formally charged with anything, so I don't see how they could insist she remains at Leverndale.'

'Is she still as bad?' Brontë asked.

'Mostly. She's just . . . very unresponsive.'

'Maybe it's you?' Brontë suggested. 'Maybe if one of us saw her, then she would be more talkative.'

This had been a source of disagreement for some time.

'I'll ask the warden again about visits from you both, but for now they're only allowing me because I'm a lawyer.'

That was a shabby lie. In truth, I couldn't allow our meagre visiting rights to be used for any other purpose than my own. Finding the truth. Finding Leland.

'That seems so unfair,' said Brontë huffily.

'I know. I'll do what I can to change their minds.'

Finlay nodded.

'I'll put in a formal request for her release at Christmas, even if it's only temporary. OK?'

'Will you tell her we're asking after her?' Brontë asked.

'Of course. I send your love every time.'

I didn't want to put her down. She was working hard and she was great with the other staff and any clients, so I cringed inside as I said, 'Em, I don't know how to put this, but would you mind not wearing jeans to the office in future?'

'I know, I'm sorry. But we are a bit behind with the laundry.'

'I know it's hard for you with Dad and Max. Would you like me to speak to Martha about getting another pair of hands to help? I'll pay for it.'

She shrugged and left. It seemed I only opened my mouth these days to change foot.

The rest of the working day passed quickly. I glanced at my watch but the hands had leapt forward. I made sure I had everything in place for the following morning's meeting – Mrs Murphy wanted our little firm to set up her trust fund.

It was a minor thing but it brought a glimmer of hope. She trusted me and was willing to put her money where her mouth was. Francis Park had personally delivered all the relevant paperwork and had offered his unofficial assistance in guiding me through the process.

I packed up my briefcase and, as an afterthought, took the Morag McCallum files with me.

When I tried to enter reception, a gigantic, ten-foot-tall, Norway spruce was blocking the door. I fought my way around it, cursing and muttering as it spiked me repeatedly.

'Where on earth did this come from?' I said as I emerged from behind it.

'Norway, I think,' Suzi replied helpfully, and continued, with Douglas's help, to wrestle the tree and enormous pot over to the window. Soil spilled everywhere.

'Isn't it rather large?'

'Goodness no! It's perfect,' Suzi enthused.

'I thought you didn't celebrate Christmas?'

'We don't celebrate the virgin birth, if that's what you mean, but I like all the festivities and decorations.'

'So I can see,' I muttered, and limped towards the main door.

'What's that wood in Shakespeare that moves about?' Douglas asked the general company.

'Great Birnam wood to high Dunsinane hill Shall come against him,' I quoted airily from *Macbeth*. 'And it doesn't move about, they used the branches as camouflage.'

Suzi popped her head around the tree and grinned.

'Is there anything you don't know?'

'Lots.'

Douglas called after me. 'We've got a new cleaner!'

'Great!'

'Suzi's gran,' was what I thought he said. Another Lu working for us? It didn't bear thinking about. And the tree would never last until Christmas. We would be deluged in pine needles.

The streets were busy. With only a month to go before the big day, people were leaving work early to do a spot of shopping. I hadn't done any yet. Normally I had my gifts bought and wrapped by the end of November, but this wasn't an ordinary year. This was the last year of the millennium, one that we should have taken special note of. Instead, we had staggered from crisis to catastrophe and back again.

A car suddenly came to a halt beside me and Paul leaned across to open the passenger door. I was surprised to see him. I had often noticed couples picking each other up from work and wondered now if that was how we looked to uninformed eyes.

Could they see we were not bound by Cupid but by suffering? For the millionth time I wished for a different life, for another chance. Leland's legacy had brought us together, but it had also torn us apart.

'Do you need a lift somewhere?' he asked.

'Thanks, but no. I'm going to do some Christmas shopping.'

I used the door of his car for support, although I could walk quite well now with only one crutch.

'I'll see you later, then. When will you get home?'

'Seven or so. I'll give you a call.' I shut the car door and hobbled off down the street.

I happened to glance back up the street while I waited for the pedestrian lights and saw Brontë jump into his car.

I tried not to let the feeling settle.

At seven o'clock I didn't go home. I went to the movies, on my own.

Maybe *Sixth Sense* wasn't the best choice. When the little boy, Cole, said, 'I see dead people,' I almost shrieked.

I see dead people, too, I thought. Except they're still alive.

TWENTY-SEVEN

Drizzle fell softly throughout his funeral. The sky was almost white but the cold December air was grey.

The interment was private. We huddled beside Father's grave wrapped in our grief. During the service we had all held hands tightly, but now our mother stood like a silhouette at the edge of his grave. Two wardens from Leverndale watched from a respectful distance.

Both Finlay and Brontë had spoken to her, but were upset by her deterioration. Occasionally, on my visits, I was rewarded with a glimmer of lucidity. Not that I shared what I gleaned. I stored it away, hoarding the tiny pieces of the puzzle. Only when I had fitted them all together would I disclose it.

She hadn't been hiding Leland for a decade as we had presumed. He had simply turned up, out of the blue, in March. 'I thought he was a ghost,' Mother had whispered.

I watched as she laid flowers at her husband's graveside. Did I imagine the flicker of a frown when she noticed the empty space left by Leland's headstone? I had arranged for its removal.

I had spent many hours with my father before he died. Reading him articles from his bird magazines, telling daft stories about the dogs and Max. Trying to be as much of a comfort to him as he was to me. Even being in the same room made me feel better. He never alluded to Leland, and I let it rest, undisturbed, as some things should be.

When he asked about Mother, he readily accepted Brontë's original explanation. It was the longest bridge tournament in history.

Media attention made the service torturous, but I was buoyed by the turnout. It was reassuring to witness so many people from his life and career paying their last respects.

DS Marshall and Michael McCabe had come, as had Paul, Liz, Douglas and Karen. They hadn't all known my father but their attendance was a welcome mark of their regard. There were some notable absentees, but who could blame them? Not everybody wanted to be associated with such a notorious family.

From behind my Jackie O dark glasses I had scanned the faces of the mourners. I had duped myself into believing Leland would attend – as an act of theatrical defiance.

We travelled back from the graveyard in a cortège of just two limousines. We could have fitted into one, but that had seemed so meagre, that I'd insisted on two.

Max thought it was a hoot having a limo in the driveway and had pressed every button, sending windows up and down, for half an hour before we had left for the funeral service. We had decided it was better if he didn't attend.

I steadied myself against the limousine's door as I thanked the driver and funeral director.

Max came dashing out of the house for yet another look.

'I wish I'd had a ride in it, Ern,' he sighed.

I glanced at the driver, who smiled.

'OK. Once around the block, but don't play with the buttons,' I warned.

Max shrieked and scrambled in. What was it with

boys and cars? I knew that the family was waiting for me, but I deliberately stayed outside in the soft mist of rain until Max came back.

According to my father's instructions, his will was to be opened immediately after the funeral. In my mind's eye, I could see us seated around the drawing room, like in one of those crap, made-for-TV movies, gasping as the executor read out the bequests.

Why we had to endure it today was beyond me. I wanted time to grieve, solitude to grieve. I didn't want to rake over the fine details of his last will and testament.

I tipped the limousine's driver and took Max inside.

'Where've you been?' Brontë asked, as she met us at the front door.

'I let Max have a ride in the limo.'

'We're all waiting,' she barked.

'Good.'

What was the great hurry? To see how much she had inherited? Money-grabbing cow.

I went to the kitchen where Martha was making sandwiches.

'Could I have a cup of coffee, Martha?'

'Do you want something stronger? They're all having sherry.'

'Any Valium?'

'Afraid not. Aspirin's about the best I can do.'

I took the pills she offered and sipped my coffee.

So much had been stolen from us since our last family funeral. I wished with all my heart that Leland had been in the casket we had buried – then none of this would have happened. Endlessly, I wondered whose body we had actually interred, whose body Mother had identified and later exhumed and cremated.

I made my way slowly to the drawing room, but Max bounced up to me.

'Ern, why don't we have a Christmas tree? Everybody else has one.'

'I know, pumpkin, but we thought it would be better to wait until Grandpa had gone to heaven.'

I smoothed his fine blond hair. Finally, Brontë had told me his father's name – and that she never told him she was pregnant. It was another indistinct hurdle that might clutter our future.

'Grandpa didn't like Christmas trees?' Max said, in surprise.

'Of course he liked Christmas trees, but maybe it would have made him sad to see a Christmas tree when he wasn't going to be here.'

He nodded slowly. 'So he knew he was going to die?'

How had I got myself into this?

'No, it's just that if we had put up the Christmas tree, then it might have made Grandpa sad because we were happy it was Christmas and he was ill.'

Max frowned and cocked his head to one side.

'But Christmas is for baby Jesus. Shouldn't we be happy?'

How come Brontë never got asked these questions? I was sure she primed Max to save the difficult ones for me.

'Yes, we should be happy. I'm sorry, Max, I think I've confused you. We haven't got a Christmas tree because . . . because . . . Grandpa was allergic to pine needles . . . and . . . we'll get one tomorrow.'

'Whoopee! Can I come with you? Can I choose it? Can it be this big? Can we have a star on top?' He stretched his arms as wide as he could.

Why hadn't I said that in the first place? If he had asked to paint me green and cover me in fairy lights, I would have agreed.

I took a deep breath and went into the drawing room.

Francis Park and Iain Halliday stood up to greet me. I thanked them for coming and took a seat beside Finlay.

Iain stood in front of the fireplace with a bundle of papers in his hands. He cleared his throat and solemnly began.

'According to the last will and testament of Sir Maxwell Laspic Ross Paterson, MBE, duly signed and recorded on the twentieth day of May in the year nineteen hundred and ninety-nine . . .'

I frowned. He had rewritten his will after his second stroke? How peculiar. I listened half-heartedly as Iain read out the usual legal jargon that went with these things. What had made him change his will?

'My estate is to be divided equally between my three children, Erin Georgina Paterson, Brontë Elizabeth Paterson, Finlay Ross Paterson, and my grandson, Maxwell David Paterson. Maxwell David's share shall be held in trust until he is twenty-one years of age. I nominate his aunt, Erin Paterson, his uncle, Finlay Paterson, and his mother, Brontë Paterson, to be trustees along with Iain Halliday and Francis Park . . .'

Brontë's mouth hung open in shock. Finlay mumbled 'Jeezus H. Christ' under his breath, and I had to stop myself from interrupting.

I was dumbfounded. I had not foreseen this. He had left it all to us. He had cut Mother out of his will.

Iain continued to read from the bundle of papers: clauses regarding our inheritance, Max's trust fund, special bequests to Martha, his favourite charities and old friends. He began to recite a list of Father's assets that were to be included in his estate. The house, any money receivable from the new partnership of Cohen Paterson, the cottage in Crail, his collection of Scottish colourists, his pension fund, his PEPs and TESSAs, his bank accounts.

I wondered how many intact assets were left. I had a quiet suspicion that Mother, with power of attorney, had been siphoning them off when cash began to run low. From what I had seen of their bank statements, they had a very depleted cash flow.

Iain paused dramatically and regarded each of us in turn. The colour had risen in Brontë's cheeks and Finlay had lit a hand-rolled cigarette that smelled suspiciously sweet.

'There's one more thing. A final clause.'

He paused again.

'It is Sir Maxwell Paterson's express wish that his beloved wife, Georgina Grace Paterson, does not benefit from their marital assets upon his death. Therefore, they are to be disposed of and dealt with as his three adult beneficiaries agree upon and see fit. Until such time as she has expired, Sir Maxwell Paterson's estate will continue to financially support her only in so far as reasonable living expenses, housing and/or nursing care.'

My first thought was, if she contested the will it wouldn't stand up in court, but more pressing questions troubled me.

'Iain, may I ask you something?'

'Of course.'

'What made my father change his will and why is there that clause at the end?'

Iain poured himself another large sherry.

'Quite frankly, I don't know. But I don't have to tell

you, Erin, that it might not stand up in court.'

Typical lawyer. He had changed the subject.

'I realise that. I realise that this is very difficult for you and for Francis. Given our present circumstances, though, any light you could shed on matters would be greatly appreciated.'

Francis pursed his lips before he spoke. I could almost see him choosing his words.

'After his stroke, your father sent word that he wanted to change his will. I have to admit we presumed that as he faced mortality he wished to include his grandson, but he wanted to redraft the will from start to finish. We were surprised by the exclusion of your, em, mother in the division of his estate, but assumed she was independently wealthy and it had been agreed between them.'

'And?' I said.

'And what?' Iain faltered.

'And what motivated this?'

'We don't know for certain,' Francis said, 'but after all the . . . nastiness, we thought that could be it.'

'But the will was changed in May. Any "nastiness", as you put it, only occurred in October.'

'I'm sorry, Erin, but we're as puzzled as you are. Perhaps your mother, fearing he was close to death, told him something. Last confession and all that.'

I refused to acknowledge the obvious reason because it would rob me of his innocence.

'When are you scheduled to read her the will?'

'Six o'clock tonight.'

Iain held my gaze. I knew what he was thinking – she might contest it, but that didn't matter to me. What mattered was the reason for the dramatic changes.

We had afternoon tea and made small talk, but I was

desperate for them to leave so that Finlay, Brontë and I could talk.

They finally departed just before four o'clock. Martha began clearing away the tea things, as I called Brontë and Finlay back into the drawing room.

'We need to have a chat.'

'About the will?' Brontë asked.

'And other things,' I said solemnly.

Finlay wiggled his eyebrows dramatically. I loved Finlay. He was so different from Brontë and me, so untainted.

'I never expected that, man. Cutting Mum out completely.'

'So, what are we going to do?' Brontë poured herself another large gin and tonic. I watched the bubbles cling to the side of the heavy crystal glass, then rise rapidly to the top.

'Do we really want to take our shares and not give them to her?' I asked.

Both of them looked at me as if I were an alien.

'I see,' I said curtly.

'Oh, come on, Erin. She's not exactly Mother Teresa. She's been hiding a murderer for the last ten years!' tutted Brontë.

'There's more to it than that, Brontë, and you know it. Most of the time she believed he was dead.'

'But that doesn't change what he's done.'

'But how does punishing her help?' I said.

'How can you be so goddamned understanding? Remember, he's still out there!' Brontë leapt to her feet, spilling gin and tonic on the carpet.

'But she thought she was doing the right thing. She's *ill*. She's not the same person—'

Brontë didn't let me finish. 'But he's done terrible

things! She was giving him money. What if her will leaves everything to Leland?'

'Don't be ridiculous, Brontë!'

Finlay was squirming. He hated arguments and any mention of Leland's crimes sent him into an agony of denial.

'Hey, girls, let's not argue . . .' he said.

We both rounded on him.

'Shut up, Finn! You have no idea what we've been through!' Brontë yelled.

'This has nothing to do with you,' I said.

Finlay held his hands up in surrender. 'I'm still your brother, man.'

'Sorry. But you really don't know the half of it,' I said. 'Feel lucky.'

'Are you going to see her?' Brontë asked.

'Tomorrow. Once she's spoken to Iain.'

'We'll just have to wait until then,' Brontë said grumpily, and sat back down.

'If she does agree to Father's will, we'll have inheritance tax to pay.'

'A lot?' Brontë asked.

'Yes. We'll probably have to sell the house. It's his major asset.'

'But, it's like our . . . home . . .' Finlay said.

'I know. But Brontë and you can't rattle about in here. Its upkeep is horrendous. Any additional capital you inherited, if not paid in tax, would be swallowed up.'

'But what if you came and lived here too? All of us in one big house. We could split the costs.'

'No way!' I said.

'Come on. What do you say, Brontë? Wouldn't it be cool?'

Brontë raised an eyebrow. 'She's like living with the gestapo, Finn. You wouldn't like it.'

'I can assure you, Finlay, you wouldn't like living with me one little bit. And put out that joint. If Mother contests it, then it will revert back to his previous will or he will be declared intestate.'

Brontë and Finlay looked blank.

'Intestate basically means that the courts regard it as if there was no will, so it reverts to Scottish law. Eventually, Mother will inherit just about everything, anyway. That means she can tell both of you to leave the house. Even if she's incarcerated, she can still legally force you out.'

I didn't explain that I could hold up such a case in court for years.

'OK, another suggestion. We don't sell the house. Brontë and you take it on and I get my share of its value from his other assets. You could live here and pay for the upkeep by getting a job.'

I knew Finlay would really love that idea.

'But I was planning on going back to Thailand, you know, to chill,' he said.

Brontë slumped further down in the sofa and slugged her drink.

'Let's call it a day and discuss it tomorrow. I'll find out from Iain or Francis how Mother took the news.'

'Cool.'

'And Brontë – don't drink too much. We've got a lot on tomorrow and you were late twice last week.'

She gave me a withering look.

I went upstairs to see Max. He was humming 'Away in a Manger' while he drew a Santa.

'I'm making Christmas cards,' he said, and held up a piece of paper.

'They're lovely. Will you send me one?'

'Yep, and Finn, and Mrs Orman at the nursery, and Grandma.'

'That's nice,' I replied vaguely.

How were we going to do Christmas? It had always been celebrated in this house. I would come over on Christmas eve and help to lay the table. The tree would be in the drawing room and the house would smell of mince pies and pine needles. It was the one time of year that I had felt part of things.

'Have you decided what you want from Santa?' I asked.

Max glanced up at me. 'Yep. I want a wee brother or sister.'

I hoped he hadn't told Brontë that.

'What about some Lego?'

'Nah, I've got lots. Ern, wouldn't you like a wee brother or sister?'

'I've already got one of each.'

'No, I mean a wee brother or sister of your own. Like a baby.'

'Do you mean a baby of my own? A son or daughter?'

Max beamed. 'Yes. That's it. A baby. Like baby Jesus.'

'Yes, I'd love one, but sometimes things don't work out the way we want.'

'You could ask Santa.'

'That's right, Max. I could ask Santa.'

I kissed him on the forehead and went home.

TWENTY-EIGHT

Brontë was annoying me, as were Suzi, Douglas and Karen.

I could have been forgiven for thinking they had never experienced Christmas before, by the way they carried on. Only Brontë had a legitimate excuse – she did have a small child – but the rest of them were irritatingly puerile. They had even asked if they could play festive music in reception.

Grudgingly, I had agreed, figuring classical choirs singing elegant carols. But I swore I would scream if I heard 'Santa Claus Is Coming to Town' filter through my door again.

I stared meanly at the Morag McCallum file and wished I had never opened it. Her parents had been in to see me and I felt genuinely overwhelmed by their case. Any festive atmosphere was entirely inappropriate.

I had gone through the prosecution's case in fine detail and couldn't find a single flaw. The case had failed simply because so much of the evidence was circumstantial. It pointed to George Kemp purely through his association with Morag, but it certainly didn't prove beyond a reasonable doubt that he was her killer. Gutlessly, I hadn't said that to them.

They had been sadly mistaken in coming to me. I simply wasn't clever enough to fight their daughter's case. And that depressed me. My secret belief that I could have been a stunning criminal lawyer was yet another self-deception.

Christmas was only ten days away and I certainly wasn't in the mood. Only six days previously, I had buried my beloved father and uncovered some things that stopped me in my tracks.

Mother had known about his will. She had helped him draft it.

When I had asked why she had excluded herself, she had leaned towards me and whispered, 'So he couldn't touch it.'

'Who couldn't touch it?' I had whispered back.

She had smiled broadly and nodded.

She claimed she had dissolved the firm to protect me – and it – from the inevitable firestorm Leland's reappearance would create.

But Leland wouldn't do those things. He wouldn't hurt a fly. Leland was dead. He drowned twelve years ago.

On it went. Mournfully, I listened as she tripped from lucidity to denial. I didn't know if we would ever get her back.

My anger with her dissipated as I witnessed her struggle with guilt and remorse, peppered with maternal defensiveness.

Yes, she had given him money, but it was only fair with him being away for so long.

Where had he been?

Leland was dead. He drowned. It was a terrible tragedy.

I confronted her with his exhumation and crema-tion, but her answer was simple. The family plot was almost full, only one space remained. In death, Father and she were determined to lie together.

'We never expected to outlive any of our children,' she said.

They had exhumed him purely to free up the space. Her mistaken identification appeared genuine.

'Why didn't you tell us?' I had asked.

'We didn't want to upset you,' she replied plainly.

Again, the police had interviewed me. I no longer felt outraged by their insinuations. I merely felt defeated and depressed.

I was jolted from my malaise by shrieks of laughter. I cursed silently and went through to reception.

The sight of Granny Lu, dressed as a reindeer, greeted me. Complete with flashing antlers and a glowing red nose.

I tried to remain calm.

'Mrs Lu. Shouldn't you be finished by now?'

Suzi Lu's grandmother was technically our new cleaner, although what cleaning she actually did eluded me. She appeared to be in the office constantly.

She beamed at me. 'Finish, yes. Play now.'

I didn't want to offend her, but the mayhem she caused was getting to me. I smiled back politely.

'Good. Thank you. I'm sure the rest of you have things to do.'

Douglas shuffled; Karen avoided eye contact. Brontë rolled her eyes expressively.

'Yes. Yes. Always work for the capable man,' Mrs Lu nodded enthusiastically.

This was another of her eccentric traits – strange, Confucius-type sayings. I was still trying to work out what precisely she meant by, 'the waters of the golden pool are covered with sleeping mandarin ducks'.

'It's only ten days till Crimbo. Lighten up,' muttered Brontë.

I ignored her.

'Douglas. A word, please.'

I marched back through to the relative sanity of my own office. Douglas stood in the doorway, looking miserable in anticipation of his dressing-down.

'Come in and sit down.'

I took one deep breath before I said, 'I can't take the McCallum case.'

'What? Why not?'

'I've been through it half a dozen times and I can't see an angle. He got off. It's unfair, I know, but that's the jury system.'

Douglas's face flushed. 'But he was sleeping with her. Doesn't that bother you? She was only seventeen years old!'

'Yes, it bothers me, but it wasn't a secret. Her parents were well aware of it, in fact they seemed quite *au fait* with the set-up.'

I pursed my lips and pressed my fingertips together like a church spire.

'OK, Douglas. This is obviously very important to you. Why?'

'I just think it's unfair . . .'

'Why did they bring it to me in the first place?'

'I don't know. Maybe they had heard of you . . .'

Douglas was a crap liar. He would never make a good lawyer.

'Tell me honestly or this will be our last discussion on the matter.'

He shifted in his chair. 'My parents know her parents.'

'Right. Good. Now we're getting somewhere. Did you know Morag?'

'Yes,' he sighed.

'Did you have a sexual relationship with her?'

He looked genuinely offended. 'No! Of course not!'

439

'How well did you know her? Do you know Mr Kemp?'

'I only knew her from family dos. I don't know him personally, but I know who he is – I mean, I've seen him.'

'In the dock?'

Douglas gave a defeated nod.

'Why didn't you tell me? Why all the cloak and dagger?'

'I thought if you looked at it independently, we would have a better chance of you taking the case.'

How was I going to admit that I wasn't as brilliant as he imagined?

'Douglas, I want to help them, but I truly don't think I'm the right person. I—'

'I know. You specialise in compensation.'

'That's not it. They need an expert.'

'But you're brilliant! You're one of the best.'

I gave a bitter laugh.

'Thank you, but you may be blinded by misplaced loyalty.'

'No,' he said quite forcefully. 'I think you've had so much shit to wade through recently that you've lost your nerve. You could do this, I know you could. If you have a rest over the holidays, you'll be your old self. Remember what you used to say? "We do not yield!" That was fighting talk. You've just had the fight knocked out of you, but it will come back.'

I blinked at him in surprise. My little Douglas giving me a pep talk. Wonders would never cease. Douglas looked equally surprised by his outburst.

'Sorry, I didn't mean to offend you.'

I waved his apology away. 'I'll tell you what I'll do – but I need your help. You write down everything, and I mean warts and all, about Morag, her family, the family set-up, her friends and her social life. Also, anything – however small and unrelated it seems – that you can find out about our Mr Kemp. I'll review the case again and try to speak to the detectives involved.'

In a civil action, we could afford to be less stringent about the types of information we used to establish guilt. Hearsay and rumour often had their foundation in truth. It was simply a case of retracing the offshoots until we got to the roots.

Douglas grinned at me, but I didn't want to buoy him with false hope.

'And if, after all that, we still don't find anything new, then we call it quits. Agreed?'

'Agreed,' he said happily.

'Good. Now go and do some work. And tell the others to get their act together.'

Douglas did as he was told, but we both knew it was bravado.

We didn't have any work. We had a few vague enquiries, a couple of simple transactions, one trust to set up and the Morag McCallum case. We weren't exactly generating business and that worried me. My anxiety metamorphosed into simple bad temper.

I couldn't shrug off the feeling of impending doom. It wrapped itself around me. The new firm was doomed, my relationship with Paul was surely doomed, and my family was doomed.

'Give me a break,' I said to any deity that might be listening, 'just for a fortnight, give me a break.'

I stood up and turned off my computer. We hadn't budgeted for the Y2K panic and had been forced to splash out on preventative software. An accumulation of things like that could tip us over the edge into insolvency.

I wandered through to reception and was surprised to see Paul in a huddle with Brontë and Liz.

They looked up simultaneously and shiftily. They were up to something.

'What is that God-awful CD?' I asked Karen.

She pulled its case from under her desk and handed it to me.

I might have guessed. I had been subjected to *The Best Ever Christmas Album Ever in the World Ever*.

'Erin, we're all going for a drink. Come and join us,' Liz said.

'I don't know. I've still got some things to do . . .'

Why couldn't I look at him? Why did I feel so awkward?

I was so aware of him, of his easy manner, of his gentle charm, that it made me blush. He was so capable in every situation, so relaxed with himself and others. But we had too much baggage. We were doomed by baggage.

'Come on! It'll be fun and we're not having an office party,' Brontë coaxed.

'There can't be anything left to do tonight,' Douglas joined in.

I caved in and went to get my coat.

We gathered in reception and trickled out the office in twos and threes. I switched off the lights and locked up. Paul waited for me and we wandered down the busy street together.

'I saw Morag McCallum's parents today. It was heart-rending. I don't know if I can help them, though. It's a tough case. Do you remember anything about it?' I asked.

'A bit. Not proven? He was much older than her, what's his name – Kemp?'

'Yes. But I think that might be immaterial.'

'What makes you say that?'

'He genuinely seemed to like her. He bought her expensive clothes and gifts. Took an interest in her education. Grooming her, almost. Does that sound odd? I know she was very young, but from what I've read she was seventeen going on twenty-six. And he wasn't her first older man. I wonder if she was looking for a surrogate father figure, which begs the question – what was wrong with her own father?'

'Sexual abuse?'

'I didn't say that, m'lud, but she was certainly savvy about the ways of the world. Her family are blue collar, respectable, hard-working people. Sound marriage, by all appearances. I think she had set her sights higher.'

'And that was why he murdered her? Was she putting pressure on him?'

'I don't know. He gave a good performance at the time, seemed honestly upset. Who knows?'

We lapsed into silence.

'Erin, there's something I have to tell you.'

I knew what was coming. He was in love with Brontë. But I didn't want to hear him say it.

'It's OK, Paul. I know.'

'How do you know?'

He tugged me to a halt and tried to catch my eyes, but I stared down the street towards the Christmas lights in George Square.

'I've seen it on the cards. I just don't want to hear you say it.'

He blew air out his cheeks and thrust his hands into his pockets.

443

'When did you find out?'

I glanced at him. What could I say? I had seen how easy they were together. I had watched their bonds grow. I shrugged.

'Come on? How do you know?'

'Call it intuition,' I muttered.

I stepped towards him to let a gang of drunken revellers pass. He placed his hands on my shoulders.

'I think we've got our wires crossed.'

The Christmas lights blurred as my eyes filled up. I wanted to be magnanimous, wishing them every happiness, but all I felt was bitter.

'I've been offered a six-month contract in the States. News 24 want me to be their American correspondent.'

'What?' I gasped.

'That's what I was trying to tell you.'

Relief swept over me.

'What did you think I was going to say?'

'Nothing . . . I mean . . . nothing . . .'

'It's only for six months and it'll give me a chance to see my daughter. I'll come back every couple of months.'

Daughter? When had he mentioned a daughter? What daughter? Had he mentioned a daughter before and I hadn't noticed?

'It's the chance of a lifetime,' I mumbled.

'You're so unpredictable,' he laughed. 'I thought you might be miffed.'

'Miffed? Not at all! Tell me about your daughter.'

'Well, we've been a bit estranged, you know, since the divorce. She's studying in New York.'

We started walking towards Royal Exchange Square again.

'Will you be based there?'

444

'Yes. Let's go to George Square. We'll catch up with the others later.'

'Wow!' I said as it truly hit me. 'You have a daughter. Wow! What's her name?'

'Angel.'

I thought about that for a moment.

'Angel Gabriel? You must be kidding!'

'I'm pulling your leg. She's called Thelma.'

I threw him a hard look.

'OK, OK, she's called Elizabeth, but we call her Libby.'

'Are you sure? Maybe she's called Cherub or Seraph?'

He took my hand and swung it in his. His strong, warm hand.

We had reached George Square where crowds of shoppers, families with small children, and groups of youths milled about. The Salvation Army was playing a carol. A choir was singing.

Oh come, all ye faithful, joyful and triumphant . . .

'When do you go?' I asked.

'Tomorrow. That's why I had to tell you now.'

Oh come ye, oh come ye to Bethlehem . . .

'Tomorrow? How long have you known about it?'

'Just a week or so, but I applied for it months ago, before I . . . in the summer.'

Come and behold Him, born the King of Angels . . .

'I would have told you sooner, but with your father and everything else.'

'Oh . . . Good luck. I'm sure you'll have a brilliant time.'

Oh come, let us adore Him . . .

'Will you visit me?' he asked.

'Of course, I mean, if you want me to.'

445

Oh come, let us adore Him . . .

'So, no additional surprises? Five more children? A two-year stint in Uzbekistan?' I gushed to cover my trembling lip.

'Nope. I'm going out there now because I need to rent a place and I want to spend Christmas with Libby. She's had a rough time of it lately.'

'I'm really pleased for you,' I lied.

She'd had a rough time? What about me? I was jealous of his daughter.

Oh come, let us adore Him . . .

I stood for a moment and then thought, what the hell?

I flung my arms around his neck and gave him a huge hug. He squeezed me tightly.

'I'll miss you, I'll really miss you,' I mumbled into his coat.

'I'll miss you, too.'

He gently tilted my head up towards him and gave me one lingering kiss on the lips.

With difficulty I smiled at him, 'I'll be OK . . .'

Something flickered in his eyes. Regret? Desire? Relief?

He released me awkwardly. 'Let's catch up with the others.'

'I'm going to give it a rain check,' I faltered. 'I've still to collect my car and go to see mother.'

He looked hurt. 'Tonight?'

'Yeah, sorry. I don't want to leave it too late, you know . . .'

'Will you call me later when you get home?'

'Yes, of course! I want to hear all about your daughter and your new job.' I said too gaily.

'I'll get you a cab.'

'I'll walk from here. It's part of the physio. I'm meant to do some every day.'

'I'll walk you home, then,' he said, and put his arm round me.

'No, you go and see the others. They're expecting you – us. We can't both not appear.'

He frowned. 'Are you sure?'

'Yes. Absolutely! I'll only be a couple of hours at most. I'll see you later. OK?'

Grudgingly he agreed.

I turned in the direction of our apartment block and swallowed the hard lump in my throat. The streets were bustling and cheerful. Smiling faces and laughter filled the air.

Oh come, let us adore him . . .

Six months was a long time. Particularly in my life.

TWENTY-NINE

The formalities for seeing Mother were swift and courteous. I was a regular face and on first-name terms now with several of the staff.

She wasn't viewed as a danger to herself or others, and was allowed to wander freely from the TV room to the bathroom to her own bedroom. That small concession comforted me. Locking her up only served to compound her torment.

She was waiting for me in the TV room.

'Hello, dear. You look cold. Is it cold outside?' she asked pleasantly.

'It's bitter. I think we may have snow on the way.'

'A white Christmas! How lovely.'

'Hopefully, it will hold off until then, so it doesn't become all dirty and slushy.'

I unbuttoned my coat and laid it over the back of a tatty armchair.

'And how was work today?'

She spoke as if we were sharing a cup of tea at a sewing bee, as though it hadn't been her husband's funeral less than a week ago.

'It was fine. Thanks.'

She picked up her knitting and began to click away.

I had never known her to knit before, but incarceration seemed to have brought out a homely streak. A closet Martha Stewart. She had already made me a hideous scarf.

'How was your day?' I asked eventually.

'Oh, fine.'

I wanted to shake her from her stupor of pleasantries and indifference.

'Have you remembered any more about what we talked about?'

She held up her knitting.

'Do you think this will fit Max? Or should I make it a tad larger?'

'For goodness' sake!'

She looked hurt. Calm down, I told myself. It's not her fault Paul's leaving. 'Yes, it will fit Max perfectly. He'll love the snowman motif and the colours.'

She smiled at her craftsmanship and happily resumed clicking away.

'Em, Mum, about Leland? Did Dad know?'

'Oh, no. Although once he thought he had seen him . . .'

'Did that cause Dad's stroke?'

'Of course not! I think it was the dogs. They were chasing sheep. Never done that before – and you know what farmers are like. Your father ran after them and next thing we knew, well . . .'

I studied her impassively. Was she lying? She had never mentioned sheep before.

'It wasn't the dogs' fault, though. It's in their nature.'

I shook my head in astonishment at her equanimity.

'Where is Leland?'

She glanced across at me. 'He's dead.'

She often said that, but if I kept on talking, as if I hadn't heard, occasionally she cracked.

I picked up a magazine and said nonchalantly, 'Didn't Dad wonder why you wanted to change his will?'

'I suppose he did, but I told him there was no point

449

in hoarding it. The four of you might as well have the use of it.'

'The four of us?'

'Yes, dear. You, Brontë, Finlay and Max.'

'Oh . . .' I had so many questions but didn't know where to start.

'Mum, when Leland came back, where had he been?'

'Travelling, I dare say. He always liked travelling. The United States, for one.'

'Em . . . How did he travel? I mean, without a passport?'

She raised a weary eyebrow. 'I don't know. You would have to ask him.'

I half expected Leland to appear from out of nowhere. It sent shivers down my spine.

'Mum, why did he come back?'

'He needed help. Oh, damn! I've dropped a stitch.'

She held up her knitting. 'Do you see that? Halfway down? Erin, be a dear and help me unpick this.'

I sat down on the saggy sofa beside her and held out my hands like a dutiful daughter.

There was a subtle scent in the air. Vanilla hand cream. She pulled out the wool and carefully wound it round my hands.

'What sort of help?' I asked.

'Help, dear?'

'You said he needed help. What sort of help?'

'Oh, well, I'm not sure. He said that somebody was after him. I think he was being bullied. You know how soft he was. Always taking lame ducks under his wing.'

Too damn right, they were after him! She mistook his coterie of freaks for lame ducks. He didn't take them under his wing – he mutated them.

'Did he tell you who it was? Who was after him?'

'No, dear, he was a bit ... That's it out now. Silly me for not noticing sooner. At least it wasn't down to the snowman. Grateful for small mercies.'

I smiled inanely. These days I was grateful for minuscule mercies.

'Here, let me take that off you ... there. As good as new.'

She took the wool bale off my outstretched hands.

'Would you knit me a hat to match my lovely scarf?' I asked.

'Would you like me to, dear? Of course. Especially if it's going to snow.'

She rummaged in her knitting bag for the hideous puke-yellow wool. Distracting her was usually quite effective.

'I wonder who was bullying him? I wish I knew. I would tear a strip off him ...' I said.

She sat back up, with the offending wool, and leaned towards me.

'Well,' she said in a stage whisper, 'it was really quite odd. He said it was an impressionist.'

She gave me a look that equated to hot-off-the-press gossip, but this time she had me completely flummoxed.

'An Impressionist? Like Monet or Cézanne?'

'No!' she laughed. 'Like Mike Yarwood.'

'An impersonator? Somebody was impersonating him?'

She scowled huffily. 'Isn't that what I said?'

'Yes, sorry, Mum. I didn't understand. It was a ... shock.'

'I was shocked too. And that's why he came back. So he could be close to you.'

I nearly shrieked.

'Close to me? Why?'

451

She sort of tutted.

'He always wanted to be close to you. Don't you remember? Even when you were a baby and I would put you outside in your pram, which is what we did in those days, he would sit outside right by your side. If you so much as squeaked, he would shush-shush you. Bless him.'

She smiled to herself.

'And when you went to nursery, he was always there, right by your side during playtime. It was a real wrench for him to go on to school without you. You should have been twins.'

I shuddered with disgust at the very thought. Being siblings was bad enough.

'He never took to Brontë the way he took to you . . . but then . . . Remember how he used to send you Valentine cards he had drawn at school?'

My eyes widened in horror. They were from him? How revolting! I had thought they were from the boy along the road.

'Mum, stop!'

She looked at me in surprise.

'Sorry, I . . . I didn't mean to shout. I was . . . upset . . . by the memory.'

'That's understandable. It's hard to lose a loved one. I know, I've lost two now.'

'Two?'

'Your father and Leland.'

'Mum, Leland's not dead. You know that.'

'Oh, no, dear, he is. Would you like to stay for a cup of tea? She'll be along in a minute.'

She was as mad as a box of frogs.

'Yes. A cup of tea,' I agreed lamely.

I had spoken to her doctors, but they claimed that

she had psychosis, was suffering from post-traumatic stress and was in denial. They were wrong. She was barking.

'Mum, I know this is very, very difficult for you, but do you know what Leland did?'

She sighed heavily.

'Erin, all siblings fight. Even close ones. He never meant to hurt you and you were a bit of a telltale. Always running to your father with a tall story about his latest mischief. He certainly got punished for it.'

I didn't remember him being punished.

'How was he punished?'

'Well, you have to remember, things were different then. Spare the rod and spoil the child. Your father would call him into his study. It was awful to hear. He would thrash the living daylights out of him. Leather strap on his bare backside. Sometimes Leland couldn't sit down for days, poor lamb.'

Poor lamb? Poor lamb?

'Mother, do you know what else he did?'

She looked blank.

'Things he did later? When he was older?'

'He didn't mean to upset us by disappearing. He had a nervous breakdown, you know. He came back.'

'Do you know about the other things he did?'

She sort of shrugged. 'I don't know how he survived for that long on his own. He was in a terrible state. He hadn't been looking after himself.'

She shook her head sadly.

'He promised he would go away if I gave him enough money.'

She had never spoken so loosely before. She looked down at her hands and twisted them in her lap. I intertwined my fingers through hers.

'Did you want him to go away?' I whispered.

'Oh, Erin! I was so happy to see him and then . . . What would the Granville-Grants think if they knew? But to send your child away, after all those years in the wilderness . . .'

'Mum? Was Leland in the basement when DSI Kelman was . . . hurt?'

'Yes,' she breathed.

'Oh, Mum! Why didn't you say? Why didn't you . . .'

'Your father would have been furious! He would have thrashed him. He didn't mean to do it, Erin. He was only protecting you. Like when you were bullied in junior one, remember?'

'Didn't mean to . . . hurt Mr Kelman?'

'Yes, it was an accident. He thought he might hurt you. That's why he came back. To protect you . . .'

'Hello there! How are we doing today, Mrs Paterson?' the nurse said gaily.

I couldn't help but be irritated.

'We were talking. I mean, we were getting somewhere.'

'Well, you know the rules,' she said briskly, and looked pointedly at her watch. 'No visitors after seven.'

'Can't she stay for a cup of tea? She was very cold when she came in,' Mother asked solicitously.

'Well . . . I'm going off duty . . .'

I smiled ingratiatingly.

'OK, then. Just ten more minutes. I'll tell the next nurse when they bring the tea. Ten more minutes, mind.'

'Thank you,' we said in unison.

'I hope they bring some cake,' Mother said as soon as the nurse left. 'I didn't like supper tonight. It was fish in cheese sauce. Can't abide that. And who knows what sort of fish it was? It could have been dogfish, for all one could tell.'

'I've got two goldfish on my desk in my new office.'

'How nice! What are they called?'

'Fang and Huey.'

She peered at me. 'Funny sort of names.'

Christ! She even had me at it now.

'Mum, sorry. I was miles away. Did Leland kill DSI Kelman?'

'What? Don't be ridiculous! Leland's dead.'

'Mum, Leland's not dead. You saw him. You spoke to him.'

She stared into space and set her face in a scowl. I had lost her again. I racked my brains for a suitable subject.

'Max is making Christmas cards. He's colouring them in and gluing glitter on them. They're really pretty,' I said.

'How sweet. Did the nursery teach him that?'

'Yes. They've been making decorations too.'

'Does he know what he wants from Santa yet?'

I got up from the sofa and went over to the window. I gazed out at the towering, oppressive shell of the original hospital. It always filled me with an irrational fear. I knew it was an empty ruin, but it clamoured with unanswered shouts from demented minds.

'He wants a . . . a little wheelbarrow and a spade, and new wellingtons and garden shears. Like the ones Leland had . . .'

'Tea and pancakes for Lady Paterson,' the male nurse declared from the doorway. These constant interruptions were getting us nowhere.

'Is there jam for the pancakes?' Mother twittered.

'Of course, ma'am!'

I kept my back to them and hoped he didn't ask me to leave. When would I get such an opportunity again? When? Maybe never.

'Would you like a cup of tea?' he said.

I didn't answer because I thought he was talking to Mother.

'Manners cost nothing,' he commented snidely.

I looked round at him and gasped.

'Jeezus!'

'Erin! Don't blaspheme!' Mother remonstrated.

I gripped the window ledge and willed myself not to faint. He was here. Right in front of me. Right now! . . .

'Leland!' I spluttered.

Mother squinted up at him. 'I had a son called Leland.'

I hissed maniacally, 'It is Leland.'

Mother tutted, 'Don't be ridiculous! Leland's dead, not a nurse.'

Leland smiled at me.

He had changed a lot but he was still a handsome, commanding man in his prime. Tall, fit, muscular, full head of dark hair, chiselled features, fine straight teeth. The sort of man any woman would be proud to call her own.

I was stunned. I had secretly hoped to see some evidence of physical decline. I wanted his rotten core to show through.

'What's that look for, Erin? You look disappointed.'

I couldn't speak.

'Oh, dear. Were you hoping I had wizened away? A Dorian Gray-type forfeit?'

How did he know?

'I must say, you haven't changed at all.'

I found it hard to breathe. I blinked and blinked uselessly.

'I see I've surprised you,' Leland said.

'Do you know each other?' Mother asked pleasantly.

'Oh, yes. We go way back. Don't we?'

'That's nice. Are you OK, Erin? You look a bit faint,' she said to me.

'I'll take care of her, ma'am,' he said.

I was rigid with fear. Hyperventilating and shaking. My skin tingled and my mouth was numb.

'What are you doing here?' I breathed.

'I'm looking after Mother,' he said.

'What are you doing here?' I repeated.

He cocked his head to one side and looked at me as if I was daft.

'I told you. I'm looking after Mother. Somebody has to.'

'She's perfectly well looked after,' I said in confusion. I couldn't believe I was having a conversation with him. Leland – the curse of my life.

'But they can't protect her,' he hissed.

'Protect her from what?'

'From him! I told you! Why are you being so fucking stupid?'

I recognised his tone. Irritation. Precursor to violence.

'Erin, the tea's getting cold,' Mother said innocently.

'Oh, right. Sorry,' I mumbled, but couldn't move. My legs were glued to the spot. I didn't know what to do. A maelstrom swirled beneath me.

'Don't you want some tea? I brought you some,' he asked. His eyes were cloaked with pretence – the pretence of normality.

'Em, no . . . I—'

457

'That's very rude,' he snapped.

'I'm sorry. I'm not . . . feeling . . . well,' I whispered. I fought the urge to scream. Calm, Erin. Be calm. Don't aggravate him. Be polite. Calm.

He narrowed his eyes and glanced furtively at Mother.

'You shouldn't have told mother about Lucy,' he whispered.

'But . . . but I didn't. The police told her.'

Leland shook his head. 'No, they didn't. You brought them Erin! How could you? After all I've done for you?'

'But I didn't. I didn't!'

I recognised the hideous ritual. Leland, the martyr, would accuse me of some fictitious crime. Retribution would follow swiftly.

'I protect you, Erin and this is how you repay me?' he seethed.

'But I didn't tell her! It wasn't me!' I cried.

'And now Mother wants me to go away. Because you just had to tell.'

He crept towards me. He was going to punish me, no matter what. There was no containing him now.

'Mum! It's Leland!' I cried finally.

Mother looked up briefly. He glanced over his shoulder at her and smiled. She smiled back.

'Still the tell-tale tit, aren't we? Lucy was going to tell too, but I showed her. Anyway, she didn't mind. She quite enjoyed it really. I'm sure she came.'

I began to retch. Dry, painful tremors from deep within my soul.

'Oh, come on, now! Don't be such a drama queen,' he scolded, and grabbed a handful of my hair, tugging my head right back. Hot tears sprang into my eyes.

'What do you want, Leland? Do you want money?'

'You don't know? And I thought you were clever. I want what's mine.'

He tugged roughly at my hair again.

'What's yours?'

'You! You were for me. Mum said so. She said you were for me. A baby for me. And didn't I look after you? Always. But you spoiled it. Telling tales and making trouble!'

His face, distorted with rage, was only inches from mine. I could feel his breath on my skin. I prayed that somebody would look through the window and see us.

'Erin! The tea's stone cold!' Mother chastised.

Momentarily, Leland glanced away and I kneed him in the testicles. He let go of my hair as he buckled in pain.

Frantically, I limped over to the security door. I rattled the handle and then thumped on the door.

'Ah-ah-ah, Erin. You need the code.'

He was on me in an instant, hauling me towards the toilet.

'Sir, unhand my daughter!' Mother ordered.

Christ Almighty! She really didn't know who he was.

'Sorry, ma'am. But you know that you're not allowed to thump on the doors.'

'She's a visitor. She didn't mean it, did you, dear?'

Leland turned back to me, a half-smile on his lips.

'I've been waiting for this, my baby. Such a long time. I did try to replace you ... but they weren't a patch. I did try.'

My whole body began to shake. I had seen his victims; I had recognised the similarities.

'Aren't you coming to sit down, dear? I've saved you a pancake.'

She looked up at me and gave a cheery smile. She was oblivious. She was useless to me. As she always had been.

'Come on!' He pulled me into the little toilet.

'You're fucking mad! I'm your bloody sister! Leave me alone!'

'Now, now, dears. Don't fight,' Mother said half-heartedly from the sofa.

I had heard her say that a thousand times during my childhood. I prayed it would trigger some memory in her, that she would recognise him.

'Yes, Erin. Don't fight. Let's play nicely,' Leland purred in my ear.

Violently I pushed him away, stumbling back into the TV room.

'Want to play? Shall I chase you?'

'Get away from me! You fucking freak!' I screamed.

'Erin Georgina Paterson. Mind your language!' Mother warned.

'Mum! It's Leland! It's Leland!'

'For goodness' sake, Erin! I *heard* you swear. Leland has nothing to do with it.'

I relinquished all hope that she might come to her senses through gentle prodding.

'NO, MUM! IT'S LELAND! IT'S LELAND! RIGHT HERE!'

She looked up at us, from one to another.

'Leland! What on earth are you doing? Leave your sister alone.'

Thank you, God, I thought. Thank you.

Leland scowled at me. 'She started it.'

We were ten and eleven again. The year it all went terribly wrong. The year his obsession turned from brotherly love to a sinister, twisted depravity.

'Mum, call the nurse,' I ordered firmly.

She blinked at me in confusion. 'The nurse is here.'

'MOTHER! He's not the nurse. He's Leland!'

She screwed up her eyes and stared at him.

'I told you not to come back. Ever again. I told you!' she said angrily.

'But I haven't finished yet,' he whined.

'Oh yes you have, my boy. I told you to stay away. What were you thinking? That nice Lucy girl? It just won't do. I'll not stand for any more.'

'Shut up! Shut up! You always take her side. Always! And so does Dad! It's always my fault, always me that gets punished. But she made me do it. She made me!'

He lunged at me and caught my throat with his right hand.

He had me up against the security door, on my tiptoes, in two steps. His fingers were tight around my neck.

'Tell her! Tell her! Tell her it was you. Tell her!'

My mouth opened uselessly. I could feel the heat rising in my face as I struggled for breath. His iron fingers were crushing my larynx, squeezing the life from me.

'Leland! Let her go this instant.'

His eyes bulged with rage and pleasure. His breath quickened with excitement.

Mum! He's hurting me! Mum! Help me!

'Tell her! Tell her! Tell her it was you. Your fault.'

I pulled at his hand, tearing his skin with my fingernails. I kicked out at his shins, but he pushed himself hard against me, his lips touching my skin.

'Tell her! Tell her!'

I could see black spots in front of me. Black spots

that rushed towards me, followed by red. Blood-red spots.

I could hear her in the background.

'Leland! Let her go! I mean it. Let her go!'

I tried to speak, my mouth opening and closing soundlessly.

I could see her over his shoulder, between the black spots that got larger and larger.

Mum! I'm scared! He's hurting me!

'Tell her, Erin. Tell her it's your fault!'

The door bumped and shuddered behind my head.

I could see her lips moving, but the noise in my head was deafening. What was she saying?

She pulled at his arm and grabbed at the hand around my throat, but the black spots got bigger and bigger until they became one.

It was quiet and I knew I had been here before.

A frightened child hiding. Be still. Be quiet. Mum! He's coming. Be still! Quiet.

A lonely child hiding. Mum! Be still. Be quiet. A footstep. He's coming! Mum!

Mum! I'm scared! Mum! I'm scared! Mum! Mum! I'm scared!

Somebody was talking to me.

He shone a torch in my eyes. Everything moved so slowly, so silently. He had a white coat with pens in the pocket.

We were underwater.

He put a plastic mask over my nose and mouth but it smelled horrid.

Take it off! Take it off!

I felt the water with my fingertips. It was warm.

There were more of them now, in white coats, some

in slate-blue. How did they breathe without the special mask that I had?

I didn't like it when they crowded round me.

I was scared and claustrophobic. I liked it better when it was just the man with the pens and me.

But then they let me float up.

I liked floating up, higher and higher. I hovered there and looked down.

A man was lying face down on the floor.

He had a half-knitted sweater sticking out of his back.

THIRTY

He sat opposite me, across the table, his hands jammed tight between his legs, his body stooped and huddled like an old man – but he rocked back and forth like a child.

He rocked back and forth endlessly. It was enough to bring on a migraine. He seemed to descend further into madness each time I saw him.

We had got very little that day. He wasn't in the mood. No amount of cajoling or argument could wheedle anything out of him.

He grinned at me and I shuddered with disgust.

'*I love little pussy cat, her coat is so warm . . .*' he sang under his breath, in time to his rocking.

'Why won't you tell me the name of the man who is threatening you?' I asked for the second time.

'*And if I don't hurt her, she'll do me no harm . . .*'

I loathed him singing nursery rhymes. My own horror story resurrected with each line.

I glanced over at the warden and gave a wasting-our-time shrug, but he nodded for me to continue. I rolled my eyes in irritation.

'*So, I'll not pull her tail . . .*'

'Leland, how do you expect anyone to believe you if you won't name him?' I snapped.

'*Nor drive her away . . .*'

'This is a waste of time,' I said to the warden.

Leland's movement was so sudden it caught me and the warden completely off guard. His hand shot up in

464

the air and towards me. I felt hot liquid splatter across my right cheek and forehead.

It took me a moment to realise what it was.

'Jeezus fucking Christ! You fucking bastard!' I screamed and leapt to my feet, sending the chair crashing to the floor behind me.

Maniacally, I wiped his sperm from my face with the sleeve of my jacket.

'Bastard!'

Leland laughed and shrieked, even as the warden manhandled him to the floor and stuck a vicious knee into his back. I hoped it hurt his wound from the knitting needles. A swarm of guards and orderlies filled the small interview room and I was bundled away to a medical room.

A doctor cleaned my face with disinfectant and cleansed my eyes in case of contact. I was furious and appalled in equal measures.

The fucking freak bastard.

'God, Erin! Are you OK?' DS Marshall gushed, as he hurtled into the room.

'No. I. Am. Not.' I growled.

DS Frederick Marshall was now my liaison officer.

'I'm so, so sorry. I don't know how that could have happened.'

'It won't happen again, I can tell you. That was absolutely the last time. I'm not doing it again,' I said forcefully.

'You're upset. That's understandable . . .'

'Upset?' I screeched. 'I'm furious! Have you any idea how revolting it is for me to sit in the same room as that monster?'

'I know, I know . . .'

Unconsciously, my hand went to my throat.

Sometimes I still thought I could feel his vicelike fingers.

'No, you don't know! He tried to kill me. He spent years abusing me! How can you, or anyone else, know what it's like not only face to him, but to try and beguile my brother into confessing.'

I felt dirty, tainted, by my very contact with him.

'Let's go and get a cup of coffee,' Marshall said softly.

'Am I done here?' I asked the doctor.

'Yes, but don't worry. He's clean. He's been tested for all transmissible diseases,' he said.

I hadn't expected to catch psychotic schizophrenia from him, but was grateful for the reassurance.

We wandered through the antiseptic corridors of Carstairs State Hospital to the canteen, showing our laminate passes at every door.

Marshall got two coffees while I took a seat. I glanced around me at the other customers. They looked as jaded as I did.

He sat down and waited expectantly.

'He's toying with us. Me,' I said eventually.

'Today he is, but you said yourself that it's peaks and troughs.'

'Don't we have enough now? I got you his trophies.'

Marshall stroked his chin pensively.

'There's more. You know there is,' he said.

'Well, I need a break. I'm going to New York next week to see Paul.'

Marshall looked slightly alarmed. And I knew why.

Leland wouldn't talk to anyone but me. Only me. I hadn't wanted to see him, never mind speak to him, ever again. But Leland had insisted. It had taken DS Marshall two weeks to persuade me to be their stooge.

'For how long?'

'Just a few days. Don't worry, I'm not planning on fleeing the country, however tempting that might be.'

'When do you go?'

'End of next week. February the sixth. I'll be back late on Monday.'

'How is Paul? How's his new job?'

'He's loving it. He's rented a place for his daughter and himself. He's mending bridges with her, as far as I can tell. I think he plans on staying for another six months.'

I didn't mention how miffed that made me.

'Do you miss him?' Marshall asked quietly.

'Yeah. I do. He was a real friend to me. I appear to be rather short of them these days.'

I wasn't feeling sorry for myself, just truthful. Headlines, such as NUTCASE GRANNY ATTACKS BACK FROM DEAD SERIAL-KILLER SON, weren't exactly generating business or social invitations.

'Do you want to listen to the tape recordings from today? See if you pick up on something?'

I sighed. 'There wasn't anything today. I spoke. He was silent apart from his bloody nursery rhymes.'

This was our routine: I would interview Leland; then Marshall would take over, followed by a psychiatrist or two; and then two more senior police detectives. And finally I would go over the recordings.

But some of them were etched into my mind. Never to be forgotten.

'But what do they look like?' I had whispered eagerly, playing my part like an amateur thespian.

'Do you want to see them?' he had said, in delighted awe.

'Do you have them?'

'*Yesss*,' he had hissed feverishly, furtively glancing at the guard.

I felt physically sick when I thought about it. When I thought about my nauseous flirting, my fake fascination. My life of lies.

Every performance drained a little bit more of my self-respect and dignity.

'It's for the greater good,' Paul had reassured me from across the Atlantic.

'I'm thinking of becoming a hermit,' I had replied.

I had sold my soul to the devil for them.

A grotesque, Damien Hirst-like collection of body parts preserved in formaldehyde. His trophies. One contained Lucy's severed tongue, another Sophie Holbrook's partial lung. And another contained the heart of charity director, Fiona Griegson.

I fought to banish the images that would haunt me for ever, but they slipped behind my eyes and dared me to see them. Lucy's tongue, Abigail's pierced eyes – the litany of desecration.

Alison's hair was braided inside her blood-soaked pants. He had slit her open with a barber's razor and cut out her intestines. He had used her intestines to braid through her hair.

But some items were conspicuous by their absence.

Leland claimed he was being set up by a 'fucking fag bastard', that this impostor had committed the crimes. We had yet to ascertain who the fucking fag bastard was. He refused to name him, for fear of repercussions – upon himself, our mother and me.

He could have been a figment of Leland's overheated imagination. He was definitely a fantasist and had been diagnosed as schizophrenic.

468

'Why does he sing the rhymes?' Marshall asked.

'To intimidate me.'

He frowned. He couldn't understand how such a seemingly harmless thing could be used as a weapon. I wasn't going to enlighten him. It had been harrowing enough telling Dr Khalil.

'Do you want to go home now?' Marshall said, although I knew he was hoping I would have another go at Leland.

'Yes. I want to visit my other loony tonight,' I said.

Marshall stood up. 'How is your mother doing?'

'A bit better. It would appear that stabbing her son in the back has done wonders for her own mental health.'

We handed in our passes and collected our belongings from security.

It was cold and blustery outside and the maximum-security hospital looked forlorn and desolate in the bleak landscape. I was glad to reach the comfort of DS Marshall's car.

'Do you think there is any credibility to Leland's claims? Couldn't they be the result of his schizophrenic state?' Marshall said, as we drove away.

It wasn't the first time he'd asked me that.

'In Leverndale, before he attacked me, he admitted he killed Lucy. And you've found her ...' I couldn't say the word. 'But, as you know, he's retracted that now.'

Marshall nodded.

'The only indication we have that he's not responsible for all the murders is the lack of evidence. Where are the rest of his trophies?'

'Maybe he didn't keep them all? He's clever. Really clever. What if he disposed of them, once he realised his number was up? Your mother wanted nothing more to do with him, and DSI Kelman was closing in,' Marshall said.

'It all goes back to his fake suicide. Paul and I are pretty sure he bumped off one of the group. Maybe there is somebody out there seeking revenge. Most lies contain a grain of truth, however minute.'

'Will you see him tomorrow?' Marshall said hopefully.

'No. I'll come back on Thursday. I've got a petition tomorrow in the Court of Session for the Morag McCallum case.'

'Are you still going ahead with that?' Marshall sounded surprised.

'We'll find out tomorrow. Mr Kemp's counsel hopes we're not.'

I thought about Morag for a moment. 'Life was but a smile on the lips of death,' Li Zhinfa had said. It was one of the few things Granny Lu had quoted that I actually understood.

'You know, Erin, you're the most remarkable woman I've ever met.'

I raised an eyebrow and gave him a half-smile.

I gazed out the window and watched Lanarkshire speed past. On the horizon the clouds gathered menacingly.

I glanced at my watch. I still had time to pop into the office and then collect Brontë. We regularly visited Mother together now. Brontë's company was an irritating but inexplicable comfort.

'Do you think anything Leland tells you is true?' Marshall asked.

I had spent many traumatic afternoons with him. I

consoled myself with the knowledge I was helping the police, but it wasn't completely altruistic.

I, too, wanted to know the truth, but he was a lying, manipulative, son of a bitch.

Leland. My brother. Cold-hearted psychopath and serial killer.

'Personally, I doubt it,' I replied.

But I wasn't a psychiatrist.

I was a compensation lawyer.

March 2000

Melissa Sawyer scraped the snow from the edges of her brother's 1982 Buick trunk and tried, for the third time, to raise the heavy, rusting bonnet.

The snow was falling again. Great, fat flakes clung to her eyelashes.

Morosely, she gazed down the twilit road, compressed into one track by snowdrifts on either side.

She was four miles in either direction from the nearest pocket of civilisation – if you could call the tiny hamlets that clung to the highway civilised.

Across country there would be single dwellings, farms, but even she knew the dangers of wandering off the track in a snowstorm.

She cursed her own car for having a flat and herself for having no spare.

She cursed her brother for not servicing his ancient jalopy. She cursed the snow and the cold and her thin-soled boots.

She cursed her aunt for dying and bringing her here for the funeral.

March in the shadow of the Catskill Mountains wasn't a place she wanted to be. She had cancelled a hot date for this – her first real date of the millennium.

She wished she hadn't taken the back road past the Scholarie Reservoir, between Gilboa and Prattsville. She should have listened to her brother and taken Route 30 through Grand Gorge.

She cursed upstate New York for not receiving a cell-phone signal.

She took her handbag and useless mobile, and retraced her own tyre tracks. She kept her head down, chin pressed to her collarbone, to lessen the sting from the icy snowflakes.

It was darker under the trees.

Laden with snow, their branches – intertwined over her head – were illuminated by the blue radiance peculiar to snow. She cursed them and thanked them equally. Less snow landed on her frozen, bare head.

She saw the headlights of a car before she heard it, the snow a natural muffler. She waved as it drew closer.

'Do you need a hand?'

'Yes, yes, please. My car, my brother's car, has broken down. I need a lift to the nearest phone.'

'Is your brother with the car?'

'No. He'll be snug as a bug at home,' she laughed girlishly. It didn't quite suit a woman of forty.

He smiled and reached across to open the passenger door of the Grand Cherokee.

In her eagerness, Melissa crossed quickly in front of the car and slipped. She crashed down painfully on her backside, but not before twisting her thin ankle.

In an instant, he was by her side and helping her into the passenger seat.

He pointed to her ankle. 'You'll need ice on that.'

'I can't believe it. I've the Ice-capades next week,' Melissa groaned, and tentatively touched her ankle. She cursed her aunt and the snow again for good measure.

'You're an ice skater?'

Melissa allowed herself an inward smile. Normally, it took half an hour to impart this information.

'Yes,' she fluttered rather obviously.

'Are you English?' she asked her handsome knight.

He was tall and well built, with a slight dusting of grey at his temples. Late thirties to early forties, she guessed. His clothes and car were expensive and immaculate. Maybe her aunt wasn't that bad for dying.

'I went to college in the UK. In Scotland,' he replied.

A graduate as well! This was her lucky day.

'My place is just around the corner. Do you want to go there first for some ice and a hot drink to warm you up? We could wait for a tow-truck there.'

Melissa smiled bashfully.

'Yes. Thank you. I don't know what I would have done if you hadn't stumbled across me,' she gushed.

'I don't know what I would have done, either,' he said mysteriously.

Melissa gave a coquettish giggle.

He smiled at her. He had an unusual smile and bright, flirtatious eyes. She hoped that meant what she thought it did.

Melissa relaxed into the heated leather seat and let her imagination run riot. Log fire, fur rug, champagne, great sex.

'Do you live out here? Or is this a weekend place?' she asked.

'Weekend place,' he replied.

'You live in New York? So do I!'

He nodded and smiled.

There was something peculiar about his smile. Wolfish, that's how you would describe it, a wolfish grin. Melissa felt a small spasm of excitement.

But it would be the very last thing she ever saw.

His smile.